CRUSADER

Hush fell on that hall as though by the dropping of some great, heavy curtain. If Queen Marie had wished to make an impact, she was not disappointed. Men stared at her, then at Henry and Alexander, then at each other – and finally over at Durward. No voice was raised, only breaths drawn and expelled, for moments on end. Few there, indeed, would fail to recognise the implications, or some of them. The eldest daughter of the late King legitimised. This Alexander's eldest sister. Heir to the throne then. He a boy of his tenth year. His undoubted successor. And ten-year-olds do not always reach maturity, especially in such circumstances. And now Henry's daughter his Queen, and this last after so much planning and contrivance. Threat to it all, indeed.

The silence continued, until Alexander himself broke it. 'I do not like that man,' he declared.

Crusader

Nigel Tranter

CORONET BOOKS
Hodder and Stoughton

First published in Great Britain in 1991 by
Hodder and Stoughton
a division of Hodder Headline PLC
First published in paperback in 1992 by Hodder and Stoughton
A Coronet paperback
This Coronet paperback edition 1997

10 9 8 7 6 5 4 3 2

British Library Cataloguing in Publication Data

Tranter, Nigel
Crusader
I. Title
823[F]

ISBN 0 340 57927 7

Printed and bound in Great Britain by
Clays Ltd, St Ives plc

Hodder and Stoughton
A division of Hodder Headline PLC
338 Euston Road
London NW1 3BH

Remembering Philip
my son

Principal Characters in order of appearance

David de Lindsay: Baron of Luffness, Barnweill, Crawford and The Byres
Lady Elizabeth: Mother of above
Pate Dunbar: Illegitimate son of Cospatrick, Earl of Dunbar
Alexander Seton of that Ilk: Neighbour and friend
Serle de Dundas of that Ilk
Donald, Abbot of Dunfermline: Chancellor of the Realm
Alan Durward, Earl of Atholl: High Justiciar and Hereditary Doorward
John Comyn, Lord of Badenoch and Lochaber: Chief of that house
Alexander the Second, King of Scots
Alexander, Prince of Scotland: Son of above, later Alexander the Third
Lady Margaret: Illegitimate daughter of Alexander the Second, attendant on Prince Alexander
Robert Bruce, Lord of Annandale: Grandfather of King Robert the Bruce
Alexander Comyn, Earl of Buchan
Walter Comyn, Earl of Menteith
David de Birnam, Bishop of St Andrews: Primate
Bishop Clement of Dunblane
William, Earl of Mar
Queen Marie de Coucy: Widow of Alexander the Second
Macduff, Earl of Fife: Hereditary Crowner
Judith Seton: Sister of Alexander Seton
Alexander Stewart: High Steward of Scotland
John de Gamelyn: Cleric. Comyn bastard
John de Lindsay: Brother of David
Walter de Grey, Archbishop of York
Henry Plantagenet, King of England: Henry the Third

7

Simon de Montfort, Earl of Leicester: Brother-in-law of above

Eleanor of Provence: Queen of Henry

Princess Margaret: Daughter of Henry. Later Queen of Scotland

Prince Edward: Later Edward the First

Robert de Ros, Lord of Wark: English Border noble

Patrick, Earl of Dunbar and March: Cousin of David.

Sir Thomas de Normanville: Justiciar of Lothian and the Merse

Sir Nicholas de Soulis: Governor of Edinburgh Castle

Bishop Richard of Dunkeld: Chancellor

John de Brienne, King of Jerusalem

1

David de Lindsay looked down at himself, hitched his belt round a little so that the handsome jewelled buckle was central and the decorative dirk hung at his right hip without dangling, and glanced over at his mother.

"Do I look aright?" he wondered.

The Lady Elizabeth nodded. "Well enough," she judged. "You will never look so fine as did your father. But that is scarcely your fault, is it? Probably mine! But you will do well enough, Davy. Especially if you can find occasion to smile. You have a warmer smile than ever *he* had!"

Sir David de Lindsay, Justiciar, Baron of Luffness, Lord of Barnweill and The Byres, had been reckoned one of the handsomest men of his age, and one of the most spectacular dressers, suitable in one who had managed to marry one of the greatest heiresses in the land, and of the ancient royal line into the bargain – hard for a plain-faced and far from elegant young man to follow and live up to.

David nodded resignedly. "I cannot think that there will be much to smile at in a parliament," he said.

"Who knows? Enough nonsense is usually talked!" The Lady Elizabeth had a mordant wit and a tongue to match. "You will scarcely need to sparkle and shine there, boy, I swear!"

"I shall say nothing, belike . . ."

"Probably that would be wisest. The less said, the less to regret. Would that so many would remember that. My brother in especial! He will no doubt much hold forth. And to little effect." She smiled and her smile, considering her style and reputation, could be remarkably warm also, on occasion. "Off with you, then. A pity if you arrive late for your first parliament." She looked as though she was going to kiss her elder son, then thought better of it. "Give your Uncle Patrick my greetings, even though he does not deserve them. And if you come across any young women at Roxburgh, remember that there are others just as fair-seeming all over this land, and possibly better endowed!"

David, who had heard that sort of advice before, made no comment. He bowed to the Lady of Luffness – who had clearly no wish to become the *Dowager* Lady of Luffness – and turned, to make for the door and down the winding turnpike stair, almost at the run now.

Out in the great courtyard of Luffness Castle he found Pate Dunbar waiting for him, with the two horses saddled and ready. Although Pate, a year older than himself, at twenty-three, was his servitor, he was also his friend – as was the more acceptable in that they were blood relations, full cousins indeed, save that Pate was illegitimate, the by-blow of the said Uncle Patrick, Earl of Dunbar and March, his mother's brother; and so, in fact, as far as blood went, of even loftier strain than any Lindsays, who were only eight generations on from the Norman adventurer who had come north with David the First two centuries before. For the Earls of Dunbar and March were direct descendants of the ancient Celtic royal line of Scotland, more authentically royal than King Alexander himself. Of so lofty lineage were they that they allowed themselves no surname, baptismal names sufficing, so that David's mother was styled the Lady Elizabeth only, not using her late husband's Lindsay; and her brother was just Cospatrick, or more usually Earl Patrick. By the same token, his by-blow Pate added Dunbar to his name, as indication of his illegitimacy.

"Roxburgh, then," David said, mounting. "How long, think you, Pate?"

"Going by the Ystrad of Gifford, over Lammermuir to the Dye Water and down the western edge of the Merse to Wedderlie and the Earlston of Ersildoune, thirty-five miles I'd say, but with the higher ground to climb. By Haddington and Humbie to Soutra and down Lauderdale, over forty, of easier going. Four hours either way, as *you* ride!"

"Aye, then. Let us take the shorter road. There is a council first, then the parliament to start at three hours after noon. We should have time aplenty."

The other shrugged and grinned. He was a much better-looking young man than was David, less square and rugged of feature. "The poor horses!" he observed.

"They grow fat, lacking work." Which was not strictly true of as fine a pair of beasts as would be seen south of the Scotwater, or Firth of Forth.

Pate mounted, and they rode together from the keep doorway across the cobbles of the courtyard and out through the gatehouse's arched pend between the twin circular drum-towers which supported the portcullis and flanked the drawbridge. This last was already down for them, and the portcullis up; and with a wave to the gate-porters they clattered across the moat and down its quite steep seawards bank beyond to the fishing hamlet of Luffnaraw. Luffness Castle was a great and powerful place, built above the shore of the wide Aberlady Bay on the Scotwater Firth, a strong position reinforced by deep ditches and the water-filled moat, its twenty-foot-high curtain walls topped by parapet and wall-walk, its angle-towers and bastions. It had been built, a century before, by the Dunbar earls to guard their vast new central Lothian lands, just as Dunbar Castle itself, fifteen miles away, guarded those to the east. David's great-grandfather, Sir William de Lindsay, had won it when he, like his grandson after him, had married a daughter of the then Earl of Dunbar, the fourth. This was her portion or dowry, on condition that the Lindsays protected the earl's nearby properties.

The two young men, greeting such of the fisherfolk of Luffnaraw as were to be seen that morning, rounded the castle's perimeter east-about and turned due southwards, to ride across the marshy levels of Luffness Muir, cattle-dotted but kept deliberately undrained and free of trees, save the odd stunted hawthorn, for defensive reasons; no enemy could creep up on the castle unseen this way. But there was a road, or rather something of a causeway across.

A mile of this and they came to firmer ground where was the nunnery of Ballencrieff, where there were the women to wave to at work in the fields, the orchards, and amongst the rows of bee-skeps, culling wax for their candle-making. Now the land began to rise in grassy folds to the Garmylton Hills,

11

amongst which folds rose the lesser castle of The Byres of Garmylton, so known humorously from the first as indication by its Lindsay lords that it was little better than a cow-byre. Nevertheless it had been raised in time to be a lordship in its own right; and now, since his father's death the year before, David's full style was Lord of Luffness, Barnweill, Crawford and The Byres. It had indeed been *his* portion until he succeeded to all, although he had never lived there. Now, in due course, he would probably hand it over to his young brother John.

Surmounting that green ridge of the Garmylton Hills, suddenly the land opened before them, the wide and fertile Vale of Tyne, reaching across miles of tillable land up and up to the long, heather-clad escarpment, dominating all, that was the Lammermuir Hills, so much higher and more formidable than those of Garmylton, the watershed which separated Lothian from the Borderland. Across that vale and that great barrier they had to go, and far beyond. This was no easy-going ride by well-trodden tracks and by-ways – and with David dressed in his best, too.

Skirting well to the east of the county town of Haddington, they crossed Tyne at the ford of the nuns' abbey, and began the long climb to Lammermuir. Thus far it was all very familiar to the horsemen, for not only were the Lindsays frequently in Haddington, where markets were held and justiciary courts sat and meetings were arranged, but the Lammermuirs themselves provided no little proportion of the baronial wealth, and not only for themselves. These long rounded hills, over four hundred square miles of them, were the main sheep-rearing area of Scotland, pasturing their hundreds of thousands of the creatures, the wool from which, exported mainly from Berwick-on-Tweed, the greatest sea-port of the kingdom, constituted one of its principal sources of revenue. The Scots lords, temporal and spiritual, however lofty their lineage or resounding their style, would have been sore deprived without these baaing sheep.

Over those breezy heather uplands, then, they rode mile upon mile, across swelling, breastlike contours, dipping into and out of empty valleys, empty that is of all but sheep and the occasional shepherd and his dogs, until at length the land dwindled and sank before them to a vast rolling plain, ridged and furrowed in minor scale but a plain nevertheless, stretching into the hazy distance where, almost a score of miles away, another line of even higher summits could be discerned, the Cheviots, the border of England. For this before them was the Merse, or March, from which the Cospatrick earls took their second title, the boundary-land, and fair indeed, save for its bloody history. Battleground might have been a better name for it; but not at this present, with no war with England and Henry the Third the King's brother-in-law.

Down into the plain they descended, to cross this western edge of the Merse, by Gimmerlaw, Lamb Hill, Ewelaw and Wedderlie and other places with sheepish names, however unsheepish were the occupants of these small Border towers and fortalices; necessarily so to survive constant English raiding, no war notwithstanding – and equal raiding from their own kind, as was the Marchmen's way of life and death. They came to Gordon, where another of the Norman adventurers had settled, his descendants having taken the name and were now great. Now they could see the wide Tweed valley ahead of them and journey's end. David reckoned that he might have half of an hour in hand.

Roxburgh might seem a strange place to hold a Scots parliament, at the very southern tip of the land, with the English borderline only ten miles away. But here, deliberately, the great David the First had established his seat, palace, and his abbeys nearby, in a determined effort to bring an end to the long-standing warfare between the two kingdoms; here rather than at one of the great fortress-citadels of Edinburgh, Stirling or Dumbarton – he who had been hostage in England for so long, and on succeeding to the throne of his brothers, had brought up all his young Norman friends to help him in his endeavours for good government and peace, Lindsay amongst them. That was well over a century ago, but his royal descendants still looked on this Roxburgh as their favourite base, indeed home. King Alexander the Second was David's great-great-grandson, and normally held his court here.

Roxburgh Castle was an extraordinary place by any standards, and extraordinarily sited. It was, in itself, a fortified

13

township crowning the ridge of a long, narrow peninsula where the great rivers of Tweed and Teviot joined, surely the longest castle in Scotland, since the ridge of rock was only some score of yards wide, dropping sheerly on each side into the two rivers, so that only lengthwise could building be extended. Thus the stronghold consisted of a series of towers, halls, barracks and narrow courtyards, even a church – for David had been a pious prince as well as all else; rather like an extended town-street in fact, one building thick, set up there on its rock spine, immensely strong since it was approachable only from its western end, and that heavily defended by three moats cut in the solid stone, each with gatehouse and drawbridge. The builder may have been a man of peace but he was versed in the arts of war.

Long before they reached the crossing of Tweed, by an artificial ford with underwater stonework, well upstream from the castle, and itself heavily guarded, David and Pate were no longer alone in their travelling, with contingents of men converging from all directions on this place. David de Lindsay seemed to be unique in bringing with him only a tail of one; the other lords, barons, lairds, churchmen and commissioners to the parliament all appeared to be intent on proving how potent they were in armed men, folk very much to be reckoned with. Perhaps parliaments were not so much for talking and debate and policy-making but for displaying strength and power?

There was quite a large town of Roxburgh half a mile west of the castle, near the fords of Tweed and Teviot, more than any mere castleton, the most important community in all the East and Middle Marches of the Borderland. Here the King's officers were ordering all attenders at the parliament to leave their followings – there was no room for them, or their horses, at the castle itself. There were sundry objections to this, needless to say, but the officers were adamant. Even great lords and bishops had to walk – although most of the greatest would already be at the council of state being held beforehand.

David, for one, was quite glad to stretch his legs after the long riding, as they strode past older, stiffer or more portly parliamentarians and their aides and esquires. It occurred to him that either this parliament was to be somewhat delayed or that there were a lot of latecomers. Perhaps such occasions never started on time?

At the first of the gatehouses and bridges they had to join a queue, while credentials for entry were checked. Although some appeared to be having difficulties here, David had none, for the guards had been reinforced for the duty by some of the Earl of Dunbar's men, the greatest lord of these parts, and his nephew was known. They moved on, past two more gatehouses unchallenged, and into the castle proper, where the Lion Rampant standard, red on gold, flew above the many towers. There was still some sneering at this emblem, amongst the native Celtic stock rather than the imported Norman-Scots; the Black Boar on silver had been a sufficient device for the age-old line of monarchy stemming from the High Kings of ancient Alba; and why the present King's father, William the Lyon – or how he got that name, although he was far from lionlike – felt impelled to change it to this ramping feline, none knew.

At one of the courtyards, the sheep were separated from the goats, that is, the parliament members were shepherded into the main great hall of the castle, whilst their attendants of whatever rank were led off elsewhere; there would surely not be room for all these in the minstrel galleries, clerestories, window-embrasures and the like? David and Pate parted.

In the hall itself David found all strictly partitioned. Up on the dais at the far end were the throne, the seats for the high officers of state and the table for the Chancellor and his clerks, at present all empty save for a few bustling churchmen. Below the dais steps were the stalls for the earls, on the right, with those of the Lords of Parliament behind; and on the left those of the Lords Spiritual, the bishops and mitred abbots. Then on the main floor were the benches for the majority of the members, in their various groupings, the holders of baronies, such as David; the ordinary abbots and priors; the knights of the counties; the sheriffs and lower justiciars. So were comprised the Three Estates of the Realm, the monarch sitting with his lords, the commoners and Holy Church.

The body of the hall was already crowded. There had

not been a parliament for long, King Alexander having no enthusiasm for them, preferring to make decisions himself, with the aid of a small council of state. But occasionally they were necessary and advisable, for council decisions to be ratified and for major changes of policy, alliances, and dealings with other nations. This one was going to be well attended, it seemed.

David was directed to the barons' seats, in front of the rest. Distinctly diffident, uncertain of his place, he hesitated, only too well aware of how differently his celebrated father would have behaved. Then he saw two men whom he knew, one a friend and neighbour, the other a far-out kinsman, sitting together. Perceiving him, they beckoned for him to join them, making room for him on their bench. They were Alexander Seton of that Ilk – Seton being the sea-town of Tranent, a few miles up the Scotwater from Aberlady Bay – the other Serle de Dundas, from the west of Lothian, he being a cadet of the Cospatrick earls and so in vague cousinship with the Lindsays, both a little older than himself and both holders of baronies. Relieved to have their company and guidance, David took his seat between them.

These two, as well as welcoming the newcomer to his first parliament, were full of news. Durward, Earl of Atholl, the most powerful noble in the land, was in a bad mood, blaming the King for favouring the Comyns – although he was married to one of the monarch's bastard daughters. Bruce of Annandale was complaining that the ever-grasping Comyns were usurping his interests in Galloway and Dumfries. David, the Primate, Bishop of St Andrews, was declaring that the Abbot of Dunfermline ought not to be Chancellor, and that as Primate *he* should have the choice of that great office. And so on. Also that there was increasing competition to wed others of the monarch's illegitimate daughters, who were now coming of marriageable age – Alexander did not seem able to father any other son than one, his legitimate heir, also named Alexander, now aged eight. The present council meeting should have been over an hour ago, so presumably there was trouble thereat.

They had time enough and to spare for talk, for the King and his councillors continued to delay their appearance, and it was almost two hours after the parliament was due to open. David asked whether this was normal, and was told that it was not. But Seton had been only at the one parliament hitherto, and Dundas at two, so their experience was limited.

That hall had become notably rowdy in the interim.

Then, at last, the High Seneschal came hurrying on to the dais, looking somewhat flustered, with his heralds and trumpeters, resplendent in the new Lion Rampant tabards the King's father had found for them. The instrumentalists blew a flourish, which effectively stilled the clamour in the hall. The Seneschal turned towards the doorway from which he had just entered.

There was a pause, and as it continued the stir and chatter began to rise again. Then a procession of proudly dressed earls and lords and robed bishops began to file in, far from orderly, indeed jostling rather for position. Most David did not recognise, save for Alan, Lord of Galloway, Bruce of Annandale, Livingstone and one or two others. This company dispersed to take their seats in the various stances, and there was another pause, again prolonged, with the last arrivals being even more vocal than the generality of members. The Seneschal was beginning to look anxious again when Donald, Abbot of Dunfermline, came in, almost at the run, clutching papers, and behind him three clerical assistants, also with documents. The abbot was the Chancellor of the Realm and would act chairman of the parliament. He went to sit at the table on the dais, arranging his papers and rolls thereon.

Now the Seneschal signed to his trumpeters, who produced another fanfare, and this time, without delay, in paced the great officers of state, the High Steward, the High Constable, the Knight Marischal, the Chamberlain, plus the Primate of Holy Church, the Bishop of St Andrews. These took up position at the back of the dais.

More trumpeting, and the Seneschal signed for all to stand. Then in came three individuals bearing the royal symbols – and these, however high they held their heads, seemed to be in some dubiety as to who should enter first. Then Alan Durward, Earl of Atholl, bearing aloft the great two-handed sword of state, distinctly aggressively, got in front, followed by Sir John Comyn, Lord of Badenoch and Lochaber, holding the sceptre, and then Patrick, Earl of Dunbar and March, carrying the crown on its cushion. These came to place their burdens on the Chancellor's table, unceremoniously pushing aside mere papers, and went to their seats, but remaining standing.

There was another and still more lengthy pause. Then a herald at the door signalled to the Seneschal, and this time a prolonged blare of trumpets shook the hall. And in strode a short, thick-set figure of middle years, undistinguished as to features and carriage but having a strange air of almost scornful authority, clad much less notably than most of his councillors but wearing round his brows the simple circlet of gleaming gold – Alexander the Second, by the Grace of God, High King of Scots. He stalked over to the throne, stood beside it for a few moments, considering all the company with a careful, indeed almost critical scrutiny, as though possibly computing supporters or the reverse, and then sat down.

Everybody else could now sit.

Then there was an unusual and unexpected development. The King glanced back at the dais doorway and raised a beckoning hand. And out therefrom, led by a young woman, the only female in all that great assembly, came a small boy of about eight years, sturdy, open-featured, round-eyed but not apparently over-awed by it all, a fair-haired lad, and a deal more good-looking than the monarch. They went over to the throne where the girl patted her charge's head and then left him beside the King and, bowing, turned to retire whence she had come, but unhurriedly, gracefully – and she was notably good-looking also. The boy, Prince Alexander, heir to the throne and apple of his father's eye, grinned at his father. He remained standing there.

In the silence which prevailed, the King raised his hand again, and pointed to the Abbot of Dunfermline at the table.

The Chancellor lifted his gavel and struck the table-top with it, as indication that the parliament was now in session. His duty was to conduct the meeting under the presidency of the monarch, who could speak, intervene or even close the proceedings, wholly in command. It could not be a parliament without the King, or, if he was under age, his regent. But the Chancellor conducted proceedings under the royal authority. This important office was almost always occupied by a senior churchman, for it demanded much writing and paperwork – and many of the great nobles could not even sign their own names, much less read and write. Seals and crosses were all they required – and swords, of course.

Dunfermline was the foremost abbey in the land, the first founded in the Romish persuasion, erected by Queen Margaret Atheling, this Alexander's great-grandmother, her initial gesture towards the replacement of the ancient Columban Celtic Church with that based on Rome. So this Donald was the senior mitred abbot. Moreover, he it was who had moved the Pope to have the said Queen Margaret canonised to sainthood. Nevertheless others grudged him the office, in especial the Primate, David, Bishop of St Andrews, who believed that it ought to be his, by right. The Scots, in Holy Church as elsewhere, were never good at agreeing amongst themselves.

The good abbot, an elderly man, cleared his throat. "This parliament is called by His Grace the King to consider and decide upon sundry matters of great import to this realm. All members and commissioners are entitled to speak to these, but necessarily with brevity and due respect, and to vote. All motions and statements will be addressed to myself, as Chancellor, and not directly to the King's Grace. Is it understood?"

The slight growl which arose could have been taken as acceptance or the opposite.

"The first issue to be decided, already discussed in council, is of the most vital moment. King Hakon of Norway is again laying claim to the Hebrides and Western Isles, despite the freeing thereof from Norse domination by the late and puissant Somerled, Lord of the Isles. And not only the Isles but much of the West Highland mainland, including the great peninsula of Kintyre, Ardnamurchan, Cowal in Argyll and parts of Lochaber, even claiming parts of Galloway, by sword-right. His Grace and council consider this to be intolerable . . ."

His voice was drowned by a great outcry and angry shouts of indignation. He let it continue for a little, then banged his gavel for quiet.

"Unfortunately Ewan, Lord of Argyll and the Isles, is scarcely of his grandfather's stature, and has not maintained the great fleets of fighting ships which Somerled built. He is in no position to give battle to any concentration of Norse long-ships, and so gives way to Hakon. As all know, the Norsemen have the greatest fleet of war-vessels in Christendom. And, to his sorrow, His Grace the King is not rich in such ship-ping."

There was silence now.

"Since the Isles and Western Highlands can be protected or conquered only by sea and ships, aid is therefore required. This aid can come only from England, from Man or from Ireland. Sadly, Ireland is in a state of great weakness and internal struggle between the petty Kings, as is usual, and the Norse influence there is also strong. King Harald Godfreysson of Man is himself held prisoner and hostage in Norway, and the Manxmen lean towards their Norse cousins anyhow. Which leaves only England . . ."

The reaction to that simple statement was as sour as it was predictable. They might not be at war with England at the moment, but inborn hatred of the Auld Enemy was there, not to be denied, and ever ready to surface. The veteran fighter, Alan Durward, Earl of Atholl, a great bear of a man, Hereditary Doorward to the Scots monarchy, of ancient Celtic line, headed it. He rose.

"I say no pleas to the English!" he barked. "Accursed be the day when we have to go cap in hand to England for aid! If they gave any, it would be to try to subdue us to their will, as they have been seeking to do down the centuries. No dealing with the English, I say!"

"I say the same!" That was Robert Bruce, fourth of the name, Lord of Annandale, whose mother had been a grand-daughter of King David, and he therefore distantly of the blood-royal. It was not often that these two great nobles agreed on anything.

There were supportive shouts from all over the hall.

The Chancellor had to use his gavel. "I do not judge my

lord of Atholl's comment to be a motion," he observed carefully. "So my lord of Annandale's declaration is not a seconding. I have to point out, as was made clear in council, that there is indeed little or no choice for us in this matter. If King Hakon and his Norsemen are to be kept from taking over the Isles again, we must have ships-of-war in large number. This realm has never sought conquest by sea, as have others, and we have built no fleets of fighting-ships, only merchanters. Do we yield to the Norsemen, then? Or swallow pride and seek aid from England? For it is certain that we cannot *build* such fleet in less than years."

"I say that we *must* so seek!" John Comyn, Lord of Badenoch and Lochaber, spoke, chief of that acquisitive and many-branched family originally de Commines, from Flanders. By a deliberate policy of marrying Scots heiresses of selected lands, sometimes by getting rid of the native male heirs, they had grown great and influential. If Durward was the most powerful individual in the land, the Comyns, his sworn enemies, were much the most powerful *family*. "We cannot fight off the Norsemen on land, for they seldom use the land. So we fight with ships, or not at all."

"I agree." Alexander Comyn, Earl of Buchan, kinsman of John, inevitably backed him, just as Walter Comyn, Earl of Menteith, rose to do the same. It was said that these three, alone, could put fifty knights into the field, each backed by one hundred armed horsemen, and more at a few days' notice – although, unfortunately, not fifty ships. What was not inevitable was the earl's follow-up statement. "Indeed I so move. I move that this parliament agrees to seek the aid of King Henry of England for the use of a fleet of ships-of-war."

"And I second," Menteith got in.

"And I move to the contrary!" Durward shouted.

A dozen lords were on their feet to second that.

The Chancellor sighed, and looked over at the King. It was obvious that this was just a continuation of a debate already argued in the preceding council.

King Alexander sat silent, eyeing his young son, in fact.

Abbot Donald sighed again. "A motion has been put and seconded. Also a counter-motion. But before I put it to the

21

vote of the assembly, I must ask for further discussion, that all may perceive the full situation. It is not enough to vote no truck with the English, without deciding what action to take in its place. Do we *let* the Norsemen take over the Hebrides? And, on the other hand, if we seek King Henry's aid, what are we to offer him as inducement, without allowing English dominance over Scotland? Consider well!"

A very different voice spoke up, and from the Lords Spiritual stalls, smooth, calm, persuasive – that of Bishop David de Birnam of St Andrews, the Primate. "Chancellor and friends all, King Henry may not require much inducement. The Norse, based on Ireland and on Man, have been assailing the coasts of Wales and even Cornwall. Henry is seeking to contain the Welsh who rise against English domination. If the Norse were to establish themselves again in the Hebrides, then they would be well placed to invade Wales in strength, not just make raids as now. Henry Plantagenet will be well aware of this. Therefore he may be well enough content to assist in defeating Hakon in *Scottish* waters, rather than in English or Welsh! And so be prepared to lend his ships."

That made an evident impression on the gathering.

Bruce jumped up. "That may be so, churchman! But once the English ships are in Scottish ports and harbours, who is to get them out again? Whilst we are up fighting the Norse, English armies could be across this border at our backs and taking over our land. *My* land in especial, in Dumfries and Galloway!"

The tide swung in the anti-English direction again.

It was another prelate who rose, Clement, Bishop of Dunblane. "What of the French?" he asked. "They are better friends to Scotland than are the English. Our present Queen is French. Can we not gain ships from there? They do not love the Norse. And they are strong for Holy Church. The Pope, I believe, would urge them to favour us, for he looks with disfavour on the Norse Primate, the Archbishop of Trondheim, or Nidaros, who claims spiritual hegemony over all northern lands which have no archbishop of their own, including this Scotland! Get French aid, I say."

That drew some support, especially from the clerical benches.

The Chancellor was about to speak when another voice halted him, level, almost toneless, but authoritative, that from the throne itself.

"Think you all that I have not considered all this, considered well? There is no time to wait for the French to decide, or the Pope, and to muster fleets – even if they would do so. It is now May month, and the Norse summer hosting season can start at any time. We have to act swiftly, if we act at all. As to inducement for the English, and assurance of them withdrawing ships and men after, I propose to gain this by *payment*. Gold!"

There were gasps from all over the hall, even though it was improper to interrupt the monarch. But money, gold and silver, were in scarce supply in Scotland always, and the royal treasury apt to be empty. Payment in money was all but unheard of.

Alexander went on in that even voice, to answer the unasked questions. "I *have* the moneys. Private moneys, *English* moneys drawn from the Honour of Huntingdon, which King David gained in marriage, and from which I gain revenue and have to pay fealty for to King Henry. These moneys, rents and dues from eleven English counties, I have kept secret and safe, but little used. For a purpose. For these years I have sought to *buy* back the Hebrides from King Hakon. He claims them by lawful tenure and sovereignty, as well as by sword-right, since our weak King Edgar yielded them up to the Norse over a century ago. The Lord Somerled of the Isles changed all that. But I have sought to counter any such claim by offering Hakon these moneys to purchase them back for Scotland, in title, while still disputing his right. But King Hakon has always refused. Now, I can use these moneys, English moneys, to hire English ships to halt the same Hakon . . ."

However flatly delivered, that extraordinary and unlooked-for announcement from the throne intrigued and fascinated; also, to a large extent, obviously convinced.

Abbot Donald, seeing his opportunity, was about to speak, when again he was forestalled. Alan Durward rose.

"Chancellor, may I ask how His Grace can ensure that once these moneys are accepted and English ships are provided, they will not remain in Scots waters and havens afterwards, to our grievous hurt?" It looked as though the matter of the Huntingdon money had not been revealed at the council meeting.

The King answered his son-in-law, older than himself, direct. "A treaty," he said. "I shall ensure it by the terms of a treaty. All ships, crews and armed men to leave Scotland peaceably at the close of the hostilities. My good-brother Henry will not break a formal treaty, signed and sealed. That is why this parliament's agreement is necessary. A treaty must be so authorised."

"And *we* command these English ships?" It was not correct thus to address the monarch in parliament, but Alexander let it pass.

"The fleet, yes. Under my personal command. But not each ship. Each will have its own shipmaster and captain. A treaty of state requires parliament's agreement. Chancellor, I suggest that you call a vote."

Thankfully the Abbot Donald nodded. "There is a motion and a counter-motion before this assembly. My lord of Atholl, yours was the counter-motion. Do you wish it to stand?"

Durward looked around him and saw only headshakes. He glanced over at Bruce, and got no guidance there. "I withdraw the counter-motion," he muttered.

"Very well. The Earl of Buchan's motion stands. Does any other wish to counter it?"

Silence.

"Then the motion is carried. His Grace seeks English aid in ships, and by treaty. It is agreed." With an almost audible sigh of relief he moved on.

"Now there follows the sequel. If English ships are required, in addition to some of our own, a Scots army is necessary to sail in them against the Norsemen, and to fight from them. Does this parliament agree to the raising of such an army? And speedily?"

All over the hall there were voices upraised now, shouts of acclaim and support. At last the lords, barons, lairds and ordinary knights, even the bishops and abbots, had their opportunity to take part, calling out how many men each would contribute, in fifties, hundreds, even thousands, rivalling each other in this, something they understood – for Scotland might be poor in gold and silver but it was rich in fighting men. David de Lindsay found himself shouting that he would provide one hundred and fifty, to beat Dundas's one hundred – although he could not rival Seton's two hundred and fifty, for Seton had the towns of Tranent and Cockenzie to draw on. The Comyns, of course, outshouted all, with their thousands.

All the ensuing noise and hubbub greatly excited and pleased the young Prince Alexander, who had been getting restive, David had noticed. Now he jumped up and down beside the throne, laughing and pointing – and from his small hand flew an object, a ball of sorts, which he had been clutching, to fall to the stone-flagged floor with a metallic clang and go rolling across and down the two steps from the dais to main-floor level, to end up not far from the first row of benches.

Probably few there noticed the incident, in the outcry and shouting, but David did, in the second row of seats. It so happened that there were gaps in the front row, few presumably eager to sit so close below the Chancellor's table and the throne. One of these gaps was in fact directly in front of David. And without any real consideration, on impulse, he rose and vaulted lithely over the bench in front, went to pick up that object, and stepped up on to the dais to hand it back to the young prince. It proved to be one of these Celtic handling-balls, carved with symbols on polished black stone, favoured in the past for turning over and over in the hand to aid in deliberation and concentration.

The boy took it, beaming, nodding his flaxen head in thanks.

David smiled, bowed jerkily to the monarch, who was looking at him rather oddly, and moved back towards his seat.

It was only at this stage that he realised that he was being eyed askance. The noise and calling-out went on, but now only from the rear parts of the hall, where what went on at the front would not be so obvious. Nearer at hand men had stopped their shouting of numbers to stare at him. The Chancellor had half risen, glaring, and was pointing his gavel at David accusingly and gesturing towards his seat. Evidently he had behaved wrongly, offended, probably broken the rules of parliament. He made another half bow towards the table, looked apologetic, and hurried back to his place between Seton and Dundas, muttering his excuses.

The abbot banged his mallet loud and long. When he had obtained approximate quiet he could be heard to be saying ". . . disgraceful behaviour! Contrary to all custom. Approaching His Grace. Could be a threat to the royal person! It must not occur again, let that be understood by all!" Then he raised his minatory gaze to the assembly at large. "Enough! Enough! This of men and arms, levies to be provided, is not the business of this sitting. It is for the Knight Marischal. All offers of men and arms, aye and of shipping where possible, to be made to Sir Hervey de Keith, Knight Marischal, hereafter, not now." He glanced over to the throne. "Your royal pardon, Sire? No ill intended, as I esteem it. Now – to the next business." He consulted his papers.

David looked at his companions, eyebrows raised. Seton grinned and Dundas wagged his head.

"Parliament has to consider the matter of Cumbria and Tynedale," the Chancellor read out. "As all know, these lands, now behind the English border, were part of the ancient kingdom of Strathclyde, which became incorporated in Scotland in due course. The English however took them by force and held them, although Scotland never relinquished claims thereto." The abbot was reading this in something of a gabble. "A century ago, however, King Stephen of England agreed to return part of them, Tynedale in Northumberland and the Penrith area of Cumberland, to Scotland. This was done, after a fashion, but his successor, Henry the Second, repossessed the lands by force. There has been constant trouble there since, with many of the landholders and people paying homage to the King of Scots and others to the King of England. Parliament has been concerned with this on many occasions. It has been the accepted decision of such parliaments that these territories remain part of the Kingdom of Scotland, although wrongously held by the English. At the marriage of His Grace King Alexander to his first wife, the

26

Princess Joan, daughter of King John and sister of the present Henry, this last monarch agreed to take steps to improve this situation. It has never been done. And with the sad death of Queen Joan, her brother has done nothing to effect. Many of the Cumbrian and Tynedale barons and land-holders would prefer to be in Scotland, which is closer to them than the rule from far-away London, and they are of the Celtic stock. Moreover, they are being required to produce troops to fight the Welsh, with whom they are on good-neighbourly terms. So His Grace here has raised the issue again." He laid his paper down, and looked hopefully at the monarch.

There was a murmuring and headshaking amongst the company. Few there were very interested in this old story, seeing no great advantage for Scotland, or themselves, in trying to regain these detached and not particularly valuable territories, certainly not worth going to war over – especially with war against Norway envisaged. This was not the time . . .

Alexander, however silent of habit and wary of eloquence, was well able to judge the temper and feelings of his subjects. He raised a hand.

"My reasons for bringing this matter before you now are twofold," he said. "One is that I judge, if we do not do it now, there will be little chance of it achieving success hereafter. For almost certainly the English are going to subdue the Welsh, finally, and these lands, just to the north of Wales, will be the more strongly Englished. Secondly, Henry, on the advice of his good-brother Simon de Montfort, whom he has made Earl of Leicester, is intending to invade France and regain Plantagenet lands and power there. So now is a time when Henry will desire no trouble with Scotland, our opportunity. I have approached him on the matter, and he is prepared to concede to me these districts of West Northumberland and Cumberland, not in sovereignty but in feudal tenure. There is a difference, as you will all perceive. I require parliament's guidance in the matter."

Men eyed each other doubtfully, wondering at the relevance of all this, at this time.

William, Earl of Mar spoke up. "Chancellor, may I ask

why His Grace considers this a vital matter, at this moment, when it is the Norse we are concerned with?"

The King answered him. "Because, my lord Earl, Henry keeps many ships based on the ports of the Cumbrian coast – Workington, Whitehaven, Ravenglass, Barrow, all for use against the Welsh. We could use those ships."

Many voices were raised. What then of his Welsh war? What of the French project? Would he not need ships for that?

Alexander stilled the noise with a hand up. "It is not fighting ships he needs for France, but vessels to carry men, horses, cannon. Merchanters will serve for that. He must make choice. Leave the Welsh conquest for a little. And Simon de Montfort is strong for the French venture, being himself a Frenchman. Henry heeds him, an able man. My envoys in England tell me that Henry will choose France, if he can. This will help him so to choose. And aid us."

That stilled the questioning.

The Chancellor resumed. "This of Penrith and Tynedale. Hitherto Scotland has claimed these lands as part of its realm, with sovereignty over them although occupied by the English power. Now King Henry offers them in *feudal* possession. This is a different tenure. Although the King of Scots will hold them, he will have to acknowledge the King of England as his feudal superior thereof. Does this parliament agree to this? Since sovereignty is involved, it has the right and duty to say yea or nay." He glanced again towards the throne, almost apologetically.

There was considerable murmured discussion amongst members. Then the Comyn Earl of Menteith spoke.

"We have naught to lose. We have no say in affairs there now, nor have had for long. This could be a large step forward, I say."

The other Comyns nodded, but all eyed, not so much the King nor the Chancellor, but Durward of Atholl.

That man sat silent. No one else raised voice.

Abbot Donald, again relievedly, went on. "Do I take that as a motion, my lord? That parliament agrees that His Grace accepts these territories in feudal tenure, not in sovereignty?"

28

"A motion, yes."

Buchan seconded.

No other voice was raised.

David looked about him, and turned to look behind him, urgently, suddenly concerned, anxious. Were none going to ask the essential question? This was crucial, surely? Must *he*, of them all?

He found himself on his feet, even as the abbot raised his gavel. "My lord Chancellor," he began, in a rush – and that was a mistake to begin with, for not being a lord or a bishop the abbot was not entitled to the prefix. "I am David de Lindsay, sitting as Baron of Luffness. I do not know . . . I must ask . . . are we assured that this decision will not prejudice us? In the future? That accepting these lands in feudal duty will not mean that we accept them as part of England? Always? That in fact we can no longer claim them as a part of Scotland. Does it make the King of Scots inferior to, paying fealty to, the King of England? I, I seek your guidance."

The Chancellor had to wait to give that guidance, for much talk and exclamation arose, some acclaiming the questioner, more pointing out that the lands in question *were* already in England, across the border, that calling this part of Scotland was a nonsense. Others that this would at least put them under Scots control. And so on.

The abbot gained quiet. "As to feudal duty, sir, His Grace already pays fealty to the King of England for his lands in the Honour of Huntingdon. Yet this makes him no way vassal or inferior to Henry for the realm of Scotland. If Henry held lands here, he would have to do the same to His Grace. This prejudices nothing. Does that satisfy you?"

Biting his lip, David forced himself to persist. "In that one respect, yes. But in the other, does it prejudice the future? Over Cumbria and Tynedale? Will this put them for ever into the realm of England? Or might the issue be reopened on another occasion?"

The Chancellor hesitated, frowning. He glanced towards the throne, at a loss.

The King remained expressionless. But he raised a finger to point at David. "Young man, you ask a fair question," he said. "This decision commits myself only, Alexander. *I* make the fealty for Tynedale and Penrith, not my successors. Any of them could, if they so desired, renounce the fealty tenure and claim the sovereignty again. *I* would not, but another could. Does that satisfy you?"

"Yes, Sire – yes. I, I thank Your Grace." David sat down.

The Chancellor announced that if no one opposed it, he would declare the motion before them carried. Parliament acceded to the proposed tenure. Was there any other relevant business?

He was answered from the throne. "I think not. The hour grows late. I judge all present to have had sufficient. I thank all." He rose. And as everyone else hurriedly stood, Alexander took his son's hand and strode for the door. The young prince looked over to where David stood and, smiling, waved a hand.

Thus abruptly was the parliament over.

David found himself the centre of considerable attention now, receiving comment, banter, some congratulation and some calculating looks from lords great and small, his two friends shaking their heads over him. It occurred to him then to wonder what his lady-mother would think of his first parliamentary behaviour?

They went to inform the busy Keith, Knight Marischal, as to their manpower offers for the projected West Highland expedition.

That evening a banquet was provided for the parliament members in a second hall of the long castle – with another, in the cleared great hall, for their esquires and attendants. With practically all the great ones of the land present, and precedence strictly enforced by the High Seneschal, David found himself, with his two companions, seated about one-third of the way down the right-hand long table stretching from the dais down one side of the hall, amongst the medium-rank lords and barons; the left-side table was reserved for the clergy, of whom there seemed an inordinate number, all equally ordered in precedence. The space in between was left open for the comings and goings of servitors with the viands and wines, and for entertainers. Up at the dais-table itself, of course, were the really great ones, earls, high officers of state, ambassadors and the Primate, these flanking two throne-like chairs. It might have been the parliament seating all over again, only now there were ladies present, not many and mainly there at the dais-table and at two smaller tables sidelong, close by.

Musicians played in the central space.

They all stood when these last lowered their instruments and a single trumpeter blew a flourish for the royal party to enter from the back of the dais-platform. King Alexander, still dressed as modestly as earlier, led in his Queen Marie de Coucy, a handsome, well-built lady, daughter of the famous Ingram de Coucy, Count of Guines in the Pas de Calais, one of the most renowned knights in Christendom. David eyed her interestedly, for his own far-back ancestors, Lords of Alost, had been kin to the de Coucys.

But his attention was quickly diverted, as behind the royal pair came the child prince, again being led by the hand by the same good-looking young woman who had escorted him into the parliament-hall. She took the boy over to one of the side-tables, where he promptly sat down – and smiling, she had to raise him up again quickly, for his father and mother were not yet seated.

The High Seneschal announced that His Grace the King and Her Grace the Queen welcomed all to their table; and then called upon the Bishop of St Andrews to say grace-before-meat.

Then they all could sit.

It proved to be an excellent repast of broth and fish and fowl and beef, with sweetmeats to follow and a variety of wines and spirits to wash it down, all partaken of to a musical accompaniment and the antics of entertainers, tumblers, acrobats, gypsy dancers, even a Muscovy bear-leader and his charge. It was fully appreciated, but it all took a long time, with so many to be served. Presently David, whose glance was apt to stray up towards the dais-table and not always to his liege-lord, noticed that first young Prince Alexander was growing restive and requiring to be mildly restrained, and then that he had disappeared altogether.

But not for long. For suddenly David felt a tugging at his elbow, and there was the boy behind him, grinning and holding out his stone hand-ball to him.

David took it, to admire the strange object, ancient obviously and worn with much handling, but still displaying the curious Pictish symbols of a ramping beast with a lappet or trunk coming out from the back of the head, and the equally strange double-disc and Z-rod.

"Very fine, Highness," he said, handing it back. "Do you know what sort of a creature that is? Not a lion. Do you think that it could dance like the bear, there?"

"It has no feet," the lad said scornfully. "How could it dance, without feet? *I* can dance. See!" And he commenced to hop up and down, with more enthusiasm than grace.

"Very good," David commented. Others were watching now, with amusement. "You are more nimble than that bear, I think."

"You, sir – I like you. You can dance, too." That was no question.

David looked in some alarm from the boy to his friends. The meal was not over, and the monarch still eating. To rise and start cavorting now was scarcely thinkable. He patted the lad's small shoulder and pointed up at the King.

"Your royal father would not like me to dance, I think, while still he eats, Highness. Later, perhaps."

"No, now! He will not mind. Nor will Mama. They like me to dance."

"I am not finished this sweetmeat yet, see you . . ."

"He cannot really dance at all, Highness," Alexander Seton put in helpfully, chuckling. "He is very clumsy."

"He is not! I saw how he jumped over that seat, before. At the, the . . ." The child could not get his tongue round "parliament", but he punched Seton's arm to emphasise his strong views on the matter. "None other did that. He is not clumsy." He turned to David again. "Come."

"I, I think, Highness, not. Your father, the King, would not like it, I am sure. While all eat . . . "

"I will go ask him, then . . ."

"No, you will not, Alex." That was a new voice, quiet, lightsome, feminine but sufficiently authoritative, as they turned to find the young woman, who seemed to be the prince's escort, standing behind them. She took the boy's hand. "Come – you have not finished your oatcake and honey. You know that you must always finish your plate." She smiled at David. "You must forgive him, Lord of Luffness. He is over-excited, I fear. Too much happening in one day! I will take him to bed."

"No! No you will not, Marget! I want to dance."

"Tomorrow we will dance, Alex. Say a goodnight to the Lord David." Firmly she pulled him away.

"You know my name!" David exclaimed.

"Why, yes. All talk of you. Even the King. He says that you provided the only real spice of that parliament! I saw you, from a corner above. I am Margaret. A goodnight to you. Come, Alex . . ."

Protesting still, the prince was led off. A few steps, and he turned to shout back. "I like you!"

The young woman smiled at them both, and shook her attractive head.

"Well, well!" Serle de Dundas said. "See what leaping over seats in a parliament can do for a man! Who would have thought it? Who is she?"

From across the table an older man leaned to speak, Sir Adam de Gordon. "She is the Lady Margaret, one of the King's bastard daughters."

"Lord!" David exclaimed.

Later, the tables cleared away, there was indeed dancing for those who felt like it – but a notable lack of females to go round, with the King and Queen retired and some ladies with them. Unfortunately the Lady Margaret did not return to take part.

Presently, the night still comparatively young, the three young men, like so many another, set off for the nearby town of Roxburgh, to see what feminine entertainment might be available there, less high-born perhaps but possibly more accessible. David, although he did not wholly neglect his opportunities, was apt to be preoccupied with the rival attractions he had perceived back in the castle, however unattainable; that, rather than his mother's discretionary advice, tending to inhibit present allures.

2

The great muster was held at that other royal castle of
Dumbarton, or at least on the low ground below it, for
the stronghold was perched on top of twin pyramids of rock
soaring above the Clyde, even less a place for thousands of
men and horses than was Roxburgh. Dumbarton, the dun or
fortress of the Strathclyde Britons, hence its name, was sited
on the estuary just below the West Highland line, where salt
water narrowed to the river, and was the second greatest
port in Scotland after Berwick, predominant on all the west
coastline. Here the fleet could assemble for the voyage up
the Hebridean seaboard; and from here the troops who
were surplus to those who could be carried on the ships
could march northwards through the mountains and round
the sea-lochs, to an arranged rendezvous.

So Dumbarton town and its environs and port were full of
men, and the Clyde waters of ships, most of these last English
– although since many were from the Cumbrian harbours,
they and their crews were looked on with little hostility by the
Scots; much less of such indeed than was displayed frequently
between various more local contingents, for instance between
the Durward and Comyn factions. Not that there were a
great many of the latter present at Dumbarton. That was
one of the disturbing features about the present muster.
The King, wisely or otherwise, had appointed that veteran
warrior Alan Durward to be commander of the land-based
forces, whilst he himself would command the fleet. And when
the Comyn lords had heard of this, they had to a large extent
boycotted Dumbarton; they were not refusing to take part
in the expedition, but were assembling their large forces
elsewhere, none knew just where – since they came from
lordships as far apart as Buchan, Badenoch, Menteith and
Galloway. Lochaber also, and since this last was nearest to

the scene of presumed conflict, indeed a Norse-threatened area, it was probably there.

That was the first ominous circumstance. The second was that Alexander was an unwell man. Never of robust health, he had in the six weeks since the parliament suffered attacks of dizziness and nausea; and the Queen Marie had sought to dissuade him from coming in person on this military and naval venture. But he had envisaged, planned and organised it all, and was not now going to leave it to others.

So there was some apprehension amongst the assembled leadership.

David, for his part, had done rather better than he had promised, having managed to bring along no fewer than one hundred and eighty horsed men, thanks to a larger response from his Ayrshire and Lanarkshire lands of Barnweill and Crawford. He still could not rival Seton, but was able to cock a snook at Dundas.

There was considerable dispute as to which contingents should go in the ships and which march overland. Some had no desire to be herded into open vessels commanded by Englishmen, and possibly suffer from sea-sickness into the bargain; others did not relish the thought of hundreds of miles of marching over mountains and round sea-lochs. Most there would have to do the latter, obviously.

The strategic situation was not quite as anticipated at Roxburgh, improved indeed. King Hakon had postponed his personal descent upon the Hebrides meantime, in curious circumstances. King Harald of Man, whom he had created, however improperly, King of the Isles, had gone to Norway to wed Hakon's daughter. On the way home their ship had foundered in a storm, and husband and wife were both lost. So the Isles and Hebrides were left without a Norse leader, and Ewan, Lord of Argyll, grandson of the famous Somerled, with the support of his cousin Dougal of Garmoran, another grandson, had appealed to Hakon to make *him* King, or sub-King. He had gone to Trondheim, been accepted, and had returned with a small Norse fleet to add to his own longship squadrons, plus the title, spurious as it was in Scots eyes – for of course Ewan mac Dougal mac Somerled was a Scottish subject, and the Hebrides lawfully part of Scotland.

Alexander, with his mustering in full process when he heard the news, decided to go ahead with his expedition, now not against Hakon himself, or only indirectly, but against Ewan of Argyll, to teach that young man a much-needed lesson.

David, and most other leaders for that matter, had no choice in the matter of his travel. There was no room for most of them in the ships. They were to march, or rather ride, with the main body of the army for Argyll. That was a large territory admittedly, a province indeed, part mainland, part islands; and just where they would find Ewan mac Dougal and his forces was highly uncertain. But it was to be assumed that they would be somewhere near a sufficiently large anchorage to provide shelter for a great number of ships, and to support and feed their crews, which much limited the possibilities. There were scores of sea-lochs and great bays on that serrated seaboard, but few having sufficiently large communities nearby to provision thousands of men. All that could be done, it was decided, was for the King's ships to sail up the coasts of Cowal and Kintyre, to Lorn and Appin, looking into the lochs; and the land-based army to seek to look likewise, from as many loch-heads as they, or their scouts, could reach. The Lord of Argyll had many strongholds and castles dotted over his widespread domains, but not all of them conveniently near large anchorages, some well inland. So it was all a matter of searching – unless, of course, Ewan either came to challenge them or headed out to sea, either to provoke a naval battle or to escape one.

This arrangement for the land force much complicated the journeying, since instead of being able to go directly by the shortest and least difficult routes, they would have to keep branching off to the west to prospect sea-lochs probing into the mountain masses; and roads and tracks suitable for taking an army over, in these Highland parts, were few and far between. Much preliminary consultation was called for.

At length, on St Moluag's Day, 25th June – considered to be a good augury, especially for venturing into these parts – the two forces parted and went their separate ways, the fleet to sail southwards, down the Firth of Clyde, to round the great Mull of Kintyre and then turn up the Hebridean coast; the main army to proceed directly northwards up the Vale of Leven to Loch Lomond, to follow that long freshwater loch almost to its head, a score of miles, then strike westwards for the sea-lochs of Long, Goil and Fyne. Not that they expected to find their quarry in either of the first two, too far south for the Islesmen, unless they were actually on the attack, which seemed improbable. But Loch Fyne, the longest in all Scotland, fifty miles of it and much of it almost a firth rather than a loch, might be different. There were sizeable communities or townships thereon, Strachur, Inveraray, Lochgilphead and Tarbert. So this was possible, even though still southerly.

Durward of Atholl made a strict commander, and required to be, with a host made up of the private levies of lords and lairds, all of whom looked to their own masters for authority rather than any overall general. And the said masters were themselves apt to be of independent mind and less than receptive to orders. Such an army was difficult to handle in the best of circumstances; on such curious and complicated a mission as this it was a task for a strong man indeed. But Alan Durward was that, at least, however unlikeable.

He had the Earls of Angus, Lennox and Strathearn with him; most of the others were either with the King or in the Comyn camp. But there were fully a score of lesser lords, amongst which were included David and his two friends, also Gordon, Fraser, Hepburn, Home and others, with lairds unnumbered, all with their various allegiances and attachments. Patriarchal and clan Scotland was much less easy to lead, in warfare as in much else, than was feudal England.

For all that, in fine late June weather, with no enemy likely to be seen for some time, David for one almost felt a holiday atmosphere prevailing as they proceeded up the lovely banks of Loch Lomond and through the mountain passes beyond. They felt in no great hurry at this stage, for although they had to cover well over one hundred miles, the fleet had much further to go, almost that distance southwards in fact before the ships could turn the difficult Mull of Kintyre and then move more than that northwards to reach the first rendezvous – for King Alexander did not intend to sail all the way up Loch Fyne, much doubting whether Ewan mac Dougal would allow *his* vessels to be trapped therein; he

37

would send up a few scouting craft to explore it, that was all, and the rest could be recalled if necessary.

David had never been on campaign before, although he had been involved in some minor Border raiding and skirmishes; this seemed a congenial way to start.

They got as far as Arrochar, at the head of Loch Long, that first day. Pasturing the horses for thousands they found the major problem. The folk of Arrochar were not to be congratulated.

Next day they did not do so well. For soon after leaving Loch Long they had to start to climb through a mighty pass, up and up, between lofty mountains, that immediately to the north with an extraordinary summit ridge shaped for all the world like some craftsman bending over his bench. This lengthy climb, mile upon twisting mile of it, strung out the army itself into a column miles long, with consequent delays, bunching, and men often completely out of touch with their leaders, bad indeed for discipline, so narrow was the mounting track. It occurred to David, and he no experienced tactician, that if Ewan of the Isles was indeed in these southern parts of his domains, he could with ease and at little cost destroy this army with a few well-chosen ambushes, cutting it up into leaderless and ineffective gobbets. Brooding on this during the long ascent, he went so far as to approach Durward on the matter, up near the front of the serpentine progress, concerned also about future passes, of which there were bound to be many in this land of steep mountains. He got little thanks for his pains.

"Fool! Think you that I do not know it?" Atholl growled back at him. "I have scouts ahead. If I judged that there was any likelihood of the Islesmen being so far south as this, I would have these lords and their wretched numb-skulls marshalled very differently, in tight groups, one group guarding whilst its neighbour moved forward, foot patrols up each hillside. I come from mountain country, and need no Lothian lordling's advice!"

David's first lesson in tactics, and possibly in tact also.

At long last, at the summit, the track forked, the left to lead down to Loch Goil, a comparatively short sea-loch; the right to sink also, through steep bare valleys, to great Loch

38

Fyne. Scouts who had been ahead prospecting declared that all was clear down as far as where the latter loch was visible, with no sign of ships anywhere as far as eye could see.

Durward led off down this right-hand track, on the long descent to salt water again.

Loch Fyne, presently opening before them, revealed a notable prospect for long distances – but no assembly of ships. They reached its banks, to camp.

To Inveraray, on its northern shore, they marched to spend the next night, a mere fifteen miles and of much easier going; but there would not apparently be anywhere more suitable to camp for many more miles thereafter. The King had been urgent that they did not "spoil" the countryside nor molest the people, all his subjects after all, despite their Lord Ewan's behaviour; but it was difficult to keep an army in check, especially a Lowland army penetrating the Highlands, whose occupants they looked upon as barbarians anyway; and it is to be feared that the territories they traversed were none the better for their passage. Inveraray town, one of Ewan's largest communities, did not escape unscathed. Durward did hang about a dozen men caught raping and looting, as example to others; but whether this was adequate compensation for the townsfolk was open to question.

All the day after they followed Loch Fyne-side, eventually to reach the arm of it called Loch Gilp, for the night. Yet even so they still were little more than halfway down its length. Still no sign of any shipping, only fishing-boats. And here, at Lochgilphead, they left salt water to turn northwards into a different kind of country, low hills rather than mountains, moorland and forest, with Pictish remains everywhere, stone circles, standing-stones, cairns. By nightfall they had reached the great plain of the Add, great for Highland Scotland, out of which rose the isolated, conical hill of Dunadd, once the capital of ancient Dalriada of the Scots, whence came the line of Celtic Kings of which Alexander was now the representative. Durward took some of the younger lords and knights, including David, to climb the steep hill that evening to inspect the celebrated footprint in the naked rock, where the early monarchs took the oaths of allegiance of their great land-holders, bare foot on sprinkled soil brought from all the various lordships, this to indicate that these held their said lands from the King; this to save him having to travel the length and breadth of the land and islands to receive their homage *in situ*. Beside the footprint was another outcrop carved with the outline of a wild boar, the symbol of the monarchy until Alexander's father William had changed it to that ramping lion. All were considerably impressed by these age-old relics, which reminded these Lowland and largely Norman-blooded lords that the genesis of this kingdom was here in the Celtic north, not in their more civilised south. Alan Durward, Celtic himself, left them in no doubt as to the significance of it all.

But even as they listened to him, the eyes of more than David de Lindsay tended to stray away to north and west, from that lofty viewpoint. For the most magnificent prospect opened thither before them, beyond the levels of the River Add, the Sea of the Hebrides, islands and cliffs, bays and lochs, mountains and headlands, stretching to all infinity, picked out in colours beyond description in the evening sun-down, enough to move even the least susceptible to scenic excellence. David had never seen anything to rival this. And this was the so-called Kingdom of the Isles which they had come to bring to heel. The entire conception and project suddenly took on a very different aspect from that visualised at Roxburgh Castle.

The next day, probing into all the farflung panorama of that seaboard, rounding the bays and heads of sea-lochs, by Kilmartin and Carnassarie, to climb through another steep pass called the Beallach Mor, they looked down on isle-dotted Loch Craignish, with more defiles and passes beyond. Now they were making a bare ten miles in a day, so difficult was the going, so circuitous, so dangerous from the point of view of ambushes. This was, indeed, no terrain over which to bring an army. Small wonder that the Islesmen dominated all, with the sea and their shipping the obvious mode of travel. Hence, too, the Norse hold over it all.

It took them three more days, by Lochs Melfort and Drimnean, Glen Callain, Loch Feochan and the passes between, to come at last to the arranged rendezvous with the King, at the great bay and anchorage of The Oban, The

Land-Locked Bay, which, screened by the island of Kerrera at its mouth, provided one of the largest and best-sheltered havens for shipping on all that extraordinary coastline. Even as they descended from the last of the passes, at Soroba, they could see that the bay was full of ships, moored and anchored.

They had taken ten days to cover those one hundred and thirty miles, desperately slow going for a mounted host, used to very different conditions. No wonder that the King and his ships had beaten them to it, with a fairly consistent south-westerly wind behind most of the way. They themselves had not had to contest an inch of their journey either, despite the opportunities for ambush, had not had to draw sword – save to intimidate and discipline some of their own unruly men.

At The Oban, they learned that all their marching looked like being unnecessary. Alexander was out on the island of Kerrera, at the entrance to the bay, and a very sick man. Ewan mac Dougal had actually come to see him there, and was now gone, and without any fighting. Their army was not required.

The lords and leaders were rowed out to the island, to report to the monarch. Kerrera was almost four miles long, which indicated the size of the bay, and perhaps half that in width, a rocky place of small hills with a very indented and cliff-girt coastline, save at the north end where it was comparatively level, and where was the landing-place from The Oban; although there was a still more sheltered haven two miles to the south called the Horse-Shoe Bays, where much of the fleet lay. The King was occupying the largest house on the island, at Ardentrive, no very noble quarters.

The newcomers were shocked at the appearance of the monarch, whom they found lying on a couch and covered in blankets, seeming to them to have aged years in the last ten days. He was shivering, despite the warm weather, cheeks sunken and haggard; but his wits seemed to be unaffected, and his speech seemed to the visitors to have gathered a strange urgency, he who had never been a loquacious man.

Alexander did not appear to be concerned with his own state, but with the situation now prevailing here, and its

41

impact upon his kingdom. Ewan mac Dougal would be little further trouble, he thought – so long as King Hakon remained in Norway. Having been sent a summons to come here, accompanied with a safe-conduct witnessed by three earls, he had duly put in an appearance, apparently from Islay, with only a few ships, professing himself a loyal subject of Alexander's, but declaring that he could in fact serve two masters, since he was forced to acknowledge the fact that the Norsemen largely controlled this seaboard, from their bases in the Outer Isles, Ireland, Orkney and Shetland, and even Iceland, a situation which could not be wished away. But he, Ewan, posed no threat to the rest of the Scots kingdom, laying no claims to Lochaber and certainly not to Galloway. He sought no confrontation. He agreed not to use the title of King of the Isles granted him by Hakon. All of which was satisfactory.

And yet, Alexander was not satisfied. Ewan was still recognising Hakon as an overlord, and so long as that persisted there was menace up here. He had refused to hand over a son as hostage for good behaviour, or to surrender any of his castles. And he had slipped away unannounced from Kerrera two nights ago, and boatmen said that he had fled to Lewis in the Outer Isles. So the situation was far from resolved. What was to be done about it? This accursed sickness of his . . .

The royal advisers had been giving differing counsel. Some, like the Earls of Mar and Carrick, were for sailing on in strength through the Hebrides, to show their power and authority, and if necessary, to destroy some of Ewan's ships and reduce his strongholds, as a telling lesson, much required. Others, including the High Steward, Bruce of Annandale, the Bishop of Dunblane and David's Uncle Patrick of Dunbar, advised a return south, in case the English did seek to take advantage of the absence of most of the Scots forces up here, and crossed the border in strength – the obvious attitude of these Border lords. A third course suggested by some of the fiercest young ones was to sail the fleet on northwards to raid not only the Outer Isles but Orkney and Shetland as well, as warning to Hakon to keep his distance – this while they had the use of these English ships which the King had paid so much for; a pity not to make good use of them.

All this fell to be considered. The situation was complicated not only by Alexander's illness but by the fact that the Comyn host had not yet put in an appearance. Durward, ever aggressive, urged an onward advance by the expedition through the Isles, to leave no doubt in Ewan mac Dougal's mind as to whom it would pay best to give allegiance. He was doubtful however about going on to attack Orkney and Shetland, fearing that this must inevitably provoke forceful retaliation from Hakon, possibly on their Scots east coasts, those northern islands being in fact Norse territory, by right not only by conquest. Most agreed with him.

Meanwhile, they had to wait for the Comyns – even though Durward demanded why. All these troops could not be carried on the ships anyway; so not a few might just as well return home now, seeing that there appeared to be no likelihood of any land-fighting. The Comyns would only add to this situation. But most declared that they must wait; the Comyns were too powerful needlessly to offend. And the King was scarcely in any state to travel in a ship-of-war.

So they waited, there at The Oban and Kerrera – and each day the royal health seemed to deteriorate grievously. They had brought no royal physicians with them, although Bishop Clement, the only senior cleric present, claimed to have some skills in the arts of healing. But apply these remedies as he would, no halt in the worsening was evident, much less improvement. Lords began to recognise that they might well be faced with the death of their soverign-lord, and the consequent elevation to the throne of a child monarch – which would, of course, imply a regency; and who knew what troubles and struggles to attain that position of power and prestige. It is to be feared that, human nature being what it is, sundry lords perceived that this might be a sensible time to get desired lands and offices into their hands, by royal charter, whilst the King was still able to sign his name to the said papers. Even the good bishop, in amongst his ministrations, was not averse to slipping in a charter, self-devised, transferring the lands and patronage of the nearby Kirk of St Bride, in Lorn, which he had noticed as rich and influential hereabouts, from the vacant see of Argyll to his own bishopric of Dunblane; a charter to which, as it happened, David de Lindsay was one of those called upon to witness the royal signature, the King's handwriting being by now, like his perceptions, notably vague.

Those perceptions, however, had a strange if brief revival on the night of 8th July, when the monarch awoke, shouting. He had had a dire dream, he announced to those nearby. Three terrible figures had appeared to him. One was dressed in royal apparel, stout and red of face; one was youthful and slender but had authority; the third was the largest, huge and terrible and fierce of face, with a frontal tonsure. They asked him, Alexander, whether he intended to go on with this invasion and devastation of the Hebrides? When he said that it was probable, they ordered him to turn back, if he valued the hereafter. He understood them to be the sainted late King Olaf of Norway, the similarly noble Earl Magnus of Orkney, and their own St Columba of Iona, who had brought Christianity to Scotland. In the name of God, then, the expedition must not go on.

As men debated this and wondered whether it was the hallucinations of a fevered brain, or a divine warning, depending on their preference, the King himself sank into a coma. Nor did he come out of it. That next day, 9th July, 1249, Alexander the Second closed his eyes for the last time on this earth, and went on to visit a higher throne.

Now of course all was confusion, shot through with tension, on the island of Kerrera, with mourning for their liege-lord, however superficially observed, far from the general preoccupation. Alexander had never been a man to inspire affection anyway, save perhaps amongst the ladies who had borne his crop of illegitimate daughters. Manoeuvring for advantage began at once – and with the continued non-arrival of the Comyn faction, Alan Durward of Atholl found himself to be in the strongest position, and, being the man he was, made full use of it. In theory the throne could never be vacant; and on this occasion there was no question as to the succession, young Alexander being the lawful and only son. All accepted that – even though Bruce of Annandale did not enjoy doing so; for years before, when the King had despaired of producing a son, he had agreed that Bruce should be the heir-presumptive, he being Alexander's cousin, his mother a daughter of William the Lyon's sister. But the child monarch would have to be proclaimed and then crowned. A council of state could do the first, and order the second. But a parliament would be necessary to appoint a regent for the boy. The royal corpse would have to be carried back to the Borderland, there to be interred in Melrose Abbey, as the King had desired. But the new monarch would have to be taken to Scone, on the Tay, for crowning, according to ancient tradition. And all offices of state, save for the hereditary ones, would be up for appointment, with all that would entail in persuasions and pressures. All thought of Ewan mac Dougal and the Isles situation tended to be pushed into the background. There were few demands now for punitive sailings on through the Hebrides, especially after that dire dream of the late monarch.

Durward himself was urgent to get away southwards, with Alexander's body, and to collect the boy-king and get him to Scone at the earliest. Undoubtedly he wanted to be off, if possible, before the Comyns arrived, stealing a major march on them, and being the first to hail and gain charge of the new young monarch. *He* certainly would not be returning overland – and there were many amongst the lords and chief men who felt the same way; their men-at-arms could do without them on that long trail home through the mountains, for they would be going more speedily, by ship.

David, with no ambitions for power and position, was not one of these, and would ride southwards with his men, Seton and Dundas agreeing to do the same. However, in this matter of getting to Scone for the coronation, there was something else to consider. Durward and the others, going ahead in the fastest ships available and leaving the fleet behind them, would have to go as near to Roxburgh as possible, then hurry overland thereto, and leaving the corpse there, hasten north again with the boy Alexander, to Tayside. Just how many days this might take was hard to calculate. But from The Oban it probably would be quicker to reach Scone by land, not the way they had come but north-about, by Lochs Etive and Awe and through the mountains by Glen Orchy to Strathfillan and Glen Dochart, and so to

Strathearn at Crieff, with Perth and Scone only another score of miles – a total of one hundred miles, less than their march north from Dumbarton. It could be quite a pleasant journey in this weather; and they would probably arrive at the coronation-place before the young monarch could. Not all the army would go that way, but some of the young lords would.

So it was decided.

There was no delay thereafter. The King's body, wrapped in its blankets and these covered with a Lion Rampant banner, was carried down in procession to one of the ships, the fastest they could find; and all crews and passengers for the other vessels recalled from The Oban. David and the other marching leaders were ferried back to the mainland, and by the time that they disembarked, Durward's ship was already heading seawards, and the other craft marshalling to follow.

There was still no sign of the Comyns. John the Red was Lord of Lochaber, of course, as well as much elsewhere, and he might have decided to descend on the seaboard in that area, which was considerably north of this district of Lorn. Or that powerful faction might have elected to absent themselves altogether? For their own purposes. Certainly they would not have done so had they known that there was going to be a change in the occupancy of the throne, and Durward in a position to take charge of all.

David and his friends went to marshal their troops from all the lanes and alleyways of the township, preparatory to moving off northwards for Loch Etive.

3

Scone Abbey lay on the east bank of the great River Tay two miles north of St John's Town of Perth, the shrine which had replaced Iona as the crowning-place of the Scottish Kings four centuries before, when the fierce Norsemen first began to invade the Hebrides and ravaged that island. Here Kenneth mac Alpin, King of the Scots of Dalriada, who became also High King of Alba and united Picts and Scots, brought the fabled Stone of Destiny and other relics of St Columba, for safety, and built this Celtic-type abbey, simpler and much less grand than the huge Norman abbeys which King David had erected in the south, but with its own special features. And here, ever since, the Kings of Scots had come to be crowned, sitting on that renowned stone.

David and his friends had covered their five score miles from The Oban in four days of good riding. They had sent their men on southwards for home, whilst they remained at the abbey awaiting the arrival of young Alexander and his escorting magnates. For how long they would have to wait they did not know. But it was no ill place to linger in, fair, and with so much of interest to inspect.

They were indeed surprised that they did not have to wait longer, for the royal party arrived only two days later – which indicated something of the haste with which Alan Durward had managed to organise all and everything. But they were even more surprised, as almost certainly was Durward, when late the same evening Walter Comyn, Earl of Menteith, also arrived, hardly expected. Presumably, since none of the other Comyn lords arrived with him, he had not been with them on their Hebridean sally, if indeed they had made one; he was the oldest of them, and of course his earldom of Menteith was not far away, a mere thirty-five miles to the south-west, so it was not strange that, if at home, he had heard of what was to be done here. Durward, for one, scarcely welcomed him.

David de Lindsay, however, was less concerned. His attention was concentrated elsewhere. For not only was young Alexander present but his mother, Queen Marie de Coucy, had come, and with her the Lady Margaret, the boy's guide, cicerone and friend – and indeed, half-sister.

Alexander, however closely confined and guarded, was not long in spotting David outside the abbot's house as he was being taken to see the renowned Stone of Destiny. At recognition, the boy broke away from the Queen-Mother and Durward, and came running, pointing and calling out – however much his mentors might have been instructing him that he must now let others come to him, not he go to them. The young woman, after a moment, came after him, smiling.

"Davie! Davie Luffsnay! There you are!" he cried, clearly mixing up Lindsay and Luffness in his mind. "Where have you been? I have looked for you. So has Marget. You were not there!"

David moved forward, holding out his hands, remembered that he ought to bow low, deeply, made some sort of a gesture of it, and then the youngster was upon him, grabbing his arm and grinning.

"Sire!" he greeted. And since that seemed rather ridiculous in the circumstances, "Alexander! Greetings!"

"You did not come." That was an accusation. "I looked for you. Where have you been?"

"I was in the north. In the Hebrides. We all were. I came here overland, not in a ship . . ." That seemed equally ridiculous, and David shook his head, aware of all eyes upon him, not all of them approving. He looked up at the girl, who had now reached them. "Lady Margaret," he said, thankfully. "I, I rejoice to see you."

"And I you, Lord David. You came to no harm on the great venture to the Isles? We were concerned for you when you did not come to Roxburgh with the others."

"That was of kind thought. But – most had to return southwards by land, with little room in the ships. My men did . . ."

"You stayed with your men? How right and good. They are fortunate in their lord, I think! We have spoken of you, often –"

"Marget says that you have an honest face," the boy interrupted. "What is an honest face?"

"I, ah, do not rightly know, Highness." Somewhat embarrassed, he glanced at the young woman – who looked not in the least embarrassed. But he also looked over at the waiting great ones, with more embarrassment. All were being detained. Durward was glaring. Yet he could hardly push the pair away, back to the others. Then it occurred to him that he did not have to. This was the King, lord of them all; and problems could be two-sided. These others could no more command the monarch to return to them than he could send him off.

"Have *I* an honest face?" the lad demanded.

"I would say so, yes, Sire. Very honest."

"Marget says that I have not, sometimes. I do not know. What is honest?"

"You will learn, Alex." She glanced over at the waiting throng. "Your mother, I think, would have you with her now. To take her to see the famous stone. She has never seen it . . ."

"Nor have I. It is big, they say, a big stone. I want to see it. Davie Luffsnay, you come too. To see it." And grasping David's hand, he turned, to pull him back to the royal party.

More embarrassed than ever, that young man hesitated. He did not actually resist – for would that not constitute *lèse majesté*? But he went reluctantly, and he looked over his shoulder at the young woman hopefully.

The Lady Margaret did not rush to his aid but came along too.

Still clutched by the small but far from weak royal hand, David sketched a bow towards the Queen-Mother, and received an amused nod in acknowledgment. She was a large woman, not beautiful but amiable in a quiet way and with strength of character. Durward, for his part, looked disapproving but could say nothing in the circumstances. Others there exchanged glances.

The progress resumed towards the abbey-church, set some distance from the monastic quarters, as was usual in a Celtic abbey. David, held firmly captive and therefore having to walk alongside Queen Marie and the Abbot Malcolm – and therefore in front of Durward and the other earls – was chattered to by the boy the while.

The elderly abbot paused presently, to point out to them a grassy mound on their right, in ground otherwise level.

"That is the Moot Hill, Your Graces," he declared. "It looks sufficiently ordinary, but there is no other like it in the land. For in four hundred years it has grown up thus, from the level – and, pray God, it will continue to grow! For it is made up of earth from all over this kingdom, soil brought from every airt. You, my Lord Alexander, will tomorrow sit on top of it, and see more soil being added."

The boy stared. "Why? Sit up there? What for?"

"It is where you receive the oaths of fealty and allegiance, Sire. From all your lords. Long ago, this used to be done at Dunadd, in Argyll, when the lords brought soil from their lordships, to put into a footprint in the rock, and the King to stand on their own ground to receive their homage. But when King Kenneth mac Alpin brought the Stone of Destiny here for safety from the Norsemen, the homage had to be done beside it. So the lords now brought the earth from their lands to this Scone, and sprinkled it here for the King to place foot on. And have done so ever since. They are apt to bring more soil than would fill a mere footprint, and so in time, over the centuries, this heap has grown into a hillock. It is made from earth from all the realm."

Alexander shook his fair head. "It looks no different from a little small brae," he objected. "See – coneys have dug in it!"

"Coneys scarcely respect traditions!" the Queen-Mother observed. "But it is astonishing that it has grown so large."

"Well, Highness, I suspect that it may have been added to, with some of our Scone earth! To make it more . . . impressive. For the King to sit upon and the lords to climb."

"Davie Luffsnay, you are a lord, Marget says. Will *you* be putting earth on that hill?"

"I fear not, Sire. Much as I would wish to. You see, I have

50

come here from Argyll. I have not been home to Luffness, in Lothian. So I could not bring earth from there, at this time. I am sorry. Another time, perhaps . . ."

"I will dig you some earth. From here. It will do finely. And we can stand on that."

"I, I hardly think that that would do, Highness. Not quite the same meaning . . ."

Chuckling, the old abbot led on to the church.

Considering the significance and importance of this edifice in the nation's story, the church of Scone Abbey was a very modest one, many a parish kirk being larger, finer. But then, the Columban Church had never gone in for great and impressive buildings, keeping up the ancient Celtic tradition that God should preferably be worshipped in His own good open air, rather than in man-made constructions, a different conception from the Romish one of building splendid monuments to God's glory. Columba himself had sometimes planted his little cells or churches within Pictish stone circles, where the Druids had led worship of *their* unknown god, the sun, thus continuing an ages-old, unbroken usage in outdoor devotion. The Scots had ever been a people preoccupied with the past and tradition.

This church certainly bore out that concern for simplicity and enduring values, devoid of ornament and elaboration. Utterly plain and functional, oblong not cruciform, with bare stone walls and stone-flagged floor, it stretched, long and narrow, from west to east, its altar at the far end equally plain and unadorned. Only a presence-lamp hanging above spoke of warmth and reverence.

But it was what lay directly below and before the altar which was bound to draw all eyes, so strange an embellishment of that church. It was a large block of stone, polished black stone, gleaming in the lamplight. Of no more than seat-height, about three feet in length and half that in breadth, it was nevertheless strangely shaped, for its top was somewhat hollowed out giving it a notably saddle-shaped appearance, but bowl-like, and at either end were rolled-over volutes, the stone carved to form handles of a sort. Also, overall it was inscribed, carved, with typical Celtic designs and interlacing, on the dark but gleaming surface. Thought to have been

51

fashioned, so long ago, out of a meteorite, so hard, dark and smooth was the stone, legend had accumulated around this enduring relic of antiquity. Some said that it was the original Jacob's pillow on which he had laid his head when he dreamed of his ladder reaching up to heaven, brought first to Spain and then to Ireland by an Egyptian princess, Scota, who had given her name to the Scots, when she eloped with the son of a Greek king and fled as far as she could westwards. But this seemed improbable, to say the least, this massive, heavy block being hardly a thing that an eloping couple would burden themselves with; moreover it would have made an uncomfortable pillow indeed for Jacob, or anyone else. There were other stories; but most likely was the one that it was in fact St Columba's own portable altar, with the hollow on top for use as a font for holding holy water, and the volutes for lifting it by. Columba had instituted the ceremony of anointing the Kings of Dalriada seated on this stone; and Kenneth mac Alpin had widened the scope of it when, two centuries later, he became High King of both Scots and the Picts of Alba. Some said that Columba had indeed brought it from his native Ireland; but nothing was known for certain. Nevertheless it was Scotland's most sacred symbol – the Stone of Destiny. To rule in this ancient kingdom, the oldest in Christendom, it was necessary to be crowned on the Stone.

David had come to view this the day previous. But now he was pulled forward, before all others, to inspect the relic, with scant respect paid to the altar behind nor the presence-light above. Alexander had, of course, been told about the Stone, and was eager to see it, and to instruct his new friend.

"See – it is for sitting on!" he cried. "Do I sit in that hole, there? It is very black, is it not. Look at that, there. Is that a lion on it? No, it has a tail coming out of its head! Like the one on my stone ball. Have you ever seen a beast with its tail coming from its head, Davie? And here is a sort of a hook thing, with a broken spear. Or is it an arrow? What is that for?" He was running his hands over the gleaming carving. "It is smooth, shiny. And cold. See – I am to sit on it . . ."

"Not now, I think, Sire," the abbot intervened gently.

"Tomorrow, it is to be. It would not be right to sit on it now."

"No, Alex – tomorrow," his mother said, in her French-accented voice. "Only to look at it today. Is very strange, is it not? This Columba of yours must have been a strong man, if this was his altar, to lift!"

"He had a white horse to carry it, Highness," Abbot Malcolm explained. "They say that he took it with him on his missions, all over, even in a boat. He loved his old horse . . ."

"I have a horse, but it is not white," Alexander announced. "My own horse, not the one I came here on. It is very old too. I have had it for years and years."

Durward clearly found all this chatter a trial. "Tomorrow, Sire, we shall come in procession here. The church will be full. We shall walk up this aisle and you will be seated on the Stone. There will be prayers and then you will be crowned, by the Abbot Malcolm and the Earl of Fife here. The High Seneschal will rehearse your descent. Then we will move outside, and the Stone will be carried to the top of the Moot Hill, where you will receive the allegiances. You understand?"

"What are alleg . . . alleg . . .? That I get, on the hill?"

"Homage, Highness. Fealty. Vows of service and loyal duty . . ."

"And earth? I get the earth. To spread. But not Davie Luffsnay's."

"Some earth will be spread, no doubt . . ."

"*I* will spread it."

"No. Not so. That is for others. You will sit and receive the allegiances of the lords, taking their hands between yours . . ."

"No. I will spread the earth."

Durward frowned. "This is a solemn ceremony, no playing, see you. It has to be done with care and order. Your Grace will be fully instructed. Now, enough talk meantime . . ." He turned to leave.

"I would have liked to sit on this stone now," Alexander said. "But . . ." He grimaced at his mother.

"No, Alex. Come."

He turned to David, conspiratorially. "I do not like that man!" he announced, in a whisper penetrating enough for all around to hear. He took David's hand again, not his mother's.

Margaret had been standing back a little way throughout. Now she came forward and took the boy's other hand, raising an eyebrow at David. Together they followed the Queen-Mother and Durward out of the church.

The man had difficulty in detaching himself from his young monarch outside the abbot's house. This was a comparatively small building, and already overcrowded with the royal party, David and the other visitors roosting in the monastic quarters, less than comfortably but better than when on the march. He was aware of the distinctly hostile looks which he was getting, not only from Durward but from some of the other earls and senior lords. This of becoming the King's chosen friend had its problems. The young woman could help, however, and did, being the boy's half-sister, probably alone with his mother in being able to call him by his name and to tell him to do this and that without seeming to infringe the royal prerogative. Now she did just that.

"Come, Alex, say a goodnight to the Lord David," she instructed. "It is almost your bedtime. You will see him tomorrow. See – your lady-mother waits for you." She looked at David. "It will be a great day for His Grace tomorrow, my lord. We must aid him as best we are able."

"I will dig you some earth," Alexander assured.

"If you so wish, Sire . . ."

"Do not call me Sire, Davie. My name is Alex."

"Very well, Alex." That was said low-voiced. "But only when others cannot hear me."

"Save only myself!" the girl said. "A goodnight." And she led the child inside.

The ceremonial commenced at noon, with all forming up outside the abbot's house to process to the church, this time in strict order and precedence. First came the sub-abbot, with a choir of singing boys and monks, to lead the way. Then the

54

aged, white-bearded High Seneschal and his heralds, with the Bannerman carrying aloft the Lion Rampant standard. Then the King. He ought to have walked alone but, in view of his aptitude for interesting distraction, it was decided that, at least as far as the church door, he should have restraining company – and this almost inevitably meant his mother and Margaret. Immediately behind came the great officers of state – the High Steward, the Doorward, the Constable, the Chamberlain, the Marischal and the Primate of Holy Church, the Bishop of St Andrews. Then the earls, including Fife, who had a special part to play this day. They were followed by the lesser officers of state – the Armour Bearer, the Dempster, the Dispenser, the Claviger, the Wardens of the Marches, the keepers of the royal castles, the justiciars and the like. Then all the lords present who did not hold particular office, followed by the chiefs of name, the knights and lairds. And finally the Abbot of Scone himself, with his priests and acolytes, and another choir to bring up the rear. On this occasion there were many amissing, inevitably, all having been arranged in haste.

The Seneschal was busy, arranging all in place.

There was an unexpected hold-up as an argument developed amongst the loftiest ones, highly unsuitable just when all were ready to move. David and his friends were near enough to see and hear what went on. It was Durward who provoked it, a man as awkward as he was authoritive, at all times. He announced that, before they started off, the young King ought to be knighted, prior to crowning – and it was evident from his hand on his sword that he himself intended to do the knighting. Why he had waited until now to declare this was unclear; possibly in the hope that any dispute would thus be avoided.

But there were immediate objections, general and particular. The MacDuff, Earl of Fife, declared that if anyone was going to knight the monarch it must be himself, the Hereditary Crowner. The Earl of Menteith objected, on principle. The High Constable said that the privilege should be his. The Earl of Carrick that this was not the time. This unseemly debate kept all waiting; but at least it gave young Alexander opportunity to escape from his female guardians and come running to David with a little bundle in a cloth which he announced breathlessly to be earth for spreading; he had gone early and dug it from the hill itself, where the coneys had made a burrow. So it was good earth for him to use when he had none himself. Bemused, David expressed reserved appreciation.

The knighting argument seemed to be settled by the Primate, David de Birnam, Bishop of St Andrews, who declared that a monarch should be knighted only by another monarch; this was the established custom and therefore none here were competent to bestow the accolade. Durward rejected that, but with almost all others tending to side with the bishop, he let the matter go.

So, the Seneschal ordering the choir to raise voice, the long procession moved off.

At the church door there was some confusion as the principals stood aside to allow the others to file in and take up their places in the nave – for here there was no chancel door for the priests to enter, as in a Romish church. Nor were there any seats, so that all had to stand. The long, narrow place was quickly filled, the heralds acting as ushers to ensure that a central aisle was kept clear.

The choir led in the chancel-party, the Seneschal and Bannerman first, then Abbot Malcolm and Bishop de Birnam. There followed Durward holding aloft the sword of state, Menteith the sceptre, Strathearn a purple mantle over an arm and in his hand a parchment roll, then Bishop Clement of Dunblane carrying a small enamel and gilt casket in the shape of a gabled building. Fife brought up the rear with the simple open gold crown on its cushion. These all paced up to flank the dark stone before the altar, and turned to face the company.

There was a pause until a trumpet blew, and Alexander came forward alone, his female support no longer in evidence. Not that this appeared to worry the boy, who seemed more concerned, as he all but trotted along, to scan the standing congregation on either side, clearly looking for someone. David de Lindsay guessed that most probably this would be himself, and raised a somewhat self-conscious arm. This was duly perceived and the boy grinned, waved back, and proceeded on his way, a very small figure to be the only lone actor in all this drama.

Up at the Stone, all bowed. Abbot Malcolm moved to help Alexander up on to the stone; but he did not wait for aid, climbing on top cheerfully on hands and knees before wriggling around to put his posterior approximately in the hollow, and calling out something – which perhaps fortunately was inaudible, for the choristers were still chanting. David guessed that it would be a declaration that the stone was cold on the royal bottom.

The Seneschal then waved to the choir for silence and the Primate turned to the altar, to offer up a prayer, sonorous and trenchant, although *appearing* somewhat odd, with the official party all with their backs to him, facing the congregation – even though Alexander turned on his seat to watch.

This over, the Seneschal tapped his staff on the stone-flagged floor and announced that they were here gathered to perform, celebrate and witness the coronation of their undoubted and gracious liege-lord Alexander, whom God preserve, in illustrious descent from the longest line of monarchs in all Christendom, as it was now his duty and privilege to proclaim.

He turned to the Earl of Strathearn and took from him the parchment roll, which he unfolded and peered at somewhat short-sightedly. Clearing his throat, he began to read.

"Alexander, son of Alexander, son of William, son of Henry, son of David, son of Malcolm, son of Duncan, son of Bethoc, daughter of Malcolm, son of Kenneth, son of Dubh, son of Malcolm, son of Donald, son of Constantine, son of Kenneth, son of Alpin." Here the old man paused for breath, as who would blame him, before going on down the Dalriadic line right to Fergus mac Erc, who first brought the Scots over from Ireland at the beginning of the fifth century. He could have gone on far beyond this, but even he, enthusiast as he was, could scarcely ignore the restlessness of the present representative of this ancient dynasty, who was finding his stone hard to sit upon and not quite the right shape for his small anatomy, and was looking round for alternative employment. The recital closed abruptly at Aidan mac Gabhran.

Relieved, the other actors in the scene moved up in line to play their parts. The sword of state was laid on the altar behind, by Durward, to indicate the monarch's support, armed if necessary, of Holy Church. Menteith presented the sceptre to Alexander to hold in his right hand, symbol of rule; he had to prop it up on the stone-top for it was heavy. Bishop Clement handed over the strange little gilt and enamel box, to be held in the left hand; this was, next to the stone itself, the most ancient relic, the famed Brecbennoch of St Columba, which had been presented to that saint by Brude mac Maelchon, High King of Alba, made to contain the sacred oil for the royal anointing, this back in the late sixth century. It was empty now, a symbol only, and indeed represented clash and dispute as well as tradition, for, since Queen Margaret, wife of Malcolm Canmore, the perfervid Roman Catholic, had managed to put down the old Columban Church and substitute the Romish one for the nation's worship, anointing was denied by the Pope for the Kings of Scots at their coronations since they did not sufficiently bow the knee to him as God's foremost representative on earth. This was still a sore point; but no bishop would dare anoint, for fear of papal displeasure, and excommunication. But at least they could present the empty Brecbennoch in token.

The boy was trying to open the roof-like lid of this to peer inside, difficult with the heavy sceptre in his other hand, and in danger of dropping both, when Abbot Malcolm took the purple mantle from the Earl of Strathearn and came to drape it over the child's shoulders. In the process he patted the said shoulder and pointed to the Earl of Fife, who now stepped forward, bowing, and took the simple gold circlet in his hand, handing its cushion to the abbot.

"I, MacDuff of Fife, Crowner of this realm by long descent, do hereby name and crown Alexander, son of Alexander, High King of Scots," he intoned to the company. He turned, and stooped to place the circlet around the boy's brows. It had been recognised that despite the wealth of flaxen curls, the crown would be too large for any child's head, and a padding of yellow cloth had been carefully affixed inside. Alexander, wrinkling his nose, had no hands available to settle the thing more comfortably, and shook his head instead, making some comment to the earl – which, probably blessedly, was drowned in the general shouts of acclaim.

"God save the King's Grace! God save the King's Grace!" This went on and on.

To that accompaniment, Fife unhitched the cloak which hung from his left shoulder and, whirling it around with a flourish, spread it on the floor beside the Stone, to kneel thereon and reach to take the King's sceptre-hand between his own two, in the age-old gesture of fealty, his the privilege of being the first to do so of all. Alexander seemed to think that he was, in fact, seeking to take the sceptre itself, and was quite prepared to give up the heavy object. It was Fife's turn to shake a head, as he rose, retrieved his cloak, and backed away.

Now it was the Primate's turn. He came from behind, to put his hand on the royal head and announced in the Name of God the Father, God the Son and God the Holy Spirit, that he consecrated Alexander, third of the name, High King of Scots. Glory be to God!

Cheers from all around indicated the end of this part of the ceremony, and the Seneschal signed to the choir to strike up again.

Thankfully Alexander jumped down from that stone, pushing the sceptre – which he did not seem to like – at Fife, but clinging to the Brecbennoch which appeared to intrigue him. He was for getting rid of the heavy gold circlet also, but Abbot Malcolm managed to restrain him, and pointed down the aisle. The boy, one hand trying to keep the crown approximately straight on his head, the other clutching the little reliquary, needed no second bidding but set off at speed down the chancel steps, shrugging off the purple mantle, and on through the bowing, cheering ranks of his subjects, not waiting for the choir to lead the way, as planned, and looking for David de Lindsay in the crowd. Duly spotting him, he seemed as though he might divert to come over and show him the Brecbennoch, which he was holding out; but David's not entirely suitable urgent pointing towards the door successfully amended this, and the boy proceeded on in less haste – to the relief of the earls and prelates who were hurriedly trying to catch up and yet retain their dignity, and tending to get involved with the choristers who were now distinctly bemused as to where they ought to be, their singing suffering.

Crowning a child monarch could have its problems.

By the time that David and his friends got out of the church, matters were under control again, Durward, sword in hand, very much in charge. The procession was being reformed, the Seneschal and heralds busy, with the choir now well in front. The King was supposed to head all thereafter, but it was evidently decided that the women would look odd flanking him at this stage, and he was to walk between Durward and Fife, his mother and Margaret behind, in case of need, the remainder forming up as before.

To rather more regular singing all moved off, their pace now also regulated by the rhythmic clash of two pairs of cymbals, hitherto not in evidence. Alexander clearly loved the noise of those cymbals, banging his hands together, reliquary and all, in time with their clangour, and laughing happily.

They reached the foot of the Moot Hill, and here the choir halted, still singing; but the two cymbalists stopped their clashing and turned to hurry back whence they had come – to Alexander's obvious disappointment, who clearly had wanted himself to take a turn at making that splendid noise. Instead, he was led by his two guardian earls to climb to the top of the hill.

There was not a great deal of room on that artificial hilltop, and all that company could not be accommodated thereon. So at this stage only the principal actors went up, the earls, the two bishops, Abbot Malcolm and the Seneschal. And there they waited, Alexander demanding where and when they were going to spread the earth. The two ladies remained below. This was definitely not their day.

Presently the boy's demands ceased as those cymbals

started to clang again from the direction of the church. All eyes turned thither. This time the clashings went at a slower pace, very deliberate. The reason for this was soon apparent, as a group of eight men appeared, the two cymbalists in front and after them six carrying between them what looked like some sort of wooden sledge on which was borne the Stone of Destiny, its evident weight precluding any unseemly haste.

The cheers rose again, to drown the singing, if not the clanging.

Getting the Stone up the quite steep hill was something of a task, the angle tending to have it slide off backwards, to the alarm of all, especially the carriers at the rear. Sundry of the watchers, including David, went up to try to help, either in the carrying or in holding the thing in place on its sled.

Panting, they got it to the hilltop, thankfully, after one or two heart-stopping slides. There, placing it in position, the Seneschal signed for the trumpeter to blow a flourish. Alexander climbed on to the Stone-top again, his crown was straightened on his head, and the second half of the ceremonial began – and this was going to take a long time, so all hoped that the young monarch would be patient.

Durward led the way, bowing jerkily before the King, drawing a handful of soil from an inner pocket of his cloak, scattering this on the ground before the Stone, unslinging the said cloak to lay it on top of this earth and then kneeling, to reach up and take the royal hands between his own and murmur the oath of allegiance, Alexander making a face above the down-bent, greying head, but saying nothing.

The earl rose, collected his cloak, and another, the High Steward, took his place, to repeat the performance. The High Constable had no cloak with him, and had to kneel on the raw earth, his own and others. On and on they came, the Seneschal calling out the names and styles in careful precedence, Menteith causing a slight delay by asserting that he should come before Strathearn and Angus.

Alexander, after the earls and great officers of state, began to look bored, his eyes on the long queue of lords and lairds stretching down the hill and around its base. He wriggled on his seat, and reached for the Brecbennoch which he had laid on the stone-top beside him – and this left him only one hand to be held between all the other pairs. He was obviously watching David's slow progress up the hill. That man found himself growing apprehensive for the many behind him; he suspected that once his own part in this monotonous procedure was over, the boy might well decide that he had had enough, and the fealty ceremony come to an abrupt and undignified end.

When at length it was David's turn to step before the Stone and produce the royal bag of earth to empty, he did so self-consciously, aware that his neighbours in the queue must well realise that this was a fraud, since he could not have been home to any of his lands, all south of the Scotwater, to collect this sample, many of them of course in the same situation, only not having soil provided for them by a thoughtful monarch. Alexander grinned at him as he knelt.

"Coneys' earth!" he said, in what was meant to be a whisper.

David nodded, and taking the warmly moist hand, uttered the required words of allegiance and homage.

He had barely finished when the boy, freeing his hand, held out the Brecbennoch. "Look at this, Davie. It is like a little house, is it not? See these round and square things, with jewels in them. It is wood inside. There is nothing in it. I am going to keep this. What shall I put in it, do you think?"

David touched the relic, but gently pushed it back. "It is very fine, Highness," he said. "But this is not the time, I think. Later we can talk of it. Have I your royal permission to rise?"

"Oh, yes. I will rise too. This stone is very hard. We have spread enough earth now."

"Sire, there are all these others who wish to pay their homage to you. It is important. For them and for you. Always it is done, with a new king. Wait, Alex, and receive them all. All to be your friends. You will much disappoint them, otherwise."

"But – it is just the same, every time. All saying the same. So many. I do not want to sit here, while, while . . ."

"Please do so, Sire." That was urgent. "It is only once, in all your life. One day, you will be glad that you did it."

"Oh, well. Will you stand here beside me, Davie? Then I will do it. You can hold this little house-box for me. You stand there."

David glanced at the earls and bishops. All would not have heard this exchange, but those nearest would, and were scarcely looking approving. But this was, after all, a royal command. Fortunately Abbot Malcolm, behind the Stone, nodded, smiling. David, with that support at least, took the Brecbennoch and stood close by, to sundry frowns. Bishop Clement came forward to take the reliquary from him, but Alexander perceived the intention and cried "No," and the cleric, shrugging, turned back. All this time Alexander Seton was waiting to pay his allegiance next.

David stood amongst the great ones, foremost indeed, while the ceremony resumed.

It certainly seemed to take an unconscionable time, and the boy made little attempt to conceal his weariness with the entire proceeding, turning to chat to David frequently, all but ignoring the kneeling oath-givers, and jerking his hands away after the briefest contact. David endeavoured to make it a little more interesting to an eight-year-old by murmuring something of where each lord and chief and knight came from, so far as he himself knew, as the Seneschal read out the names.

At length it was over, and the boy awaited no permission to jump down from the Stone, to retrieve his Brecbennoch from David, and go running down the hill to show it to his mother and Margaret.

The Seneschal clearly had intended to marshal all again to head back to the abbot's house in procession, but with the King already starting off in that direction, more or less dragging the Queen-Mother, Margaret and David with him, it was wisely recognised that enough was enough, and by mutual consent all just dispersed without formality, to make their own way to their quarters.

Probably there had not been a coronation quite like it before, in all their ages-old series.

It was usual to hold a banquet after such an important celebration, but the abbot's house was much too small for such an occasion, and the abbey had not the necessary facilities anyway. The nearby town of Perth was the obvious place to hold it; but it seemed that the Earl of Fife, considering that this was *his* especial day, had had a feast prepared for as many as would care to come to it, at Abernethy, about ten miles further south, and conveniently on the way home for the royal party. So, with the hour still comparatively early, despite the seeming length of that second part of the ceremonial, it was agreed that a move there should be made with as little delay as was possible. Fife hastily sent a messenger ahead at speed, to warn his chamberlain of their coming.

For the twelve-mile ride, David was summoned to accompany the King, his mother and half-sister. His had become a peculiar and distinctly difficult position, not approved of by most of the great magnates, particularly Durward. But he was most evidently the favourite of the young monarch, however oddly that friendship had started; and all that day's doings had been engaged on precisely to establish the authority and prerogative of Alexander. With no regent as yet appointed, none were in a position to deny his wishes – and he was a fairly strong-willed youngster anyway. So David had to ride at the boy's side, near the head of the long column, with Queen Marie on the other side and the Lady Margaret close by.

The Brecbennoch of St Columba went in a pouch at the royal saddle-bow.

Alexander, after being dissuaded from deciding to keep sweetmeats in it, wanted to know all about the reliquary, where it came from and what it had been made for. Marie de Coucy did not know, had never before seen it, and Margaret was not much wiser; so that David, although no expert on the subject, had to explain as best he might about Columba's conversion of the sun-worshipping High King Brude of Alba to Christianity, and this being the sacred chrismatory for holding the anointing oil for that significant occasion, six centuries before. Which, of course, led to questions about Columba himself, Alba and Dalriada, which Alexander's ancestor, Kenneth mac Alpin, had united to form Scotland, all of which taxed David's knowledge and memory considerably – but which served to lighten the journey, for his hearers at least.

Not that it greatly required lightening for David himself, in fact, for he appreciated the boy's enthusiastic friendship, however much it rather worried him as to arousing enmity elsewhere; and still more perhaps, enjoyed the company on his left hand, the King's half-sister.

"You are very good with Alex, my lord," Margaret told him, when the boy was chattering to his mother. "Patient. He can be headstrong. But there is no harm in him. Just overmuch spirit perhaps. His father let him have his head too often, I think."

"I like him. And his spirit. But I fear that not all around him, the important ones, approve of his interest in me now that he is King. Perhaps I should seek to keep my distance, hereafter?"

"Why that? I would not think that you would greatly fear their scowls and the like? Alex will need such as you, I judge. Many of these great ones will seek to use him, for their own ends – that is sure. They will pull him this way and that. He is not yet nine years. I fear for him, my lord."

"Do not call me my lord – you, a king's daughter . . ."

"A king's *bastard*, sir!"

"The blood is there, nevertheless. And, and the spirit, I swear! Alex is not alone in that! The King is fortunate in his half-sister, I say!"

"*One* of them! There are . . . others. Older than I am. And not all loving each other. The eldest is Marjory or Margaret, Countess of Atholl, wife to Alan Durward. Which could make my position with Alex difficult. She is his half-sister also – and her husband could seek to use that to his own advantage. Take him into *her* care, rather than mine. And so hold him all but prisoner, controlling the monarch."

"You think that there is danger of that? Dear God, could he do it?"

"He seeks the power in this realm. Always has done. Why he married Marjory in the first place." She spoke low-voiced, for Durward rode quite close behind.

"But . . . Her Grace?" David also spoke quietly, glancing over beyond the boy, at his mother.

"So long as the Queen is here I think that she would be against it. She is kindly towards myself. We agree well. But – she talks of returning to Flanders. At least for some time. The widows of Kings do not always fare so well in their adopted lands. And her brother is such a great man, the First Knight of Christendom. They are fond. She would be happier there than here, now. But she cannot take her son with her."

"M'mm. I did not know of this. You think that she will go?"

"I would say so. Perhaps not for very long. But . . . long enough for Alan and Marjory to get their way."

"What can be done, then? Do the King's own wishes matter nothing? I would . . ."

Alexander turned back to him. "Where are we going now, Davie?" he demanded. "This Aber . . . Aber . . .? I have never heard of it. Nor my mother either."

"Abernethy is not now very important, Sire – but it was a great place once. In the days of your long-ago forebears, the Picts. Abernethy, where the Nethy stream enters the Earn River, was one of the main seats of government for the southern Picts, or Albannach as they called themselves. Pict was not their own name but one the Romans gave them. Alba was their kingdom and Albannach their name, and this Abernethy important. For their Columban Church also. There is still a strange round tower there, only one other like it in the land. Tall and slender. You will be able to see it soon, I think. What it was built for I do not know . . ."

"How big? As high as the towers of Roxburgh Castle?"

"Higher, I would say . . ."

"You are very knowledgeable, Lord David," Queen Marie said. "Where do you learn it all? *I* am very ignorant."

"I know no great deal, Your Grace. But about the Albannach and the Celtic Church I know a little. My mother has taught me. She was a daughter of the former Earl Cospatrick of Dunbar, sister of the present earl, and so a direct descendant of the ancient Celtic royal house. The first of her line was Maldred, an elder half-brother of King Malcolm Canmore, who was stronger and drove him out of Scotland to Northumbria, this during MacBeth's reign. The good King David allowed Maldred's son Cospatrick, the first of the name, to come back, and made him Earl of Dunbar. My mother is very proud of her Celtic heritage, and has taught me some of it."

"So you are half-Celtic and half-Flemish, my lord?"

"Well, it is eight generations since the de Lindsays came out of Flanders, Highness. With William of Normandy. I scarcely see myself as Flemish!"

"I think that we need the Lord David to teach Alex about his kingdom and its story, Highness," Margaret said.

"You are right, *ma chérie*. We must see to it. My royal husband told me little of all this of his earliest forebears. All those names the old man read out in the church at Scone! I was lost after the first three or four!"

"*I* could not have named half of them," David admitted. "Although they were all Kings of Scots. I think that my mother could."

"There was one was not a king," young Alexander declared. "For one was a lady, was there not?"

"Ha, Sire, you were listening, then! Yes, Bethoc was the daughter of Malcolm the Second, called The Terrible. He had no sons, but two daughters. The other was Donada, who had a son called MacBeth. But Bethoc was the elder, and married Crinan the Thane and produced Duncan, who became King after Malcolm. He had two sons, Maldred my mother's ancestor, and Dolfin. They were legitimate. Then he had Malcolm, called Canmore or Big Head, by the miller of Forteviot's daughter, and *he* slew MacBeth and became King himself. David was his youngest son."

"A miller's daughter?" the Queen-Mother wondered. "His lawful wife?"

"No, Your Grace. They were not wed. Malcolm was illegitimate."

"But he got the throne? A usurper? And your ancestor, this Maldred, was legitimate? The lawful, elder son. Then, then . . .? Then *your* line should have the throne, not this Malcolm's?" She wagged her head. "Not my husband's and Alex's!"

67

David cleared his throat. "It is an old, old story, Highness. None now question the rightness of it."

"Save perhaps your mother, my lord!"

This of ancestry was boring Alexander. "This high tower at Aber . . .? Can I climb up it, Davie?"

"I should think so, yes. *I* have never done so . . ."

"We go there to see this tower?"

"Oh, no. Abernethy is the nearest house of the Earl of Fife, the Crowner, to Scone, that is why. He provides a coronation feast. He is the chief of the house of MacDuff. It was an ancestor of his who helped Malcolm Canmore to kill MacBeth. As reward, he was given much land, including this royal palace of Abernethy. So we go there. You see that rise ahead, Sire? Once we have topped that, we ought to be able to see Abernethy and its tower, across the levels of Strathearn."

They reached the little town on the hillside above the level plain in early evening, clustering around and below its rambling palace and the extraordinary tower which rose beside the church which was even less pretentious than that of Scone. More than seventy feet high, slender and cylindrical, the tower was free-standing, no more than nine feet in diameter. Almost like some great chimney it soared above all, its weathered stone speaking of the mysterious priorities of the ages long past. Beyond it, within the grass-grown ramparts of an ancient fort, stood the hall-house of the former palace, long and comparatively low-set, only the two storeys high, unlike the lofty Norman-type castles.

Nothing would do but that Alexander should explore and climb that tower right away. His mother thought that he should wait for the morrow, for it was almost dusk now; but she did not forbid it – and no one else could, whatever the frowns and headshakings. Until a regent and governor was appointed, this boy was in a position to have his own way.

Obviously no crowd could enter that slender funnel of a tower, and when David hurried after the dismounted monarch he found only Margaret at his back.

"I had better come," she said. "He pays heed to me – sometimes!"

"Help me up," Alexander shouted back to them, which

was not like him. However, they discovered the round-headed doorway of the strange edifice was fully three feet above ground level, for some reason, with only a narrow ledge as doorstep, so aid was required. The seamed old wooden door was not locked, fortunately, and the boy pushed it open, its creaking immediately lost in a great flapping and fluttering – and a strong smell of bird-dirt. Clearly, whatever its original purpose, it was now adopted by pigeons as a doocot.

Amidst down-floating feathers, and on a heap of odoriferous droppings, they found the inside tiny indeed, for the walls were three feet in thickness, which left only a three-feet interior, so that there was barely room for the three of them to stand, especially with a wooden ladder rising in the middle. There was no other stairway, nor room for one. Alexander, at least, did not monopolise the space, for he was mounting that ladder without delay, encrusted as it was with droppings – which might not do his fine clothing any good.

"Careful!" David called up after him. "This is a very old ladder. Some of the spars may be broken." He got no answer, as the boy disappeared through a trap-door above.

"I had better go after him. You wait here."

Climbing up, about ten feet, David emerged on to another dirt-covered flooring, with a second ladder, halfway up which Scotland's King was already mounting. As the boy's head and shoulders passed through another trap-door, he shouted down.

"There is light here. A window."

When David reached this second floor he found Alexander shouting with laughter at an open, unshuttered window out of which pigeons were flapping and brushing past him to get out. David grabbed him, for it would have been easy to fall out of the man-sized aperture, with no sill and the birds buffeting.

"This is a splendid place, is it not?" the lad exclaimed. "Could I catch one of these doos . . .?"

"Better not, I think. It is their home, after all."

When they turned to face the next ladder, it was to discover the young woman's head and shoulders appearing through the trap.

69

"You should not . . ." David began, but did not go on, as he aided her up.

"Think you I was going to be left standing down there? Only . . . this riding-skirt is too long and heavy for climbing ladders!"

"Then take it off," her half-brother advised helpfully, as he started on the next stage of the ascent.

"Do not embarrass the Lord David, Alex," she returned, but easily.

There were four more ladders and platforms to negotiate, the last tiny landing lit by four small windows, before they finally emerged on to the flat roof. Alexander, crowing with excitement and rushing to the parapet to peer over, David seeking to hold him secure and at the same time help Margaret out – not so difficult as it might sound, with the platform roof only three feet across and the trap in the centre.

In better light and a clear day the view from here would be superb, the wide spread of Strathearn to the gleaming Tay estuary and the Highland mountains beyond. Alexander was not especially interested in the view, however, more concerned with the circling pigeons, and pretending to fly off a hawk to swoop on them, as in falconry. It was strange how much more aware of height and drop they were because of the narrow girth of this summit than they would have been on a wider roof, any tendency towards dizziness much enhanced. Margaret took David's arm in consequence, and *he* took the opportunity to hold her closer. Her well-built person was heaving gently after the exertion of climbing all those steep ladders.

The boy was waving towards the palace, hoping that somebody was watching and admiring. But receiving no answering gesture that he could see, he was in as big a hurry to get down again as he had been to climb up. David urged him to be careful going down, as it would be easy to miss a rung in the backward progress, and fall. Needless to say, that was ignored.

Margaret reacted rather differently. Gazing down, while David held her one hand and she kilted up her long skirt with the other, she ventured one foot down, groping as it

70

were. The ladder did not project above roof-level, so she needed that hand to reach for it. She withdrew her grip of David, but holding up the skirt and feeling for the next rung down with her boot-clad foot, and peering down into darkness, had an unbalancing effect on her, and she came clambering out again.

"I feel a fool!" she announced. "It is this wretched skirt, David. It is too thick and heavy for this. I cannot see where to put my feet, and it all makes my head spin. A fool, yes!"

"Do not say that. You are certainly not clad for climbing ladders." He felt like seconding Alexander's advice that she should take off the riding-skirt, but recognised that this would hardly do. Instead he suggested that he might go down before her and guide her feet step by step.

She seemed happier with this proposal.

So he climbed down the first four rungs, backwards, and then grasped one of her slender, leather-booted ankles, very much aware of a notable length of shapely white leg above. This was an experience he had not enjoyed before. Carefully they commenced the descent.

"As well, perhaps, that it is so dark," she observed – which called for no answer.

Step by step he guided her, and then rather more than guided when they reached the ladder-foot, more or less lifting her down bodily and carefully holding her close thereafter, just in case she was dizzy.

"You are very aware, David, of . . . the possibilities!" she mentioned.

"I . . . ah . . . would not have you endangered. Or fall."

"There are falls . . . and falls!" she returned obscurely, but she did not thrust him away – indeed she could hardly have done so in that so confined space.

For his part, the man guided her down the next ladder with no less attention, and enjoyed the process and the so necessary woman-handling at the foot.

Completing the full descent, almost reluctantly he let her go. "Safe now," he said.

"Am I? Do not sound so disappointed," she told him, letting down the heavy skirt. "But, I thank you. A man of some foresight, no? I must remember it! Not that we are likely to be ascending more such places, I think. Although, with Alex, who knows!"

He helped her down the final three-foot outside step more discreetly.

The King was hopping about impatiently. "You are so *slow*!" he exclaimed. "That was good."

They took him over to the palace.

Unfortunately, from David's point of view, the remainder of that evening was less productive of challenge and opportunity. For now the Earl of Fife, as host, was very much in charge, and the other earls and magnates able to manage the situation more to their satisfaction. The hour being what it was, and Alexander's bedtime already past, it was thought fitting that after so exacting a day for him, he ought to make only a very brief appearance at the celebratory banquet, and then was led off by Margaret to his couch. He managed a farewell wave to David, placed now well down the hall from the dais-table, but evidently spotted by keen young eyes – but that was all.

The feast thereafter was adequate, but for one guest at least the spice had gone out of the day.

In the morning Alexander again insisted on David riding beside him, but now, on the wider roads of Fife, Durward and the MacDuff made a point of riding alongside, flanking the Queen-Mother and Margaret – which, although it did not inhibit the King, did David somewhat, he feeling his presence there to be unsuitable. Menteith and Strathearn struck off now to their own bailiwicks, as did other lords of these more northerly parts, with their trains. Fife himself was only to accompany them to Queen Margaret's Ferry across Forth, to as it were see them off his territories. So the royal party was considerably reduced.

By Glen Farg and through the Ochil Hills and round great Loch Leven, it was some twenty-seven miles to salt water at the Queen's Ferry, where a flotilla of flat-bottomed scows could take passengers and horses across the mile of the narrows to the Lothian shore – to the boy's enjoyment. Thereafter it was only another ten miles to Edinburgh, where its old royal fortress crowning the lofty rock beckoned from afar, and was considered to be far enough for one day's riding for an eight-year-old. However, that citadel was a strong but stark place, with but little comfortable accommodation for visitors, in especial unexpected ones. So David and Seton were to ride on to their Lothian houses – Dundas had already dropped off at his castle near the southern ferry-terminal – and the royal party would proceed on southwards to Roxburgh next day.

So it was farewell there beside the North Loch at the foot of the frowning castle rock, Alexander all but tearfully urging David to stay with them, his mother pointing out that his friend had his own affairs to see to at Luffness, but that they would see each other again soon. Margaret added her assurances.

The boy was not consoled. "You *must* come, Davie. Soon. Very soon. I want you to come. I need you, for, for all kind of things."

"Do not be tiresome, Alex," Queen Marie said. "The Lord David will come when he can. He has been away from his houses and people and lands for a long time now. There will be much to see to. Lords have many responsibilities. You must not think only of yourself. Especially now that you are King."

"If I am the King can I not *command* him to come?"

"I will come, Sire, never fear. One day. Before long, I hope."

"You *promise*?"

David glanced from one woman to the other. This was difficult. He could not just appear at a royal court unannounced and unsummoned, when it suited him.

Margaret came to his aid. "The Lord David might come to teach you more about those Picts and Albannach that we descend from, Alex," she said. "As a, a preceptor. Is that the word? So that you know more of your kingdom and where it, and we all, came from. You would be prepared to do that, my lord?"

"Indeed I would! If, if I was asked, summoned."

"Yes – oh, yes. Tell me more about Columba and his little box. I have it here." And the boy patted the bag at his saddle-bow. "And about his old white horse that carried that heavy Stone."

"Why, yes, that is an excellent suggestion," Queen Marie agreed. "We shall summon the Lord David to be your preceptor, Alex – and we shall all learn more from him. If he will be so good?"

"I will be highly honoured, Your Grace. Whenever you so command."

"Good! Good! Soon!" The King clapped his hands, grinning now.

David looked at the younger woman, was about to speak and then thought better of it. He bowed to the Queen, then to her son, and carefully did not look at the stony-featured Durward.

"Have I Your Graces' permission to retire . . .?"

4

It was good to be home at Luffness. Travel as he would over the land, he was always glad to return here, to this red-stone castle at the head of the great bay, a place with an atmosphere and character all its own, withdrawn somehow, remote-seeming however strong the fortalice itself, amongst its wind-blown trees, with the unending sigh of the waves on the far sand-bar at the mouth of the bay, the calling of the sea-birds, the quacking of mallard and the honking of the wavering wild-geese skeins which criss-crossed the sky. And he got on well with his formidable mother – although all did not – found his young brother John, aged twelve, bearable, and was fond of Pate Dunbar, who was much more than any attendant and esquire. Pate had not come with him on the Hebridean expedition, for the Lady Elizabeth had required him at Luffness, where he acted also as land-steward, with no other man, apart from servants, about the castle – he was her nephew, after all, if from the wrong side of the blanket. Since the late Sir David's death, Pate, old for his years and responsible, had filled a role of growing importance. Save when there were guests in the house, he lived with them as one of the family.

David had much to recount, and to hear also, of course, and after Johnnie's bed-going, delayed as it was on this occasion, they sat up late that night, the Lady Elizabeth anxious to hear all, asking shrewd questions and making pointed comments. She was interested in these links with the young King, naturally, but warned against the suggestion that he might become some kind of tutor to Alexander.

"That way lies danger," she asserted. "The making of enemies. And powerful enemies. It would be well enough for some cleric or other lesser man. But you are a lord, although not a great one. You would be resented by other lords, as like to gain much influence with the new monarch, and therefore power. There will be great rivalry now in this land, to manage the King and so rule all. A child on the throne leads ever to trouble. The earls will be at each other's throats, or some of them, seeking the regency, that Durward of Atholl foremost. And a young lord so close to the sovereign will be seen as a hindrance, a danger."

"But I have no wish to wield power in the nation," her son objected. "Why should *I* seek anything such? I would but seek to aid the boy and act his friend, not to push myself into any position of influence."

"It would not be what *you* wish, David, but what others would fear. All rule in the land is done in the King's name. So he who controls the King is master. And if you could sway the King, you would become powerful whether you sought it or no. And so represent a menace to others. You are not a fool, are you? Can you not see it?"

"You would have me refuse, then? Despite their urgings? If they sent a royal command, *could* I refuse?"

"A boy of eight years' urgings need not be obeyed, I say. They would scarcely rank as a royal command. But – you say *their* urgings? Who are they? Is it the Queen Marie and this bastard daughter of the late Alexander? One of that brood?"

"Margaret is good, kind, honourable. She is closer to the boy than any, closer even than his mother, I think . . ."

"But *she* does not issue royal commands, I warrant!"

"No. But the Queen-Mother agreed with her. And she – "

"So there we have it! It was this young woman's proposal? Lord, David, do not tell me that it is this Margaret who beckons you to the King's side? That *she* is the magnet! That would be folly indeed. I have feared that you are weak about women. I have warned you . . ."

"I am not weak about women! You have it wrong, all wrong. Margaret is Alexander's companion and guide. Her father so appointed her. Queen Marie trusts her more than any other. They asked me to do this, for the King's sake. He knows but little of much of his kingdom, in especial of your Celtic line, of the past. I can tell him . . ."

"David, use such wits as you have! This girl has smitten

76

you. You seek to be near her, and this of being the boy's preceptor is all that you need for excuse. But – do you not see it? If being so close to the King is dangerous, almost more so would be to seek any attachment with the late King's daughter, illegitimate though she may be. *You*, no great lord. Think you that the powerful ones, the earls and magnates, will not be after her, for themselves or their sons? His other bastard daughters, older than she is, are wed to the highest in the land. Even Durward's wife is one of them. They will mislike you the more."

David wagged his head, frowning.

Pate, listening to all this, put in a word for his cousin. "If David is careful, discreet, might not all be well? Indeed, all to the good? For him. If he has the young King's ear, men may come to him for help in their ploys and needs. It need not all be jealousy and resentment. And if this Lady Margaret is so sought after, she may not be there very long, but be taken and wed."

David frowned the more, which was unkind.

"You should have more sense, Pate," his aunt reproved. "Do not encourage him in his folly. David has ample to attend to here, in his baronies of Luffness, Saltcoats, The Byres of Garmylton, and Barnweill and Craigie and Crawford in the west. Enough for any young man to see to, without seeking to put a noose round his neck by getting in the way of powerful and dangerous nobles. Let us hear no more of this. For there is going to be strife in Scotland very soon – you will see. War, even. Between rival factions. They will battle for supreme power, nothing more sure. Durward and the Comyns, in especial. Even my otherwise foolish brother, and your father, Pate, sees it. He has chosen the better path, for once – and is to go on crusade!"

"Crusade! Uncle Patrick?" David exclaimed. "Why? Why that? He is not great for religion, is he? Crusading! He did not come on the sally to the Isles. But . . ."

"Patrick smells trouble ahead and will get out while he may. He hates Durward and the Comyns equally. He did not go with King Alexander to the Highlands because he feared that the English would take the opportunity to invade in force while Scotland's strength was elsewhere – and Patrick's lands are the first that would be overrun and ravaged, nearest the border. If he was not there in strength to protect them."

"Others could have said that!"

"Perhaps. But others are not Patrick of Dunbar, who is less than urgent to aid this present line of Kings, since he believes that *he* should be sitting on their throne, if he had his rights, Malcolm Canmore's bastard line! An old story, but my brother never forgets it. Now that Alexander is dead and this boy succeeds, Patrick recognises that he not only never will be considered for the regency, but will be eyed askance by the others, in case he has designs on the child's throne. After all, there is no other true heir. The claims of Bruce and Comyn are all through women. So – he goes off on crusade to the Holy Land, for the sake of his immortal soul, or so he says. And will come back when the troubles are over. And none will despoil a crusader's lands, while he is gone, for fear of the Pope's anger, anathema and excommunication! My normally foolish brother!"

David sought his couch that night with much mentally to digest.

In the days that followed, the Lady Elizabeth was proved right in some of her contentions at least, for there was indeed much for a lord of baronies and manors to see to after a fairly lengthy absence, requiring his personal attention and decision. Pate made an excellent land-steward and manager, but there were matters he could not deal with, particularly where baronial rights were concerned, where only the baron himself could decide. Within his barony, the baron's powers and responsibilities were extensive and even daunting. He had the power of pit-and-gallows, for instance – meaning that, for quite a wide variety of offences he could imprison or even hang, without reference to a higher authority. He and he only had the right to hold sales of cattle and sheep, fairs and the like, within his barony, and receive commission on all transactions. He had the fishing rights in all rivers and lochs, and only he could let these out. He had his own mills, and only in these might his tenant farmers' grain be ground – at a price. Luffness had the salt-pans at Saltcoats, a mile to the east, where the sea-water was boiled, and all the barony must buy their salt here – important for the salt-fish trade. And so on.

Then there were decisions as to tenants' disputes and claims. It was surprising how often these cropped up and how reluctant the said tenants were to abide by any other than their lord's own judgments, the most frequent to do with riggs and pasture. The system of land cultivation was by rigg and common grazing, that is, the tillable ground was in the main divided up into riggs, long narrow strips, separated by gutters or shallow ditches for drainage. These riggs were allotted by rotation to the various tenants, and changed seasonally, this to ensure that no one tiller monopolised the best and most fertile land. So a man might have half-a-dozen riggs, some of them possibly quite some distance apart, even on another part of the estate. Each year the tenants met together to decide on the allocation of these, and always there were grumbles and complaints of unfair decisions, and only the baron could alter these. The pasturing of cattle, horses, sheep, goats and even geese was less troublesome, since common grazing was the rule, large areas set aside for these commons. But even here there could be disputes, for the animals had to be watched and watered and prevented from straying off on to the tilled land, to damage the crops; and the providing of rotations of cowherds, shepherds, coltherds and the like, usually boys and old men, was a responsibility of each tenant – and some were less reliable than others, and great were the recriminations when beasts were allowed to wander off, with the herd fallen asleep perhaps, and corn or roots were trampled. Enclosed fields were the privilege of the lord only.

So David had no lack of duties to attend to, although happily there were no serious offences requiring the baron's court and sentencing. He had never, so far, had to condemn a man to hanging on the gallows-hill, and prayed that he never would, doubting whether he would be able to harden his heart to do it. Once his father had forced him to watch the grim process, when he was a boy, to learn his trade as it were, and the effects still were with him. Even the confining of a prisoner to the fearsome pit in the thickness of the

79

castle keep's walling, without light or heat, was something of a dread for him, a thought to disturb his sleep in more comfortable parts of the building. His mother declared that he was over-soft to be a worthy baron; his father had not shrunk from such duties.

It was not all duty and responsibility, of course. It was now August and the season for wildfowling started. David, reared where he had been, would have been an oddity indeed had he not been a devotee of this sport, hawking for mallard, widgeon, wild-geese and herons, with the occasional swan, giving him great satisfaction. Shooting the wildfowl in flight with bow and arrow demanded still more skill, as did stalking roe-deer in the woodlands. He and Pate pursued these activities then, especially the duck and geese flighting in the great bay at dusk and dawn, and sometimes they took young Johnnie with them. Also they went fishing, spearing flounders in the shallows or going out of the bay into the Scotwater, beyond the three-mile-long sand-bar, with lines and nets, sometimes alone in a small boat, or more often with some of the fishermen of Luffnaraw in their large sea-going cobles, venturing as far out towards the Norse Sea as the mighty Craig of Bass or even the distant Isle of May if the wind was in the right airt for a sail to be hoisted.

David, the while, awaited a summons from Roxburgh Castle with mixed feelings. There was no question but that he wanted to go there; but he realised that there would be strong objections from his mother, and he still tended to be much influenced by her authority, for it was only a year since his father's death and he had not been in any position to controvert her. Not that she was really a stern parent, and on the whole they got on very well together; but she was by nature an autocrat, and her ancestry did not help.

In fact, the Lady Elizabeth had her own methods of implementing her good advice. One evening, when David and Pate returned from a long day's fishing, she announced that she had been to Seton Palace, six miles to the west, while they were away, to see their good neighbours, and she had invited David's friend Alexander Seton to come over to Luffness two days hence to sample the wildfowl hawking, which was amongst the best on all the east coast of Scotland. David would have an opportunity to display his expertise.

The next day, it so happened that a courier indeed did arrive from Roxburgh with a summons – but not bearing a command to wait upon the King, but to attend another parliament, in mid-September, this in the name of the realm's Chancellor. Forty days' notice was required for the proper calling of a parliament. This assembly, so comparatively soon after the last, was very important, it seemed, not only as the first of the new reign, but necessary for the appointment of a regent. So at least David would be going to Roxburgh again in six weeks' time, and with no maternal inhibitions able to restrain him.

The following forenoon, then, Alexander Seton arrived as expected – but unexpectedly he had with him his sister Judith. David knew Judith, of course, a cheerful and outgoing young woman, something of a tomboy, and quite handsome in a strong-featured way. Apparently she had come to learn the refinements of shoreline hawking, something she had not attempted before. Her brother seemed just a little embarrassed at her presence with him. David, although surprised, welcomed her.

There was a further surprise. The Lady Elizabeth, not an enthusiast for falconry nor wildfowling hitherto, turned out to be joining the party this day. Her elder son could not recall when last she had accompanied him down to the bay. The fewer present, actually, the better for this sport.

Normally, hawking was done on horseback, with the sportsmen flying or launching their birds, the falconers carrying them and tranters to act as retrievers, both for the hawks and their kills. But Aberlady Bay was no place for horses, save at low water out on the firm sand bar. The inner bay, all fifteen hundred acres of it when the tide was out, was part mud-flats and part salt-marsh, with the Peffer Burn winding its sluggish way through to its mouth at the bar. This wide and flat area was the haunt of wildfowl innumerable; but it was without cover, in the main, and the pitted salt-marsh and soft mud poor riding ground indeed. Moreover, the fowl were wary and easily scared into flight, which was why the fewer the sportsmen the better, two being less obvious than a party. Another reason why horsemen, much more visible at any distance, were not advisable. Also extra falconers and tranters had to be dispensed with, and trained dogs used as retrievers.

Eight of them, then, went down into the bay below the castle walls – too many for the best sport, by far – David, Pate, Seton and the two ladies, with three men carrying the hooded peregrines, and three dogs. More dogs might have been useful, but Luffness had only three trained for this work, since it was normally a solitary sport – and untrained animals would be worse than useless. David feared, with this kenspeckle company, that there might be little sport in it. He wondered at his mother. Johnnie had wanted to come too, of course, but even their mother was dismissive today.

Wearing long riding-boots coated with beeswax to keep out water and wet mud, if possible, they waded the Peffer, about a score of yards across here, the women kilting up their skirts, and out on to the saltings. The tide was two-thirds out, and ebbing. They had not gone for more than two hundred yards before they saw ahead of them duck rising and winging away northwards, far too far off to fly their hawks against. Pate looked at David and shook his head.

That young man had to assert himself. "This will not serve," he declared, halting. "We are too many, too evident. We shall never get near enough for a kill. We must split up, go in pairs, three pairs, each with a dog, and spread out, far apart. There is sufficient bay for all. Keeping on the salt-marsh, not out on the mud. You will find cover, of a sort, mainly tree-trunks washed up by the tide, and other flotsam. Pate, if you and Dod go furthest out, circling inland a piece and then turn and work back, you will help to put up fowl, which should fly towards the rest of us."

"Good," the Lady Elizabeth approved. "I will go with Alexander. You, David, take Judith and show her how it is done, this being her first essay. Will and Tom, with the extra hawks, can take up some central position."

Blinking at having all this taken over and arranged for him, David could scarcely controvert. The hooded hawks, or rather falcons, peregrines, legs strapped with their jesses, were transferred to leather-padded armlets, and soothed by gentle stroking. Then it was dispersal.

So David found himself alone with Judith, rather obviously by arrangement of his mother. She appeared to be quite happy with the situation, and told him that she had long wanted to do this. She had flown hawks often, of course, but never on foot and in tidelands. He must instruct her.

With their dog close at heel, they moved further out towards where the sea-grass and greenery of the salt-marsh ended at the reddish mixture of sand and mud of the tidal ats, and there found one of the many tree-root stumps washed up in storms to crouch behind. On the way, they put up sundry waders, dunlin and redshank and a pair of widgeon, but these last too far off to set hawk at. David found a log for them to sit on, behind the stump, and they settled down to wait.

"As well that it is but August," he mentioned. "This can be a cold ploy in different weather, later in the season. You are warm enough, in this breeze off the sea?"

"To be sure." She laughed. "If it gets cold, we can always huddle closer! If these hawks will let us."

That sounded an aspect of the sport he had not thought of before.

He told her of the problems of wildfowling with hawks. It was mainly duck, mallard, widgeon, teal and the like that they were out to catch. Except at the dawn and dusk flighting, to and from their inland feeding-grounds, these, when raised, tended to fly low; and hawks preferred to stoop on birds flying high, naturally enough – since, if the quarry was to swerve at the last moment, near the ground, the hawk, diving fast on to it, could dash itself on the said ground and possibly cripple itself. So the higher the duck flew the better, many a hawk refusing to stoop otherwise. Geese were different, flying much higher; but there were not many geese in August, and such as there were would be inland, feeding, during the day. As for heron and swans, they were only occasionally to be had, slow-flyers but strong, and capable of putting up a fight.

Judith listened, but with only moderate attention for one eager to learn the rudiments of the sport.

"Yes," she said. "Meantime we but wait?" She edged a

little closer on their log. They had settled the hawks on their tree-roots in front. "It is long since we saw each other, David. You have been much venturing, and meeting the great ones, Alexander tells me. I hope not so much as to forget old friends and neighbours?"

"No. No – of course not. Never that."

"Good. You must come to Seton soon. I have looked forward to this day." She patted his hand.

That could not have been for very long, for it was only two days since his mother had gone to Seton and arranged this. But he could hardly say so.

"I hope that the sport does not disappoint, then," he told her, a mite carefully.

"We must not let it, David!"

"It rather depends on the fowl, does it not?"

"And ourselves," she amended.

"And the hawks!"

"Even lacking wildfowl and hawks we could still enjoy the day, no?" And she patted his hand again – and this time *her* hand stayed on his.

David certainly could not snatch his hand away. He liked women, too, and their attentions, and was no prude. And this Judith was attractive enough, spirited, forthcoming and clearly prepared to be co-operative. If it had been some other young female . . .? But this was Judith Seton of that Ilk, sister of a fellow-lord, friend and neighbour. Any closer association with her could lead to complications, indeed to almost the presumption of marriage. Was that his mother's intention? The reason for this day's activities? What had these two women been saying together? Or was he just being over-suspicious and difficult? He would hate to be that. He patted her hand, in turn, but not lingeringly – and promptly raised it to point.

"Oyster-catchers and dunlin," he said. "And a flight of sanderling. See how they swerve and bank, all without colliding. Is that not a wonder? But these are no use for the hawks."

"Alexander tells me that you are far ben with the young King," Judith went on. "And that he has a governess, his half-sister. Good-looking. Do you find her handsome, David?"

He hesitated. "Scarcely handsome – but good-looking, yes. Fair. And kind."

"Not too kind, I hope! Since that would be *unkind*, no? In that she is a king's daughter, even though bastard. And no doubt destined for some great earl or other. Not for such as Davie de Lindsay! But perhaps her kindness is . . . otherwise?"

"I did not mean that she was kind to *me*! Or not in that way." He looked away. "I am not . . . concerned."

"I am glad of that," she said. "A pity if you were to suffer rejection when, when you could be better . . . suited."

"I am not . . ." he began, when he was spared, at least for the moment. Two mallard were winging their way in their direction, from the bay-mouth. Probably they had been put up by Pate and Dod, had swung out seawards and were now coming back towards the inner bay. They were not high, but were not too low-flying for sport. Swiftly he grasped his own peregrine, whipped off first the jess strapping its legs, to free it, then the hood off its head, and turning it towards the oncoming duck, gave it two or three little jerks in that direction, then launched it up and away.

The bird, trained and eager, was sufficently hawk-eyed, despite having been as it were blindfolded, not to miss the sight of quarry in an otherwise empty sky and, wings beating fiercely, rose up and up in a continuing corkscrew motion.

The girl cried out. "It does not see them! It is not going towards them. Foolish creature – it goes in the wrong direction."

"It will have seen them, never fear. It but climbs, gains height. It needs height."

Sure enough, the falcon, rising incredibly swiftly, soon, at fully two hundred feet perhaps, halted its climb and swung off towards the pair of duck. But mallards have keen eyes too, and the pair knew predators when they saw them. Promptly they swung off westwards, wings beating fast, out towards the open mud-flats, rising higher as they went.

That meant that the hawk had to climb higher also, which was a delaying factor. David would have expected the duck to go low. But although mallard can fly more than twice as fast as a horse can gallop, a peregrine can fly faster, even climbing. By the time that the quarry was halfway across the bay, and soon would be a little difficult for the watchers to see, the hawk was above them. The duck knew it, and in their panic now separated, one swinging landwards, the other seawards.

"Which . . .?" David exclaimed.

That hawk had no doubts, at least. They saw it circle towards the sand-bar, seem to halt suddenly in the air, wings winnowing, then close them and drop abruptly, like a plummet, so fast that the watchers could not actually follow it down. What they did see was something like an explosion of feathers, as peregrine and mallard hurtled towards the mud together.

"A kill!" David cried. "Well done! A notable first kill!"

The dog at their side was whining in anticipation.

"Save for the poor duck!" the young woman observed.

"A quick death. It would know nothing. A better death than battered in a storm or wings frozen in winter ice. They all must die . . ."

"So must men and women! But not before their time . . ."

He could have asked why she had wanted to come wild-fowling, but he was now peering out there to the flats. What happened now was important. The hawks were trained, after a kill, to return to their falconer; but instinct or hunger could triumph, and the killer could go down after its quarry and use its sharp, hooked beak to tear itself a meal. Passage-hawks, as birds captured from the wild and then trained, were called, were more apt to fail in this respect, and sometimes thereafter to fly off and return to the wild; but birds like this one, bred in captivity, were better.

With a nod of relief David saw his peregrine flapping and corkscrewing up again, and was praising it when suddenly it swung off seawards and still gaining height. He frowned, and then perceived the reason. Three smaller duck, teal by the size of them, were flighting out from the shoreline, fairly low, and the hawk had seen them. This represented complication.

All this time the dog had been whimpering and trembling. David now unleashed it, and pointed. Like an arrow from a bow it was off, heading in the direction of the fallen mallard.

It had keen eyes too, plus a useful nose. It would find the kill almost certainly.

The hawk went after those teal, and they, quickly becoming aware of it, turned seawards again and skimmed lower. David shook his head.

"Bad!" he said. "They could go far out. And once a hawk has started on a chase it will be loth to give up. It could kill over the sea, and not only do we lose the game but we have the hawk gone for some time."

"Look!" Judith exclaimed, clutching his arm, and pointing. A tight group of fairly large and heavy-seeming fowl were coming towards them, again from seawards, keeping low. Pate obviously was making an impact out there.

David shook his head. "Those are eiders," he said.

But she had already whipped off her hawk's hood and the creature was straining at its jess.

"No use eiders," he told her. "You cannot eat them. Taste of fish."

She had already loosed the jess, however, and the bird was off. The duck swerved away inland, and the hawk turned to follow, rising.

"We will not see that one for a while, either!" David commented. "They will go amongst the sea-buckthorn and trees, in that direction, and your hawk will go hunting them. Could be long before it returns."

"Never mind. Eider give fine down for stuffing cushions, do they not?" she excused herself.

"Save that we have no dog to retrieve any," he pointed out. "When our beast comes back it will not know where to go after them."

Judith did not seem unduly upset over this fiasco. She laughed, indeed. "We will just have to entertain each other until the first hawk returns," she announced, and huddled up closer still. "That wind off the sea is not very warm, is it?"

David could not but grin at this shameless opportunism, and duly put an arm around the girl – the least any man could do. She snuggled in and laid a head against his shoulder.

"I think that I like wildfowling," she informed. "You do it usually at dusk and dawn, Alexander says? I do not know about the dawn, but I think that I would like it at the darkening. In the right company, that is."

What was he to say to that? He said nothing.

Their dog came back with a mallard drake in its jaws, the handsome green, grey and white plumage but little damaged, if somewhat slobbered on by the retriever.

"See," David said, taking it. "The hawk kills expertly. Only the neck is broken. Astonishing that it can drop from such a height at such speed and strike a fast-flying duck just where it will do that."

This subject did not seem to enthral his companion. She pushed the clever dog away and did some retrieving of her own, getting his arm back around her and adjusting her person so that his hand ended up most naturally cupping her left breast, and a pleasing handful too.

"Lady Elizabeth tells me that you like women's company, David," she mentioned. "That is good. But . . ."

"My mother appears to have been busy, two days ago! Likewise, your brother! What else did they tell you?"

"Why, no more than kindly talk of those who are fond of you. No harm in that, is there? No harm in liking women's company, either. Save that . . . there are women and women!"

"I am aware of that, yes. Just as there are men and men! Perhaps *you* should be warned, Judith Seton!"

"Oh, I am quite safe, I judge. I *use* my judgment!"

"So! And I rank where in that?"

"Oh, high, David – high. And might rank higher, I think." And she stroked his wrist more than companionably.

While it was admittedly tempting to encourage this process, David felt, perhaps belatedly, that caution might be called for. And he did not like to feel that he was being manipulated, especially by his well-loved mother. He looked around.

"Perhaps we should move to another position," he suggested. "To see how the others fare?"

"We are very well here, are we not? And if we move, will our hawks find us again?"

"Oh, the hawks will find us. And if not, they will return to their castle lofts. Nearer to Gulan Point we might find

88

more sport. And you might feel warmer with the movement."

"Is that not a long way to walk, David? In these heavy boots. I am quite happy here."

"Very well." She was his guest, after all. He launched into a disquisition on the advantages of peregrines over other hawks and falcons for wildfowling on the tidelands.

She rearranged herself after his beginnings of a move, replacing his left hand on her conveniently swelling bosom. "I like being held. It feels . . . secure," she said, ignoring falconry. "Do *you* like the feel of a woman, David? Playing the man? Protecting her from winds and cold . . . and other things?"

He could not in honesty deny it. And her frankness was refreshing at least. "To be sure. And you are shapely, Judith. I, I appreciate . . ."

"You might be the more appreciative – who knows? Perhaps not out on this salt-marsh!" She rubbed a cheek against his, and her lips were very close.

He did not want actually to turn away, and those lips were enticing, red, moist. But if he fell now, who could tell how difficult it might be to call a halt? And the further this went, the nearer he was to commitment. And he was not ready for commitment yet, however suitable a match they might make in most respects. He was contemplating some not too obvious avoiding action when his peregrine came to play the part of rescuer.

"See – here it comes!" he exclaimed. "And with . . . yes, with a kill. Here is a wonder! Noble bird!"

Whether Judith Seton thought the same was question able, as the man started up. But she put a good face on it.

The falcon came over them, circled. David, standing now, held out his arm with the leather gauntlet and whistled gently. The bird dropped what was held in its talons, a teal, a small duck admittedly but as large as the hawk itself, to fall at the man's feet. Then, using its wings in a flapping motion, it sank down, to hover for a moment above his head, then settled exactly on his arm.

"Good bird! Fine bird!" he commended, stroking the back

feathers. "Put on the hood, Judith," he directed. "And the jess . . ."

On his feet, David decided that he should not sit down again. He looked around him, and standing, could now see, over the levels of the salt-marsh, to where his mother and Seton were crouching behind another tree-trunk, almost half a mile away. And still further seawards, two walking figures were visible, Pate and Dod, coming back towards them.

"That must serve, then," he announced, with something between relief and regret. "Pate is returning. There will be little more sport now, I think. I wonder where *your* hawk is?"

"If we wait here, it will come back to us, no?"

"Not necessarily. Once it goes hunting amongst woodland and buckthorns, it may stay away for some time." He picked up the mallard and the teal, to put in the game-bag slung over his right shoulder – and which had been rather in Judith's way hitherto, to be sure. "Let us go and see how my mother and Alexander have done."

She did not actually sigh as she shrugged.

They found that the Lady Elizabeth and Seton had in fact done distinctly better than they had, with no fewer than five kills, two mallard, two widgeon and another teal; they had been nearer to Pate, of course, and rather more game would have come their way. They had indeed had to call on the extra hawks from Will and Tom. There followed arch and knowing glances at David and Judith, and remarks anent lack of attention and the like, to account for *their* modest bag. Seton had noticed David's peregrine flying back with the teal in its claws, unusual. One of their extra hawks had not come back, like Judith's.

Pate and his companion arrived soon after, and it was agreed that there would be little more sport to be had without much walking, not enticing for the ladies in heavy boots. So a move was made back to the castle, with Dod, Will and Tom sent, carrying the bag, to look for the missing hawks. Pate had a pintail duck, a widgeon and a shoveller. So altogether they had ten fowl, which was a fair catch for tideland hawking.

Judith announced that she had much enjoyed herself.

Thereafter, in the castle, they passed the time pleasantly enough, with no problems surfacing for David. Judith, in good spirits and making lively company, sang for them to the Lady Elizabeth's accompaniment on a lute. When, eventually, the Setons departed on their six-mile ride home, David elected to accompany them part-way – and got the kiss he had shirked earlier, full on the lips, and lingering for a horseback salute, this at Fernieness, near to Longniddry. There were urgings for him to come to Seton, and soon.

On the ride back, alone, in the gloaming, he had opportunity to consider. This was a situation which would not go away, he foresaw. Obviously his mother was pushing this young woman his way, and with a view to marriage certainly. Probably she had been thinking that it was time that he married, ever since his father's death. Baronies required heirs. As evidently this preoccupation of hers had been enhanced by his perhaps unwisely evidenced admiration for the Lady Margaret. That admiration was, he had to admit, itself unwise – at least any contemplation of it going any further than respectful regards. But . . .

He decided that, since there were those six weeks before the visit to Roxburgh for the parliament, and in the circumstances much could develop in six weeks, he would do something in the meantime which he really ought to have done before this – and to which his lady-mother could not object. He would go and visit his west country baronies and properties, and display their new lord to his tenants and representatives there, at Crawford, Barnweill, Craigie and the rest. That would fill in the time.

As expected, his mother was not long in remarking upon the virtues and excellences of Judith Seton, her suitability as a wife, and the advantages of having the two neighbouring estates linked. The Setons were, like the Lindsays, originally of Flemish origin, but they had acquired good Celtic blood also, by marriage. Marriageable and attractive young women of their standing were not thick on the ground, by any means, in their area. And so on.

David was carefully non-committal. He decided not to mention his resolve to make an expedition to the west country baronies until a day or two later.

91

5

As it turned out, the tour round those distant properties, all
gained by the Lindsays through judicious marriages, more
than adequately filled in the time before the parliament
and avoided possible developments with the Setons. Indeed,
David had to cut short his surveying and exploring, for he
had inherited wider lands and more extensive estates than
he had realised, especially in the upper Clyde valley in
the Crawford and Lowther Hills area, with great sporting
possibilities as well as notable cattle and sheep country.
And still further west, in Ayrshire, Craigie and Barnweill
proved to be prosperous lairdships with quite large villages
and much tilled land – and more still, tillable – with an old
castle at Craigie. It was the under-use of much of this possible
farming ground, lack of drainage and general laziness or lack
of initiative on the part of land-stewards and grieves, which
mainly delayed him. He had left Pate at Luffness, to look
after matters there, and could have done with him in the
west, for advice and support. Clearly David's father had
neglected supervision of these properties – he had been
Justiciar of Lothian, of course, and held other offices, so
that his time had been otherwise occupied.

So David got back to Luffness only in time to make hasty
arrangements for his departure for Roxburgh, his mother
suggesting that he had been away for too long and wondering
what he had been up to. Fond as he was of her, her son felt
that she was taking overlong to recognise that he was now
of full age, a man, and a lord, master himself of others and
wide acres, not just a youthful son to be schooled.

Taking Pate with him on this occasion, he did in fact call in
at Seton, but only to pick up its lord on his way southwards.
He could not fail to see Judith, of course, was duly embraced
and as duly reproached for having delayed so long in coming.

She had been to Luffness twice, it appeared, in the interim; so he had not been forgotten.

Thereafter, as the three young men rode for the Borderland, over the Soutra moorland plateau and then down Lauderdale, Seton managed to indicate, elaborately casual, that women could be difficult, and even embarrassing creatures on occasion, however delightful; and that he had had no hand in manoeuvres to involve David in their little plots and intrigues, benevolent as he was towards all concerned.

He was reassured as to understanding.

Inevitably there followed some remarks as to the young King and his half-sister, with comments which neither probed nor warned but were not wholly adventitious. David listened attentively.

Their arrival at Roxburgh, into the bustle of assembly for the parliament, made little mark, for after registering their presence at the castle's outer gatehouse, they retired to the nearby township to spend the evening and night there, official proceedings not to start until the next day's noon; little mark, that is until at table with sundry other lords and commissioners not of the first rank, a bellman came ringing his way through the streets and wynds, and into the many crowded hostelries, calling for one David de Lindsay, Lord of Luffness, to attend at the castle forthwith, at the command of the King's Grace.

Not a little perturbed at being thus brought to the attention of all, David returned to the castle with the bellman.

This time he passed all the guards unchallenged, and was led past the various towers and keeps to the palace block itself almost at the far eastern end of the narrow, elongated stronghold between the two rivers. Here he was left in a first-floor chamber before a well-doing fire of birch logs.

He had not long to wait. An inner door was flung open and the small figure of the monarch came rushing in, clad in a bed-gown, to hurl himself at David and to pummel him with tiny fists.

"Why did you not come? Why did you not come?" the boy demanded. "Davie – why? Where have you been?"

"I, I could not come unsummoned, Sire. I have come now for the parliament. But . . ."

"You *should* have come. I have been looking for you. All this long time. And you never came. Where have you been?"

"At home, Sire. Just at Luffness. And other places to the west. Places I had to visit . . ."

"Every night I told God to send you!"

He held the boy close. "I am sorry, Alex. It is difficult, you see. You are the King now, and . . ." He glanced up. The Lady Margaret had followed into the room and was shaking her head, whether at him or at her half-brother or at them both.

"A good evening, my lord David," she said. "You must forgive Alex. He just would not go to sleep, once he heard, from the gatehouse, that you were here, until he saw you. Very determined, very wicked. But then, you have been wicked also, have you not? In not coming."

"I could not just present myself at your door, at the court, unbidden, Lady Margaret. You know that that is not correct behaviour in a subject. I would have wished to come . . ."

"You were told that you were welcome, that time when last we parted. Queen Marie herself said so."

"She was kind. You both were. But that is not a royal summons, I judged. To court. I could not presume . . ."

"At least you could have come early for this parliament, no? And when you reached here, come to see us." She amended that. "To see Alex."

"Yes, you should. You should! Why did you not, Davie?"

"Perhaps I have less high opinion of myself than has Your Grace! Only names were being taken at the gates. I am not one of the great ones, Alex. Just a small lord."

"But of broad acres, I hear." That was the young woman. "Be not *over*-humble, David."

Noting that she had dropped the lordly prefix, he smiled. "In *your* company I might require to be, lady!"

"And what does that mean?"

He was not quite sure, himself. "I might be tempted to be over-*bold*. Be too . . . forward. To a king's daughter."

"A king's bastard," she reminded him, but easily. "If you become too bold, David, I will tell you!"

"What does forward mean?" the King demanded.

The adults eyed each other.

"Er . . . speaking too freely, Alex. Lacking in, in respect, perhaps. Taking liberties."

"What are liberties?"

"Well . . ."

The young woman came to his rescue. "Being rather too . . . wilful, he means. Making his wishes too evident, to others' displeasure. Not that I have noticed anything such in our David! Unlike *you*, Alex! You took liberties, this night, big liberties. Refusing to lie down and go to sleep until David was brought. Shouting at me. That was forward, see you."

The boy scowled. "If you had let me go look for him, in the town . . ."

"That would not have done at all. You will have to learn, Alex, that there are things a king *cannot* do. As well as those he, and only he, can. It is difficult, I know, but you will learn."

"Just as *I* could not come seeking you unbidden, Sire, so you, the King, could scarcely come seeking me," David put in.

"Why not?"

This could go on indefinitely, obviously. Margaret took the boy's hand. "Because it is the way matters go," she said. "Now, back to bed. You are much too late as it is. And tomorrow, you have much to do and sit through, at your first parliament. So say a goodnight to David . . ."

"Davie must come up with me. I will say goodnight to him in bed."

"But you will see him tomorrow . . ."

"I *want* him to come. And, and I am the King!"

Again they exchanged glances. "A royal command!" David said, with a smile. "I will come."

They left that room, the boy's hand in David's now, to climb the twisting turnpike stair, up past the second-floor hall where, by the noise and music, some sort of feasting was in progress; and up two more storeys to an attic floor which contained two intercommunicating bed-chambers, both with fires burning. The first clearly was a woman's room, by the clothing and gear on bed and chests.

"I would have made it more tidy had I known that I was going to have a visitor here!" the girl observed.

"I . . . I . . . am privileged," he said.

"Then do not be over-bold and forward, to your friends, over seeing my bedchamber, sir!" she told him.

"Never that!" he assured, earnestly.

They passed through to the next room, even less tidy, garb-strewn, with the bedclothes of the great royal canopied couch a heap.

Margaret pointed to the bed. "In you get," she ordered. Alexander climbed up, and promptly started to kick his heels in the air, to the unseemly disarray of his bed-gown, the opposite of a sleep-starved child.

"Settle, now. Quiet, you." She rearranged the bedclothes to cover him. Then she blew out the two candles which had lighted the room, so that there was only the fire's flickering glow. "Goodnight, Alex. Sleep well. God keep you."

"God did not hear me before," he reminded.

"He probably did, but decided that this way was best for you."

"I think that He does not always listen."

"Perhaps you do not always ask properly." She stooped to kiss his flaxen head. "Now – shut your eyes and go to sleep."

"I have to say my prayers."

"You said them before. Do you not remember? You see what I mean by not asking God properly?"

David fisted the boy lightly on the small shoulder. "Goodnight, Alex. Tomorrow we will see each other."

"Do not go away. Not until I am asleep, Davie."

"You will never go to sleep if David waits," Margaret said.

"I will. He can tell me about those, those people. Who had the Stone. And the little box. See – it is over there. The, the Bannock. And, and Colum."

"The Brecbennoch," David amended.

"And Columba," the girl added.

"In fact, Colum *was* his name. Columba he got called, because that means dove. And he was an unusual dove indeed! More like an eagle."

"We both stand corrected, then. But no stories tonight, Alex. It is over-late." And, as protests began, "We will go just into my room, there. Close by. But do not call to us, or talk. Or David will go away. You must sleep. I will not shut the door."

In the adjoining chamber she began to tidy up. "That young man needs a strong hand, King or none!" she observed. "A man's hand, I think."

"Has he not a tutor, a teacher?"

"A young monk, yes. But he is much too gentle. Alex orders *him*, not the other way. He needs a stronger hand than Brother Anselm."

"I would think that his sister's would serve!"

"You judge me a strong woman? Hard, perhaps?"

"Lord, no! Or . . . certainly not weak. But never hard. I, I much admire."

"Ah, but then you do not know me very well yet, do you?"

He was noting that word "yet", and savouring it, when she added, "Despite being in my bedchamber!"

"I, ah, recognise the honour you do me in this."

"It is scarcely an honour. More a necessity! With our liege-lord there demanding. He is very fond of you, David – as you must also recognise."

"I see it, yes. And wonder at it. Why? I have done nothing to warrant it – save leap over a bench at a parliament and retrieve a ball. Why me?"

"No other would have done that, I think. But do not you start asking why this and why that, David! I get a sufficiency of such questions each day of my life! Why, why, why? But – I have a question of my own. Tell me, how fond of our Alex are you? I mean, as a person, a child, not just as your sovereign-lord to whom you owe duty and have sworn allegiance?" Her voice was lowered, but none the less urgent.

He eyed her thoughtfully. "I think . . . very fond. I like him well. And, and feel for him."

"Feel, yes. But – how much? You see, he needs much help. From a man who cares for him. Not just for the King but for Alex himself. Many will serve him well enough, no doubt, as monarch. Many will seek to please him, for their own ends, to gain place and preferment. Some will try to use him, appearing his friends. But he needs better than that. He needs caring. And guidance."

"He will have a regent to guide him. That is why we are here. To appoint a regent."

"In affairs of state, yes. But how much caring will such regent give? There will be struggle for the regency tomorrow – all know that. But these great ones will not be struggling in order to help young Alex, but to gain power and rule in the land, in his name. Can you think otherwise?"

He did not answer.

"To be eight years old and a king will be no happy fate, I think. He will require friends, true friends."

"He will find none better than his sister, I say."

"Perhaps. But I am only a woman. Young, and born out of wedlock. He will need more than that."

"His mother . . .?"

"Queen Marie is strange in this. She loves Alex well, I have no doubt. But she seems to keep her distance from him. He is not close to her. And she is going away, leaving him."

David spread his hands. "I will do what I can."

"Yes. Do that. It may not always be . . . a joy!"

"When it is aiding *your* efforts, I think that it will be!" What made him say that?

She considered him with that calm scrutiny of hers. "I wonder?" she said.

There was a murmur from next door. Margaret tiptoed over and peered in. She came back.

"He is not asleep yet. His eyes are open. He will hear something of our voices. Perhaps if we remain quiet for a little he will settle. He is excited at seeing you." She moved to the bed and sat, patting it. "Sit you, while we wait." And she put a finger to her lips.

He went to sit beside her, in something of an emotional stir. Here he was, in her room, alone with this young woman, on her bed, close, in silence. She, who so greatly attracted him – he was past denying that now. Out of reach she might be, a king's daughter – but she was near enough for him to touch her nevertheless. She clearly trusted him entirely –

98

although that might have its less exciting aspect. What would his friends say if they could see him now? What would his mother say? And Judith Seton? If it was she who was sat beside him on a bed in flickering firelight, there would be not much doubt about what would happen! Whereas here . . .

Margaret rose, went to the fire, and quietly put on another couple of small logs, which had the effect of setting up some brighter flames, lightening the room somewhat. She came back and sat again – and was it just his hopeful fancy or did she not sit just a trifle closer than before? She nodded to him and smiled, companionably rather than encouragingly perhaps.

For his part, the man, in leaning back a little to support himself on an elbow, managed to narrow the distance between them by another inch or two.

So they sat, watching the licking flames, and the wavering shadows on the walls, making movement of the tapestries. David realised that he was breathing rather deeply and tried to stop that.

But presently, that being unsuccessful, he could contain himself no longer. He leaned over and whispered, "This is good!"

She seemed to consider that, then nodded. "Hush!" she said, but not censoriously. "Not long now, I think."

If that was meant to temper his enthusiasm it had the opposite effect. He leaned still closer, and almost of its own volition his hand reached out to pat her leg. And when she did not immediately draw away, that hand settled and rested there, on a warm soft thigh.

For a moment or two she let it lie there. Then gently her own hand settled on it in turn, and lifted it, to return it to his own lap. "Better not," she murmured, with what might just have been a sigh. Or was that imagination on his part?

She rose again, then, and moved to the door, to slip inside. When she returned, she remained standing. "He is asleep now."

Reluctantly he got to his feet. "I suppose, then, that I must be on my way," he said.

"I fear so, David. You go back to the town?"

"To my regret, yes."

"We shall see you tomorrow, no doubt."

"But not *here*, perhaps!"

"Probably not. This must not become a habit, sir!" But she smiled as she led the way to the outer door.

On the threshold they paused. "You had better go down alone," she decided. "Some might be leaving the hall now, the feasting over. And it would scarcely do if we were seen descending together from up here, at this hour! No?"

"To be sure. I see that." He rubbed his chin. "Margaret, you have greatly honoured me, and made me very happy, this evening. It has been . . . something that I have never known before. Thank you!"

"I realise, David, that you would have liked to . . . have to thank me still more! But . . ."

"Perhaps, yes. But – I understand."

"Do you?"

At her tone, he hesitated.

She shook her head. "A goodnight, then. And *I* thank you for your . . . patience." Touching his arm, she turned away. "Sleep well." Then, as he began to descend the stair, she called again. "Do not forget what we spoke of – Alex's need for a friend, David."

He had plenty to think about as he made his way back to Roxburgh town that night.

This time, there was a notably large attendance for the first parliament of the new reign, and with momentous decisions to be made, decisions which would affect the lives and possibly fortunes of all. For if the monarch was, at this stage, comparatively unimportant, whoever was appointed to be regent, to rule in his name, was not. The rise and fall of many could hinge on today's deliberations and votes.

David, Seton and Dundas, who had arrived before them, found their way, in good time, to the same seating they had occupied previously – and there were the inevitable remarks about keeping a space in front clear, the height of the bench-back, and so on. Actually, the said space was soon occupied, for the hall was crowded indeed today.

When the earls filed in, it was evident that the Comyns had rallied their fullest strength, for as well as their earldoms of Buchan and Menteith, they had links by marriage with four others. Their less lofty supporters were already there in force.

The Chancellor, when he came in, scanned the assembly somewhat anxiously, it seemed, if not prepared for trouble certainly anticipating it. The great officers of state followed, then the bearers of sword, sceptre and crown, and the High Sennachie and heralds, these last signing for all to stand.

The trumpets sounded.

There was a pause and then Alexander appeared in the dais doorway, obviously being guided in by a feminine hand and arm. Hesitating therein and biting his lip as he stared at the great gathering, a final push sent him in almost at the run, to climb on to the throne and sit, scowling, whilst the Sennachie led in the chant, "God Save the King's Grace, God Save the King's Grace."

The boy's gaze quickly found David, and he grinned and waved, the scowl disappearing. David noted that the hand which waved on this occasion held Columba's Brecbennoch, not the stone ball. At least it would be less likely to roll away. He smiled back, but could scarcely return the wave.

After Bishop de Birnam's prayers, on this occasion seeking not only God's help in their deliberations but blessings on the new monarch and reign, the Chancellor, almost reluctantly, announced that the business of this parliament was to choose, elect and appoint a regent for their esteemed and well-beloved sovereign-lord, Alexander, the third of the name, High King of Scots, His Grace being only in his ninth year. The regent's was a most important and responsible office, as all present would appreciate, and demanding of great strengths, wisdom and understanding on the part of the chosen individual. Their Scotland had not required the services of a regent hitherto in men's memory, all her monarchs having succeeded to the throne when of full age; so this was a decision of great significance, all but historic. Let none approach the matter without due thought, care and recognition of responsibility.

It is to be feared that David de Lindsay, for one, failed rather to pay fullest attention to this due and admirable exhortation, for his regard rose and remained on the gallery

101

where Queen Marie and the Lady Margaret had come to sit and watch the proceedings.

Abbot Donald was scarcely finished when Robert Bruce, Lord of Annandale, jumped up. "Chancellor, I say that there is little need for choice in this matter of regency. None is better fitted nor more entitled to the position than Alan Durward, Earl of Atholl, High Justiciar of this realm. I so move – Atholl for regent."

"And I second that," the Earl of Strathearn declared. "None better, the most experienced commander in the land, the longest-serving officer of state, and wed to the late King's daughter."

There were murmurs of agreement, scarcely hearty but fairly general.

"I have a motion and seconder," Abbot Donald said, although he did not sound confident about it.

William, Earl of Mar rose. "I say otherwise. I propose John Comyn, Lord of Badenoch and Lochaber as regent. None more worthy, none more able." Mar was married to a Comyn.

"And so say I." That was Alexander Comyn, Earl of Buchan, younger brother to the said Red John. He had gained the earldom of Buchan through marriage.

"As do I," the Earl of Menteith added, a cousin.

There was a great shout of agreement from all the Comyn supporters. They were not necessarily more numerous than the Durward ones, but they were definitely more vocal.

"I have, then, two nominations, both seconded," the Chancellor said. "Is there any other name proposed?" He did not sound hopeful.

Silence, while men looked at each other.

"Then, it must be a vote . . ."

"Chancellor." That was Alexander Stewart, the High Steward. "The regency means the rule. And the rule in this land was always, from the earliest times, vested in the High King and the lesser Kings, the mormaors or earls. These appointed the High King and aided him in rule. So, surely, the ruler appointed for His Grace should be one of the earls. My lord of Badenoch and Lochaber, however puissant, is not that. I feel that it is my duty as Steward of the royal lands to say so. I therefore would vote for the Earl of Atholl."

This time the Durward support was a little louder.

Meanwhile, the monarch was running the Brecbennoch up and down the arm of his throne, and making faces.

"Chancellor, the Steward may be right as to earls, in the days of old." This was Bishop de Gamelyn, despite his name an illegitimate Comyn. "Those ancient earls held the power and rule because they could field the greater numbers of armed men. Strength in men and lands is as necessary as ever today for the King's support. My lord of Badenoch may not have won an earldom in marriage, but he is head of the most powerful family in this land, and can field almost forty knights of his own name, as well as many others, all with their tails of armed men. Can my lord of Atholl do as much?" That may not have been a typically clerical point of view, but it was typically Comyn.

Again the applause, fists beating on seat-backs.

"If there are no other nominations, I must put the matter to the vote of this parliament," Abbot Donald said, on a sigh. "I will put the counter-motion first. Those who vote for the appointment of John, Lord of Badenoch and Lochaber show hands."

They did more than show hands. Many jumped to their feet, waved and shouted.

Abbot Donald banged his gavel. "Sit! And silence! Only show hands, that the vote may be counted."

His clerks stood, to peer and count.

In that slow business, Alexander also rose, to stand on his chair, and gazing about him began to count on his fingers, at last finding something to interest him in the proceedings.

The clerks at length agreed, and the Chancellor announced, "Sixty-two in favour of the Lord of Badenoch."

Cheers.

"For the motion?"

More counting.

When the clerks reported, the abbot looked uncertain, unhappy, questioning his acolytes. Even then he hesitated. Then, "Here is a close-run vote," he declared. "Sixty-one in favour of the Earl of Atholl . . ." As the yells of triumph began, he banged his gavel for quiet. "*I* have the casting vote," he reminded. "But before I cast it, I would point out that in this most important issue for our realm, by my calculations at least fifteen of those present have not voted. This is . . . irresponsible."

Silence greeted that, as men considered.

He went on. "All ought to vote on so vital a matter. Think well, and then vote, as care for His Grace, your wits and conscience dictate." A pause. "Those in favour of the Lord of Badenoch, show."

The clerks declared, "Sixty-six."

"For the Earl of Atholl – vote."

Whispering between the clerks, then the announcement. "Sixty-six."

The hall seemed to erupt in excitement, challenge, agitation.

The gavel again. "My lords and commissioners, this is . . . unfortunate. An equal vote. No clear decision. And at least six still have not voted. I judge these in error. I still have the casting vote. But in so equal a choice, I am loth to use it. This is grievous. The parliament and nation seemingly equally divided. Whatever way I vote, the Chancellor would seem to go against the will of half the nation. This is no way to decide a regency." He looked around him for guidance – but on this occasion the throne could not help. Certainly no aid came from either of the two would-be regents, who glared at each other but said nothing.

The abbot sighed. "If vote I must, I do so with much sorrow . . ."

"Chancellor, may I speak?" John, the Lord of Home rose, an elderly man and head of that powerful Borders house. "I agree – we must all agree – that this situation is an ill one, not in the best interests of the nation. I say that we must think again. Not as to which of these two lords, but otherwise. I would have proposed a third name, as one of the ancient royal line, who could, perchance, have won the support of both sides. That is my Lord Cospatrick, Earl of Dunbar and March. But, alas, he has departed on crusade." The Homes were themselves descended from the Cospatrick earls. "Since I cannot nominate him, I make bold to offer another suggestion – a *council* of regency. Not one regent but, say, three. My lord of Dunbar to join it when he returns from the Holy Land."

There were exclamations from all over the hall at this novel proposal, most of them seemingly favourable, as a way out of the impasse.

Abbot Donald clutched at this lifeline gratefully. "Good!" he exclaimed, "Good! Do you make that a motion, my lord of Home?"

"If there will be seconders, I do."

A dozen were on their feet to second, including David and his two friends.

"Is there any counter-motion? I, I pray not!"

Silence.

"That is well, then. This parliament agrees to appoint a council of regency. Such council to consist of the Earl of Atholl and the Lord of Badenoch and Lochaber. But also, surely, another? At least one other. Or, or . . ." He left the rest unsaid.

None could disagree with that, even the two principals, however much they might otherwise disagree.

"Nominations for a third member of the council?"

Now all considered each other. This would be difficult. Since all there, at least all who had voted, were in favour of one or the other, any nominee also would be bound to favour one or other in the council. Yet to elect *two* more members could result in a further stalemate. Two against two would be as bad as one against one. So, what?

A figure rose, from the bishops' benches, none other than Clement of Dunblane. "Chancellor, I was one of those you criticised for failing to vote. This, not out of irresponsibility – the reverse, rather, I contend. I feel that Holy Church ought not to take sides in such matters. Clearly, not all think as I do! But, on the same reasoning, I suggest the wisest choice for a third member of the council of regency should be a churchman, one uncommitted to either side. And so make a useful balance. Is it not so?"

There were murmurs of agreement from many.

Another cleric rose. "I support that proposal as wise and right. Indeed, I make it as a motion. And, who better as third member than he who made it? As representing Holy Church. I nominate my lord Bishop of Dunblane for that position. He was, forby, a friend of the late monarch." That was the Abbot of Melrose.

There was no lack of seconders, even though Durward and Comyn looked unenthusiastic. And none thought further to complicate the issue by proposing any further nominee.

Sighing with relief, Abbot Donald pushed aside his papers. "That disposes of the main business of this parliament," he declared. "There are sundry matters, especially as to appointments, sheriffships and the like, but since these should first be considered by the regents, and they will undoubtedly have to make many changes, this present assembly need not deal with them. So, if Your Grace agrees, I will adjourn the session, and –"

A tapping noise, not loud but insistent, interrupted him, and turned all eyes towards the throne. Young Alexander was sitting again, and banging his little Brecbennoch on the arm of his chair – although his glance was directed upwards towards the gallery where sat his mother and half-sister. In the subsequent hush, he gave voice, in something of a rush.

"I want, I want a cup. A, a cup-carrier. I want a cup-carrier."

The stares of all were on the boy, wondering.

When none spoke, he thumped again. "A cup-carrier. For me." He looked hopefully from the gallery to David and back.

And into the non-comprehending quiet, a quiet voice from up there spoke the words, "Cup-*Bearer*, Alex."

"Yes. Cup-Bearer. I want it. Him."

Abbot Donald blinked. "Sire, I am sure that your royal wish will prevail. But I do not see . . ."

Serle de Dundas rose. "Chancellor, in accordance with His Grace's wish, I propose David de Lindsay, Lord of Luffness, Barnweill, Crawford and The Byres. That he be appointed Cup-Bearer to the King." He sat, not looking at David.

Seton rose. "I second." And sat.

Into the silence which followed, the Chancellor spoke. "Your Grace, this is scarcely a matter for parliament. Your royal wishes are our command, to be sure. But appointment to your royal household is not for parliament to decide. Yourself and your regents . . ."

"I want Davie Lindsay," the young voice cried, and again the Brecbennoch banged.

"Then undoubtedly you shall have him, Sire. My lord of Luffness – you hear? Now, Your Grace, if you will permit the adjournment . . .?"

The High Sennachie signed to his trumpeter, who sounded the required flourish, and all stood.

But still the monarch had his own royal will to display. When the Sennachie, bowing, gestured him towards the dais door, Alexander jumped from his throne and ran down in the other direction, calling "Davie! Davie!" So, while the standing and bemused gathering watched, David de Lindsay was grabbed by the hand and led off to the door, past the bowing great ones, and out.

"Cup-Carrier Davie! Cup-Carrier Davie!" the royal chant went; and he was given the Brecbennoch to carry, in token, meantime.

In triumph he was conducted out and back to the palace keep by an excited liege-lord.

When, presently, they were joined by the Lady Margaret, David eyed her warily.

"This, I must think, was *your* doing!" he all but accused. "All contrived by you, was it not?"

"With a little help, perhaps, from my lord of Dundas," she admitted. "It seemed to be the best arrangement, for all. Is it not so, David?"

He frowned, in two minds. Probably she was right – but he did not like being manipulated, used, without consultation and his consent.

She evidently recognised his dubieties. "Alex's need is undoubted," she said. "And our duty towards him, the duties of all." She rumpled the boy's hair, lest this swelled the size of his head too much. "The King's service demands our best endeavours – however ill-behaved this present young monarch may be on occasion! He must be kept in order, so that he grows into a good King, not a bad one! And that requires a man close to him. And he wanted you." Clever, she was, in using them both thus. "So it had to be David de Lindsay."

"You could have warned me."

"I did, yesterday. After a fashion. But – you might have refused!" It was her turn to look almost accusing.

"I . . . I do not know." That, even in his own ears, sounded feeble indeed.

"What cup is Davie to carry?" Alexander demanded, impatient at all this discussion. "There are lots of cups."

"No particular cup, Alex. Cup-Bearer to the King is an ancient royal office. Your father had a Cup-Bearer when I was young. One Sir Oliver Fraser. But he died and I do not remember another being appointed. There are other positions like it, which one day you may fill. Keeper of the Wardrobe, Groom of the Bedchamber, Master of the Horse . . ."

"What horse? There are lots and lots of horses."

"*He* would be in charge of all the horses. These are but appointments, you see. At a royal court. And we thought that Cup-Bearer would be the most suitable for David. Closest to yourself."

"I am thankful that you did not have me appointed Keeper of the Wardrobe, at least!" That was heartfelt.

She smiled. "I thought of it! But . . ."

"I must find a cup for Davie to carry. A special one. Could we have a gold one?"

"That will not be necessary, Alex. It is only a title, after all. And you must say it rightly – Cup-*Bearer*, not cup-carrier."

"But this of the parliament?" David put to her. "That was not necessary, surely?"

"Not necessary – but advisable, we felt. We recognised that once the regent was appointed, he could choose his own officers and people at court . . ."

"We? Who were we?"

"The Queen Marie and myself. This could not have been done without her approval. We decided that it had to be done thus, at a parliament. And by the King's own command. Before all. Accepted by all. Then no regent, or regents, as it turns out, could overturn it. Not without much upset. We do not think that the Earl of Atholl greatly approves of you, and we expected him to be the regent. But the same could apply to the Comyn. So we planned it this way."

"Women!" he exclaimed – but not too censoriously. He even mustered a smile. "And what now?"

"Now you require no royal summons to come to court. You are *part* of the court. You can come and go as you will. And we hope that you will prefer to come, rather than to go!"

"Yes, you must not go, Davie. You must stay with me. Carry my cup. I will find one . . ."

"I have my own duties and tasks to see to, Alex. Luffness Castle and the other baronies. I cannot just forget them. I have my mother and brother to think of. Barony courts to hold. Herds of cattle and flocks of sheep to see to . . ."

"Then I will come with you and see to them. I would like that. I like sheep. Better than cattle-beasts. And goats. Do you have any goats, Davie?"

"*I* have not. But some of my tenants have."

"When will we go?"

"Enough of talk just now, Alex," Margaret said. "We will show David to his chamber. And you will change your clothes. These are too fine to wear all the time."

"Chamber?" David wondered.

"Yes. You must have your own chamber, now. Here. Close to Alex's."

She led the way upstairs.

On the same upper landing at which was the door to the intercommunicating bedchambers which David had visited previously, there was another door. This opened into a third room, rather smaller, but adequately furnished with a large bed, the walls tapestry-hung and a fire laid ready to light.

"Yours," the girl said, gesturing. "Will it serve your lordship?"

He nodded. Various thoughts chased themselves through his mind. One, that there were only these three attic rooms at the top of this tower; the stair went on only to a caphouse giving access to the parapet-walk. Two, that his chamber was next door to Margaret's. And three, that every time he desired, or was desired, to go to Alex's room, he would have to pass through the girl's one. He nodded again, with enhanced approval.

"I hope that you will find all to your satisfaction, David. It is no very grand chamber, but it is best that you be near to Alex, in this tower."

"Yes. You are ever thoughtful. I shall do very well here, I think."

The boy was climbing on to the bed, to bounce on it. Shaking her head over him, Margaret led him off to change his clothing.

Left to consider his situation, David came to the conclusion that, despite being manipulated, he was not doing so badly, all things considered.

That evening, at the usual post-parliament banquet, he found that he was now expected to sit up on the dais, not at the main top table of course, but at the little side-table there which Alex and Margaret had shared on the previous occasion. Only now, the boy was King, and had to sit beside his mother at the main board; so that David and Margaret had the lesser one to themselves – which suited the man very well. Alex clearly would have liked to sit there with them, but the Queen insisted that he could not do so. He was seated therefore between his mother and Bishop Clement, with the two other regents to right and left, seeking to ignore each other more or less.

Soon after the meal began, Margaret decanted a very little of the wine from a flagon in front of them into a goblet, and used the water in one of their finger-bowls to much dilute it.

"Alex is too young to be drinking wine," she whispered. "But this will do him no harm, I think. If you took it over to him now, he would like it, I am sure. And it will demonstrate your position."

Somewhat doubtfully he nodded and rose, with the goblet. "Do I just hand it to him?"

"With a bow."

He moved across the dais, his coming not escaping the kingly eye. Alexander rather spoiled the effect by getting down from his chair of state and coming to meet him – which unfortunately complicated matters, for it was of course

110

the custom that when the monarch stood all must stand. In consequence there was much uncertainty, some rising, some merely raising bottoms, while the Queen sought to retrieve her son, unsuccessfully, with David feeling vaguely responsible.

"Is that my cup, Davie? What is in it? Is it real wine?"

"Yes, Sire. Or . . . partly. An admixture."

The boy took it, and nothing would do but he must sample it there and then. He made a face. "Not very good," he declared. "I like my honey wine better. I have some there." He pointed.

David led him back to his chair, and bowed apologetically to the Queen. All standing could sit again.

Back at his own table, Margaret smiled. "As you can see, Alex needs teaching, Cup-Bearer! You will be busy." She paused. "He cannot remain for long at this feasting. I will have to take him away presently. He will want you to come too, I have no doubt. But if you came just through the doorway there, that would serve. And then you can come back."

"No, no. I will leave with you both. I soon can have enough of feasting."

"As you will . . ."

As course succeeded course and the wine flowed, Alexander soon became restless, and Queen Marie glanced round. Margaret nodded, and she and David rose to go forward to collect their charge, Alexander jumping up immediately.

This time, on a trumpet-blast, everyone had to rise as the trio headed for the door, the boy without a backward glance. His mother grimaced.

Up in the tower-rooms, by royal command, David attended the undressing process and listened to a somewhat gabbled prayer-saying. Thereafter he was urged to tell a story, presumably sleep-inducing. He was not so venerable that he did not remember some of his own childhood tales, and recounted an old favourite about the boy's ancestor Malcolm Big Head who had moved Birnam Wood, or at least seemed to, in order to hide his army's approach and attack on King MacBeth's force at Dunsinane Hill, each man carrying a tree-branch – although whether

111

this was calculated to close young eyelids was open to question.

When it was finished, another was demanded. But Margaret said no, one story each night was sufficient. There followed the anticipated request for Davie to stay next door until sleep came – to which the man found no objection.

So once again the couple sat in the firelight on Margaret's bed, the room a deal tidier this time. They were silent for a while. Presently she said, "If this is going to become a habit, I think that I must needs find a chair or two, no?"

"Why?"

"Not all would esteem this . . . suitable." She shrugged. "Even, perhaps, with chairs!"

"Who will know?"

"None, I hope – save perhaps Queen Marie, who comes sometimes to see her son abed."

"M'mm. And she would disapprove?"

"Who knows? But she and I are good friends. It does not usually take long for Alex to sleep. So your waiting need not be prolonged, David."

"A pity!" he said.

"You are sure that you do not wish to return to the hall, the banquet?" she wondered. "It will go on for long yet."

"I much prefer this."

"Even so, the night is young."

"*You* must remain here?"

"Oh, yes. I stay near to Alex. This is my duty, my calling."

"Calling? You mean, it is required of you? Always?"

"Yes. My father laid this charge on me. Alex was his only son, lawful or otherwise, although he had many bastard daughters, myself the youngest. He was fond of me, after his fashion, and entrusted Alex to my care. *He* did, rather than Queen Marie. Which was strange perhaps. But she never has seemed to resent it. I promised him that I would always cleave to Alex and watch over him. And so I shall."

"Always?"

"So long as I may. And he wants me, needs me."

"But . . . what of marriage? You will most surely wed. Fair

112

as you are, and a king's daughter. Wed some great one. As have your sisters."

"As to that, who knows? I seek no great marriage."

"Others may seek it for you."

"Perhaps. But I have a mind and will of my own – as perchance you have noticed? And who can *force* me into such? Only the King could do that, I think. Certainly no regent."

"Then I am glad," he said.

"You are not concerning yourself with my marriage, David?"

"Er . . . no. No. I have no right, no concern. Or, not that – no call, or, or . . ." He floundered.

She patted his arm but said nothing.

That pat encouraged him to edge slightly closer on the bed. "I greatly enjoy your company," he told her.

"Do you? As well, probably. Since we both are to be so close to Alex."

"*You* do not find that . . . tiresome?"

"Not as yet, no. So long as your behaviour is, shall we say, agreeable!"

"Oh. And what constitutes agreeable behaviour?"

"You are very earnest tonight, David."

"I but wish to know where I stand. With you. Now that I am part of the same household, as it were."

She gave a little laugh. "You seem to be sitting, rather than standing, with me, here and now! But as to agreeable, why that is what we both agree to be to our wishes. As simple as that, no?"

"*My* wishes may sometimes exceed yours." He reached to take her hand.

"Then I will tell you so, sir!" But she did not withdraw her hand immediately, but only after a few moments. She was good with her gentle indications, that one.

So they sat for a while, unspeaking – and while he did not take her hand again, he contrived to edge that little bit closer, which brought his thigh to just touch hers, to which she did not seem to object.

Presently he sighed.

"What is that for?" she wondered. "Do you weary of waiting? Perhaps Alex is asleep now."

113

"Lord, no! It is but that I must go back to Luffness shortly. Perhaps tomorrow. I left there only for a day or two. This parliament was not likely to take long. There will be much to see to before I can leave to come to bide here."

"Yes, I understand that. And, since you sigh, I must take it that you no longer regret the biding here? As when first you were faced with the prospect."

"I did not regret. It was but that I was . . . unprepared. Taken by surprise."

"Poor David! And now? Now you are reconciled to your fate?"

"So long as you are part of it."

"Ah, but am I? *You* are Alex's Cup-Bearer, not me."

"Your friend, at least?"

"I think that we can agree on that! The agreeable ones! Now – I shall go see if Alex is asleep. There have been no murmurs . . ." She took his elbow to raise him up – which he took as an indication that this present interlude was over.

She came back, nodding. "All well. Your room there is ready for you. I hope that your bed proves comfortable."

He almost said something there, but wisely forbore. Instead, "I will go down, first, and have a word with my two friends. Who I think deserve it! You suborned them?"

"They were not hard to convince."

"We men are but feebly armoured against your feminine wiles, I reckon."

"Not even David de Lindsay?"

"Especially him, the weakling."

"Then goodnight, weak one! As well that one of us is strong, no?"

He took her hand to raise and kiss it. "Goodnight, Margaret. Sleep well. I will come back up to my room here the happier for knowing that it is but through a single wall from yours." That he allowed himself, at least.

She had the last word. "Do not mistake the door, then," she advised, as she started him down the stair.

114

6

Back at Luffness, David had his mother's opposition to contend with. Not only was she not enthusiastic about his appointment as Cup-Bearer to the King; she shrewdly guessed that it was not wholly devotion to the young monarch which had brought this about.

"This bastard daughter of the late King – it is her you want to be near, is it not?" she demanded. "I warned you about this, David. She is not for such as you. She will be given to some great noble, and . . ."

"Who will give her?"

"Why – those in charge of the kingdom now. These regents you have appointed in your parliament."

"They have no hold over her. Only the King could command her. And young Alexander will not do that, for he greatly needs her. But – that is not my concern. I admire her, yes. But my duty is towards the boy. He needs also a man's hand close to him. And for some reason he likes me, wants me with him. His position is like to be hard enough, all know. The King is in his ninth year. And ambitious men all around him . . ."

"To be sure. That is why I warn you. These ambitious, powerful men, such as Durward and the Comyn themselves, with others, will not love you, for your influence with the young monarch. Any more than allow you to court his half-sister. You are seeking trouble in this."

"I shall not seek to interfere in affairs of state."

"Perhaps not. But others may try to use you. Try to reach the boy through you. I say that you are being foolish, David."

"I am committed now. Even before parliament."

"This young woman – how does she behave towards you? Is she . . . forward?"

"No."

"But she approves of you. That much is clear."

"As her half-brother's guide and companion, yes."

"And therefore *her* companion also!"

"Only on . . . occasion."

"David, young women can entrap men, in all seeming innocence. If you are determined to go on with this, you must beware. I do not want you to become embroiled in matters too high for you, and of danger. I think that, before you take up this appointment, if so you must, you should wed."

"Wed!" He stared.

"Yes. That would be best, safest. Judith Seton would marry you, I think – she seems to like you well. And she would make a most suitable wife for you. It would have to be a hurried wedding – but she is a sensible girl, and would agree to that, probably."

"No!" That was quite a bark.

"Do not be obdurate as well as foolish, boy! You have your responsibilities as your father's eldest son. And mine. A suitable marriage is one of them, and important. Go and see Judith . . ."

"I will not! And if you bring her here, I will not have her talking of it. I had a sufficiency of her methods last time! You talk about forward! Although I think that *you* were behind that?"

"I want to see you happy, David. Settled, and living the life that you were born to. Not at court, amidst intrigues and folk who would use you . . ."

"I think that I find the intriguing a deal nearer home!" he jerked, and, turning, left her standing.

Thereafter, he managed to keep the subject of marriage at arm's length, although with so determined and formidable a mother it was not easy. But at least she did not invite Judith over from Seton. Indeed he was apt only to see the Lady Elizabeth in the evenings, so busy was he with putting matters in order on the properties, so that all could be left in Pate Dunbar's care during his absences. He was thankful indeed for honest, reliable and eminently sensible Pate, who probably would have made a better Lord of Luffness and the rest than himself. He was going to miss his company and support at Roxburgh.

116

The wildfowling season was now at its height, with the geese flighting over in their wavering ribbons night and morning, in their thousands, and the mallard ever growing in numbers also, the former filling the skies with their wild honkings, spending the nights out on the Aberlady Bay bar, and the days feeding on the inland stubbles, the ducks' quacking a constant background of murmurous sound when the noise of the waves permitted. David and Pate did go down to the saltings two mornings, just before dawn, to await the early flighting, with their crossbows and dogs. They had to go a fair distance out, for the geese rose at quite a steep angle from the sand-bar and soon got too high to shoot at. They managed to bag eight birds between them, which was satisfactory sport. It was cold, waiting hidden, out on the mud-flats before a November sunrise.

A week of activity and David was ready for his southwards return. His parting with the Lady Elizabeth was strained, she recognising his determination but unable to prevent herself from reiterating her warnings; he anxious not to hurt her unduly, and assuring her of his care and caution, but not to be dissuaded. Pate thereafter rode with him as far as the Lammermuir rise of Soutra Hill. He too was mildly admonitory, as he turned his horse's head back.

"Watch how you go at that court, David," he advised. "It may well come to blows between those two regents, and take more than any bishop to keep them from each other's throats. You do not want to be thirled to one side or the other, for the loser's supporters could suffer. There could even be war, I judge. With that young boy the prize. You, close to him, will be . . . endangered."

"Think you that my mother has not sufficiently instructed me in all this, Pate?"

"Yes. I should hold my tongue! But – it is permitted that I be concerned for you?"

David punched his cousin's shoulder by way of answer and reassurance, and they went their separate ways.

David found Roxburgh town in a state of alarm and upheaval. The Comyns had ridden off, the day before, for the north, after a night of riot and bloodshed. The two regents could, it seemed, agree on nothing, and their followers were not slow to translate their enmity into action. None expected the Comyn retiral northwards to be the end of it, by any means.

On arrival at the castle, such nation-shaking matters were subordinated to the excitement of welcome, Alexander hurling himself on David's person and pummelling him with fists, Margaret rather more restrained, but not so much so that she did not take his arms and plant a kiss – admittedly only on his cheek, but very well received nevertheless, and heartily returned.

"What have you been doing?" the boy demanded. "You have been away for long, long. I have been waiting and waiting for you. Days and days and days! You should have come . . ."

"I came so soon as I could, Alex. There was much to see to at Luffness."

"I have told him of your many duties, David – or some of them. The matters only a lord can see to. He is very selfish . . ."

"I am not! Davie is my Cup-Bearer." He had got that right now. "I need him."

"I am glad that my presence means so much to you." David glanced sidelong at the girl also. "And perhaps a little to *you*, too? But – I am here now. To bide. For a while . . ."

"You will not go away again?"

"Well – not for some time. I think that they will manage at Luffness without me now, for a while."

"All was well, there?" Margaret asked. "Your mother . . .?"

"My mother is . . . difficult. She is good, kind – but she has different notions for me than, than cup-bearing!"

"I see. I am sorry. So there was disagreement?"

"Yes." He took a chance. "She would also wish me to marry."

"Ah! And you feel otherwise?"

"I am not against marriage. In due course. But not to the young woman she suggests."

"Who is . . .? If I may ask?"

"My friend Alexander Seton's sister, Judith. A near neighbour."

"And so . . . suitable. And willing?"

"Oh, sufficiently willing! But not my choice."

"Poor David! You have not enjoyed your time at home, I think."

"I am not a child any longer. My mother appears to forget it. She is a proud woman, proud of her ancient blood. And would have me to follow her lead. But I have been of full age for over two years now, and will choose my own way. Not have it chosen for me." He paused there, it occurring to him that Margaret might take that rather personally, since, after all, she had been not exactly guiltless in her manipulations likewise.

"I will remember that!" she returned, smiling; and somehow, contrarily, that seemed to make an added bond between them.

Alexander was becoming restive at all this talk. "What did you do while you were away all that time, Davie? Were you herding your sheep? I saw some sheep one day, when we went riding in the hills."

"Well, no. You could say that I was ensuring that others were doing the shepherding properly. And matters like that." He nodded at his liege-lord. "As one day *you* will have to ensure that your kingdom is properly governed."

"I will do that. If you will help me, Davie. Not like that man!"

"He means my lord of Atholl," Margaret explained. "He does not like his Hereditary Doorward, I fear. Who is scarcely . . . patient."

"The other man is not good either. The one with the red hair. But the fat one is better. He smiles."

"That is no way to refer to the good bishop, Alex. He is a man of God, and kindly."

"God does not help him much. With the other men, does he?" That was a fairly shrewd royal observation.

"Perhaps more than we think. At least the Comyn has gone, now – the Lord of Badenoch. And there is talk that the earl will go north soon also. That will leave only Bishop Clement here."

119

"Is that so? The regents do not intend to stay together?"

"Evidently not. As well, since they agree on nothing. It is crazy-mad. No way to rule a nation. Enough for one to propose some action for the other to oppose it. However sensible or necessary. The bishop always in the middle, and unhappy with it."

"Where has the Comyn gone?"

"Back to his own lands in the north, they say. Badenoch and Moray. And his brother's in Buchan. They have large territories in Galloway too, in the south. The Earl Alan Durward fears that they are going there to assemble men. As does the bishop."

"For what purpose? There is no threat from the Norsemen at the moment, is there?"

"Not that I have heard of. No, the fear is that it is to gain the sole regency, by force of arms. To oust Durward."

"Civil war? Surely not that!"

"Well may you say so. But that is what is feared here. Durward is said to believe that the Comyns will attack and ravage his lands of Atholl and Deeside. Not so far from their own. Destroy his armed strength there. Then come south to unseat him here. So, he goes north himself to muster, before they can do so. Is that what the realm has come to, lacking a king – or a grown one? We do not need the Norse and English threats, it seems!"

"I hope that they have a fight and kill each other," the monarch declared cheerfully. "Did *you* kill any of the birds, Davie – the goose-birds you told me of? They will be very easy to kill, I think. For they walk about on the commons, like ducks. *I* could kill one, I am sure. But Margaret says no."

"Those are not the same kind of geese, Alex. Those are tame geese, belonging to folk who farm the land. You must not kill *them*. Those I shoot are wild-geese, very different. They fly in thousands, high in the air. Not easy to get within arrow-shot. But we did get eight, down on the salt-marsh of Aberlady Bay. I have brought two, for us to eat here."

"Oh, good! Good! When will we have them?"

"Better be soon – for they have been shot three days, and carried on horseback."

"I will see to them," Margaret said. "Have them plucked

and cooked." She smiled. "Two will not go very far amongst many. How think you if we have them to ourselves? Roasted and brought up to our rooms in the tower-top? A little feast of our own, tonight. To celebrate David's return."

It would have been hard to say which of her hearers greeted that suggestion with most enthusiasm.

So that evening, the boy's bedchamber – which was the largest of the three – was lit by more candles than usual and had a table brought in to set before the fire, and thereafter smelling of more than birch logs and beeswax when servitors came up with venison soup, roast goose and sweetmeats made of plums, pears and apples, just flavoured with brambles, stewed in honey, and with honey wine to wash it down. David was a little disappointed when Margaret informed him that she had told Queen Marie, who had expressed the wish to come and join them, at least for a little.

So he had to be on his best behaviour and fairly formally correct, when she arrived. But she quickly put him at ease, declaring how glad she was to welcome him to court and, smiling, how much she looked forward to her son's improved behaviour hereafter. David had not seen her so forthcoming, for she normally had a strange air to her, of detachment, almost as though she was not fully present with the company, her mind somehow elsewhere. But this night, although she told them that she would not stay long, as she must dine with the two remaining regents and other lords, she sat down at table with them, declining the soup but accepting one goose-leg to nibble, and asserting that it was all most delightful, and how fortunate her son was in his attendants.

When she rose to go, and David escorted her to the door, she would not let him take her downstairs, but patted his arm.

"Be good to Alex," she said. "Firm, but kind. I think that I will have easement of mind, knowing that you are with him."

"I am much honoured, Your Grace. And will guard and cherish His Grace with, with my life! I greatly esteem him."

"That is well. You will, I believe, have much effect on him, for good. Which he needs, fatherless. And that will make him a better king for your Scotland. So you have opportunity much to serve your country, my friend."

He could only wag his head at that.

Going back thoughtful, through Margaret's room, he was not so bemused as not to notice that two chairs now were set at either side of the fireplace.

After that, the meal went most happily, even merrily, with just the three of them, the servants dismissed; Alexander indeed growing boisterous, but the other two, on this special occasion, letting him have his head. He expressed himself as finding wild-goose meat very much to his taste, and, after three helpings, having to be diverted to the sweetmeats, with the inducement that he could have as much cream to pour over it all as he liked.

David could not recollect when he had enjoyed a repast more. All agreed that they should do this again, frequently – which in turn produced royal demands that Alex should be taken to Aberlady Bay to help shoot the required geese.

The sweets and honey wine consumption became distinctly strung out as Alex recognised that it was now past bedtime and delay was called for. Then they had to send for what was left of the viands to be cleared away, before the boy, thoroughly excited now, could be got to bed, his evening's devotions sketchy. It looked as though the others might have a long sit next door this night.

David, ushered to one of those chairs, eyed it less than enthusiastically. "I was well satisfied with the bed," he observed. "Or, shall we say, not quite satisfied, but . . ."

"No doubt. But we have to observe correct behaviour, do we not? Since we are that young man's guides and ensamplers. Some would say that we are being indiscreet, as it is." She sat, and gestured him to the chair opposite.

"Such would be better minding their own affairs!" he said.

Nevertheless, it was very pleasant sitting by the fire across from her, all but one candle snuffed so that the light did not keep Alex awake. The man could not touch her thus, but he could see her features and expressions the better; and of course it was really more comfortable than sitting up on a bed with no back-rests.

"Tell me about this would-be bride of yours, David," she said presently. "Judith Seton, was it? Is she well favoured,

as well as well disposed? Of what age? And . . . size?
Bearing?"

"Oh, she is sufficiently good-looking. In a way. Not to be
compared with yourself, to be sure. A little taller, perhaps.
And, and larger in her person. Of my own age."

"She sounds to make a most worthy wife!"

"For some other, no doubt. Not for myself."

"You have known her long?"

"Since childhood, yes. But . . . not closely."

"And what would you *require* in a wife, David, which this
Judith lacks?"

"What *you* have got," he answered simply.

That silenced her. He was about to go on, but thought
better of it. She put another log on the fire.

So they sat and watched the flickering flames, thinking
their own thoughts – but every now and again their glances
met and they smiled quietly to each other. Which held its
own satisfaction for the man.

Presently Alex called, and Margaret rose to go to him.
When she came back, it was to tell David that the boy was
asking if he was still there. Hearing no murmur of voices,
he feared that David had gone.

"I told him," she said, "that he could not expect you to
sit through here every night, waiting for him to sleep, King
or no King. You are a man, with a man's concerns. Other
men to talk and drink with. Other women, perhaps."

"I make no complaint," he assured her. "This is . . . good."
Then, "Talking of other men, how do these regents behave?
Not to each other – to Alex. They scarcely seem to throng
him! Keep their distance. But they *are* his regents, appointed
to rule in his name."

"They do not see much of him, no. Perhaps they are
unsure of what is required of them, as to the boy. After
all, there have been no regents before, to guide them –
not in memory, leastwise. Durward avoids Alex, if he can.
And when he cannot, is curt, stiff, unbending. The Comyn
was more . . . flattering. In an almost mocking way. And
Bishop Clement – he is different, kindly, patient. But he
is unused to children, a man of books and papers. When
they require anything from Alex, they are apt to get it

through his mother or myself. They have had a royal seal made for him, a small one, to serve instead of the Great Seal, which Chancellor Donald keeps. They often require papers and documents to be sealed with the royal authority. Alex quite likes doing that, the melting of the wax and the stamping of the seal. He would seal everything in sight, if we let him!"

"And you think that Durward is going away? He will not take the King with him, I hope?"

"No. There is no word of that. He will leave a secure guard here, I am sure. I believe that he thinks that if he is in the north, on his own lands, the Comyns will be less inclined to attack them. This, for the next month or two. After that, in the deep of the winter, hosts cannot move about in the Highlands, in Badenoch and Atholl, for the snowed-up passes, and there should be peace of a sort between them. After that, who knows . . .?"

"The bishop will remain here with the King, then?"

"Queen Marie thinks so, yes." She looked at him. "Are you going to find the life here very dull, David? Tied to a boy. No other duties to perform. Save what you may make for yourself. I feel . . . afraid for you. Belatedly, perhaps! A man requires his activities."

"I shall make do, I think."

"There will be ridings afield, to be sure. Visits to Border magnates. Hunting and hawking. Fishing in the great rivers. You can teach Alex these. Archery. And skills which his tutor, the monk, cannot give him."

"It sounds as though I shall be sufficiently occupied! And you seldom far off?"

"Oh, I shall be about, yes. You could well soon have had enough of me. Like your Judith!"

"That is not possible."

As he tended the fire again, she went to the next room. "All is well," she reported. "He is asleep. Once he is over, he seldom wakes again until morning. So – now you can go about your man's affairs, David. You will have friends, or at least fellow-lords, about the castle and town."

"I am well content here . . ."

"Nevertheless, I think that it might be well if you were

124

seen down in the hall and about the palace. To prevent . . . talk. No? We must watch for that."

"Must we? I suppose so, yes. I wish . . ."

She put up a finger to his lips, a nicely intimate gesture. "We must keep wishes under due rein, David. Meantime . . ."

He nodded. "If so you say." He rose. "I will go down. But only for a short time. I will seek my couch early tonight, after long riding. The more gladly in that it is but a few feet from yours, here."

"As well that there is good stone walling between!" she said, but not sourly.

"Aye. So – it is goodnight, again?"

"It is indeed. Sleep well."

"And dream, perhaps? Of, of delights nearby?"

"As to that, sir, I cannot constrain you. Nor . . . would wish to!"

He reached to bring and hold her close to him, then, for a moment, before turning and striding off.

She watched him go, nibbling at her lower lip.

In the morning, David was surprised to receive a summons to attend on the Earl of Atholl, in another of the many towers of that elongated castle. When he presented himself, he perceived that there was much bustle about these premises, men coming and going. He was kept waiting for some time in the lower hall.

At length Durward came in, clad as for the road. He wasted no time on preambles. "Young man," he said, "I leave for Deeside. I may be gone for some time. I leave the Lord of Erroll in charge here. He has his orders. You will obey him, as you would myself." No mention of the third and clerical regent. "You appear to be much esteemed by the young King. But he is only a child – forget it not. Do not presume. You understand? You could be removed at a snap of my fingers."

David eyed the older man levelly and said nothing.

"The boy requires attention, schooling in more than letters, keeping in hand. For he is over-forward for his years. See you to it. Do not let him get above himself. But – nor

125

you either! You are warned. And that applies also to the Lady Margaret. Since she is the boy's governess, you will be much in her company. Watch you your step there. She is not to be played with, however kindly she may act towards you, on occasion. She is my good-sister – remember you that!"

David took a deep breath, but restrained himself as to words.

"I will be kept informed as to what goes on here, in my absence." That was grimly said. "So heed my words, Lindsay. I have accepted you thus far, because I knew your father and worked well enough with him. He was a sound man and a good soldier. He served with me against the English in Henry Plantagenet's invasion and our victory at Ponteland. He fought stoutly. Sir David knew his place, and filled it well. See that you do likewise."

"I shall do my duty, my lord. To my liege-lord the King. And shall not forget what you have said. And how you have said it!" That was as far as he let himself go.

The other eyed him with a hard stare. "Do that," he said, and waved a dismissive hand.

David turned on his heel and left him. These two would never love each other.

He had plenty to consider as he went back to his own quarters. He was receiving a sufficiency of warnings, that was sure. He was perhaps not as receptive to them as he might have been; but he was not a fool either, and recognised that care was essential, considerable care and circumspection.

7

In the weeks that followed, David de Lindsay had much cause and opportunity for care and circumspection. He did not go as though treading on eggshells, or ever on the watch. But he was aware that *he* was being watched and tested, and no doubt reported on. He told Margaret, of course, of his interview with Durward, and she admitted that she had expected as much. She did not add that this was why she had been gently moderating towards his more personal advances, but that was implied. Not that she was not incensed against Durward, especially over him calling her his good-sister and all that implied. She had had no dealings with her half-sister, the Countess Margaret, for years; all King Alexander's bastard daughters were named Margaret, allegedly because of his admiration for his great-great-grandmother, Queen Margaret Atheling. But Durward had the power and ruthlessness to make life difficult for them all. And his minions were everywhere about the court.

That said, it did not mean that much enjoyment was not had by the trio, much achieved, much progress made in sundry directions – even though, as far as David's emotions were concerned, there had to be a continuing degree of frustration. For that he was wholly and deeply in love with this young woman he could not deny, and probably made obvious, at least to herself. In that, although he was not encouraged, neither was he actively discouraged. Margaret was never amorous nor consciously tempting; but nor was she over-guarded nor dismissive. They continued to live in close proximity, inevitably.

Alexander, to be sure, remained unconcerned by all of this. His preoccupation was with geese, wild-geese. Ever since that first evening's feast in his bedchamber he had decided that this was joy and gladness, this dining of just the three of them before the fire. Only, to be just right, the main course had to be wild-goose. Other meats might serve at a pinch, but only as substitutes for the real thing. So the royal command was for such game to be shot. Which, of course, was not so easy.

David explained that the geese, although there were thousands of them, were not only hard to shoot but not to be found in many locations – for instance in the Tweed and Teviot valleys. The creatures were not like ducks and most other wildfowl; they flocked only in large numbers and only in certain places. Although they could feed over wide areas of stubbles, grasslands and moors, they were almost impossible to approach there, always with their lookouts posted; they would roost for the night only on sea sand-bars and mud-flats, where none might approach them easily unobserved. And there were not so many of such places available on the east coast of Scotland. Indeed, south of the Scotwater or Firth of Forth, there were only the two likely haunts, and these two fairly close together – Aberlady Bay and Tynemouth, both in Lothian. As far as David knew there were no other resorts of the creatures south of the Tay estuary.

The result of this lecture, of course, was a demand to be taken to Luffness and Aberlady Bay to shoot some – a proposal made not infrequently before. But nearing midwinter, although very much the goose-shooting season, this was not perhaps the time to take an eight-year-old on such an expedition. Temporising, David suggested that they might try making a few shorter sallies into nearer-at-hand areas, in the hope of perhaps discovering a small flock of the birds. They might even venture as far as the Tweed estuary, their nearest coastal location – although he really had little expectation of finding any there. Margaret, always concerned to keep her young and energetic charge occupied, was fully supportive in all this; indeed saw no reason why, if David was willing and Queen Marie had no objections, they should not pay a visit to Luffness for a day or two. Alex was good on a horse, and if they made the journey in two stages, there ought to be no difficulties.

Queen Marie's agreement was necessary. She did not refuse, but pointed out that there could well be opposition to any taking away of the King on the part of Durward's minions left at Roxburgh. It might seem to them as suspicious, possibly a device to get Alexander into the hands of other ambitious men, the Comyns for instance.

David saw the danger of that. He suggested that it might be got over by a process of gradualness, and of seeking the co-operation of the said guards. A number of short ride-outs, as it were to prepare the way, looking for geese, and wildfowl in general, and asking for a small escort of Durward's men to accompany them. Get these used to the process, and there should be little difficulty, even though these had to go with them to Luffness. Since his duty was to educate and entertain the monarch, none could say that this was out of order.

First, however, Alex had to be instructed in shooting. Normal archery was rather beyond him as yet; but the crossbow was different. Smaller, its bowstring was drawn back by a lever which even an eight-year-old could manage, and its weight not too much for the boy. There were two sorts – or the one could be adapted for two uses – for shooting arrows or stones, the latter a sort of catapult, but much more accurate in the aiming. So, in the outer bailey of Roxburgh Castle, the King was instructed in the use of both, and proved an excited but apt pupil, keen of eye. Margaret was well content to attend these practices also, and although already used to crossbows, improved her aim and learned the technique, new to her, of shooting selected stones and pebbles. Alex was good at finding suitable ammunition, and much time was spent down at the two adjoining riversides searching for water-rounded pebbles which would fit the bows' stone-holders.

This stage over, they ventured out in search of sport, to gain further practice – no geese, to be sure, but plenty of duck, mallard and teal in the main, and the occasional swan. And now, as anticipated, guards accompanied them, but seldom more than half a dozen, under one or other of Durward's knights and lairds. These David encouraged to join in any sport, so that all became quite friendly. Even Queen Marie joined in once or twice.

Actual sport was limited, to be sure, for these river-banks were not ideal conditions for wildfowling. The duck were apt to rise well in advance of the sportsmen and fly off at a great speed, usually upriver and mid-river, too fast for arrow-shooting, especially for novices. Hawking would, of course, have been much more profitable – but that was not the object of the exercise. Alex wanted to be a wild-goose-shooter, and this was merely a leading-up process. Actually, the boy never managed to hit a duck, but enormous was the excitement when one day a swan rose out of reeds at a bend in the Teviot, and being much heavier and much more slow-flapping than duck, and flying off over the land not the water, Alex was able to let fly with a stone and brought it down. Never was monarch more gratified over a victory. Now he would shoot geese, he assured all.

They ate the swan two evenings later, in a bedside dinner. It was not so tasty as wild-goose – although some declared swan-meat an especial delicacy, indeed with English royal favour. But Alex was not satisfied, goose he wanted and goose they must have. They tried tame goose; but though his elders were well enough pleased with this, their young liege-lord was not. It was not the same, he declared. When were they going to Aberlady Bay? This became all but a chant.

Queen Marie was not against an expedition to the Lothian coast. The problem was Yuletide. It would very soon be Christmas, with its customary celebrations, and these tended to extend over two weeks. Alexander, a single-minded youngster, saw goose-shooting as the first priority, however, and was much against waiting for weeks. Tentatively David suggested that, with his mother, they could hold their Yuletide at Luffness – and was surprised when Queen Marie declared that to be an excellent notion. She would accompany them. She would enjoy a change of scene from Roxburgh Castle, where she had been all but immured for overlong. They would all go.

David began to wonder what he had let *his* lady-mother in for, and her reactions to the royal household descending on her house for a couple of weeks – and that did not mean just the King, Queen Marie and Margaret, but a sizeable guard which would be bound to be sent with them. She might well be upset and scarcely welcoming, being the woman she was.

However, he reminded himself that he was now the laird, and the decision was his.

Margaret, for her part, deemed the whole project excellent.

So on the Eve of St Thomas, quite a cavalcade set out, with an armed escort of a score of the royal guard, and Queen Marie with a lady-in-waiting. So there were three women. Alex was highly elated, shouting his glee in having got his way. They would not cover the fifty-odd miles to Aberlady in one day, in the circumstances, but ought to get as far as Soutra Hospice for the night.

Fortunately the weather was kind, dull and windy but not very cold, the winter snows forfending – which was as well, with the high ground of the Lammermuirs to cross. They were all excellently mounted, and all much used to riding, with Queen Marie perhaps the least active although no old woman. Her son rode with a crossbow hanging on each side of his saddle-bow, one for arrows, one for stones; he was not to be parted from these.

The party made good time, up Tweed and over into Lauderdale, reaching Soutra before the winter's dusk.

The hospice was staffed by Augustinians, experts in the treatment of sickness and disease. But their hospitality was useful and welcoming for travellers also. They were suitably impressed to receive royal visitors. Alexander took a lot of getting to sleep that night, with David actually sharing a bed with him, overcrowded as the place was. The women were disposed in a different building altogether.

In the morning light, the boy was further roused by the fact that they could now see all of Lothian spread before them from Soutra hill, the wide Scotwater and much of Fife beyond; and although not Aberlady Bay itself, hidden behind the Garleton ridge, they could identify the area where it opened, a dozen miles away only. He was eager to be off.

Just what Alexander had imagined when they reached Luffness and the bay was unclear; but undoubtedly he was disappointed, unlike Margaret and the Queen. For the tide happened to be in, and all the mud-flats and saltings covered, so that its great expanse looked merely like a wide curve of the firth itself between the green horns of Kilspindie and

Gulan Points. A wintery noontide sun shone today and white clouds scudded, making a picturesque scene, backed by the distant twin Lomond Hills, known as the Paps of Fife. But this was not what the boy had come to see – and not a goose was in sight.

The arrival at Luffness Castle was not without its drama. Leaving his guests exclaiming over the size and almost splendour of the place, soaring above the shoreline and clearly much larger than they had anticipated, David rode in ahead over the drawbridge across the moat and between the drum-towers into the courtyard, to inform his mother. The approach of so large a party had not gone unobserved, however, and under the Lion Rampant banner, and the Lady Elizabeth had come out from the keep to investigate. Pate was already waiting.

"David, what is this?" she demanded. "I am happy to see you. But – who are all these?"

"I have brought you guests, Mother, notable guests. Your liege-lord, no less. And his royal mother. Also the Lady Margaret. We have come to shoot geese!"

She stared at him. "God save us! The Queen? And her son? Come to Luffness. Geese? Have you lost your wits, David?"

"His Grace is eager to try to shoot wild-geese. Or at least to see them shot. So we have come to pass Yuletide here."

"Yuletide? But . . .!"

"Come, Mother. Greet Their Graces." David had dismounted, and now turned to lead her back to the gatehouse. He was being very firm, the Baron of Luffness.

Lady Elizabeth, shaking her head, followed, with Pate a little way behind.

The royal party was drawn up, still mounted, on the drawbridge, Alexander exclaiming at the pink stone of this castle as against the grey of Roxburgh.

Lady Elizabeth dipped the required curtsy. "I greet Your Highness. And you, Sire. And, and . . . all!" It was not often that that one was hesitant for words. "Er . . . welcome!"

Queen Marie smiled her somehow otherwhere smile. "I fear that we descend upon you unexpectedly, Lady de Lindsay. And over-many of us. But the good David, here, assured me that we would not too greatly upset your arrangements. If so, we shall remain only a day or two, and return to Roxburgh."

"Oh, that will not be necessary, Your Grace, I am sure." It was scarcely a hearty welcome, but would serve. David let out a sigh of relief.

"Come," he invited, and waved all the cavalcade on and into the courtyard, Pate calling for men to take the horses.

Actually there was no great difficulty in coping with this invasion, at Luffness. A very large fortalice, it was capable of housing and providing for many more than its present normal complement, the family and retainers. There was ample accommodation in the keep for the royal group; and the guard would be lodged partly in the angle-towers and lean-to outbuildings and partly down in the castleton hamlet of Luffnaraw, with the fisherfolk, although they would eat at the castle. Sadly there was no exact parallel to the three contiguous bedchambers of the Roxburgh palace tower, but there were two topmost rooms with access to the keep parapet-walk, one of which was David's own bedroom. He arranged for an extra bed to be put in this one, for Alexander; and Margaret could use the room next to it – even if Lady Elizabeth rather raised her eyebrows at this.

Alexander was impatient over this arrival and settling-in process. It was the geese that he had come for, and the geese he was concerned with. When, when? David pointed out that it was only at the dawn and dusk flighting that they could be shot, and only when the tide was out, normally. Fortunately the tide should be two-thirds ebbed by this late afternoon, so they might be able at least to have a try then – although it was really best in the early morning flighting. The boy could hardly wait.

A minor crisis developed presently. A single small skein of geese, no more than a score, happened to come honking their strange wild cries over the castle area, heading inland from the bay, not high but of course well out of bow-shot. Alex, who had never heard the sound, looked up, and, wanting to know what these were, became considerably worked up when told that these were what he was looking for, he demanding his crossbow there and then. It had to be explained that this was not the way. Those were far too high up, and only an odd little group. He must be patient. Later.

David, for one, was thankful when, with the light beginning to fail, they could make an initial venture down into the bay, the tide sufficiently far out for most of the saltings and mud-flats to be uncovered. Just the four of them went, Margaret insisting on coming along to see what it was all about, and Pate accompanying them, with two dogs. The fewer the better at this sport. The visitors' long riding-boots would not be improved by the deep mud, but that would wash off.

They crossed the Peffer Burn by a long and shaky foot-bridge below the castle, Alex exclaiming that it was shoogly, and set off to plowter across part of the salt-grass, dodging its holes and puddles, and then on to the mud-flats, the boy loud in exclamation, Margaret intimating that she could think of other ways of enjoying themselves. Parallel with the eastern shore of the great bay they trudged for fully a mile. David was saying that not too far ahead they would move in towards the actual tideline on their right where tree-trunks and roots were apt to be washed up to provide them cover to hide behind, when a distant honking sounded landwards. The boy positively danced with excitement, but had to be warned that this was premature; this lot would not be for them. They were not far enough out yet, and these would pass over too high for shooting. But there would be more, never fear.

Soon a large skein was passing overhead, a long V-shaped wavering ribbon of the fowl, the sides of the V each perhaps eighty yards in length, and so all covering quite a wide area, possibly over two hundred birds all told. Because he could see them clearly, even in the half-light, Alex wanted to start shooting straight away and had to be restrained. They were well out of crossbow-shot, and the fowl were seeing *them* and sweeping upwards. Patience was the watchword in this sport. There would be thousands of geese yet to come.

Another lot came over, to the right of them, before they found a suitable uprooted and washed-up tree to hide behind. Now the entire evening sky seemed to be filled with sound, in various directions, together with a sort of contented gabble

134

from the geese already settled on the sand-bar, all above the muted roar of the waves breaking on the said bar. Margaret admitted that it was somehow exhilarating, challenging. But – it was getting ever darker. Soon would they be able to see their targets?

David assured that they would. The darker it got, the lower flew the geese; and their own night vision was improving all the time. If the birds were within range, they would be able to see them. Only for moments, of course; so they had to be ready, arrows and stones in place in their bows. She said that she would leave the shooting to the males.

A louder honking, coming closer, had them all crouching low behind their tree, the dogs eager as the monarch. But, although this was obviously a very large skein, and they could even hear the swish of hundreds of wings, all passed too far to their left to be seen. Great was the royal lamentation and protest. And when another lot passed fairly close on the other side, unseen, there were almost tears behind that tree.

"It is a difficult sport, Alex," David told him. "Not for feeble folk or impatient ones. You have to be the best to shoot geese – hawking is different. I am sure that no one else at court is a goose-shooter. So, do not expect too much this first time."

"Could we not run over to them? If more fly past to the side? So that we could see them . . ."

"No use, Alex. They have better eyes than we have, and would see us moving, and would sheer off. But, fret not. There are still many to come. Some, who try to count them, think that there may be as many as five thousand and more in the bay of a night. And I . . ."

"Hush!" That was Pate, quietly. "I think . . . yes, I think . . ."

One of the dogs whimpered.

Listening intently they could hear not only honking coming close but a sort of throaty chuckling. Then, suddenly, they were over them, visible, perhaps forty feet above, not a large skein, twenty or thirty and not in a V but in a fairly straight line. Three crossbows were raised and aimed, and three twangs sounded in quick succession. Immediately there was a great commotion above, a mighty flapping of wings, a croaking and squawking as the birds banked and swerved off and up. But there was also a distinct plop somewhere not far in front of them, and the dogs' urgent whining.

Pate released them.

Alex began to shout in elation.

David nudged his cousin. "Leave this to me," he said quietly.

The dogs were back in only moments, one dragging a goose along, its wings still feebly flapping. David quickly rose and went to take the bird, swiftly and effectively twisting its neck. He saw that it was transfixed by an arrow. He had feared as much. Pate had used the arrow, he and Alex stones. Pretending that he had to pat the dogs, he stooped and snatched out that arrow, hoping that this was not seen. Then he turned to the boy, thrusting the great bird at him.

"Your first goose, Sire!" he declared. "Cleanly shot. Good shooting!"

Alex reached out to take the heavy trophy, almost choking with emotion and actually hugging the goose to him. For once that youngster could find no words.

Margaret was beginning to add her congratulations when Pate once again hushed them. More were coming. Hastily they reloaded. Alexander, with his goose, was not in time to fit another stone into his bow when another flight came over, much larger. David and Pate both loosed off shots into the dense mass of fowl, and this time they could hardly miss. Two more thuds sounded amidst the abrupt wild beating of hundreds of wings, and the dogs were off again.

Great was the excitement.

Alex was urgent to reload now, gabbling to rival the geese. But although they waited, and heard other skeins passing, some quite nearby, no more actually came over their hide. After some twenty minutes of it, David, concerned that Margaret would be getting chilled, said that the flighting must be nearly over and that they were unlikely to get any more sport that night. Time to return home.

So, with a goose each for the males to carry – almost too heavy for the boy, but he was not to be parted from his – they picked their way back over the dark saltings, still with geese filling the night with their cries and wing-beats. For King Alexander the Third it was sheer triumph.

That night Scotland's sovereign-lord slept with a goose-wing on his pillow.

The Lady Elizabeth quickly got over her shock at the royal invasion, and indeed proved herself to be an excellent host-ess, obviously taking to Queen Marie, if remaining a little less forthcoming towards Margaret. Yuletide celebrations began almost immediately after St Thomas's Day, so there was no lack of activity, not a few of the observances pagan in origin, pre-Christian preoccupation with sun-worship and the winter solstice, the rising of the reborn sun after the shortest day of the year. Yule-logs were to be gathered and ceremonially brought in; there was great collecting of candles to blow out symbolically at sunrise on Christmas morning; lantern-lit processions were made through the villages of Luffnaraw, Aberlady and Gulan, singing carols; and feasting was provided for all, high and low alike. In all this, young Alex joined in happily enough; but not to the exclusion of his preoccupation with the wild-geese. That came first with him. So frequent visits were made down into the bay, when the tide was right, not always with as much success as on that first one, but only once without any sport at all. One dawn flighting they tried, with the geese going in the other direction, rising from the sand-bar to fly inland for the day's feeding and it was on this occasion, with a group of the birds rising from quite near at hand, that Alex actually hit his first kill – although of course he thought that it was his second. His pride was highly vocal.

Margaret did not usually accompany the shooters, this not really being a woman's sport, she asserted. But she did join in all else, with her quiet enthusiasm. David relished this.

Geese, like other game, are best eaten after a few days' hanging, and there was an ice-house in the base of one of the castle's angle-towers for keeping the meat fresh. So they had a special bedroom-feast on Christmas Eve, before the fire in David's room, to eat Alex's first bird. To this they invited Pate, to whom the boy had taken a liking, as a fellow goose-shooter. It made a happy occasion.

Pate was not invited thereafter into Margaret's bed-chamber for the pleasing custom of remaining within earshot, with open doors, for Alex to sleep. This evening there was a musical party down in the great hall, followed by a midnight Mass for family, visitors and retainers. So that David and Margaret could both attend this, Pate volunteered to come back and sit by the King's bed, when he was asleep. This was, in fact, the first occasion when the couple were able to spend the evening together in others' company. It was a change, and pleasant – but David preferred being part of the vigil upstairs.

For his mother's benefit, when after the Mass service Margaret announced that she would go up and relieve Pate Dunbar, and said goodnight to all, David did not accompany her. Later, when he did mount his stairway, he tapped at the girl's door and called a quiet goodnight, getting a murmurous reply. It took quite a lot of self-discipline not to open that door and go in.

Christmas Day was filled for all with activity, religious and secular, only Scotland's liege-lord complaining that there was no goose-shooting amongst the celebrations.

Queen Marie was now talking of returning to Roxburgh. But the Lady Elizabeth's attitudes had changed markedly and she urged a longer stay, until New Year's Day at least. Visits to their neighbours at Seton and Dirleton were proposed; it seemed that, despite her rather superior view of the old Celtic dynastic family to which she belonged, as compared with this one, she was not averse to demonstrating the quality of her visitors.

The call at Seton was, for David at least, somewhat uncomfortable. Judith, after her initial curtsies, hurled herself into his arms with exclamations of joy at seeing him, with no sort of inhibitions, with Lady Elizabeth beaming and the Queen-Mother raising her eyebrows. Margaret looked on interestedly. Oddly enough, the only spoken comment came from King Alexander.

138

"Who is she?" he enquired, eyeing Judith a little askance. "Is she your sister, Davie? Why does she do that?"

"The Lady Judith is an old friend, Sire. That is all. She is the Lord Seton's sister," he said, disentangling himself.

The royal stare was hostile. "Margaret does not do that," he said.

Alexander Seton hurriedly changed the subject. "Sire, I have some fine hawks in the yard here. Would you care to come and see them?"

Alex took David's hand, and they went off together.

The visit was otherwise successful enough, with David managing to keep his distance when it came to parting.

That evening, at the ritual waiting in Margaret's room, she referred to the Seton incident, in an interested rather than a challenging way. "Judith Seton has a great affection for you, David. And she is handsome, a full woman. And your friend's sister. You have been close?"

"No. Not so. From childhood we have known each other, to be sure. But that is all. She is . . . hearty!"

"I saw that, yes. She would make a worthy wife for you, would she not? And I think that your mother much approves of her."

"But *I* do not!" That was flat. "Not as a wife."

"Then, as a lover, perhaps?"

"Never that. I, I would look elsewhere." He reached over to take her hand.

She did not withdraw hers for a little. "Poor David!" she said, gently.

He peered at her in the firelight. "What do you mean by that?" he asked.

"Only that you have your problems. I know. Difficult for you, I think."

"Dear God, yes! I wish, I wish that you were not a king's daughter, Margaret!"

"King's bastard," she corrected. "*I* could wish it too. But we cannot choose our fathers! Nor, always, whom we woul• wed."

"Aye, there's the rub! But – I will not wed Judith Seton."

"You might do worse."

"I might do better – a deal better! If only you . . ."

She rose. "This talk but troubles us both, David. To no good purpose. I am sorry, very sorry. Queen Marie has warned me. I am not free to, to choose my own way. Let us not hurt each other, if we can help it. Now, we will go see if Alex is asleep. Then say a goodnight."

Thereafter she allowed him to kiss her brow, at her door, a very frustrated young man.

Hogmanay, New Year's Eve, was a great occasion, at Luffness as elsewhere in Scotland, a time for especial celebration, essentially pagan in origin but with little of even that religious significance remaining, the feasting and entertainment carefree, untrammelled, and frequently developing into licence, with behaviour accepted, or at least winked at, which would not be so on any other day of the year – however unsuitable a way it was to start a new year. It was said that there were more babies born in September than any other month, in consequence.

Although the Lady Elizabeth did not permit excesses and unseemly ongoings, common in many castles and great houses, she was no spoilsport, and the Luffness festivities were far from dull or lacking in spirit. The feasting was on a generous scale, in quantity and variety, venison, wildfowl, beef, pork and salmon from the ice-house available. Sweetmeats in abundance, wines, spirits and ale all but unlimited. There was a masque on this occasion, especially devised by David and Margaret for Alex's benefit, comprising a dozen young girls dressed in suitable colours and provided with wings and beaks to represent a skein of geese flapping round the hall in a V, with young men lumbering in long boots after them, capering, with crossbows to aim and pretend to shoot their chosen quarry, to music and much honking and crying, the girls at the end duly collapsing to the floor with dying wing-flaps, to be picked up and kissed and carried from the hall, to cheers and intimate advice. There was other entertainment, singers and instrumentalists, acrobats, gypsy dancers and a man with performing dogs which walked on their hind legs round the hall – to Alex's delight. There was dancing for all both before and after the repast – the latter for those still able, and these gradually

140

growing fewer, with the survivors ever more abandoned in their performance. The King, who was permitted to stay up until midnight this once, watched all with interest and considerable comment. He produced a few solo capers of his own, and joined Margaret and David in one of the dances, scarcely to their advantage.

Midnight celebrated, and the year 1250 ushered in with acclaim, the over-stimulated boy was taken upstairs and got to bed. His two guardians were afraid that, in the circumstances, he would take a long time to sleep, but David told him a story about St Columba and the strange beast in Loch Ness, and presently the eyelids drooped.

When David returned to Margaret's room, he found her standing before the fire, gazing down into the flames. He went to her, and put an arm around her shoulders.

"So we commence a fresh year, turn a new page," he said. "What will it bring us, I wonder." He emphasised that "us".

She did not answer at first. Then, "What do you wish for it?" she asked. "It is a time for making wishes and resolutions, is it not?"

"You *know* what I wish," he said. "For us . . . to come closer. Closer than this!" He held her more tightly. "As to resolutions, I fear that I must strive ever to hold myself back, like any reined-in horse. Keep fighting all that is in me, lest, lest . . ." He left the rest unsaid.

She did not. "Lest what, David?"

"Lest I offend. Lest I forget that you are not for me! Lest I do what every part of me longs to do. *Take* what I want!" He did not realise how fiercely he was now clutching her shoulders, all but shaking her.

She started to speak, and then stopped and abruptly turned within his arm to face him, but to bury her face against his chest, gripping him in turn. She did murmur something, but it was lost against his doublet.

"Lassie! Lassie!" he all but groaned. "Help me! Do not . . . hinder!"

She looked up then. "I am past helping, David, I think. You . . . or myself," she got out. "Past all pretending. I am . . . I fear . . . as bad as you!"

141

His breath catching, he stared down at her, at that face so near his own, into eyes that even in the firelight he could see were now filled with tears.

"Margaret!" he gasped. "Margaret, my love! Is it true? True?" And before she could deny it, or resile, he stooped to kiss, and this time not on her brow.

Her warm moist lips met his own, met, stirred and opened.

They stood there before the fire, holding each other convulsively, kissing and kissing. And time stood still, stiller than they did. If their monarch stirred or even called out, next door, they did not hear it, knew nothing but the ecstasy of the moment, that they were together at last, not questioning the future, not questioning anything just then, lost in each other.

Eventually David led her over to her bed and sat her down, not ceasing to hold her. Questioning, of a sort, did come then.

"My dear, my dear – why? What made you . . . what brought you to this? Why now? What changed you?"

"Nothing changed me, David my heart! I have loved you almost from the first. I sought to fight it, but could not. But I *could* prevent myself from letting you know it, and did. Until tonight. Was I a fool? Or am I the fool now? Knowing that . . . knowing what we know. That nothing is changed. And yet, and yet, everything is changed! Is it not?"

"Changed, yes – God be praised! Here is joy! Wonder! As good as His heaven! But – why now, Margaret?"

"I do not know. Or, perhaps, I do. Some of it. I have wanted to come to you, for so long. And tonight it somehow had to be. The start of a new year. A fresh beginning." She gave a little laugh. "I do not think that it is the wine! I did not drink so much! Perhaps it was all the revelry below there. Everyone letting go of themselves, dropping their guards, care laid aside. It, it just had to be, my dear . . ."

"Praise be, whatever it was! I, I . . ."

But words, further feeble words, were unnecessary, a waste for lips which could be better employed. Eyes, hands, persons, could be eloquent too, even if still a sort of moderation was mutually accepted without any actual saying so. They had so much, now, that they need not seek for more, not

142

yet. Nor voice the questions which must arise. Time enough for that.

Some awareness of time did eventually come to them, of course, that night, and Margaret found the strength to point it out. Alex was an early waker, as they knew to their cost; and although he might well sleep later for once, after his late night, if they themselves were to have any sleep, then they had better get it while they might, for it could not be far off dawn, the new dawn for them. So . . .

David made the inevitable male suggestion about the lack of need for sleep at all – or even the bliss of sleeping together. But she closed his lips with a lingering kiss and a gentle but firm goodnight, and sent him back to his room, to dream.

He assured her that he would not be able to sleep for what was left of the night. But he did.

8

Back at Roxburgh, life settled into its accustomed routine, for, although all was changed for David and Margaret, in one respect, in another nothing was. He was still very much only the King's Cup-Bearer and she was a king's daughter, a princess in all but title. They of course discussed the situation from every angle and reached their conclusions, however reluctantly. In private they were lovers, not in the physical sense, for that would have been folly and almost certainly have led to dire trouble; but in public they remained only good friends and partners in the royal service. If any others came to suspect their closer relationship, in especial Queen Marie, who despite her seeming vague manner did not miss much, nothing was said, and all assumed to be as before.

By a sort of equally unspoken understanding between them, David learned just how far he might go in his affectionate gestures. Cupping a shapely breast in an embrace was acceptable; but slipping a hand within a bodice and fondling was not advisable, as apt to lead to further advances, which however mutually agreeable must be avoided. And the like. The man recognised that any hint of this getting to the ears of Durward, or of the other regents or even privy councillors, could result in the very development they dreaded, namely the speedy marrying-off of Margaret to some great one, before she became less acceptable as a prize.

Young Alexander found no fault with his guardians' behaviour, although more than once he came on them in each other's arms.

Bishop Clement remained the only regent at Roxburgh – which was a blessing. They heard little of the other two, in their respective northern fastnesses, these presumably waiting for the winter snows to clear the Highland passes to enable hostile attitudes to express themselves in action.

There was no more goose-shooting meantime, but promises for the future. The monarch had to content himself with alternative and less exciting meats for their bedchamber feasts – although David sent for, and Pate Dunbar delivered, a couple of the birds from the Luffness ice-house for Alexander's ninth birthday, a notable occasion in more than that.

Then, to emphasise this, they had a brief visit from Durward himself. He brought a great collection of documents, charters and notifications of appointments, which it seemed required the royal endorsement. To display this, and mark the birthday, he had taken upon himself to make a new royal seal, cast notably small, to emphasise the youth of the monarch, he keeping the Great Seal of Scotland in his own hands. Obviously he was acting as though he was the sole regent and ruler. The Comyns' reaction to this was unknown; but presumably the Lord of Badenoch did not take his duties very seriously anyway, since he remained where he could effect little on a national scale. As for Bishop Clement, he seemed well enough content with his nominal and all but grandfatherly role at Roxburgh, left to pursue his studies in peace.

Durward had little to say to David, nor indeed to any of them save Queen Marie, whom he treated with more respect than he did others, his dealings with young Alexander short and wholly concerned with royal authorisation. He did announce however that there was to be a great celebration at Dunfermline shortly, to mark the canonisation of the blessed Queen Margaret Atheling, the King's great-great-great-grandmother, notification of which had recently arrived from the Vatican, the first saint Scotland had produced since she herself had established here the Roman Catholic Church to replace the Columban one. The King, his mother and the court were expected to attend. He would send word as to dates and arrangements.

With that, Alan Durward departed. At least, thankfully, as far as David was concerned, he had announced no plans for marrying Margaret off to some suitable husband.

All at Roxburgh Castle breathed sighs of relief when he was gone. Queen Marie declared that she hoped that this Dunfermline project would take place soon, otherwise it might interfere with her plans. It seemed that she, strange woman, had decided to make her visit to her homeland of Flanders in the later spring, length of stay away unspecified. She seemed little concerned about leaving her young son.

So life returned to normal at Roxburgh, with little happening of relevance to the management of the affairs of the kingdom, a curious situation for a royal court. Rumours reached them, of course, of controversial activities, the appointments of Durward's friends to high office, rumbles of revolt from various parts of the realm, and so on. But none of this seemed greatly to affect the royal entourage – and no complaints at that. Possibly Durward's strong hand at the helm of state had its advantages as well as its problems. In fact, of almost more concern to them at Roxburgh, so near the borderline, were stories emanating from England of unrest and insubordination in that realm, where Henry the Third was proving to be no strong monarch, and troubles developing, especially in the north. Unrest in Northumbria and Cumbria was apt to spill over the border into Scotland. Moreover, Henry, it seemed, had now claimed, in a letter to the Pope, that he was Lord Paramount of Scotland, and seeking archiepiscopal jurisdiction over the northern kingdom for the Archbishop of York, this presumably in a move to appease the northerners.

Then, just as the Queen-Mother was beginning to display her own form of agitation, a courier arrived from Durward to summon them to Dunfermline. All was now in readiness there.

The journey was not so very much longer than to Aberlady Bay, for, by striking north-westwards from Soutra Hospice instead of north-eastwards, they could reach Queen Margaret's Ferry over the narrows of Forth in about twenty-five miles, by skirting to the south of Edinburgh town. Doing so, Alexander exclaimed at the great upthrusting hill of Arthur's Seat, so like a crouching lion, and the fortress-castle atop its rock, so like that of Stirling which he knew.

They found the ferry busy indeed, for great numbers of folk, high and low, appeared to be using it today, the four flat-bottomed scows comprising it, all in use, and with extra small boats pressed in as reinforcements. Even the royal party had to wait, their horses requiring the largest scows. As it happened, they found Serle de Dundas more or less superintending the traffic here, for his castle of Dundas was only a mile or two away, and he had been asked by the monkish ferry-operators to aid them control the situation. These were rueful, he told David, that because of this unusual surge of ferrying, they themselves would not be able to attend the celebrations at Dunfermline, they of all people, whose predecessors had been especially appointed by the Queen Margaret to man and work this ferry so that pilgrims could visit the first stone abbey erected in Scotland, beside her husband's palace at Dunfermline. As they waited, Dundas also mentioned that Durward had just come from founding a hospital at Kincardine O'Neil, near his main seat of Coull Castle on Deeside, to the glory of God and out of his regard for Holy Church. David was not the only one who wondered why Durward had suddenly become so interested in Church matters, he who had hitherto shown little concern with religion.

Once across the estuary, it was a mere five miles to Dunfermline, the capital of Fothrif, a sizeable town occupying higher ground above the Forth plain. Here had been the fairly rude palace-fort of Malcolm the Third, Canmore or Big Head, to which he had brought, all but his captive, Margaret Atheling, sister of Edgar Atheling, who should have been sitting on the English throne had not William of Normandy, the Conqueror, dispossessed him. And here Margaret had tamed that rough and savage monarch, the slayer of King MacBeth, married him and set about changing his Scotland, in particular in substituting the Church of Rome for the ancient Columban Celtic Church – which was partly what they were to be celebrating now, even though some wondered whether that had been a change for the better.

As they approached, the visitors could see the great abbey she had built, so different from the modest little Columban abbeys and churches, a vast monument in stone, quite overshadowing the palace nearby, with even the abbot's house more splendid than the King's. Holy Church had cause to thank Queen Margaret.

Alexander and his mother were ceremonially received, on this special occasion, by Durward, major clerics and members of the Privy Council. There was no sign of the Lord of Badenoch and Lochaber, but the Earl of Menteith had come to represent the Comyns. Bishop Clement, the third regent, had of course accompanied the royal party.

By this time it was late afternoon. The palace was full to overflowing with great ones and their trains, and David was despatched to monastic quarters where he found Seton and other acquaintances of a like rank. But for the subsequent banquet in the palace great hall, he, as Cup-Bearer to the King, was permitted to sit up on the dais again, where presently Margaret joined him.

Twice David had to lead Alexander back to the main table and his mother's side, to mixed frowns and smiles.

There was no accompanying Margaret and the boy to bedchambers that night. The company in the monastic dormitories prepared themselves for the morrow by drinking wine well into the small hours of the morning, at Holy Church's expense.

The Primate, Bishop de Birnam of St Andrews, assisted by the rest of the episcopate and the Abbot of Dunfermline, had organised all for the next day, in the abbey. The great church was packed, even to the clerestory galleries, all having to stand save for the greatest lords and earls and senior clergy. Alexander was led, behind a choir of singing boys, by Queen Marie and Durward, to a throne-like chair in the chancel, these seating themselves close behind, with Bishop Clement nearby. The Earl of Menteith sat as close to the chancel steps as he could get.

At precisely noon the officiating clergy filed in, to more singing and the clash of cymbals – of which latter the monarch obviously approved, clapping his hands in time.

Bishop de Birnam took charge. A brief and token Mass was celebrated, only for the participating clerics, all others being offered a comprehensive benediction. Then the Primate made his peroration.

They were assembled, he declared, to rejoice in God's great mercy and goodness in giving to their land and nation, one hundred and eighty-eight years before, the blessed, beloved and saintly Margaret, sister of the rightful but dispossessed King of England, granddaughter of St Stephen, King of Hungary, and wife of Malcolm the Third of Scots, who had come to Scotland as it might seem by mischance when on her way back to Hungary with brother, mother and sister, but in fact had been sent by the providence of the Almighty. She had, after her wedding to the King, devoted her life not only to the care of her new people and the improvement of their condition, but to the amendment of their faith and worship, replacing the old and error-prone Columban Church by the true Holy Catholic and Apostolic Church of Rome, to the everlasting good and benefit of all, establishing the due orders of ministry – one of which he had the great honour to fill. She built this magnificent abbey that they now filled, planned others which her sons, in especial the youngest, the good King David of blessed memory, erected thereafter, so nurturing true religion in their ancient kingdom. Also correcting the erroneous date for the celebration of the Feast of Easter. All this and more they owed to the blessed Margaret.

The bishop paused, and at a sign from the abbot, the cymbals clashed and a hymn of praise was raised by the choristers.

The Primate resumed. Always, then and thereafter the people of Scotland had indeed called her blessed, for great had been her love for the common folk. But now she was the blessed Margaret indeed, for His Holiness the Pope, with all his cardinals, had duly canonised her and elevated her to the formal sainthood. They were gathered here to praise God and to celebrate this glorious translation of Saint Margaret of Scotland.

Cymbals and praise.

As the bishop went on to further speech, those in the chancel heard a small but penetrating voice say, "Was not Columba a saint too?" And the King of Scots held up his Brecbennoch, which he always carried with him on official occasions, towards his mother.

There was just a moment of hesitation before the Primate went on – for, after all, when the monarch raised his voice, subjects were supposed to heed if not respond. But clearly this royal intervention was not one which could be dealt with there and then; so de Birnam contented himself with a brief bow towards the throne, and resumed.

This long-desired and due canonisation had largely been expedited by the representations to the Vatican of the noble Alan, Earl of Atholl, regent for His Grace Alexander here present, untiring in his efforts for the realm and Holy Church. He now invited the said Lord Alan to come forward and uncover the memorial which had been contrived to mark this very especial and blessed occasion.

Durward rose, and with no bowing nor ceremony strode past bishops and clergy to the high altar, and there drew a fine embroidered covering from a handsomely carved box of dark wood; and, opening the lid, lifted out therefrom a gleaming silver casket on a chain, held this up towards the congregation for a moment or two, replaced it in the box, slammed the lid, and went back to his chair unspeaking. He had never been an eloquent man.

Since the great majority present would not know what this was and its significance, Bishop de Birnam went on to explain. This was the famed Black Rood of Scotland, part of the piece of the Lord Christ's true cross, given to his granddaughter Margaret by St Stephen of Hungary and brought by her to Scotland, the only such precious relic in a dozen kingdoms. Her son, King David, had ever carried it with him, and by it was saved miraculously from being gored by a wounded stag in the royal hunting-forest below Arthur's Seat at Edinburgh, and there founded an abbey, in gratitude, which he named the Abbey of the Holy Rood. Now they had had carved this good kist to contain it, and brought it here to Margaret's own abbey, to be placed above her earthly remains, for she lay buried before this high altar. So Margaret and her Black Rood would be reunited.

That, to cheers, completed the celebration, and after hymn-singing Durward rose to lead out the King and his mother. There was a slight hitch, however, with Alexander loudly demanding to see what was in the box that that man had held up, and hurrying over to have a look. So all stood, while the bishop of St Andrews went to open the little chest and show the monarch the silver casket and chain, himself being given the Brecbennoch of St Columba to hold while the boy examined the Black Rood. He did not seem to think much of it and handed it back saying that he liked more his own Breck-thing. Thereafter the royal group was able to make an exit and less exalted folk could leave.

There was to be more feasting, but before that, David and Margaret managed to abstract Alex from the palace and take him for a walk down into the nearby Glen of Pittencrieff, where his ancestress had used a cave for a sort of private retreat for her devotions. This they found, the boy declaring that he had seen bigger and better ones, and then they climbed to a viewpoint above the town.

As they went, David expressed his wonderings about Alan Durward to Margaret. What had come over him? All this concern for things religious, he who had never displayed any religious tendencies hitherto, indeed only contempt for the priesthood. Now he gave a hospital on Deeside to the Church, and pressed the Pope for this of Queen Margaret's sainthood. He did not look as though he might be ailing, and thinking of his latter end?

Margaret had few helpful suggestions. She cordially disliked the man, but perhaps even he might have his better feelings, and be concerned to demonstrate them? It might be that Bishop de Birnam was being a good influence? After all, Birnam was in Atholl, and they might be kin of a sort.

Alex had his own questions. Why was this other Margaret being called a saint, the *only* saint, when Columba was the real saint? And was there not a Saint Andrew with a cross, too? That man in the long hat was not telling truth, was he?

David tried to explain. The word saint had different meanings, so there were saints and saints. The ancient Celtic Church, to which Columba belonged, used to call all their missionaries saints. And of course Christ's apostles and disciples got called saints too. But Holy Church in Rome was different. They *made* saints. Only very special people, to be sure, and it took a lot of arranging and time. They probably did not approve of the Celtic Church saints; but that was a matter of opinion.

Alex announced that he liked Columba best, anyway.

151

The banqueting and entertainment thereafter did not reflect any very religious element. Probably Malcolm Canmore rather than his saintly Queen would have approved.

Next day the royal party was off on its way back to Roxburgh.

9

That summer of 1250 was bedevilled by the news from the north and the south. A form of limited civil war was in progress in the Highlands. This was nothing unusual amongst the feuding clans, to be sure, but now it was on a greater and more serious scale, since it was between the great nobles, Durward and the Comyns – and this could well spread to other parts, for both sides owned great lands elsewhere in the kingdom and large manpower, the Comyns especially in Galloway. The fact that both were led by co-regents for the King did not seem to concern either. Not that repercussions of this greatly affected the court at Roxburgh, save as to concern for the future.

But the news from the *south* did. For this was ominous, and had its effect on Queen Marie. For Henry Plantagenet of England, in his efforts to smother troubles in his own realm, was using the ages-old remedy of rousing patriotic fervour against a common objective, in this case Scotland. He was not only claiming to be Lord Paramount thereof, merely because King David and his successors had paid fealty to the Kings of England for the rich lands they had acquired in that realm by David's marriage to the great English heiress, Matilda, Countess of Huntingdon; added to the fact that there was no archbishop in power north of York, and therefore York must have ecclesiastical jurisdiction over archbishopless Scotland. But as well as this absurd claim, he was now asserting that the coronation of young Alexander was invalid because not authorised by *him*, as Lord Paramount; and he had applied to the Pope to have it annulled, a folly which would have been laughable were it not for its dangers as an excuse for possible military action and invasion. Moreover he had renewed the one-time proposal that Alexander should be wed to his own daughter, the Princess Margaret, forthwith, obviously so that he could exert guardianship over the child couple.

All this much upset the Queen-Mother, not seemingly so much on account of its implications for her son and his realm as for the fact that Henry was delaying sending her the requested safe-conduct for her passage through England on her way to France and Flanders. She was eager to join her brother.

There was other dire news, from even further afield. The present crusade in the Holy Land had suffered a major defeat at the hands of the Infidels, largely, it seemed, on account of rashness in the leadership of King Louis the Ninth of France, and terrible were the casualties, amongst the dead being David's uncle and Pate's father, Cospatrick, Earl of Dunbar and March – to the great distress and anger of his sister the Lady Elizabeth at Luffness. David was summoned home, not so much to comfort her as to share her indignation.

Since Alexander was ever clamouring to return to Luffness and Aberlady Bay, David took him and Margaret with him, although having to explain that this was not the season for the wild-geese, which migrated northwards to colder climes for the summer. Queen Marie did not accompany them.

Their greeting, in the circumstances, was a mixed one of warmth, concern, doubts and criticism – Margaret of course the reason for the last, even though not put into words. But the younger woman was left in no doubts on the matter, and she was allotted a room much removed from the one she had occupied, next to David's, when last she had been there.

Whilst Margaret was putting Alex to bed that night, David was detained downstairs for a private conversation, his mother in a determined mood – not that this was unusual with her.

"David," she said, without preamble, "in all your concern for that boy, and others, you are not to forget that you have responsibilities towards your own family. I am not referring now to the estates and baronies. Nor to myself, although my concerns should be yours also. But to this of my brother, your uncle, slain by those godless Saracens. He must be avenged."

David blinked. "Avenged . . .?"

"Avenged, yes. The heathen cannot slay the representative

154

of the true royal house of Scotland without paying for it. My brother was a fool to go crusading, as I told him. But to die thus! The evil sons of Satan, after the defeat, captured the crusading lords and knights, first humiliated them and then beheaded them, Cospatrick amongst them. We cannot let that challenge go unanswered."

"I do not see . . ."

"*You* must make the gesture, for the honour of our line. My nephew Patrick, who is now Earl of Dunbar and March, is a poor shallow creature. *He* will do nothing. He is no credit to his blood. But you are different. You have more spirit, even though often misguided! Someone must maintain the honour of our house."

"But – what can I do?" David had never been particularly fond of his uncle. 'What is there to be done?"

"You must go on crusade. Yes, you! One day. Wipe out the dishonour done. Promise me, David! I know that it may be long before another crusade is mounted, especially after this disaster. But one day the leaders of Christendom will go back, to punish the Infidel and free the holy places from their evil sway. You then to go with them."

"But, Mother, how can I do that? I have my own life to live! So much to see to, here. I guard and teach the King. I have these lordships and lands to look to, and their folk . . ."

"It may not be for years yet. It took long years to rally, gather and get this crusade to the Holy Land, as it has others. But I require your promise, David, that when the time comes you will not be found wanting. Without such promise, I will have no peace. Our line and blood demand it. You are a Lindsay, yes – but you are also of the blood of the Cospatricks, the Celtic rulers, right back to ancient Alba, whom Columba converted to Christianity. *You* will not fail them, when they look down from Paradise on their descendants? Promise me."

He wagged his head helplessly. This mother of his had always been obsessed, all but deranged on the subject of the dispossession of the eldest royal line, the older and legitimate brothers whom Malcolm Canmore, Queen Margaret's husband, had so wrongly superseded and banished. It looked as though this had now become some sort of madness. But

155

that it was very real to her was obvious. He was fond of her, owed her his devotion. And he could hardly push off the responsibility to his young brother John.

"If you so wish it, I will seek to go, one day, on a crusade, Mother," he told her, less than heartily.

"Not *seek* to go, but go, boy!" she said. "Your promise. Otherwise I shall never live, rest, nor die in peace."

He bit his lip. That word die, of course, hit hard. She was not an old woman, by any means, little more than fifty; but she had bouts of a recurring sickness. His father, on his deathbed, had told him to look after her. He inclined his head.

"Very well, I promise," he said.

"Good! You much ease my mind." She waved that subject away with a hand. "But not altogether, David. It is time that you married, high time. You have your responsibilities there, also. If you will not wed Judith Seton, who would be the most admirable, then some other who would make a worthy and suitable match. The Lord of Luffness, Barnweill, Crawford and The Byres should be married and produce an heir. But *not* to that young woman upstairs, of whom you are seeing far too much! You know that. She is not for you. If, because of this of the young King, you are going to continue to be in her company so much, then you should have a wife. Otherwise your names will be linked. And that way lies dire trouble. For her as for yourself. You are not witless. You must see it."

He closed his lips tightly, looking away.

"David, do not play the fool! She is not, cannot be, for you, half-sister of the King. It is strange that she has not been married off to some earl or great magnate before this. As she will be, Durward or the Comyn will see to that. You must accept it."

"I love Margaret," he said then, simply. "And she loves me."

His mother came to touch his arm, an unaccustomed gesture with her. "Oh, lad, I am sorry. Sorry indeed. But love, like sorrow, alters nothing. You will not be allowed to marry her, that is sure. You cannot fight it. So – play the man, not the fool. For her sake as well as your own. And find a bride of your own station. Judith would be best, but . . ."

"Do not name Judith Seton to me again!" he burst out and, swinging around, left his mother standing there.

Margaret must have found him a very silent and unforthcoming attendant when he accompanied her to her bedroom door that night – and to some extent in the two days following.

When they rode southwards thereafter, with the last of the geese from the ice-house, Pate accompanying them as far as Soutra, it was Margaret who broached the vexed subject, with Alex in deep discussion with Pate on how the wild-geese knew to come back to Aberlady Bay each autumn from their faraway summer quarters, and why always to the same bay?

"Your mother, David, I think was warning you again about myself and our . . . association? You have been restrained. Was it a sore trial? Leaving you so grieved."

He had not realised that he had been so obviously preoccupied. "I am sorry. Did I behave so ill? Yes – my mother is . . . difficult. She is not unkind, but she is very set in her ways and wishes, her notions."

"And she does not approve of me!"

"She does not mislike you, I think. Only believes that you are not, cannot be, for me. Which, to be sure we also . . . fear! But she believes that we could come to dire hurt and trouble, in this. That I am endangering *you*, by my fondness. And *that* I dare not think on. We know all this, to be sure. But she is strong on it."

"Poor David! What have I brought upon you? What would your mother have of us, then?"

"That I wed! Just that! Only so, she says, will others, Durward and the great ones, accept our close association. If I am wed to another . . ."

She rode silent for a little while. "Perhaps she is right," she said at length.

"No! Or – she may be right in one respect. That might appease those in power. But, in all else, she is wrong. I will *not* wed another! That is the end of it! I will not."

"The good Lord knows that *I* do not want you to do so, David," she told him, a quiver in her voice. "But . . . it would be for the best, perhaps. Since we are placed as we are. I am but a drag and danger in your life. And, and I cannot see betterment. Judith Seton would wed you. As, no doubt, would many another if asked."

"I could not yield up my love for *you*. Could you stop loving me?"

"No, I could not. But . . ."

"Then, if we were still together, caring for Alex, as is our simple duty, we would be living a lie. You must see that. And would that be fair on, on the other woman, whoever she might be?"

Margaret shook her head helplessly, she who was no helpless one.

He was concerned to change the subject. "She, my mother, was hot on another cause also. She made me promise, one day, to go on a crusade."

"Crusade! The Holy Land? You . . .?"

"Yes. To avenge her brother, my uncle of Dunbar and March. And for the credit of our line. She is all but crazed on this. She sees it as a matter of honour, little to do with religion I think."

"But, David, why you? If any must go, the Earl Cospatrick had a son, had he not? The new earl. What of him? *You* are a Lindsay . . ."

"She despises Patrick, my cousin. Considers him weakling."

"And you promised?"

"I had to. Perhaps it is I who am the weakling! But – she made it as though she would be broken in spirit, die a woman bereft . . ."

"She could be bereft of a *son*, if you went and suffered the fate of your uncle!"

"But she would conceive the Cospatrick honour to be saved! Which seems to mean more to her than aught else. Or almost so."

"She believes that *our* house and line – I mean my father's and Alex's – are usurpers, and yours, or hers, should be sitting on the Scots throne? Your cousin Patrick, king. No?"

"I fear so, yes."

"So she has that against me, also! I see your problems, David. Malcolm Canmore and *his* Margaret have more to answer for than abbeys and sainthood, by dispossessing his elder brothers!" She frowned. "And this of a crusade? When?"

"The Lord knows that! It could be sufficiently long. Perhaps never. After this disaster. It took years to muster and contrive, to suit all the princes of Christendom. And . . . I promised only that one day I would go. *If* a crusade was mounted. Not necessarily the first one . . ."

Alex reined back, shouting. "Pate says that I could hawk for the geese. But big hawks are needed. Goose-hawks. No, goshawks. He says that you have none of these, Davie. Why? Will you get some big goshawks, and we will do that? I would like it . . ."

That was a safe subject for their onward riding.

10

The summer passed into autumn, at Roxburgh, without major incident, however disturbed was the kingdom in general. No invasion from England took place, and it was rumoured that Alan Durward had come to some understanding with Henry Plantagenet, details undisclosed. But if there was truth in that, it did not expedite the granting of the safe-conduct for Queen Marie to travel through England, to her increasing frustration and gloom. She was even contemplating trying to arrange for a sea-passage in some merchanter, lacking in dignity as this would be for a Queen, and hazardous because of the prevalence of English pirate-ships which preyed on traffic to the Continent. Then, on All Hallows Eve, the last day of October, a courier did arrive, from Henry at York, with the precious document, no explanation given for delay.

The Queen-Mother was a changed woman, her motherhood not her evident priority.

It took only two days, to the Commemoration of All Souls, for arrangements for departure to be completed; and next morning it was farewell.

Alexander, with Margaret and David, accompanied his mother the twenty-eight miles to Berwick-on-Tweed and the borderline. There, at the heavily guarded bridge, where the river was still crossable before it widened to the estuary, it was goodbye. There was remarkably little evident emotion about the parting, despite their amity and friendship. Alex's and his mother's relationship was ever undemonstrative, on both sides, and remained so, he in fact being much closer to his half-sister. The Queen kissed him briefly and patted his shoulder, he looking away.

"You will be your father's good son," she said, a perhaps peculiar way of putting it. "Remember always that you are the King, but heed Margaret and the Lord David. They will look well to your care. And remember me in your prayers also, Alex. We will see each other again, one day, before overlong."

He nodded. "When?"

"That I cannot say, at this present. Much depends on . . . others." She turned to Margaret. "You will care well for him, I know, as always, friend as well as sister. I have no fear for Alex in *your* care. You will write me letters, when you can? At my brother's court."

"When I can find a courier, I shall, Your Grace."

"Yes – that may be difficult. The ambassadors will help." To David she addressed herself, oddly enough, at rather greater length. "My friend, I am the happier leaving Alex in that I know that *you* are with him. He is greatly advantaged in having you. He needs such as you. He loves you well. Protect him from . . . those others. I have much trust in you. In Margaret and you, both. Guard and instruct him . . . and cherish him."

"That we will, Your Grace. Have no fear."

She glanced at Margaret but still addressed David. "You two – I feel for you. You have my good wishes. I think that you are close. Fond. Is it not so?"

He inclined his head, unspeaking.

"I wish that I could aid you both. Perhaps the time may come, who knows? If you are *given* time! I shall pray for you."

He swallowed. "Your Grace is kind. And, and understanding. You think that there is . . . hope?"

"There is always hope, David. And for us all. Myself also. And since love is of God Himself, love can triumph, I believe. We *must* believe."

Margaret and David exchanged quick glances.

"So now I go on my own hoping way," the Queen-Mother said. "I leave you, with God. Pray for me, as for yourselves. We will meet again. Do not forget me, Alex." And without more words, Marie de Coucy turned in her saddle and rode onward, with her escort of the royal guard, to display her safe-conduct to the waiting English bridge-captain. Those had been more words than any of them had ever heard from her previously, and more revealing words.

They watched until the Queen's party disappeared beyond the bridge-end and into the township of the Hospital of Tweedmouth. She did not once look back, although Alex raised his hand more than once.

"Why did she not wave?" he asked.

"I think because she might not see you, having tears in her eyes," Margaret told him gently.

"Why?"

They reined their horses round.

Alexander chattered as they rode back, clearly far from dejected. The other two were less talkative.

When, back at Roxburgh Castle, they could speak alone, David was not long in referring to that parting conversation.

"Queen Marie spoke strangely," he said. "She assuredly knows of our feelings for each other. And does not frown on them. Indeed, she seemed to wish us well, in it all."

"Yes, clearly she has not been deceived. Although she has never spoken of it until now. Why, I wonder?"

"She keeps her thoughts to herself, that lady! Unlike *my* mother! Until today. What think you she meant? When she said that of hope? Hope for us, but hope for herself also? Love and hope. She was going on her hoping way, she said. She is ever a strange woman – but that was strange talking indeed."

"Who knows? But she is not a happy woman is Marie de Coucy. I judge that she has not been happy for long. I heard stories, as a girl – what truth in them I know not. That she was wed to my father by design – as are most royal marriages, as we all know too well. But that she was already in love with some man in her own country, deeply in love. So she came to Scotland against her will, to marry my father after he had lost his first wife, Joanna, daughter of King John of England, who died childless. Possibly Marie and he never loved each other? Which might explain something of her way with young Alex. Perhaps not – who can tell? But that may be why she is so eager to return to France or Flanders. She still . . . hopes! After ten years."

"So-o-o! That would account for a lot, yes. And why she

162

understands and feels for *us*. But – it is good that she does, for whatever reason. It might help us."

"I fear not. She has little to say in the affairs of Scotland. And she is not even in the country now. It is Durward and the other regents and magnates who decide matters. Who will decide *my* fate!"

"The accursed folly of it . . .!"

David learned that a fellow-lord, Aymer de Maxwell, used goshawks for sport on his Solway marshes near Dumfries, where there were greylag geese by the thousand – their own at Aberlady Bay were the pinkfoot variety – and, for a Yuletide gift for Alexander, rode right across southern Scotland, over one hundred miles, by Teviotdale, over the high watershed, down Ewesdale and Eskdale and by Dumfries itself to Caerlaverock near the Solway Firth shore. There he persuaded that young lord to sell him a male and a female goshawk, as a duty towards his monarch. Indeed Maxwell, an enthusiast, took him out on the following evening to sample hawking the geese at their flighting, demonstrating the especial procedures and departures from the normal hawking activities, new experience for David – although he could have guessed most of it.

He learned something else at Caerlaverock. Aymer de Maxwell had his own sources of information, from both sides of the Western March of the borderline – from the Comyns, who owned much of Galloway and the south-west, and from across the Debatable Land line, at Carlisle where, since Cumbria had been part of Scotland and Strathclyde until not so very long ago, there was much less animosity towards the Scots than on the Northumbrian eastern side, and indeed considerable coming and going. He learned that the Pope, Innocent the Fourth, allegedly in response to Alan Durward's approaches, had appointed three English bishops, of Lincoln, Worcester and Lichfield, as a commission of enquiry into the suppression and superseding of ecclesiastical jurisdictions in Scotland by the civil justiciars and baronial courts, to the financial loss of Holy Church, especially in Galloway and the south-west, and by the Comyns in particular.

David was as indignant as was Maxwell himself. *English*

bishops appointed to enquire into Scottish affairs! Clearly all part of the attempt to have the Archbishop of York and the English Church placed in authority over the Scots, aiding Henry Plantagenet's aim to be Lord Paramount of Scotland, the Pope now involved. And, possibly, Durward! What curious game was that man playing? Any move against the Comyns could be understood; but aiding the English claims was scarcely believable. And all this interest in Church matters, and Rome?

David had ample opportunity for thought on it all as he rode back to Roxburgh with his goshawks, but came to no conclusion other than that Durward was a menace, probably to Scotland as well as to himself and Margaret. If all this represented statecraft, then the less of it they had the better. He would tell Bishop Clement this of the Pope and the English bishops.

Alex was, of course, elated over the goshawks, and inevitably urgent that they should go to Luffness forthwith to try them out against the geese. It had to be explained that they could not impose themselves on the Lady Elizabeth for two Christmas seasons running. After Yule they would go for a few days. Meantime, they would do some hawking at lesser game.

That festive season was a strange one for David and Margaret, enjoyable in some ways, stressful in others. The lack of Queen Marie's presence was the cause of this. They were much more on their own, in consequence; but this put more strain on them, or on David at least, in holding back the physical demonstration of his love. To be living so closely to each other, with so little in the way of other intimate company save for Alex himself, was taxing in the extreme for full-blooded young people. Bishop Clement was really their only associate in daily proximity, and by that man's nature and calling he was something of an anchorite, mind apt to be far away on interests and studies of his own; moreover he was sometimes absent in person as well as in mind, for he had a diocese to superintend, at least in theory, and although he had an efficient and reliable deputy at Dunblane, he had to visit there occasionally. The permanent court officials were in residence at Roxburgh Castle, to be sure, the Chamberlain, the Master of the Household, the Dispenser, the Captain o the Royal Guard and the Keeper of the castle and others, but these had little to do with the couple save in an official capacity. The young monarch's monkish tutor was a very shy and modest character, more apt to serve as clerk to Bishop Clement than to instruct Alex – who tended to be a less than eager and obedient scholar anyway. No doubt David and the girl were watched, perhaps even spied upon in some degree, to be reported on; but in the circumstances there could not be any very comprehensive scrutiny. And they made a point of being on reasonably good terms with the other castle denizens.

Since part of David's duty was to try to teach Alexander how to behave as monarch, he had to beware of letting the three of them develop into too much of a cosy little group, keeping themselves very much to themselves. So, although the boy would have had almost every winter evening a feast in his bedchamber by the fire, they ensured that most nights he dined in the great hall, with the castle staff and any visitors, Bishop Clement joining them on occasion. With his mother gone, and himself the sole recipient of royal respectful address, Alex very quickly became more aware of his unique rank and station, and might have grown objectionably so had not he remained wholly devoted to and in the main amenable to David and Margaret; they were his friends and allies, never his subjects. He was growing up fast, however, his tenth birthday approaching.

Yuletide and its celebrations over, they duly made the journey to Luffness, with only a small escort this time, their watchers' suspicions evidently lulled. The Lady Elizabeth seemed to be in a less disturbed frame of mind, more welcoming if still scarcely effusive towards Margaret or even Alexander. On this occasion David's brother John, now aged thirteen years, seemed to take to the younger boy, largely, it seemed, on account of those goshawks. John, who had never shown any great interest in goose-shooting in Aberlady Bay, had developed a passion for hawking, engaged in on horseback, with dogs. These new larger birds intrigued him, and he was as eager as was Alexander to try them out. So the boys, with this mutual interest, suddenly became associates.

David, for one, was glad that his royal charge should find someone nearer his own age to be friends with.

There was pressure, of course, for an immediate trial of the goshawks. But since this was a totally different sport from the wildfowling on the salt-marsh and tidelands, a daytime not a dawn and dusk activity, and the January days were short indeed, this had to be postponed until the morrow. But with geese already beginning to pass over the castle on their dusk flighting to the sand-bar, nothing would do but that an all-male sally be made down into the bay there and then, Pate and Johnnie enlisted. They were really too late to get sufficiently far out for effective shooting, the main flighting over and the light gone; but they did get a shot or two at a late-coming skein and bagged one goose – whose it was remained in doubt, since all four drew bow, but by general consent it was Alex's, to the royal satisfaction.

Next forenoon the hawkers were off, mounted now and accompanied by dogs, this time Margaret coming along. As well as the two goshawks they took a couple of their ordinary Luffness falcons in case there was a lack of the hoped-for sport. This goose-hawking was pursued inland, where the skeins flew to feed, by day. First the sportsmen had to locate their quarry, which was not always so simple as it might sound with the thousands of birds involved. Some chose to feed on the stubble riggs of farmed land, pecking up the fallen grain-heads, mainly oats, left after harvest. But they required fresh water for drinking also, so that such stubbles had to be near to streams, ponds or lochans. Some preferred grasses, especially by mid-January, when most of the fallen grain had either been picked up or ploughed in, and so frequented rich grasslands and pastures, usually well away from human habitations. Still others went away to the lofty valleys of the Lammermuir Hills, too far off for reaching on short days.

So it was a matter of sending out scouts to try to locate the geese, Pate and some of his henchmen dealing with this. They had to be careful about it, of course, for horsemen appearing anywhere near a flock feeding could arouse it and send all flying off elsewhere. The same would apply to the hawkers themselves, when their turn came.

On this first occasion, Pate returned before too long to the impatient waiting party, sitting their horses on a frosty morning on Luffness Muir, to announce that he had located a flock less than two miles away, in the Vale of Peffer near enough to the hamlet of Druim. This was good, but it held its problems, for the wide vale, the flood-plain of the River Peffer which reached the sea at Aberlady Bay, was bare and open, with little of the necessary approach-cover available. The only way to get near the area unobserved was by using a belt of scrub woodland which had survived around an ancient Pictish burial-site; but this meant fording the Peffer which, although it was no deep or rushing river, because of its marshy banks and muddy bottom was difficult indeed to cross, with only two passable fords in miles. A start was made, therefore, for the first of these fords.

As they rode, David recounted to Alexander the significance of these two Peffer fords for other than just the convenience of travellers, for they were in fact notable in part of Scotland's history, no less than in helping to establish the Apostle Andrew as the nation's patron saint. For near here, back in the distant ninth century, an army of Alexander's predecessors, the High King of Alba and the King of the Scots of Dalriada, had been attacked by a larger host of Angles and Saxons from Northumbria whilst crossing the easternmost of these difficult fords. They were in dire danger of defeat and annihilation when, by using the other ford over a mile to the west, Kenneth mac Alpin, grandson of the Dalriadan monarch, he who eventually united Picts and Scots, was able to turn the enemy flank; and at the same time a white cloud formation in the blue sky, in the shape of a St Andrew's Cross, gave heart to the defending force, and they achieved an unexpected victory, with Athelstan, the Saxon leader, slain. The two Kings had there and then sworn that St Andrew should be the new patron saint of their realms.

Alex, although his mind was rather preoccupied with finding geese, was sufficiently attentive to pick up that adjective "new" as applied to patron saint. Who was the old one, then, he demanded. Was it not Columba?

David had to admit that it probably was – which produced a royal declaration that his ancestors had been foolish in replacing the splendid Columba with this Andrew; and when *he* was of age and ruling Scotland properly, he probably would replace Andrew with Columba again.

David wondered whether he had been wise to refer to this subject.

By making a detour well to the west and splashing across that ford, they were able to reach the woodland cover unobserved; at least no geese flew up from beyond. Pate said that a flock was feeding on grassland not far to the east, not much more than quarter of a mile. Once they halted the horses, and listened, they ought to be able to hear them.

That was a strange wood they entered, not the usual oak, birch, hawthorn or rowan, although these were represented, but many dark evergreen yews, tall and clearly very ancient, producing a brooding oppressive atmosphere. Amongst these sombre trees were the standing-stones of druidical sun-worship, most fallen and overgrown with gorse-bushes and bracken, but telling their own story. This wood tended to be shunned by local folk, the belief being that it was a burial-place of the Picts, and haunted. It was called Mungo's Walls, no doubt after another Celtic saint, Mungo, who came from these parts.

The present intruders were not concerned with such superstitious ideas however. In the cover of the trees and undergrowth they reined up and listened. Sure enough they could hear, above the whisper of the light wind in the branches, the sound of geese, not the wild honking nor yet the gabble of their nightly roosting out on the sand-bar, but a throaty murmur, continuous, contented, as the birds in their hundreds fed. The dogs whimpered at the sound, and the hawks began to stir under their hoods.

Alex was equally affected. Could they now ride out and raise them? he wondered. Fly their goshawks?

Pate explained. That would not do. The geese always posted sentinels, usually old female birds, to keep watch, and they were very keen-eyed. The moment people, on horses, emerged from this wood they would be seen, the flock instantly warned, and all would rise. Admittedly the goshawks, loosed, would wing swiftly after them; but the geese would fly away from the danger, in this case eastwards, and it might be a mile or more before the hawks caught up with them, and as far again perhaps before they made a kill, if any. And they, the horsemen, would probably never catch up, see any sport, or even their dogs find the kills. No, it had to be done otherwise. He, Tom and Will would go off, on foot, skirting round south-abouts, seeking to keep hidden, creeping behind any cover available, to try to get to the *east* of the flock, unseen. Then, in position, show themselves. The geese would rise and fly off westwards, it was to be hoped, at least some of them over this woodland area. They, the hawkers, would station themselves on this far west side of the wood, and when the geese came over above them, release their goshawks from directly below. Then follow geese and hawks, at speed.

Alex, impatient as ever, thought that it was all sounding a very drawn-out process, lacking in excitement.

Dismounting, then, Pate and his two assistants left on their circuitous stalk, and the rest moved to the western edge of the woodland to wait. Alex and Johnnie, eager to watch any developments, went on foot to the other edge, with warnings to remain well hidden.

They had quite a long wait, with even David admitting that there was overmuch inaction about this sort of hawking. But when something happened, at least there were no doubts about it, no more delay. Suddenly there sounded a great honking and squawking and crying, loud and maintained, indeed growing with every moment. Alex and Johnnie came racing back through the trees, stumbling over fallen stones in their haste, calling out the unnecessary information that they were coming, coming, quick, quick!

The first fowl were overhead and into view before the boys could scramble up into their saddles. There was no V-formation yet, just a mass of flapping, loud-mouthed protesting birds, still not one hundred feet up and rising fast with every wing-beat. The goshawks should have been loosed right away, but Alex had to be waited for.

Hurriedly mounted, he sought to snatch off the hood from one of the creatures, all but throttling it in the process; then to unloose the jess-strap round the legs which attached it to David's wrist. Johnnie was quicker with his, and his great hawk sprang into the air and beat upwards, all but ungainly at this stage, with furious wings. Alex's followed some seconds later, to cries of elation.

Still the tail-end of the goose flock was passing over, but to the surprise of the boys the goshawks both seemed to ignore these, still beating upwards, upwards. Through the scatter of fowl they rose, and kept on climbing.

Alex shouted aloud his reproaches, declaring them stupid birds; but Pate urged him to wait. They knew what they were doing. But – time *they* were moving.

So, spurring their mounts, they set off to follow the route of the now fast-flying geese, westwards. This was not so simple as it sounds, for while the fowl flew in approximately a straight line, they could not ride that way, with many obstacles in the way, ponds and marshland to avoid, burns and ditches to cross, thickets to negotiate. And all the time, with the geese outdistancing them, hard as they rode, Alex was letting his horse pick the way, for he was staring upwards, exclaiming that the wretched goshawks were still just climbing, flying off on their own, not interested in the geese at all. Admittedly they were now very high and seeming to get left behind. Soon they would be mere specks in the sky.

The horsemen rode on after the geese, the dogs now well in front. They were splashing through an extensive wet patch of that undrained level vale when Pate shouted, reining in, to point upwards and ahead. The goshawks were now just visible, but no longer together. One seemed to be stationary, hovering, wings winnowing; but the other was dropping, wings folded, hurtling, plummeting down so fast that the eye could barely follow it, a living missile. The geese were only a dark line now half a mile away and the riders could not see the goshawk actually strike. But they did see the flock abruptly break up and part, right and left.

Pate yelled for the dogs to speed forward, pointing and waving. The beasts seemed to know what was expected of them.

Margaret, gazing upwards, cried that the other goshawk was stooping now; but it was almost too far away to see any impact. Alex cried aloud his frustration. It was all wrong,

wrong! They were seeing nothing, doing nothing, those stupid hawks far too late, showing them no sport.

As they rode on after the dogs, Pate explained that the goshawks had to operate that way. Large birds as they were, they were not one-third the weight and size of a pinkfoot goose. And ordinary attack would be quite ineffective, beaten off by the quarry's powerful wings. It had to be this dropping at speed from a great height, with exact accuracy, to hit their prey just where the impact of talons would break the neck. The hawk would then either follow its victim down and remain with it, or drop it and soar up for another assault.

All of which was informative but left the boy unsatisfied.

Matters did not greatly improve for him when, after some further riding, one of their dogs came back to them dragging a goose, and with no sign of the killer, the hawk presumably having gone after further prey. And when, presently, another dog with another goose arrived proudly, and no goshawk, Alex's disgust was unrestrained. This might be a very good way of filling a larder with meat, but there appeared to be no sport in it. He much preferred the flighting for geese on the tidelands. Let them go down into Aberlady Bay for the evening flighting.

So, leaving Pate and Johnnie to link up with Tom and Will and eventually retrieve the goshawks and any further kills, the others returned to Luffness. David could have spared himself the long journey to Lord Maxwell on the Solway shore.

Alex and David got another two geese that evening on the mud-flats, so whatever else, they would return to Roxburgh with an ample supply of the preferred feast-meat.

The early spring months thereafter were bedevilled with news of national import, much of which affected Bishop Clement's peace of mind, in especial. Alan Durward seemed to have the Privy Council eating out of his hand, however little he considered his fellow-regents. He had for long been Justiciar north of the Forth; but now he had had himself constituted sole Justiciar of the Realm, doing away with the justiciarships of Lothian, Galloway and the south-west. This of course put him in a very powerful and influential position, since he now was the final authority in all matters of law and order, to whom all sheriffs and heritable jurisdictions were subject, and all the attendant revenues accrued. Bishop Clement believed that this was just a first step to having himself proclaimed sole regent, even though this last would require parliamentary endorsement. What the Comyns thought of it could be guessed at; but they did not seem to be very effective at restraining their rival. To be sure it was said that Red John Comyn of Badenoch and Lochaber was a sick man. The good bishop feared that his own regency would soon be coming to an end – not that he made much impact on affairs as it was. But he was concerned for the young monarch's weal, with Durward sole ruler of the land.

The next news caused him further anxiety, with Alexander himself angry, not to mention David and Margaret. It was that the Prior of St Andrews, with the support of Durward, was raising a papal action against the *keledi* there, as infringing the rights of Holy Church and retaining revenues which ought to come to the said priory, in especial against one man, Master Adam Mackerston, who called himself Provost of St Mary's. These *keledi*, literally the Friends of God in the Gaelic, often misnamed Culdees, were a relic of the ancient Celtic Columban Church, which had somehow survived St Margaret's process of Romanisation, having obtained from that Queen a special charter establishing them in a little religious colony at St Andrews, endowed with lands for their support. They alone, of what had been the national Church, remained, a mere seven of the priests; but they claimed certain rights, particularly that they were canons of the cathedral church of St Andrews. Now, it appeared, they were to be done away with. It seemed an odd way of celebrating the recent elevation to sainthood of the blessed Margaret, who had, for some reason, expressly cherished them, at least their predecessors.

Bishop Clement could not understand it, noting that the application to the Pope was not in the name of Bishop de Birnam of St Andrews but by the prior thereof, and Durward backing it. And Alex, with his preoccupation with Columba, the Stone of Destiny and the Brecbennoch, was indignant. David noted one more indication of Durward's curious concern with Church matters, and wondered.

The third upsetting development was an unannounced visit to Roxburgh by Alan Durward himself. He came to make an important announcement and issue his instructions. There had been a council meeting in Edinburgh to hear a special envoy sent by King Henry of England, and to consider his message. He, the Plantagenet, had decided to activate the understanding reached years before with the late King Alexander the Second, that his son, the present monarch, should one day wed his own, Henry's daughter, this for the good of both realms. He proposed that the marriage should be celebrated this next Christmastide, at York. The Privy Council had debated the issue and come to the conclusion that this would be a major step towards establishing peace, understanding and amity between the two nations, and an end to cross-border raiding and the like. Moreover, it seemed that the Pope had sent his blessings upon the proposal. So young Alexander was to be prepared for this great event during the months to come. Full instructions would be issued in due course.

Astonished, all but appalled, Margaret and David heard this announcement. They had known, of course, of the suggestion that one day Alex might wed the young princess, but never taken it very seriously, certainly never contemplated it happening to a ten-year-old boy.

Alex himself was less concerned, not really taking in the full implications, the word marriage meaning little to him, and anyway next Christmas a long time ahead. He was more interested in the idea of the long journey to York. And why York? Was England very different from Scotland? Were the people very strange? That Frenchman who came to see his mother said that they had tails. Was that true?

Prepare the King for the great event, Durward had ordered. How did one do that? Alexander was developing fast, but he was still a child.

Doubtfully, David and Margaret faced those summer months. Bishop Clement was of little use to them.

11

Instructions of a sort did arrive from Durward in the following months, not as to preparing the boy in mind and spirit, but as to clothing for him, special garb to be made, gear to be assembled, numbers involved, horses to be provided, and the like. Clearly it was all to be a very elaborate and carefully organised expedition, and very much a showing of the Scottish flag, due impression to be made on the English.

Oddly, instructions arrived in the autumn from the Plantagenet also, brief but significant, in the form of a safe-conduct for the Scots party to travel through England, with the exact route to be followed. It seemed an extraordinary notification for one monarch to send to another, especially when one was coming to marry the daughter of the other, and might imply either supreme arrogance or very unruly conditions in the southern kingdom and lack of royal control over his subjects.

Another message, more welcome, came from France, in November, this from Queen Marie, to say that she hoped to be at her son's wedding, and wished him well.

The escorting Scots company began to arrive at Roxburgh early in December, and steadily numbers grew. One of the first large groups to appear were Comyns, surprisingly, under the Earls of Menteith and Buchan, strangers there indeed. Their chief, the Lord of Badenoch, was apparently too ill to attend, but the clan was evidently going to be well represented on this special occasion, many of their allied lords putting in an appearance also. When Durward and *his* supporters arrived, there was no attempt to hide the animosity between the two factions, frigid relations being the best that could be hoped for – and even this did not tend to apply to their retainers and men-at-arms, for there were nightly scuffles and disorders in Roxburgh town, with the royal guards trying to keep the peace. The hatred between these two lines did not stem wholly from the ambitions of their leaders; there was an ethnic and hereditary rivalry also. Durward and his people were of the ancient Celtic Highland stock, whereas the Comyns, originally de Comines, were Normans who had come to Scotland with King David after his long exile in England, and had judiciously married Celtic heiresses, gaining their great territorial possessions that way — although of course a large proportion of their retainers were as Highland as the opposition; but clan warfare was normal anyway.

The Church was well represented in the gathering, the Primate, Bishop de Birnam, leading a covey of prelates with Bishop Clement, intent on showing the Archbishop of York that he could forget his deplorable pretensions to hegemony over the Scottish Church.

In all the preparations and assembling, the principal actor and reason for it all, King Alexander himself, was strangely unaffected, detached, looking forward to the journey and seeing new places, but otherwise unconcerned; also finding the inevitable association with his senior nobles and clergy far from his taste. David and Margaret had to try to hold him to his royal duties.

At length, on St Drostan's Eve, 13th December, the date specified by King Henry to enter England, they set out. So large a cavalcade, and with many elderly clerics, they would not travel fast, and it was reckoned to be just over two hundred miles to York by the route laid down, stopping-places arranged for at named abbeys and priories at approximately twenty-mile intervals, Henry's orders very definite. With the wedding scheduled for Christmas Day, they were due to arrive in York three days earlier. It was all strictly arranged for them — not entirely to the satisfaction of the Scots, who saw it not so much as kindly forethought on Henry's part as the would-be master's hand directing. David guessed that it was partly that, but also that the Plantagenet, ever having difficulty with his unruly northern lords, had heedfully planned a route where he could be fairly confident that there would be no trouble.

Durward saw no reason why Margaret should accompany them on this visit, but Alexander was adamant that she should, declaring that he would not go without her. There were very few women involved.

They were to cross Tweed, and the borderline, at Wark, where the ford was guarded, on the English side, by a powerful castle; and here the travellers found a large escort awaiting them, bristling with arms, under no less than the Earl of Warenne and Sussex, John Plantagenet, and Henry Percy of Alnwick. Since the latter, the greatest lord of Northumberland, was more apt to lead hostile raids into Scotland than to act host, and not a few there had suffered at his hands, no doubt Henry's kinsman, Warenne, had been sent north to ensure approximate harmony. Nevertheless the meeting was less than cordial amongst all ranks.

It was a very numerous company indeed, therefore, which set off south by east across country, making for the valley of the Till, the major English tributary of Tweed, under the banners of the Lion Rampant and the Leopards of Plantagenet, but with very little association between the two groupings. Up the Till they proceeded, by Milfield and Akeld to Wooler, their first night's destination. Here, in the name of the Bishop of Durham, the Earl Warenne took over a priory dedicated to St Cuthbert. He explained carefully to Alexander that it was a small, poor place, unlike the other religious houses in which they would lodge, this because of its nearness to Scotland and liability to attack therefrom, holy place as it was. However, David, close by, was able to inform earl as well as boy, thanks to his mother's teaching – for the Cospatricks had been Earls of Northumbria once – that this Cuthbert was in fact a Celtic Church saint who had missionarised the pagans of these parts. This information Alex gleefully retailed to any English he could find, however sourly it was received.

Only the senior members of that joint company could be installed in the priory, the monks ejected, and most of the travellers had to quarter themselves in the little town of Wooler – to the disadvantage of the inhabitants.

Next day, skirting the Cheviot foothills, they rode on to Brinkburn Priory at Rothbury, a much more ambitious establishment, where Warenne and Percy thankfully handed them over to the Bishop of Durham, and thereafter departed without ceremony. From now on it appeared they were to be in the care of Holy Church.

As it happened, despite a more resplendent escort, with this prelate actually travelling in a magnificent horse-litter such as no Scots cleric had ever aspired to, the said clerics were less than elated at this development. For one thing, this Durham prelate called himself the prince-bishop, and treated the Scots, even the Primate de Birnam, as underlings. Also he made no attempt to hide his assumption that his colleague, the Archbishop of York, in fact their host for this journey, was spiritual overlord of Scotland, an attitude not calculated to make for warm relations, and a warning as to things to come.

However, they were handsomely entertained and housed at Brinkburn, and the non-ecclesiastical visitors found no fault.

Newminster Abbey, near Morpeth on the Wansbeck, was their next stopping-place, a still more splendid foundation. But here no women were permitted to enter, and Margaret and the few others were hived off to a nearby nunnery, something never experienced in Scotland. It was with difficulty that Alexander was persuaded not to insist that he and David did not go with her.

They were surprised, next day, not to head due southwards for Newcastle-on-Tyne, as they expected, but southwestwards, through low hilly country to much further up the Tyne valley, making for the Priory of Bolam, near Belsay, and dedicated, they were interested to discover, to St Andrew. Why they were brought here they were not informed. There were large religious houses around Newcastle; but it might be that these were very much under the authority of the Percy family of Alnwick, or of Warenne himself, and the visitors less than welcome. Or it might be the prince-bishop himself who was unwelcome.

Not only Alexander was highly interested, before they reached their next day's destination, to cross the great Roman Wall, which locally was known as the Pechts' Dyke. It was explained to the boy that this was their pronunciation of Picts; and the Romans had built this great barrier across the land, from sea to sea, and staffed it with their legions, in order to keep out the Picts or Caledonians, as they called the Albannach, from the English or Anglian settled lands to the south. Alex quickly picked up the message that if the Romans reckoned that this enormous, fortified barrier, with all its mile-stations and forts, was necessary here, then the said Picts or Scots must have held sway right down to this area. Why, then, was *this* not the border with England, and all to the north *his* kingdom of Scotland?

The Prince-Bishop of Durham had some difficulty in answering that. It was something to do with King Stephen, he suggested.

Hexham Priory, where they halted, was quite the finest establishment they had yet visited, with a great cathedral-like church attached; and Alexander was delighted to learn that this too was dedicated to St Andrew, Scotland's patron saint. Clearly, in his opinion, all this Northumbria ought to be in his realm; and when he learned that Tynedale had indeed once been so, with its land-holders paying their allegiance to the Scottish King, he was loud in his assertions that this English usurpation must be rectified. He would speak to King Henry about it.

The cavalcade thereafter followed the East Allen River up through moorland country now, high, unpopulated land and quite a lengthy ride of it, to Weardale and the Durham border, where, some weary, they settled in at the monastery of St John's, a more modest place as befitted these uplands. But according to the prince-bishop, who seemed to be concerned over the size and impressiveness of the religious houses of his Palatinate rather than with religion itself, this would be the last of the minor establishments; hereafter, once out of these wretched moors and hills, they would find more worthy overnight accommodation.

Certainly the abbey of Egglestone, near to Barnard Castle of the Balliol family and the Yorkshire border, was a fine place; and a score of miles further the following day, Easby Abbey near Richmond bore out the prelate's forecast. But their final stop on their journey, Fountains Abbey, was the most notable of all, a magnificent Cistercian minster in a fair countryside.

Fine as it was, however, they scarcely saw it at its best, for it had been a long ride from Easby and they had arrived at dusk; and they left again before the December dawn, for the prince-bishop was now concerned about timing, for they were, it seemed, running a day late, and they must not keep the archbishop and monarch waiting. They had been going to stop at Kirkham Priory for the last night; but now it seemed they must press on the full distance to York. There were grumbles on the part of the senior Scots clergy, especially as to folk who rode in horse-litters, but the non-ecclesiastical riders made no complaints, for they had indeed found the short journeys and modest pace somewhat trying, used to more energetic horsemanship.

So it was 23rd December when at length they rode into the great city of York just as the sun was setting, quite the largest town most of the Scots had ever seen, and dominated by its vast minster. Trying not to be too overawed by the size, edifices and obvious wealth of the place, they threaded the narrow streets to the huge archiepiscopal palace.

Their reception was scarcely what might have been anticipated as welcome for a crowned head, only a chamberlain of the archbishop greeting them, with a platoon of uniformed servitors and officials, all wearing the crossed keys on red emblem of York archdiocese, who were to conduct the various visitors to their respective quarters in the enormous palace, where, they were told, refreshments would be served. The King of Scots and his close entourage would be accorded an audience in due course, and would receive a summons.

This reception by no means pleased the Scots; but there was nobody to complain to at this stage, for the prince-bishop promptly disappeared. However, at least they had no complaints as to their accommodation, for the quarters allotted were little less than princely, in an entire wing of the establishment, Alexander being taken to a noble suite of rooms with its own hall, kitchen, ante-rooms, as well as bedchambers. So David and Margaret were able to remain with him. They had been afraid that they would be separated – with inevitable protests from their charge.

There was a surprise in store for them there, for before any so-called summons arrived for an audience, they had a royal visitor – not King Henry but no less than Alex's own mother. Queen Marie, it seemed, had arrived at York two days previously, from France.

She was all but a changed woman, her reserve largely gone. She threw her arms around her son, hugging him – something not seen before – to his evident embarrassment, kissed Margaret and clutched David's arms in warm greeting. And she talked, almost chattered. Clearly her visit to France had been good for her. She was going back there, after the wedding, she informed them, with evident satisfaction.

But she had news of a different sort for them, and was not long in imparting it. She wanted the three of them to hear it at once, for it was important – before Alex and his lords were involved in arrangements and negotiations with Henry Plantagenet. She had learned from John de Brienne of Acre, titular King of Jerusalem, who was close to Pope Innocent, that Alan Durward had applied to the Vatican for a decree of legitimisation for his wife, the Countess of Atholl, Margaret's half-sister, and was offering large moneys for its speedy concession. Legitimisation. Did they see what that could mean?

David and Margaret saw indeed, and stared at each other. If this eldest natural child of the late King was officially declared to be legitimate, she would thereafter become heir-presumptive to the throne, since young Alexander had been the only lawful offspring; and Durward's children by her next in the succession. This would put that earl in an all but unassailable and permanent position in the rule of Scotland, with the monarch still a child and unable to produce an heir of his own for years to come.

David saw more than that. With Durward the hard and unscrupulous man he was, Alex's very life could be endangered. If he was gone, disposed of in one way or another, Durward's wife would become Queen Regnant, and her husband able to assume the Crown Matrimonial.

"You think that this is possible, Highness?" he demanded. "That this Pope might grant the request? *Can* he? Can he make legitimate one born out of wedlock?"

"He can, yes. By papal decree. It is not infrequently done. And Durward has been seeking to please the Vatican for some time now, playing the friend of Holy Church, winning the Pope's approval."

So that was it, the reason for all the religious fervour, hitherto less than evident – the canonisation of Queen Margaret, the support for the three English bishops to form a commission of enquiry in Scotland, the demotion of the *keledi* at St Andrews, and the rest. All a carefully planned campaign to influence the Vatican in his favour. For this.

"When?" David asked. "When is this to be?"

"That Jean – my friend John de Brienne – did not know. But it could be before long. He, Jean, thought that I ought to know of it." She paused, and uttered a little laugh. "He and I intend to wed!"

They caught their breaths. Suddenly so much more became clear to them. Here was the reason for much that had concerned and mystified, her years of restraint and pre-occupation after her widowhood, her desire to get back to France; she had had this earlier lover, this John de Brienne, and he had presumably waited for her. Marie de Coucy was a whole woman again.

Margaret started forward to kiss her late sire's unwilling wife, and David murmured his felicitations, however unimpressed Alexander appeared to be.

"Why are *you* to wed?" the boy wondered. "You are my father's wife. This King, this John – does he command it? Like the King Henry here?"

"Not command it, Alex, no. Jean and I have known each other for long. He is only called King of Jerusalem because his father was; he has no kingdom. It is our wish to marry, now that I have lost my husband, your father. And, see you, King Henry cannot *command* you to anything, Alex. You are a sovereign monarch. None may command you."

"Then why must I wed this girl? I have never seen her."

"It is a difficult matter to explain. A matter of state, between realms. Kings must marry, to have heirs to their thrones. And they usually wed princesses, high-born. This of Princess Margaret was considered by your father and Henry years ago, at a meeting at Newcastle, as, as suitable. To help bring Scotland and England closer together, to heal the enmity so often shown between the two kingdoms."

"Why?"

"You will understand, one day."

"This man, John – why is he called of Jerusalem, when you say he has no kingdom?"

"His father was a great crusader. And was created King there by the princes of Christendom. You know of the crusades . . .?"

"Will you be *Queen* of Jerusalem, then? Go and live there?"

"Scarcely that, Alex! Jerusalem is held by the Infidels, sadly, the Saracens. These crusades are to try to drive them out, to recover the Holy Land for Christ's cause. Until then, I fear, Jean remains King only in name."

"*I* would like to go and kill Saracens."

David brought the conversation back to what was pre-occupying *him*. "This of legitimisation of Durward's wife, Your Grace – it could be . . . dangerous."

"Well I know it, David. Why I hastened to tell you."

"Henry, I think, will not know of it. And will not like it, either!"

"No. None knew of it, as yet. All secret. Shall I tell him?"

David took a pace or two up and down, thinking hard. "Would that be best? Now? Or after the wedding. I think, once Henry's daughter and Alexander are wed, this will seem the worse to him, the greater threat. *Before*, he might change his mind. Not allow the wedding, at all. Or come to some arrangement with Durward. They *have* been working together, all believe. But this would change much. So – do we *want* this marriage to take place?"

The two women looked at him.

"What is best for Alex?" he went on, urgently. "If Henry learns of this legitimisation and Durward's wife becomes heir-presumptive, Henry might think to gain his ends, his ambition to be Lord Paramount over Scotland, not by having Alex as his good-son but by having a compact with Durward. Cancel the wedding and support Durward and his wife, in return for an admission of his superiority over Scotland. Which the marriage of his daughter and Alex will not give

182

him, however much more increase of influence. And then, then there would be danger indeed!" He glanced at the boy, needing to say no more.

"You mean . . .?" Margaret exclaimed.

"Danger, yes," he said briefly. "Alex . . . disposed of!"

"I see it, yes." Queen Marie bit her lip. "The marriage should stand, yes. You are right, David. Better, so. But afterwards . . .?"

"Afterwards, yes. Tell Henry, when it is too late to change it." He continued with his pacing. "This news, you see, alters everything. Everything. It can bring down Durward. So long as it becomes known by all *before* the Pope acts. This to Scotland's great advantage. The man is an incubus, a menace. Not only to Alexander but the whole realm. We could get rid of Durward, I think!"

"How mean you?" Margaret asked. "How get rid of him?"

"Do you not see it? Few love Durward in Scotland – although many fear him, and support him because of that fear. For he is strong. But this of the legitimisation will make it evident to all that he aspires to the throne, for his wife if not himself. Why, otherwise, seek such decree? The secret, once it becomes known, will unite all against him as nothing else would. And, once his daughter is married to Alex, Henry Plantagenet also. I can think of none, save Durward's own kin, who would approve it."

"Yes, yes. I see it. So – what do we do?"

"Let this child marriage, foolish as it seems, go on. Then, when it is done, let Her Grace tell Henry. And *we* will tell the Scots lords and bishops. There will be fury, uproar, indeed!"

They all gazed at each other as the full implications dawned, even though the bridegroom-to-be did not comprehend, although he did see that there seemed to be some way of disposing of Alan Durward.

"What will they do to him?" he wondered. "Will they chop off his head?"

"Hardly that," David said, with the first smile of that conversation. "But he will be much cast down, I feel sure. Probably could lose his position as regent. *You*, Sire, could possibly demand that you need a new regent, or council of regency. That would help."

"Yes, yes. But why will Durward heed us? And what has the Pope in Rome to do with it . . .?"

They were seeking to explain something of it all to the boy when the same archepiscopal chamberlain who had greeted their arrival came to announce that His Majesty King Henry and His Eminence the Archbishop Walter would now grant audience to the King of Scotland. Let them follow him.

"This of granting audience," David protested. "It is wrong, quite wrong. His Grace the King of Scots, not King of Scotland, needs no granting of audience. He is as much monarch as is Henry Plantagenet. More so, in that his is a far more ancient monarchy and throne. Tell you your archbishop that!"

Doubtfully the other eyed him, before leading the way, by passages and corridors, to the central block of the great quadrangular palace.

They were conducted through an enormous hall thronged with folk, all seeming much more richly dressed than the visitors, to an ante-room where they found awaiting them Durward, the Bishops de Birnam and Clement and the Earls of Menteith and Mar. These were surprised to see Queen Marie, the bishops at least greeting her warmly. The chamberlain left them. Durward was scowling, impatient at all this waiting to be received.

Presently an inner door opened and the chamberlain reappeared, with behind him a resplendently garbed cleric, elderly but tall and stern of feature.

"His Eminence the Lord Walter, Archbishop of York," they were informed, with bowing – but the bowing was towards the archbishop not towards the visitors.

The Scots party, in consequence, showed little reaction, certainly no bowing. Alexander it was who spoke.

"Is an archbishop older than a bishop?" he wondered, comparing the newcomer with the Scots pair.

That at least produced smiles – though none from His Eminence. He inclined his grey head.

"You are the King of Scotland?" he said, thinly. "Welcome to my poor house.' He glanced round the others. "Queen Marie I know."

That lady took the hint and introduced her companions,

commencing with the Bishop of St Andrews, whom she emphasised was Primate of the Scottish Church, then the Bishop of Dunblane, regent, and the Earls of Atholl, Menteith and Mar. Also the Lady Margaret, a daughter of the late King Alexander, her husband, and their son's Cup-Bearer and guardian, the Lord David de Lindsay.

The archbishop eyed them all without warmth, but particularly David, whose presence he clearly felt to be superfluous.

"His Majesty the Lord Henry will see you now," he announced flatly and, turning, went whence he had come.

They followed on.

They passed into a smaller hall, empty save for two men occupying a dais at the far end, one sitting on a throne-like chair, the other standing a little behind. These made no move.

The archbishop bowed. "Your Majesty, be graciously pleased to receive in audience Alexander, King of Scotland, his mother, the Lady Marie, and his . . . attendants." That last held its own eloquence.

The seated man, wearing the golden circlet of kingship over his brows, raised a hand. "Welcome, Alexander. I am Henry of England," he said, and smiled faintly. He was a man of middle years, slenderly built, long of face, especially of jaw, with large dark eyes, good-looking – but despite the chin, not strong of feature, with some looseness about the mouth.

The boy had been well instructed as to his part to play. He did not bow. "I, Alexander, High King of Scots, greet you, King Henry," he got out in something of a rush, but remembering to emphasise that word "high". "I have come far to greet you."

"Ah, yes. I trust that your journey was comfortable, Alexander? My Lord Chancellor would see to that."

That title of chancellor puzzled Alexander, as it did others; but clearly by his glance Henry was referring to the archbishop; so that stern man must be Lord Chancellor of England as well as metropolitan. The boy looked at David, to see whether he should answer this. It was the archbishop Chancellor who spoke next, however.

"It is customary to advance, kneel and kiss the King's hand," he said coldly.

None of the Scots could move before their sovereign-lord, and he, after another glance at David, remained where he was.

The man standing behind King Henry broke the uncomfortable silence. "His Majesty of Scotland can no doubt dispense with that," he said pleasantly, in an accented voice. "Perhaps reserve his kissing for another!" And he smiled at the boy.

"Yes, yes," Henry agreed. "He will meet my daughter later." He half turned. "Here is the Lord Simon of Leicester."

They had all heard of Simon de Montfort, Earl of Leicester, the foremost statesman and soldier of England, even though French-born, who had married the King's sister.

Alan Durward now elected to go forward, to kneel before Henry and kiss the outstretched hand. The others, eyeing each other, accepted that as sufficient gesture from them all.

There was a pause. This was proving to be an uneasy interview. Again it was the Earl Simon who spoke. He addressed Alexander.

"Do you, Sire, find this England very different from your own Scotland?" he asked amiably. "Not so many mountains?"

"Your hills are very small," the boy agreed. "But you have lots of people. And towns, big towns. And bishops." Alex looked over at his own two prelates, wondering clearly whether that was not the right thing to say.

The smiles produced – save from the archbishop – seemed to prove that it did not go down badly. King Henry held out his hand again, not to be kissed but to beckon the boy to him.

"Come, Alexander, tell me of your journey and what you liked and misliked" he said. "You are to be my good-son, so we must come together."

Doubtfully the boy went forward, his mother with him.

As the others stood waiting, uncertain what to do now and getting no help from Archbishop Walter de Grey, Simon de Montfort came down to chat to them, clearly a man of parts and able to put others at ease. He was of an age with Henry, but very different in other ways, stocky, strong-featured, with an air of natural authority tempered with geniality.

Their host, the archbishop, stood aside, distancing himself from them all. The Earl Simon paid particular attention to Margaret.

Presently the English King rose, to indicate that the audience was over, and nodded to his Chancellor, before turning and leaving the hall. That man announced that there would be a banquet shortly. His chamberlain would come for them. He then also departed, without ceremony, and it was de Montfort who escorted the party to the other door and the waiting chamberlain. He kissed both ladies' hands as they left.

The banquet that evening in the large hall was quite the most ambitious the Scots, at least, had ever attended, both as to the numbers present and the provender and entertainment provided; also, of course, the celebrity of the guests. Everyone of prominence in England seemed to be present, along with the ambassadors of almost every state in Christendom, including the Holy See. And all was organised down to the last detail – even though not always exactly as the said Scots would have had it.

The dais-area was crowded indeed, with *two* tables thereon, one behind the other. At the front one sat only royalty – save for the archbishop Chancellor who was, after all, the host. Henry's Queen, Eleanor of Provence, was there, with their daughter, the bride-to-be, and two sons, Edward and Edmund, aged twelve and ten years; Simon de Montfort and his princess wife; and of course, Alexander and his mother. So there were ten of them. And behind, room only for another dozen, with so many English notables, including their prince-bishop, the Earl Marshal and kin of the royal house, allowed only two of the Scots entourage to be there, Durward and Bishop de Birnam. Three very long tables stretched lengthwise down the hall, below, with earls, ambassadors, bishops and great lords nearer the dais. David and Margaret found themselves seated far down the central table.

Alexander and his mother had young Princess Margaret seated between them. She was aged eleven, six months older than Alex, a quiet, plain-faced child, tall for her age. They did not seem to have much to say to each other. Her elder brother Edward, heir to the throne, was very different, an eye-catching youngster, well-built, good-looking and with an air of confidence which verged on the scornful.

Course succeeded course of every variety of fish and fowl and meat, wild boar, venison, peacocks with tails displayed, swans, every kind of duck, woodcock, partridge, quail, snipe – but no wild-geese, which Alexander would be noting. Between these courses there were entertainments, of jugglers, acrobats, dancers, instrumentalists, even a horse which danced, after a fashion, to the timing of its rider's pipe-music. Prince Edward much appreciated this last and, getting up, insisted that the horseman ride his beast right up to the dais-platform edge and dismount, the boy to take his place and to proceed down between the tables, singing lustily, to the applause of the gathering – even though the horse failed to recognise the melody and respond adequately.

All this eating and entertainment, with wine to assist, took up a lot of time, and many, weary from long riding, were longing for their b.... But it was Christmas Eve, and it seemed that there was to be a midnight Mass over in the minster. Fortunately, however, the children present were excused this, and David and Margaret managed to avoid it also on the pretext of putting Alexander to bed.

Before leaving the hall, they learned that the wedding was not to be celebrated next day, as they had expected, but the day following. It seemed that there was to be another Christmas service in the minster and then some sort of ceremony in the palace, followed by still another banquet.

Alexander informed his two friends, before closing heavy eyes, that he did not think much of this other Margaret that he was to wed; she was very dull and hardly said a word. What would they do with her afterwards? They could only say that she was probably very shy, and would improve once they got to know her. He did not much like Edward Plantagenet either, who was too pleased with himself. But the other, Edmund, was all right.

The Christmas Day service in the vast, crowded minster, presided over by the archbishop, was conducted by the prince-bishop of Durham and a host of clergy, officials, acolytes and choristers. The Kings and Queens sat in the chancel, with Henry's children. Alexander and Prince Edward were clearly restless well before the long celebration ended, and indeed were presently making faces at each other. The young princess, however, was decorum itself.

Returning to the palace, refreshments were served to sustain them until the banquet, and then the Earl of Norfolk, Earl Marshal of England, with trumpeters, made an announcement. His Majesty the Lord Henry graciously deemed it fitting that, before bestowing his beloved daughter, the Princess Margaret, on Alexander, King of Scotland, he should also bestow the honour and dignity of knighthood on tomorrow's bridegroom, who was not yet knighted. Twenty others, including the Princes Edward and Edmund, would also receive the accolade in honour of this especial occasion, after the King of Scotland. Would the said King of Scotland therefore step forward.

Taken by surprise as the Scots were, Alexander himself was by no means bereft of speech.

"Knight?" he said, in scarcely a whisper. "Me? Can he do that? Am I old enough? And why do they always name me King of Scotland?"

Henry answered that himself. "I am King of England, Alexander, so we name you King of Scotland, no? And knighthood does not depend on age. Whomsoever I elect to knight becomes a knight, even an infant. It is an honour which I can bestow on you. Suitable that you should be knight before your wedding."

"Are all these others to wed also?"

"No, no. But – it is a great occasion and worthy to be celebrated thus, to be remembered by others also. But you first. Come then, Alexander, King of Scots, and kneel before me and I will dub you knight."

"Kneel?" Alex stiffened, and looked quickly at David, nearby, who had well warned him about never allowing himself to be put in a position of seeming to make gestures of inferiority to the English monarch, who was seeking to call himself Lord Paramount of Scotland. Almost imperceptibly David nodded, meaning that on this occasion he *should* kneel, that being always done when knighthood was conferred, whomsoever by. But the boy took the nod to mean otherwise, that he should produce the required statement which he had learned, to avoid having to make gestures of submission.

"I, a King, kneel only to my God!" he jerked, embarrassed but definite, thereafter nibbling his lip.

There was silence in that great hall for moments on end, until, once again, Simon of Leicester came to the rescue.

"Bravely spoken, Sire!" he said. "Here is a young monarch indeed."

Henry Plantagenet looked at his friend and brother-in-law doubtfully, then shrugged. "Very well," he said. "Come, Alexander."

So the boy went forward, to stand before the other King, not exactly defiantly but set-faced nevertheless. Henry turned to the Earl Marshal. "Your sword, my lord," he said.

The only man who could wear a sword, indoors, in the presence of his sovereign, handed him the weapon. Taking it in both hands, Henry raised it, higher than was usual, and intoned the formula.

"I, Henry, knight, as is my right, do hereby, before all, dub and create you, Alexander, knight." He brought down the sword to tap the boy with the blade, first on one shoulder then on the other. "So, and so! Arise, Sir Alexander. And be thou good knight until thy life's end."

The boy stood there, wary-eyed, waiting, in the hush.

Simon de Montfort maintained his helpfulness. He stepped over, to touch Alexander's arm. "That is all, Sire," he murmured. "You are knight now!"

The boy looked at him, and back at Henry. "All? Only that?"

"Only that. But much done in brief moments. Knighthood is a great matter, an honourable stature indeed. By rights you should have held your vigil beforehand, for faith is required of knights. But, no doubt, the service we all attended in the minster will serve. You are truly knight now, and can create your own knights. For a knight can create a knight – and only a knight can do so." And he led the boy back to his mother's side.

Thereafter the other postulants to knighthood lined up to

receive the accolade, all grown men save for the two princes, Edward Plantagenet leading the column with quite a swagger. None of these refused to kneel.

Watching and listening, Alexander, interested, tugged at David de Lindsay's sleeve. "That man said that now I am a knight I can make knights too, Davie. Is that right?" He was not very good at lowering his voice, that one.

"So I understand, Sire," David answered. "Only a knight can make a knight, as my lord of Leicester said. I suppose, in fact, that any knight could knight another. But it is customary for only Kings, great lords and commanders in the field to do so."

"Then I *could*!" Alexander grinned. He listened intently as the last of the score was dubbed.

Then, as the applause of the company greeted the new knights, and Henry handed the sword back to the Earl Marshal, the boy darted forward unceremoniously to that earl's side and held out his hands.

"Will you give me the sword, my lord," he said.

The other stared, as did all there. But the boy's hands remained out, demanding.

Glancing at King Henry, the other hesitated. But it was a royal command, and he could scarcely refuse, before all. He handed over the weapon doubtfully.

It was heavy, but Alexander was strong for his age, and gripping it with both hands, at haft and blade, he bore it back in triumph.

"See!" he exclaimed. "I can do it also. Davie, you kneel!"

David gulped. "Alex! Sire, no! Not, not . . ."

"Yes. You must. I want it. I command it. Kneel."

Looking around him helplessly, at all the astonished throng, David, wagging his head, sank on one knee – for, after all, this was his sovereign-lord speaking.

The boy, holding the sword unhandily, raised it, to bump it down on one of his friend's shoulders. There it rested. "Davie Lindsay, I, Alexander, King of Scots, do, do dub . . . do make you a knight," he got out. "So!"

The recipient was in dire danger for a moment, as the unwieldy weapon got lifted over his head to descend heavily on the other shoulder. "Rise up, Sir Davie. Oh – and be a good knight until, until . . ." Alexander clearly could not remember that last phrase .

"Get up, Davie – *Sir* Davie!" he urged.

Into the ensuing silence, as David rose, a single voice was raised, a female voice. "Splendid, Alex!" Margaret cried.

Her acclaim was joined by one other. "Bravo! Bravo!" That was Simon, Earl of Leicester.

With that lead, there was a scattering of applause, mainly from the Scots present, although by no means all of these. Surely never had so newly created a knight created another quite so swiftly thereafter, and a ten-year-old knight at that.

King Henry was looking less than pleased, whatever his brother-in-law's reaction. He turned away.

Alexander was laughing happily. "I did it," he declared. "We are both knights now, Davie. Did I do it well?"

His mother it was who answered him. "Very well, Alex. And it is excellently well deserved by Sir David, now a true chevalier!" She came forward to kiss David on both cheeks – which allowed Margaret to do the same. They both then kissed Alexander.

Henry was seen to be speaking sternly to his son Edward, who presumably had been thinking to follow Alexander's example.

The banquet thereafter was held, not in this archiepiscopal palace but in the nearby Abbey of St Mary's, York being rich indeed in ecclesiastical establishments, with no fewer than forty churches. This Christmas Day pre-wedding repast was on a smaller scale than on the night previously; and although Margaret was invited, as Alexander's half-sister, Sir David de Lindsay was not.

12

The marriage ceremony next day, in York Minster, was very grand but mercifully short, in view of the youthfulness of the two principal participants, who could not be expected to maintain any very prolonged behavioural stance, especially Alexander who was not the most patient of youngsters. The archbishop conducted the service, which scarcely helped the boy, who made no pretence of liking the prelate, nor of enjoying the entire proceeding, certainly showing no particular empathy towards the bride, who seemed uneasy and depressed throughout, as was hardly to be wondered at.

King Henry gave his daughter away. There was no grooms-man – even though Alex would have had David in that role, if it had been permitted. Durward and Bishop Clement, as regents, took their stance in support of their young monarch, but were more or less ignored by him. He kept gazing around the huge, crowded church, by no means giving the impression that this was an important milestone in his life. He made the required responses as instructed, but without emphasis or conviction, and let the princess look after herself. He did seem to appreciate the music, however, especially the trumpet fanfares which followed the proclamation that the royal pair were man and wife. That was a prolonged flourish, to which Alexander beat time.

When, eventually, the procession formed up to move down the central aisle and out, Queen Marie came forward to urge her son to take the new Queen's arm, which reluctantly and grudgingly he did – to drop it the moment they got out of the minster. The girl registered no reaction one way or the other.

The wedding feast in the palace thereafter was endured by bride and groom, with speeches by Henry, Archbishop de Grey and, very briefly, by Durward. When Alexander was called upon to make some reply, he merely rose, inclined his head right and left, and sat down again. The impression given was that he was not greatly interested in the day's programme.

That changed, however, once the meal was over. The wedding having been at midday, it was still only late afternoon, and there was ample time for the developments which undoubtedly were the real reason for the entire proceedings. They all moved into the adjoining lesser hall. And now the archbishop changed hats, as it were, and became the Lord Chancellor of England. And he was not one for beating about the bush was Walter de Grey. Raising his hand for silence, after a glance at the Plantagenet, he came to the point promptly.

"Your Majesties and my lords," he began, ignoring the ladies. "It is, on this auspicious occasion, right and proper that the two realms, now happily in a unity through the marriage of Alexander of Scotland and Margaret of England, should celebrate and demonstrate more than just that marriage. The harmony of this day's union should be reflected in harmony between the two kingdoms, and all cause for dispute and enmity put away. Now is most assuredly the time for such necessary and desirable improvement, all will agree."

He paused for the required applause – which was hearty on the side of the majority, the English; less so amongst the northern visitors.

"Disagreements and disputes most frequently arise on two scores, in matters of state and matters of Church government," he went on. "These could and should be resolved, for all time coming, for the benefit of both realms and of Holy Church. As to the first, King Knud, or Canute, King of England and Emperor of the Anglo-Saxons and the Danes, obtained the submission and fealty of King Malcolm the Second of Scotland, in the year of our Lord 1031. Ever since then the Kings of England have been entitled to use the style of Lords Paramount of Scotland. This entitlement . . ."

The rest was drowned in cries of protest from the Scots, to the great offence of all the others. There was unseemly disturbance in that hall, in the presence of the two Kings, and Henry had his Earl Marshal banging on a table with his useful sword, for silence.

Frowning, the archbishop Chancellor proceeded. "I say that this of the royal paramountcy is a fact, a historic fact, which cannot be denied. The said Malcolm bowed the head and bent the knee to the said King Knud or Canute, accepting him as overlord. That fealty has never been abrogated by deed or statute. And now is the time, all should agree, for it to be acknowledged and accepted in amity and goodwill, on the occasion of this illustrious marriage."

"No! No!" came the shouts from practically all the Scots. But they nevertheless were in a difficult position to express themselves more fully on the issue, with their monarch present and none able to speak before he did; except perhaps, as regent, Durward – who chose to remain silent.

Alexander, darting glances right and left, scowled. "No," he declared. "It is not so."

"You cannot deny the facts of history, Highness," the archbishop said sternly. "It happened. The Scottish King paid fealty to the English King for his kingdom. Admitted him as superior. Which superiority has been asserted and retained ever since."

Alexander looked unhappy. Old history was not his particular study. He turned to seek David's aid, who, in that lofty company, was standing well back.

It was another Walter, however, who came to his aid, the Comyn Earl of Menteith. "Sire, may I speak?" he asked. "That of King Malcolm the Second, as I understand it, was not homage for Scotland, the kingdom, but only for Lothian and the Merse, which Knud Svenson had overrun. It was but a device to get the Dane out of the lands south of Forth which he had invaded and was occupying. Lothian and the Merse were themselves not part of Alba, ancient Scotland. So, to get rid of the invaders, Malcolm did homage for them, at Stirling. Them only. Nothing of old Scotland. And only to the Dane –"

"Moreover," William, Earl of Mar, broke in, "the English King Stephen, grandson of William of Normandy, abandoned any such claims to Scots territory, and indeed ceded *English* territory to Scotland – Tynedale, Penrith and Carlisle. So this archbishop's claims are false, wholly false."

"You both greatly err!" that prelate declared angrily. "Tynedale and Carlisle were *not* ceded to Scotland, only to

King David, who had himself been Earl of Cumbria before succeeding to his throne. King Stephen was a weakling and usurper. His failures did not prejudice the rights of the Kings of England."

"You cannot hold your sword both ways, my lord Archbishop!" Bishop de Birnam put in. "If your King Stephen was a weakling, and his deeds can be ignored, so can Malcolm of Scotland's! This of harking back is folly. We live today, not two centuries ago."

Simon de Montfort was speaking quietly to Henry Plantagenet, who inclined his head.

"This is unseemly," the latter said, "This dispute in our royal presence. On this day of all days. Let us have an end to it. My position and style as Lord Paramount is *beyond* dispute. Let it be acknowledged by my new good-son, and be done with it. A simple word is all that is required."

David had moved nearer to Alexander, in answer to the mute appeal. The boy was looking agitated indeed.

David's position was difficult. Amongst all these great ones, his was a very minor role, however much Alexander relied on him, merely Cup-Bearer to the King. He could by no means raise his voice in that company. But he could shake his head, and did.

"No!" Alexander said promptly, to his new father-in-law.

As Henry frowned and tapped a foot on the floor, the Earl Simon did his share of advising. "His Majesty of Scotland could pay homage for his English lands," he suggested. "That is required, is it not? For any lands held in another realm."

The Scots eyed each other. That was correct, lawful. And, as well as the English feudal territories of Tynedale and Carlisle, Alexander had inherited estates in the earldom of Huntingdon held by King David and his successors. Durward found his voice.

"That is so," he said. And to make it sound better, added, "If King Henry owned lands in Scotland, he would make homage for them to King Alexander." Which was a safe enough observation, since that situation did not arise.

David had to nod now.

Alexander reluctantly moved forward to face Henry, tight-lipped. He did not kneel, although that was normal.

Henry held out his hand, and the boy took it between both of his, muttered something vague, head lowered, and then dropped the hand, drawing back. It could have been the briefest oath of homage ever.

The Plantagenet looked displeased, but Leicester smiled and made an easy gesture, a wise man.

And that, apparently, was that. Despite the disapproving looks of the archbishop and others, Henry had had enough for one day, it seemed. He turned and quickly left the hall, to hasty bowing, his Queen and family hastening to follow after him.

The archbishop Chancellor had the last word, however. "Because of unworthy disturbances and ill behaviour in the town on the part of the Scots soldiery and men-at-arms, and other ill-disposed persons, to avoid further clashes and distress to the citizens, the said Scotsmen have been allotted new quarters in the barracks of the old fortress of York," he announced in a steely voice. "This is being attended to." And bowing briefly, he too left the hall.

Back in their own apartments, Queen Marie, after some discussion on the afternoon's events, and praise for her son's stance, wondered whether this was the time to acquaint King Henry with the Durward request for papal legitimisation of his wife. David and Margaret both agreed that probably it was not, that the morrow would be the wiser choice. Today had produced sufficient upsets. The Scots were due to start their return journey two days hence, so there was time enough. Possibly a word with Earl Simon beforehand might be useful. He appeared to be a man of good sense, vision, and influence with the Plantagenet.

It was Margaret who commented thereafter on the fact that Alex's new wife was not in evidence, and had remained with her parents. Not that this disconcerted any there, certainly not the bridegroom. It had been that sort of a wedding-day.

At least there was no difficulty about finding occasion next day for the Durward revelation. There was to be a final banquet that evening, and before that, another ceremony, that of the presentation of the bride's dowry, which would constitute something like an official handing over of the girl to her husband. That would be the occasion for their dramatic disclosure, it was agreed.

That ceremony proved to be rather more than just the formal handling over of five thousand silver merks from one sovereign to the other; actually it was already owed to Alex's father by Henry, so was hardly a munificent dowry. That sum, in silver coinage, was of course too bulky and heavy to be transferred there in the hall, so a token pouchful was proffered – and it was Durward who stepped forward to receive it on his monarch's behalf.

This exchange seemed apt for Queen Marie's revelation, and she was taking a deep breath to announce it when she was prevented by Henry making a statement.

"This of dowry will, no doubt, on our daughter's arrival in Scotland be matched by the provision of a suitable portion and house for her in your kingdom, Alexander, as is customary for a Queen. And she, being young, will take with her, as guardians, my lord John de Balliol, Lord of Barnard Castle, and my lord de Ros of Wark. These will ensure for me her well-being, whilst she remains under full age. They will also act as my own counsellors to you, Alexander, in the interests of both realms."

The last statement raised Scots eyebrows. English counsellors for the King of Scots was a conception not hitherto envisaged. It could be merely another device to assert this lord paramountcy claim? But the two counsellors were cunningly chosen, for both had Scots connections. Balliol had married a daughter of the Lord of Galloway; and de Ros of Wark's mother had been an illegitimate daughter of King William the Lyon, Alexander's grandfather.

As they were all pondering this, Henry went on. "As well, Queen Margaret will have with her the Lady Matilda de Cantelupe, as companion and lady-in-waiting. And as her secretary and chaplain, Robert de Anketil who, no doubt, will be found a suitable benefice in Scotland."

These last appointments were unexceptionable and, with Henry apparently finished, Queen Marie was again priming herself to make her own momentous statement, when Archbishop de Grey spoke.

"Your Majesties and my lords, these matters of state having been dealt with, those of Holy Church now require the attention of all." He looked around him, at his most belligerently authoritative. "For long years the Church's position in Scotland has been unsatisfactory and in grievous error. That Church was ill-founded by Irishmen, in pagan times, and it adopted many pagan and outlandish customs and rites, in its worship and priesthood, notably at what it calls Yuletide, and in the wrongful celebration of Easter. Moreover, it paid no allegiance to His Holiness the Pope. This was partially corrected by the Queen Margaret Atheling, but not wholly. There are still so-called priests of that mistaken religion officiating in Scotland, even in the city and diocese of the chief bishop, here present, of St Andrews. I had to send up a commission of enquiry of three of my own bishops recently, to seek to regulate this matter. And other mistaken practices."

As Bishop de Birnam began to protest, the archbishop held up his hand commandingly.

"This all is a matter of grave concern, indeed of scandal! The Church in Scotland is in gravest error, and frequently fails to act in step with the rest of Christendom. And it has no lawful head." He glared at de Birnam. "This bishop calls himself Primate. But who made him Primate? Or his predecessors? Not the Holy Father in Rome. I say that this is shame and folly, and to the spiritual detriment of all, the people of Scotland in particular. There is no metropolitan north of York. And I am that metropolitan, and so have the responsibility. Holy Church requires metropolitans, archbishops, to oversee bishops and lesser orders. Therefore until His Holiness should think to appoint a metropolitan for Scotland, it is my duty to exercise the metropolitan authority there. Can any deny that most evident fact?"

Out of a number of raised Scots voices, de Birnam's prevailed, although his was not a dominant character.

"His Holiness the Pope appoints his papal representative to Scotland," he declared. "You, my lord, cannot deny *that*! And he sends him, in the first instance, to me, the Primate. Therefore he accepts the Scottish Church in full communion with Rome. If he requires an archbishop, or metropolitan,

199

to preside over our Church, he could appoint one, myself or another. He has not done so. Therefore your assumption is in error. You have no more spiritual authority in Scotland than had the three bishops you sent. Nor can have. Save by papal decree. Which has not been granted – even though we know that you have applied for it, and more than once!"

"Nor ever will be, I think!" It was not often that Bishop Clement raised his gentle voice, regent though he might be in name. "So long as two other archbishops contest your claim before His Holiness. The Archbishop of Nidaros, in Norway, sits further north than do you, and claims to be metropolitan of all northern lands, including Scotland. Folly, yes – but no more so than yours, since the Norse claim rule in the Hebrides and in Ulster, and of course Shetland, Orkney and Iceland. Moreover, your own colleague, the Archbishop of Canterbury – not present, all will note – is also metropolitan, and contests your claim to spiritual authority extension, which could outmatch his own! Of all this His Holiness must take account. As well as his concern for the Church in Scotland. I say . . ."

He got no further, in the resultant hubbub. The rivalry between the two English archbishops was known to all, something of an ongoing scandal indeed. So a raw nerve was touched here. De Grey was all but speechless with anger, and Henry himself was looking perturbed and resentful, whispering to Earl Simon.

David de Lindsay took the opportunity to do some whispering also – to Queen Marie. "*Now* is the time, I think, Highness," he said. "This folly could be halted by your *greater* announcement. Referring to the Pope. Before King Henry marches out, in offence. Now, speak."

She nodded and held up a hand, a royal hand, even though it trembled a little. The Earl Simon saw it, and raised his powerful soldierly voice for quiet.

"Hear *me*," Marie de Coucy appealed. "I also have word of His Holiness in Rome as to Scotland. By the mouth of the King of Jerusalem. His Holiness has been approached by one here present, the Lord Alan Durward, Earl of Atholl, one of the regents for my son Alexander, to have a papal dispensation, not concerned with rule in the Church but rule in the state. He has sought the legitimisation of his wife, Margaret or Margery, eldest illegitimate daughter of my late husband, King Alexander the Second – for which legitimisation he, Durward, is prepared to pay much, and has already paid, in some fashion. To make his wife legitimate. With all that could and would entail."

Hush fell on that hall as though by the dropping of some great, heavy curtain. If Queen Marie had wished to make an impact, she was not disappointed. Men stared at her, then at Henry and Alexander, then at each other – and finally over at Durward. No voice was raised, only breaths drawn and expelled, for moments on end. Few there, indeed, would fail to recognise the implications, or some of them. The eldest daughter of the late King legitimatised. This Alexander's eldest sister. Heir to the throne then. He a boy of his tenth year. His undoubted successor. And ten-year-olds do not always reach maturity, especially in such circumstances. And now Henry's daughter his Queen, and this last after so much planning and contrivance. Threat to it all, indeed.

The silence continued, until Alexander himself broke it. "I do not like that man," he declared.

Durward himself, still clutching the leather bag of silver merks, himself seemed struck dumb, his features working but no words coming. Thunder-struck he stood, fists clenching, glaring at Marie de Coucy. He might have denied his guilty secret there and then, but even he could not accuse royalty of lying, in the presence of royalty.

The other monarch spoke. "This is fact, Highness? Not but hearsay? True tidings?"

"King John of Jerusalem does not tell untruths, Sire. And he is close to Pope Innocent."

"Then . . ." Henry left the rest unsaid.

Others were more vocal, Walter Comyn, Earl of Menteith, in especial. "Here is infamy! Dastardry! If not treason!" he cried. "He seeks the throne, no less! Durward betrays us all. He would have his wife the Queen."

"The Crown Matrimonial!" Mar elaborated, in case there were those who did not fully comprehend. "Regent for young King Alexander, he does this! As good as, as . . ." He did not finish that, but few failed to get his meaning.

Durward pulled himself together. "Not so!" he denied. "You are wrong, wrong. I but seek my wife's well-being. She mislikes to be considered bastard. That is all." Never an eloquent man, nor caring for eloquence, he could have done with it now. "You err."

Henry and the Earl Simon had had their heads together. "Then why did you not tell us of this, my lord of Atholl?" the former demanded. "You come to this marriage of my daughter, yet do not tell me of so important a matter. Think you it is no concern of mine? A new heir to the throne of Scotland!"

"That was not the reason, Sire."

"Then why the secret?" Bishop de Birnam put in. "And should not any plea to the Pope have been made through me, the Primate?"

If Archbishop de Grey snorted at that, no one else did. Even Bishop Clement, so often ignored and slighted by his co-regent, joined in the denunciation.

"It is ill done," he said. "And in a regent."

There were further cries of offence and anger from all around, English as well as Scots.

Durward, recognising the realities of the situation, and that all there seemed to be against him, did not further resort to explanation and excuse, but drew on his dignity – for he was a man of strength and dominance, whatever else. "Your permission to retire, Sire?" he got out. And without waiting for answer, bowed briefly and, turning about, strode from the hall, alone. Few, if any, felt sorry for that man.

Thereafter, the final banquet was a somewhat subdued affair, only one subject apt to preoccupy the minds of adults, even if probably the young people involved did not recognise its fullest implications. Durward himself did not put in an appearance. Henry Plantagenet was very reserved, although he did cross-question Queen Marie at some length. Nothing more was said, then, as to metropolitan authority in Scotland.

Back in their own quarters, the little group round Alexander were agreed that their plan could hardly have worked out more effectively.

"You turned the tide today, Highness," David told the

Queen. "I think that Durward will not survive this. Not as regent. It will bring him down. Few, if any, will support him now. He was a fool to do it, unlimited ambition the ruin of him."

Margaret, who hardly knew her half-sister the countess, agreed. "He will have offended even his own people," she said. "I cannot think that my sister had much to do with all this. From all that I know of her, she is quiet, no seeker of high place. Alex, I think that you will be having a new regent!"

"Who?"

"That I do not know. Perhaps Walter of Menteith. Or William of Mar. The Comyns will make much of this. Their opportunity."

"Why not Davie?" the boy asked. "*Sir* Davie! I would like that."

They all smiled.

David told him, "I am not of the stature for a regent, Alex. Not an earl, nor even a great lord. Only a small one. And too young. The Privy Council and parliament would never consider such as myself."

"You are my Cup-Bearer. Could I not make you greater, Davie? As I knighted you?"

"I think not . . ."

"One day perhaps, Alex," his mother said.

"These counsellors whom King Henry is sending to Scotland with the new Queen?" Margaret asked. "Balliol and Ros of Wark. What does that mean? What part will they play? Englishmen. Is it only for a short time? Or will they stay with her always? And to counsel Alex also, he said!"

"I cannot see that they can remain in Scotland always," David said. "Even if Alex allowed it. After all, they are both lords of great lands in their own country. Wark is just across the Tweed, yes. But Barnard Castle is in Durham, not greatly far from here. Perhaps they will take it by turn to wait on young Queen Margaret? And Alex need not *heed* their counselling!"

"No!" that youngster agreed. "I do not want English lords telling me what to do. I will do what Davie and Margaret say, not these."

"Well – *I* say bed, Alex, at this present!" Margaret announced. "You have had too many late nights. And tomorrow we start early, on our long riding. You need a good sleep . . ."

In the morning, there was something of a sensation. Durward had departed, ridden off, presumably for Scotland, during the night, a few of his people with him including Abbot Donald the Chancellor, and Sir Robert de Menzies, the Chamberlain. So *all* were not abandoning him yet.

Henry was angry at this leaving his presence without royal permission. And the rest of the Scots company wondered what would be the situation once they were back in their own land. Would Durward accept eclipse without a struggle?

The actual leave-taking was somewhat delayed over this, but it was made into no very elaborate occasion. Henry and his wife had presumably said their farewells to their daughter in private, as had Alexander and his mother – who would be returning to France without delay; and the Archbishop of York was less than forthcoming, obviously glad to see them gone. Without any actual discussion on the matter, they formed up in two distinct parties of travellers, the Scots and the English separate, the young Queen Margaret riding with her two lords, her Lady Matilda de Cantelupe and her chaplain, plus a quite large armed escort. On this occasion it was not the Prince-Bishop of Durham who accompanied them, his place being taken by a lesser light, the Bishop of Carlisle. Some such cleric was required, it seemed, for once again they were to spend the nights in abbeys and monasteries, not necessarily the same ones. It was noticeable that English lords' castles were not available, not even Barnard Castle, which would be on their route.

There were few tears at the parting, the bride showing little more emotion than she had done at her wedding, a reserved, silent child, so unlike her elder brother. Queen Marie hugged her son and kissed Margaret, but was most evidently looking forward to resuming her chosen association with King John of Jerusalem. Queen Eleanor of Provence did not put in an appearance, this early morning; nor did Prince Edward.

Undoubtedly the entire proceedings had been something of a disappointment and upset for the English interests. As for the Scots, they would see.

13

Long before they won home to Roxburgh, it was evident to all the way the situation there was going to develop. Menteith and Mar, the two most senior earls present, one a Comyn, the other married to a Comyn, would grasp the opportunity presented by Durward's almost certain downfall. A council would be called forthwith, Durward demoted and new regents appointed. And not only regents; almost all Durward's appointees would be dismissed and replaced, no doubt, by Comyn nominees.

Bishop de Birnam who, as leader of the Church, could not be unseated by the said Comyns, was concerned that a better regime should be established, and all power not concentrated in the one great family, as had been the case hitherto. He and Bishop Clement came to Alexander's quarters at Hexham Priory on the third-last night from home, with proposals. Ostensibly they were to put before the King; but David's influence there being evident to all, and seemingly approved of by the two prelates, much of their converse was addressed obliquely to him and Margaret.

"It is important, Sire, that too much power is not allowed to be given into the hands of the Comyn party," de Birnam said. "We have seen the dangers of that. They will undoubtedly sway the council. But Holy Church has a say therein also. We must use it to moderate matters, for the good of your realm. Almost certainly they will appoint one of their people to be Chancellor, a key position. Along with others. So we must seek a balance, if possible."

Alexander looked at David.

"The Earl Alan Durward may not accept such demotion, my lord Bishop," that man pointed out. "It may be war, civil war, whatever the Privy Council may say."

"That is possible, Sir David, but I think unlikely. I believe

206

that Durward will have to lie low, up in his own Highlands. For a time, at least. When this of the legitimisation appeal becomes known in Scotland he will find his support melted away. It was too near to treason; and supporters of treasonable acts themselves, by law, commit treason. He was never popular – only strong. Now his strength will be like a tree felled. No, I think no war."

"We could go and kill him! Kill Durward!" Alexander suggested hopefully.

"I scarce think that the best course, Your Grace," de Birnam said gravely. "Leave such attentions to the Comyns! No – but there are other things that can be done. For one, I think that more power could be vested in your royal self, Sire. Your eleventh birthday is in a month or two. It could be celebrated by giving you – or, more properly, by your *taking* – more power and authority, in person. Therefore less power to a regency."

"Oh, yes. That would be good," the monarch agreed cheerfully.

"All appointments of state are made in your name, as it is. If you were to make some yourself, with good advice, that could help limit the Comyns' power."

"Would the council agree to that?" David asked.

"If the Church was strong on it, and those who formerly supported Durward against Comyn would add their weight, then I think that it could be accepted."

"What appointments could His Grace make which would be effective? To restrict the Comyns."

"Not a few, probably. I think of the justiciars first. Durward assumed to himself the role of sole Justiciar of the Realm – a source of some offence. Previously there were a number of justiciars, for different areas of your kingdom. All to act in the name of the King. So could any deny the King's right to appoint them?"

"Davie shall be justiciar!" Alexander declared.

There was throat-clearing. "Let us not name names just yet, Sire," Bishop Clement put in. "Time enough for that. Appointments of sheriffs or shire-reeves, keepers of royal castles and forests, certain officers of state, and others, could come direct from the crown."

"How would this be done?" Margaret asked.

"A parliament should be called, at the soonest. The Privy Council will have met first, to be sure – since parliament requires forty days of notice," de Birnam said. "But if I call together the bishops and mitred abbots immediately, we can ensure that the Church's wishes and proposals are known first, and many will take their lead from that. The Comyns themselves will take some little time to meet, for they are scattered all over the land. And to see what Durward may be doing. I believe that, thus, the Comyns, may be . . . contained."

"This of the lords de Ros and Balliol?" David wondered. "How are *they* to be dealt with? And this child Queen? Are they to lodge at Roxburgh? Or have their own establishment elsewhere? She, and His Grace here, can scarcely . . . cohabit!"

"What does cohabit mean?" Alex demanded.

"Shall we say, live in the same house, Sire. Or, at least, the same rooms."

"I do not want *her* in my house!" That was definite.

"Yet she is now your wife, Sire," de Birnam said. "The Queen. You must surely act kindly towards her. But – Roxburgh Castle is large and has many towers, spread wide. Apart. Surely the Queen and her lords can occupy one of these, and so be . . . convenient. As to the said lords, I think that they will not prove too awkward. De Ros I have long known, and found amiable. Indeed, I think him almost more Scots than English! Living as he does on the south bank of Tweed, his castle faces Scotland and seems to turn its back on England. And he had a Scots mother. As for the Lord John Balliol, he has such great lands in the south to manage that I would not think to see much of *him* in Scotland. It will be Robert de Ros who is most with the Queen. And should, I hope, cause His Grace little concern. She, the Queen, may be as often at Wark, perhaps, as at Roxburgh."

They were relieved. But Margaret shook her head.

"I am sorry for the child. *She* comes worst out of all this. We must all be kind to her. You also, Alex. For none of it is of her choosing. She is young for her age, I think, and must feel lonely and bewildered. Why not ride beside her tomorrow, Alex. You will have to grow to know her, after all. And she needs some understanding and friendship now."

The boy scowled and said nothing.

"If you are going to assume more power and rule now, Sire, you will have to learn to do things that you do not especially *want* to do," David put in. "Power without thought for others, goodwill and kindness, is but tyranny. You could well start with your young Queen."

"But she never speaks nor smiles, nor anything."

"She will be frightened, Sire. All but lost. All her family and friends left behind. Save for this Lady Matilda. How would *you* like to be in her place?"

Alexander shrugged. "I will ride with her tomorrow, if you and Margaret will also," he said.

So the final two days of their return to Scotland saw an improvement in Scots-English relations. The girl Queen did not actually blossom out in friendship and cheer, admittedly, but she did become less warily reserved and even once smiled, if shyly. And Alexander, if not effusive, did speak to her occasionally; and once indeed, when a skein of wild-geese passed over, high, flying north, launched into an exposition of the joys of goose-flighting at dusk and dawn, even though he received little encouragement – except from de Ros, who seemed interested, and admitted that he had never attempted such sport, and knew of no location where it could be engaged in, in the Tweed valley area. He was told to come to Aberlady Bay.

David, in fact, in these last days, found himself getting on well with Robert de Ros, a man almost old enough to be his father but of a cheerful and forthcoming nature and easy to talk with – unlike de Balliol, who was moody, proud-seeming and silent. If they had to put up with English counsellors, then de Ros was as good as any they were likely to get. As it happened, that amiability and friendliness was demonstrated the second day thereafter when, on account of bad weather and a delayed start, they reached Tweed later than expected, and de Ros urged that all should halt and spend the night at Wark Castle instead of pressing on to Roxburgh – no doubt to his wife's consternation, who had to provide, without notice, for this large company. It was the first English castle to entertain them. Lady de Ros did well, in the circumstances.

It was at bedtime, apt to be the occasion for confidences and discussion, that Alexander conceded that he was finding the Plantagenet girl less trying that he had feared, even if scarcely exciting company. She was quite good on a horse, at least, and did not complain about going too far each day, as did her Lady Matilda. But what was he to call her? He had to use her name sometimes – and he was not going to call her Margaret.

"But that *is* her name, Alex," his half-sister said. "You cannot avoid calling her that."

"I can!" the boy announced, at his most obstinate. "*You* are Margaret. I will not call her that. Only you. I must call her something else."

"All others will call her Queen Margaret, Alex. I do not see how you can do other. You cannot *invent* a name for her."

He set a stubborn jaw.

David had a suggestion. "Margaret, you named your half-sister, the Countess of Atholl, Margaret or Marjory, I have noticed. It is the same name, is it not? Why not use that?"

"Well . . ."

"I will not call Margaret Marjory," Alexander declared. "She *is* Margaret. But I will call this girl Marjory, yes. That is good."

"But others will name her Queen Margaret, Alex," his sister pointed out. "You will not change that."

"It will be accepted, from Alex," David thought. "A special name between them. Like Meg."

So it was settled, Alexander prepared to try it out on the morrow.

In the event, it all produced an improvement in the situation. In his eagerness to have his own way, Alexander made a point of riding beside the girl, chattering and repeatedly calling her Marjory, which did not seem to upset her – the boy's increased attention eliciting some slight response indeed. Probably she took it to be the Scots form of Margaret. And Robert de Ros took it to imply a growing closeness in the pair's relationship, with the adoption of this pet-name, which clearly pleased him. Balliol had no comment to make.

So they arrived at Roxburgh Castle in half a day's ride, and Marjory saw her new home stretching along its precipitous rock-top between the two rivers. What she thought of it she did not reveal, even though Alexander pointed out that they could fish from the castle-walls on either side, in different rivers, and that there were not many houses where that could be done.

The others, for different reasons, were thankful to be home. Now – what was the news of Durward?

Little indeed was known about Alan Durward's doings, at Roxburgh. But the prelates went to nearby Kelso Abbey, and found out more – for, as usual, the monks were the best-informed folk in the land, this because of the comings and goings of wandering friars, sometimes called tranter-priests, who ranged the country with their begging-bowls, providing much-needed ministerial services, baptisms, weddings and burials for the remoter communities, and gaining and imparting news in the process. At Kelso, across Tweed, it was learned that the Earl of Atholl and a small party had indeed passed through the town, without stopping, some days before, and had gone on northwards at speed. He had crossed Forth at Queen Margaret's Ferry and proceeded on, making evidently for the Highland Line and his own territories in Atholl, the Mearns and Deeside.

These tidings, more or less anticipated as they were, concerned the Comyn lords, especially Mar whose lands marched with Durward's on Dee and Don. Was the miscreant gone to muster his forces, to restore his position by force of arms? If so, the sooner they themselves got their power assembled, the better. They were for off.

The prelates, too, at de Birnam's bidding, were eager to get away, for he was calling an important meeting at St Andrews to decide on the Church's part to play in this crisis. The other lords and officers of the royal party all were desirous of getting home, after their long absence, and to prepare for eventualities.

Two days after their return, then, Roxburgh Castle was

all but deserted, save for the King and Queen and their immediate attendants and permanent staff, even Bishop Clement going with the other clerics. It all made an extraordinary change in conditions for Alexander and his two friends, a sudden quiet and hiatus after all the activity, clash, excitements and travel. Calm descended, inaction, leisure – so much so that, after three days, John Balliol departed south-westwards, for Galloway, where he had inherited large lands from Devorgilla, daughter of the last Celtic Lord of Galloway. He was not missed, even, it seemed, by de Ros.

Marjory and her little party were allotted a tower two along from the gatehouse and two more apart from Alexander's own. So they did not have to see overmuch of each other. In fact, Robert de Ros was more often in the King's company than was his ward, she seeming to be well content to keep her own company, learn from her lady-in-waiting and chaplain tutor, work at tapestry, embroidery and needlework. Alexander tried to interest her in fishing, without much success; but she did reveal that she played on the lute, and an instrument was found for her. Often thereafter they could hear the rather plaintive notes issuing from her tower. Margaret frequently visited her when de Ros was with David and Alexander.

This period of waiting held its own worries. Rumours reached them, of course, but little firm information as to what went on on the national scene – extraordinary, really, when it was being proposed that the young monarch should assume greater authority in the rule of his kingdom; but it seemed to be nobody's business to inform him as to developments. Bishop Clement remained away, and the other regent, the Comyn Lord of Badenoch, was now believed to be at death's door.

Oddly enough, most word of what went on came from Robert de Ros, who seemed to have his own sources of information. Through him they gathered that Durward was indeed lying low, not trying to assemble an army, presumably aware that his fortunes meantime were in eclipse. He remained in his northern fastnesses, at the castle of Coull on Deeside. The Comyns, on the other hand, *were* mounting all their power, whether to attack Durward or just to prove to the rest of the realm that they were now the power to be reckoned with; probably both.

It was a full month after their return from England before official information arrived, this in the person of Bishop Clement, coming from St Andrews. He announced that there had been a Privy Council meeting at Edinburgh, at which he had attended. Durward had not done so, and had been, as expected, duly demoted and expelled from the regency. The Lord of Badenoch and Lochaber had resigned, and the Earls of Menteith and Mar substituted. These changes and appointments had to be confirmed by the King-in-Parliament, of course, to become lawful, and a parliament had been called for mid-April, giving the due notice, which would conveniently fit in immediately after Alexander's eleventh birthday, allowing them to use the occasion to call for an increase of the royal authority.

The Comyns were now largely in control, admittedly; but the Church had consolidated its position, with the Primate determined to take a greater share in government, and to support the King's increasing authority. With the solid backing of the bishops in this, he had so informed the council. Therefore, although the Comyns would undoubtedly put forward a host of nominees for most offices of state and positions of power, before parliament confirmed this they would have the *King's* proposals to consider, and this ought to ensure that all did not go the Comyns' way. Already Bishop de Birnam was himself listing names for possible appointments which would support the royal authority. Throne and Church would be more strongly linked.

David de Lindsay, whilst a good, or fairly good, churchman, was just a little concerned at all this having the effect of making the clerics just too influential in the state. So long as de Birnam and Clement were in charge, well enough; but they were both elderly men and in the nature of things would presumably be replaced before so very long. Who might succeed them? Ecclesiastical dominance could be almost as bad as that of Comyn or Durward.

Alexander's own preoccupation now was in elevating David to some suitable eminence – this was *his* conception of increased royal power. Could he not make him a justiciar? David's own father had been Justiciar of Lothian, had he not? Why not that, then? And once he was that, perhaps he could promote him further, to High Chamberlain, or even a regent?

Much toning down of youthful ambitions had to be engaged in before a compromise was reached. David was much too young to be a justiciar, but perhaps an assistant or deputy justiciarship might be acceptable?

For his part, David concentrated on seeking to impress on his sovereign-lord the need for good and due behaviour at the important forthcoming parliament, to give a suitable impression of the looked-for authority and maturity. He probably need not do much actual speaking, but what he did say should be delivered clearly, firmly and with dignity if possible. Bishop Clement, the sole remaining regent until the others were confirmed, would be at his side, and he, David, would seek to be somewhere nearby where he could help to give guidance if necessary. Alexander declared that, yes, he would show them all who was King of Scots – an averment which did not entirely reassure his Cup-Bearer.

The eleventh birthday celebrations, despite the significance being attached to the occasion, were modest indeed, being confined to the little group at Roxburgh Castle, with nothing which might really be called a banquet and festivity, and the entertainment afterwards, devised by Alexander himself, fairly elementary, games and play-acting and singing of songs. Margery was prevailed upon to play her lute before all, shy about it as she was. David and Alexander engaged Robert de Ros and the Castle's keeper in a mock tournament, with wooden swords, whilst Margaret encouraged the young Queen to cheer them on. De Ros's wife, who now spent much of her time at Roxburgh, a comfortable and motherly soul, proved to have an aptitude for story-telling and entertained them with tales of the Borderland, with supernatural overtones; she was a Scot, from the Merse, a de Normanville of Maxton, and indeed proved to be a distant relation of David, through the Cospatrick earls. She and Margaret rendered ballads in song, all seeking to join in the choruses. It all made a pleasant and enjoyable evening, although scarcely momentous an entry into the monarch's so significant twelfth year.

Of course, whether the year itself would be momentous remained to be seen. They would discover, presumably, in a day or two.

The all-important parliament was to be held in the great fortress-citadel of Edinburgh Castle, so the royal party had to ride north for the occasion. Alexander, eager to prove his mettle on a horse, was for covering the fifty-mile journey in one day, and as a way of testing out his new wife's staying-power in the saddle – for it was decided that this was an opportunity for Scotland's young Queen to be shown to her people. However, Bishop Clement was long past the age for major horsemanship, if ever he had been, and Soutra Hospice was quite as far as he could manage in one day, to his liege-lord's ill-concealed scorn. So they arrived in Edinburgh by noon on the second day, with parliament to meet the day following.

The town, of course, was crowded, the lords and commis-sioners having almost all brought their trains of men-at-arms, partly to demonstrate to the new regime their potency and partly in case the deplorable Durward, whom all men still feared, might elect to come and take a heavy-handed part, after all. There was no sign of that as yet, however. The Comyns' three wheat sheaves banner flew everywhere, a deal more prominent than was the Lion Rampant of Scotland.

The royal party was greeted, up at the great rock-crowning fortress, by the Earls of Menteith, Mar and Buchan, the two former obviously already considering themselves to be regents, and all but ignoring Bishop Clement. Alexander was advisedly cool towards them, however familiar they had all been on the long journey from York.

De Ros, who had never been to Edinburgh Castle, was much impressed by its size, strength and the stupendous views seen from its battlements: but he did ruefully declare that the quarters allotted to them were more like prison cells than a royal palace.

On the morrow, at midday, then, all assembled for the vital session, the Comyns assuring that their strategically placed scouts reported no sign of Durward making an appearance. At this stage, it was all distinctly tentative and uneasy, as to arrangements, for few now in charge had had experience in organising a parliament. The High Sennachie and the Chancellor normally saw to this; but the old sennachie had died, and Abbot Donald had discreetly vanished – and taken the Great Seal of Scotland with him; possibly he was with Durward. Neither could be replaced without parliamentary approval. So all the initial procedure lacked precision and a guiding hand, although the Comyns sought to ensure that their dominance did not go unrecognised. They were apparently putting forward a churchman, one John de Gamelyn, said to be a Comyn bastard, as Chancellor; but he was not yet in a position to take charge. This temporary void in direction had the effect of enabling the royal group to take the lead, since there was no question as to the King's and Bishop Clement's authority; and David found himself more or less acting as sennachie, on the royal behalf, marshalling the official procession and entry to the parliament-hall and arranging for Margaret and the young Queen to take seats at the other end of the dais from the throne and Chancellor's table, where they could see and be seen.

With most of the former officers of state amissing, the formal entry was much curtailed; but the trumpeters could still make their resounding flourishes, and the great lords and earls filed in to take their foremost seats. The Primate entered alone, and then the crown, sceptre and sword of state were carried in by the three Comyn earls, Menteith, Mar and Buchan. Finally, to the clash of cymbals – Alexander insisted on this – David ushered in the King and his remaining regent, the boy to sit on the throne, Bishop Clement to stand behind him. David himself went to stand nearby, but decently back. Alexander had not forgotten to bring his Brecbennoch of Columba.

After a final blare of trumpets, Alexander himself spoke. He had been well rehearsed in this, but even so it came out in something of a rush.

"My lords, commissioners and leal subjects – greetings! To this parliament of my realm. It is one of great, great . . ." He paused, trying to remember the word. "Of great *moment*."

Pleased with himself at that, he nodded, and repeated, "Moment. I call on the Bishop Primate to speak." And he sat back, relievedly.

De Birnam bowed and raised a hand. "Let us praise God Almighty, and seek His blessings on our deliberations on this notable, and as His Grace has said, momentous occasion." He launched into a prayer of some length, indicating to their Creator the heavenly guidance required this day, with so much to be ordered and settled, for the realm's weal.

Then, again bowing to the throne, he went on, in a different voice. "As all know well, the rule and direction of this kingdom has been rudely shaken of late, men in positions of power have behaved unworthily, and changes are called for in direction and offices of state. Moreover, His Highness, our well-beloved Alexander, by God's grace High King of Scots, has now entered his twelfth year, and has been married to the gracious Margaret, daughter of the King of England," and he bowed in the other direction. "This most significant situation calls for major changes in the governance of the realm. The Privy Council has met, as has the Assembly of Bishops, and come to decisions to put before the King-in-Parliament for confirmation, as by law required. Or otherwise."

He paused and looked around him.

Belatedly Alexander remembered. "Proceed!" he jerked.

"Firstly, it is right and proper that His Grace the King should now take a more prominent part in the rule of his kingdom. To this he and his regent agree. And this, to be sure, does *not* call for the confirmation of parliament!" That was significantly said. "His Grace will, hereafter, select and appoint certain officers of state and others and, while heeding the advice of his regents and the Privy Council and parliament, will himself give due decision. Not in all matters, but in some. And, as agreed at York, on his royal marriage, he will also have the counsel of lords appointed by King Henry of England. Which should help to ensure peace and amity between the kingdoms, to the benefit of all."

That last had men eyeing each other distinctly doubtfully.

De Birnam went on. "Decision first has to be taken as to the regency. Until His Grace comes of full age, a regency is required by our law. The Earl of Atholl has, by his unworthy activities, forfeited his position as a regent, and the Privy Council advises that he be dismissed therefrom, His Grace agreeing. Does this parliament also agree?"

A great shout of approval emphasised that there were few, if any, Durward supporters present.

"We need no vote on it, I think. Then, John, Lord of Badenoch and Lochaber has resigned by reason of prolonged sickness. Which leaves only Bishop Clement of Dunblane in the regency. He, and His Grace, consider one regent to be insufficient at this stage, and on the advice of the council the names of Walter, Earl of Menteith and William, Earl of Mar, are put forward for parliament's approval. Both are able and worthy lords, and well calculated to support and advise the crown. Is it agreed?"

The assent was less general and enthusiastic than for Durward's dismissal, although the Comyns all cheered loudly; but there was no vocal dissent.

"Then I call upon my lords of Menteith and Mar to come forward and take their due places behind the throne."

That was done with alacrity, even though Alexander scarcely showed signs of welcome.

"There but remains to myself one duty," de Birnam said. "On the demission of Abbot Donald of Dunfermline, a new Chancellor of the Realm must be appointed. The Privy Council proposes the name of Master John de Gamelyn, of our college of St Andrews. Is this nomination accepted by parliament?"

Apart from one or two cries of confirmation, there was silence at this. Few there had ever heard the name, undoubtedly. And some college official was scarcely a normal nominee for such an important position. But if the council recommended it, this Gamelyn must be a Comyn supporter.

At the continued silence, Menteith raised his voice. "Master de Gamelyn is a man of great ability, learning and discretion," he declared flatly. "I have every confidence in him."

De Birnam had mentioned to David beforehand that Gamelyn was thought, in St Andrews, to be Menteith's own bastard nephew.

"Does any object to the appointment of Master de Gamelyn as Chancellor?" the Primate asked.

Silence still, but it could be taken for assent.

"Then I ask Master de Gamelyn to come forward and take the Chancellor's chair at this table."

There was a stir in the hall now, as from the back limped a young and slender man, garbed as a cleric. There was nothing obviously distinguished about him, save perhaps for a clever, sallow face and heavy-lidded dark eyes. But he had a certain air of authority, strangely. He bowed to the throne, to the Primate, and turned to sit at the table, almost as though by right.

De Birnam went to join the group behind the King.

Alexander said, "Proceed!" as instructed.

"Your Grace, my lords spiritual and temporal, commissioners to this parliament, friends all," the young man said clearly, carefully. "I am greatly privileged to take up this onerous appointment, and will use my best endeavours to fill it to the satisfaction of all. This session of parliament is highly important, as all are aware, and I crave indulgence if I fail to do justice to the occasion. So – to our deliberations. What is first?"

He had scarcely got that out when Menteith spoke, strongly. "All will agree that there has been much of injustice done in this realm in the years just past. And the righting of the wrongs, where possible, should be amongst the first of our duties. The regency having been renewed, the justiciary must surely be our next consideration. Alan, Earl of Atholl, amongst his other offences, wrongously took to himself the position of sole Justiciar of the Realm, putting down all the other justiciarships, long established. Now, I say, these should be restored, for the different provinces of the kingdom, for the better administration of justice and the rule of law, all under the office of Justiciar of Scotia. For that office I propose Alexander, Earl of Buchan."

"And I second," Mar declared.

"Do you accept such nomination, my lord of Buchan?" Gamelyn asked.

"I do."

Thus swiftly and effectively the thing was effected. No voice was actually raised against the appointment, backed by two of the regents, although there were murmurs.

"As Justiciar of Scotia, have you any names to put forward for the lesser justiciarships, my lord of Buchan?" the new Chancellor asked.

"Yes, Master Chancellor. It is important that sound and worthy men be put in charge of the administration of the realm's justice, to supervise the jurisdictions of sheriffs and baronial courts. To this end I would nominate Sir John Comyn, son and heir of the Lord of Badenoch and Lochaber, as Justiciar of Galloway. Sir Reginald Cheyne of Inverugie, to be Justiciar North of the Mounth. Sir William Comyn of Kilbride to be Justiciar South of the Mounth. And MacDougall of Lorne to be Deputy Justiciar for Lochaber, Argyll and the Isles. Also Sir Andrew . . ."

David Lindsay coughed significantly, to attract Alexander's attention, to make intervention. But before the boy could find the words to halt this obviously prearranged catalogue of appointees, he was beaten to it. A strong and angry voice was raised from the great lords' benches, that of Robert Bruce, Lord of Annandale.

"Your Grace! Chancellor! I protest! This is too much! Is all justice in this land to be the preserve of the house of Comyn? These being named are all of that line. Cheyne's mother is a Comyn and MacDougall is married to one . . ."

Noise erupted in that hall, the Comyn faction vociferous, others supporting Bruce. Thus early in his career, Master Gamelyn had to bang his gavel on the table for quiet.

"My lords," he said. "Let us have order in His Grace's presence. The Earl of Buchan has the floor and must be permitted to finish. Objections and counter-motions may be raised thereafter, if so desired. But –"

He himself was interrupted, and by one he could scarcely use his gavel against – the monarch himself. Alexander did the banging, with his Brecbennoch, on the arm of his throne.

"I want Davie to be a justiciar," he exclaimed. "Er . . . assistant justiciar. *Sir* Davie Lindsay," he amended. "Of, of Lothian."

There was a pause as men eyed each other. Gamelyn coped.

"Yes, Sire. Certainly. Justiciars can have assistants, or deputes. Sir David de Lindsay, Justiciar-Depute of Lothian. Assistant to whom, Highness?"

Alexander looked round at David. This was not just as it had been arranged. No name for Justiciar of Lothian had been decided upon.

Into the silence, Buchan spoke again. "Sire, if I may continue, I would propose Sir Thomas de Normanville to be appointed Justiciar of Lothian."

This was the baron of Maxton, in the Merse, and incidentally the brother of Robert de Ros's wife. Did he have a Comyn connection?

The King looked uncertain, and Buchan went on. "He would, to be sure, accept Sir David de Lindsay as deputy Justiciar."

"Yes. And I want another." Alexander glanced again at David. That man, distinctly embarrassed by all this, produced a penetrating whisper. "Walter FitzAlan, High Steward."

"Yes, I want Walter the Stewart to be keeper of Stirling Castle." Alexander, at David's mouthing, added, in a hurry, "The Earl of Lennox to be keeper of Dumbarton Castle. And, and Patrick, Earl of Dunbar to be keeper of *this* castle. Edinburgh Castle."

That certainly produced something of a sensation. These three were the greatest fortresses in the land, and whoever controlled them was in a powerful position. And the three named were all independent of the Comyns. These were royal citadels all, although Durward had hitherto appointed their keepers. None could very well contest the King's right to nominate, if so he chose. Menteith and Mar exchanged glances but had to shrug.

Gamelyn looked all around him, enquiringly. "Are there any other nominations?"

Menteith spoke, quickly. "There are many appointments to be made. But none, I think, requiring the confirmation of parliament."

"Then can we take it that this parliament accepts the nominations here made?"

221

"I, for one, do *not*!" That was Bruce of Annandale again. "All these justiciarships – Comyns! And, no doubt, other Comyn appointments to follow! I contest them."

"As do I." Nigel, Earl of Carrick seconded. Bruce's son was wed to Carrick's only child.

There was a pause.

"Then, my lords, have you alternative names to put forward for each position?" Gamelyn asked, respectfully.

That held the protesters. Clearly they had not come with any prepared list of possible justiciars.

When he got no answer, the Chancellor spread eloquent hands. "We cannot take your objection in general as a motion, my lords. Lacking . . . details. Other nominations. Names for the various offices."

"We would require time to consider such," Bruce said.

"This parliament cannot wait on your consideration, my lords," Menteith intervened. "Which, it must appear, will take time! But – if you will submit names and offices to us, His Grace and his regents, they will be considered."

David, out of no particular care for Bruce but anxious to encourage resistance to a Comyn hegemony, stepped closer and whispered to the monarch.

Alexander, impressed by the Chancellor's gavel for making satisfactory noise, thumped his Brecbennoch again. "I have another royal castle. Dun . . . Dundonald, yes. I make the Lord of Annandale keeper of Dundonald."

Menteith and Mar shot baleful glances at David. Dundonald was a strong and strategically placed fortress near to Ayr, occupying a position between the High Steward's lands of Renfrew and Carrick, and adjoining the Bruce lands of Upper Annandale. Such a block of country, set between the Comyn lands in the north and their properties in Galloway, could be a considerable stumbling-block to any expansion of their powers. Hitherto it had been little used, all but abandoned, but . . .

"This parliament cannot approve or deny His Grace's appointments to keeperships of his royal castles," Mar said, frowning. "Indeed parliament's main concern is the appointment of a new regency and the restoration of the full justiciary. And that has been done. At this stage, other matters

222

can be dealt with in council. I propose, therefore, Sire, that parliament adjourns."

"I agree," Menteith said.

Alexander once again looked at David, his guide and prop, and then at Bishop Clement. Both nodded, since nothing was to be gained by prolonging this battle of wits meantime.

"Yes," the boy acceded.

Gamelyn took up his cue promptly and efficiently, as he had done all else. "Then, Your Grace, my lords and commissioners, I declare the parliament adjourned. And call upon my lord Bishop of St Andrews to close the session with prayer and a benediction."

Accordingly, de Birnam stepped forward again, and briefly thanked their Creator for what they all hoped were wise decisions, and added a blessing upon all.

David signed to the trumpeters and clashers of cymbals to lead the King and his regents out, as all stood.

A new page had been turned in Scotland's story.

14

It did not take long for the two new regents to make their authority felt. That very evening of the parliament they came to the royal quarters in the castle and announced that, since His Grace was now to assume more personal power and say in the affairs of his realm, and they must needs frequently consult with him, they were of the opinion that Roxburgh Castle, situated at the very southern tip of the kingdom, was unsuitable and inconvenient as the royal domicile. They would therefore have His Grace come to take up his residence in this more central castle of Edinburgh, from which the realm could be better governed. They urged, therefore, that the King and Queen, on return to Roxburgh, prepare to move their court to this Edinburgh at earliest convenience.

Surprisingly perhaps, Alexander found no fault with this suggestion – or, perhaps coming from his regents, almost an order. The reason was not far to seek. The aforementioned wide views from the castle battlements had much impressed the boy, especially that to the east where, clearly visible, were the conical hill of North Berwick Law and the ridge of Garleton. Between these prominences, only sixteen miles away, lay Aberlady Bay, haunt of the geese. He could therefore ride there in under two hours. On such can decisions of state hinge.

For his part, David de Lindsay was well enough content to make the change, recognising as he did how grievously he had had to neglect his duties at Luffness and The Byres of Garleton; now he would be able to go there frequently. As for Margaret, while she would have preferred to remain at Roxburgh, in pleasant countryside, rather than be immured in the midst of a city, she made no complaints. And Margery produced no comments, either way. Whether Bishop Clement had been consulted on this was not clear, but he was delaying his return to Roxburgh for a few days, presumably to confer with his new fellow-regents.

On their ride to the Borderland, able to do it in one day at Alexander's urging, and lacking the bishop's hampering presence, there was much discussion on the parliament – which indeed had been one only in name, with no real debating, merely a formalising of decisions already taken – also the situation now prevailing, and how much improvement, if any, the Comyns were likely to be over Durward's regime. Alexander was pleased with himself, and of his new authority, and announced that he would keep the Comyn earls in their places. He had to be warned that, in fact, he had little real power as yet. In a parliament he could make an impression and influence decisions; but the Privy Council was another matter, meeting in private and now very largely under Comyn domination. For the day-to-day rule of the kingdom, the regents' and the council's decisions were what would count.

"And the Chancellor's," Margaret put in.

"The Chancellor only acts as secretary to the council," David pointed out. "He does not preside, as at a parliament."

"Perhaps. But that one will influence much, I think, young and unknown as he is. You will have to watch Master de Gamelyn. He is clever, shrewd, with more wits to him than those earls. He is the one to keep your eyes on, I feel sure."

"So say I," de Ros, who was riding south with them, agreed. "There is a young man who has the ears of his betters and masters – or they would not have made him Chancellor – and who will go far. If the others heed him, he could effect much in Your Grace's kingdom."

"Could we not say that I do not want him, and have another Chancellor?" the boy suggested.

"I fear that it is not so simple as that, Alex," David said. "The Chancellor, although proposed by the Comyns, was *appointed* by the parliament itself, always is. Only a parliament could dismiss him. You would have to convince another parliament that he is unworthy. And your regents would object. Or two of the three would."

"I made the keepers of three castles. No, four. And made you a justiciar."

"That is different. Royal castles could not be denied keepers *you* appointed. You took the Comyns by surprise, there. As for the justiciary, I am not so sure . . ."

"Ah, yes, David – how does it feel to be a justiciar?" Margaret asked. "You are a judge, now, not just a cup-bearer. Must we all go in awe of you?"

"Lord, I had almost forgotten! But I am only a *deputy* justiciar. I know naught of the justiciary. My father was Justiciar of Lothian, yes – but I paid no heed to that. I cannot think that it was a wise move, Alex."

"It was, it *is*, my royal will!" the King said loftily.

"Your Grace's royal will requires some tempering on occasion, I think!"

"What does tempering mean, Davie?"

"Well . . ."

"You will have to seek instruction from your senior justiciar, David," Margaret said. "This Thomas de Normanville of Maxton. I do not know him. Do you? Sir Robert, *you* will know him. He is kin to your wife, is he not?"

"Yes. He is a sound man. Able. Honest. Sir David will not find him difficult to work with, I think. His elder brother, Waleran, has long been a sick man, so Thomas acts Lord of Maxton."

"Has he Comyn links?"

"His mother was a Comyn, yes. But I do not think that he is close to those three earls. It is but that the Comyns have no lands in Lothian and the Merse, and he is best that they can appoint."

"Where is Maxton?" Alexander demanded.

"It is on the Tweed, Sire. Only eight miles or so west of Roxburgh Castle. A goodly lordship."

"I will go with you, Davie. And see this man."

Margaret, ever mindful of the young Queen's silent presence – her Lady Matilda had not gone with them to the parliament – turned in the saddle. The others, it is to be feared, were too apt to ignore her. "How think you – will Your Grace enjoy to live in Edinburgh Castle instead of Roxburgh? It will be very different, I think. We must get better lodging than we had these last three nights. Alex can demand that."

The girl merely nodded.

"She can play her lute as well there as at Roxburgh," her husband announced casually.

That evening, at Roxburgh, with even Alexander tired after their fifty-mile ride, David, adjourning to Margaret's chamber, took her in his arms.

"Has the thought come to you, my dear, as it has to me, that matters are not now as they were? With us? he asked, kissing her brow.

"You mean . . .?"

"I mean that in all this of change of power in the land, *our* position could have much changed also. Yours and mine. We could not think to wed, you a King's daughter, myself but a lord of modest degree. But now . . ."

"What has changed, David? *We* are still the same. Durward has fallen, yes. But . . ."

"See you – the new regents may not be so strong against it. Even if they should be, they know that I am in Alex's favour – that is clear enough. And he is now to have more power. I say that we should wed. Wed, lass! Hazard it."

"Oh, David!" She clung to him. "Could we? Dare we?"

"We could, yes – and *should*. And quickly. Before the Comyns think of finding a *Comyn* husband for you! It was that that came to me. They might well so decide. So – let us do it first."

"But – would it not be as with Durward? They would have it annulled. Appeal to the Pope. They would use the excuse that we are in kinship, however distant. Your great-grandsire, another Sir David, married a daughter of King William the Lyon, did he not? That would be enough for the Vatican. A, a prohibited relationship – is not that the word for it? Then take me away from you."

"The Pope may not be so pleased with the Comyns, lass. After all, Durward was paying him well for his wife's legitimisation. That may still be granted. Durward had been doing much for Holy Church. Rome may well frown on the Comyns for replacing him. Not grant any appeal for annulment, if asked."

"You think it so? David, David . . .!"

"Forby, if we got Bishop Clement to marry us! If it was done by a regent? The Comyns will despise him, yes, as did

Durward. But still he *is* a regent, senior in years to them. They might well hesitate to go against it, if Clement married us. New as they are to the regency."

"Would he do it? The bishop?"

"I think that he would. Especially if Alex *commanded* him to do it. He is friendly towards us."

"David, I dare not think that it is possible! If it is, if it is . . .!"

They kissed and clutched each other in an ecstasy of love, hope, anticipation. He led her over to her bed, to sit and embrace the more comprehensively.

Inevitably, perhaps, the man's embraces were fairly quickly becoming comprehensive indeed, one hand loosening her bodice to reach for and fondle her breasts, the other reaching lower, when Margaret placed her own fingers on his too eager lips.

"My love, not, not now! Not yet! Oh, David, I know. I want you, as you want me. But – let us wait. A little. We have waited so long, yes. But just a little longer. If you will? Till we are indeed wed. Soon, soon, yes. But, let us do this . . . rightly. When we *have* the right. As man and wife. Not, not stealing it, secretly. When all can be ours, honestly. In just a little time. No?"

He drew a deep quivering breath, raising his head. "If, if you wish it." That was a very reluctant concession. "It is no great sin, is it? And . . . and you are so lovely! I have *needed* you, for so long. And now, and now . . ."

"Only a small while, my heart. Perhaps I am foolish. I am yours, yes. But I would be the more happy when I can give myself to you as your wife. Not just your lover."

"Very well," he said, even if his tone belied his words. He bent head again to kiss those warm, rounded breasts lingeringly, before tucking them back in their hiding-place. Also smoothed down her skirt, as he rose. "You are probably right," he declared, if lacking in conviction.

"Dear one, I thank you. I am sorry. But this is best, I think. We shall wed, God willing, the more blessedly for the anticipation. And this memory!"

"Then – the sooner the better, woman! When does Bishop Clement return?"

"He said within the week . . ."

"A *week*, confound him! Seven more days. And nights!"

"Perhaps sooner, my love . . ."

With a curious mixture of elation and frustration, David Lindsay sought his own chamber.

They did not have to wait quite a week, for Bishop Clement arrived five days later. David hardly allowed him to enter his own quarters before he hurried to approach him on the vital matter, armed with all his arguments in favour, plus Alexander's enthusiastic assertion that he would make a wedding his royal command. *He* was wed, now – so should be Davie! The prospective bridegroom said that he did not think that an appeal to the Pope for annulment would follow, in the circumstances. Especially if Bishop de Birnam supported the match, as he quite probably would. Clement admitted that relations with the Vatican were difficult at the moment, and representations from the Comyns against the episcopate would probably not be welcomed.

The good bishop, however, was a little surprised at David's plea that the wedding should be the very next day. Why the haste? He was told that, since they would have to be returning to Edinburgh shortly, and there would be much of packing and upheaval, this matter should be dealt with expeditiously – an explanation which did not wholly banish Clement's surprise. But he did not refuse to act.

So, on a fine afternoon of early May, with the cuckoos calling from the wooded slopes around, the couple were at last made man and wife, in the castle chapel. It was the short and simple service which both requested, before a very small but select company, in that, besides the King of Scots and his Queen, his tutor, the castle keeper and the Lady Matilda, there were only the de Roses. It might seem a strange choice to have the English Lord of Wark, King Henry's representative, as groomsman; but David had come to respect and like this man. Margaret had no one to yield her up, but Lady de Ros stood at her back, and none there complained of lack of support. Bishop Clement had not conducted any weddings for many a year, and was somewhat absent-minded about it all, repeating himself once or twice and pausing on occasion, but not omitting the vital vows and declarations. Alexander involved himself to the extent of calling "Good! Good!" at intervals.

The bridegroom, at least, was scarcely aware of the details of it all, so elevated was he in his emotions. Margaret, on the other hand, was quietly competent, heedful – and looking as lovely as she was happy. When they were pronounced one, in the sight of God and man, she was grasped almost fiercely by her husband, there and then, and smilingly had to restrain him so that the benediction might be decently received.

As the bishop stepped back, duty done, Alexander hurled himself forward, to pummel both of them with his fists, in an access of enthusiasm. This was a *real* wedding, he cried, the implication as to his own very obvious. In having to sober the boy down, David managed to recover some of his own calm, and behaved more as a bridegroom should.

The wedding feast which followed was not held just for the three of them in his bedchamber, as their liege-lord suggested, but in the lesser hall, with the garrison and servants of the castle invited to take part, with entertainment, music and dancing afterwards, the festivity tending to become somewhat out of hand as the evening progressed, inevitably. Bishop Clement retired early, as did Margery and her lady. David wished that he and Margaret could do the same, but recognised that that would not do. So it all went on much too long for his taste.

When, at length, they felt that they might make their escape, and it be hardly noticed, there was still the problem of Alexander. He, excited, was the reverse of sleepy, and seemed to consider the evening to be young yet, with much of interest to be discussed and celebrated. It was difficult to explain to an eleven-year-old boy that newly-weds might seek privacy on such an occasion.

Eventually, the monarch safely in bed if still very wide awake, David announced that he and Margaret would not be sharing *his* room that night; but that first they were going to take a walk in the May half-dark air, to clear their heads of the day's ongoings. He, Alex, would undoubtedly be asleep before they got back. The likelihood of this was strenuously denied; indeed the boy reproached them for letting him get undressed and into bed, when he might have gone with them on their walk.

They lingered on that stroll rather longer than David would have wished, pleasant as it was by the shadowy riverside. When they eventually got back and climbed the stairs, carefully silent, he tiptoed to the door of Alexander's room, to listen – not so much out of an excessive sense of duty as to ensure that they were unlikely to be disturbed – for if the boy heard them, he was quite capable of coming along to impart some notion which would not await until morning. But happily he was fast asleep – and once that, he seldom woke.

David got back to his own chamber and thankfully closed the door. It is never really dark in Scotland's May, and Margaret had not lit the lamp. She was standing silhouetted against the window, looking out, her back to him. He went to take her in his arms.

"At last!" he exclaimed.

"At last, yes." Her voice was all but tremulous. "Oh, David, my dear. I am . . . a little frightened!"

"Frightened? You! Lassie – why? Why? We have waited for this for so long. And we know each other so well. What could affright you?"

"That is it. *Because* we have waited so long, I fear. I fear that now I may fail you. That I will disappoint, after all your patient waiting . . ."

"*Impatient* waiting! But – how could you fail me? You! My Margaret, my love, my *life*!"

"Because you will be looking for, for so much. And I may not reach your expectations. It is all new to me, you see. And I am all . . . unpractised!"

"Woman, dear, it is not often that *you* talk folly! We have not been so long together without knowing much of each other. You are the most lovely and desirable creature I have ever encountered, your every inch a delight . . ."

"I may *look* aright, perhaps. But more than looking is called for this night, David – and I could prove less than you hope for. That is my fear. You see, just because I *am* a King's daughter, I have little experience of men and love-making, or even the pretence of it . . ."

"But we have been not so far from it, many a time, have we not? Had to restrain ourselves? Or I have. And you – do not tell me that you have not felt something of the desire for it? You have never rebuffed me. Only said to wait."

"Yes. Oh, yes – I have felt the need, the urge. It is just that in this matter I do not *know* myself. And fear to disappoint. Perhaps I am being foolish . . ."

"That you are! Enough of this talk, Margaret-mine. We have better to do than air foolish fears!" And loosening his hold of her person, he changed to loosening her bodice.

She began tentatively to help him with its fastenings, but he pushed her hand away.

"No. Leave this to me! This is your husband speaking! I have long desired to do this. I will undress you, in fact not just in my mind!"

She mustered a little laugh at that. "Are you so expert, husband?"

That called for no answer. And he certainly proved to be fairly effective in divesting her of her clothing – not that, in warm May weather, she was too closely wrapped. And despite his command, she aided a little, stepping out of items where necessary.

Finished, he too stepped back, to admire his handiwork. And he actually uttered something of a groan at what he saw in that wan twilight, a groan of sheerest wonderment, rapture, delight, overwhelming emotion. For she was lovely indeed, fair beyond words, all of her, sheer splendid womanhood in her every proportion. Much he had guessed at, of course, being a man of some imagination, but the actuality surpassed even his vivid expectations. The full and shapely breasts he knew, but lower was enough to catch his breath, all in an excellent physical harmony, rich, rounded but slender also, as though sculpted by a master, length of leg not the least of it all.

Shaking his head, he began to tear off his own clothing.

She came to him, then, offering help before he damaged his fine gear in his unseemly haste. And, although he probably would have been speedier without her assistance, some part of his avid mind recognised that this co-operation might well aid her own further co-operation. Her warmly enticing proximity and touchings indeed rather got in the way of his disrobing process, especially when she stooped to his hose, and his hands strayed and clutched and went exploring.

Presently, naked as she, all but panting, he picked her up bodily and carried her to his bed, there telling himself to be gentle, gentle, however urgent his manhood. So he caressed and fondled and kissed comprehensively, until he could no longer hold back. Whether thereafter he was as gentle as were his good intentions, she uttered no complaint, and after an initial tense holding of herself, in a little began actually to stir in some sort of rhythm beneath him.

That, although so to be desired, had its perhaps inevitable effect on an over-eager man, and with a gasped apology he came to a premature conclusion.

Lying prostrate thereafter, and blaming himself, it came to him, by Margaret's own reaction, that perhaps this was no grievous calamity, and *he* the failure, not her, for it was giving her time and experience of a sort; and nothing was surer than that he would be able to redeem himself before too long, and, it was to be hoped, pleasure her the more effectively. And meanwhile he could stir himself to fondle and ready her. She responded, to his increasing satisfaction.

And, in due course, his strategy proved a success for them both, and he rejoiced indeed when she cried out in abandon at last, and he could forget conscious discipline and care and let his natural vigour again take its course.

Thereafter they slept, replete, in each other's arms, aware only of love, mutual love.

15

The removal of the court to Edinburgh duly took place in mid-May, a tiresome and prolonged business for those responsible – which did not include Alexander, who felt no need to concern himself with such boring matters. He certainly was not going to accompany the slow-moving procession of folk, goods and gear to the city. Kings were not for such. When David asserted that he felt constrained to travel with the lengthy cavalcade, the boy was put in a quandary. Either he had to back down, or go on without his friend. His obstinate streak prevailed, and he rode on ahead with Robert de Ros and a small escort. It was the first time that he had made a journey without his chosen mentor.

It took three days to get all to Edinburgh. There they found David's cousin, the Earl Patrick of Dunbar, duly installed as keeper of the great castle. He was not David's favourite relative, a moody, prideful young man who seemed to bear a general grudge at life. They had not expected him to take his unanticipated appointment as keeper as one demanding his personal presence therein, the usual custom being to use a deputy-keeper, save for special occasions; but he seemed to have taken up residence, and in the fortress's best quarters – not that these were in any way magnificent.

Finding accommodation for all in that stern rock-top citadel was no easy matter, and productive of many complaints. Roxburgh had been infinitely more commodious and comfortable. It was decided that much of the so-called court should be found lodgings in the town, including Bishop Clement. There were twin gatehouse towers, and although one was essential for the guard and the manning of the drawbridge and portcullis, David took over the other, its three storeys providing a circular chamber on each floor, the basement to serve as an eating-room or tiny hall, the top floor Alexander's bedroom, and the middle one for himself and Margaret. The idle garrison was set to work to clean up all, and find plenishings. The young Queen, with de Ros and her lady, was installed meantime above the armoury. Improvements would have to be made. It was notable that the Comyns had more or less taken over the Abbey of Holyrood, down at the other end of the town, considerably better premises for living in. Earl Patrick's men-at-arms and theirs had already come to blows, it transpired.

It all hardly seemed to constitute a change for the better; but they would no doubt manage to remedy matters. As it happened, David and Margaret were so happy with each other that they were nowise inclined to grumble; and Alexander revelled in the wonderful views from his tower-top and was not overmuch concerned with creature comfort anyway. What Queen Margery thought of it all, after her father's splendid palaces in England, was not divulged.

They had a visitor that very first day, in the person of Chancellor de Gamelyn, who came in his capacity as secretary to the Privy Council, with a sheaf of papers, deeds, orders, charters and the like for Alexander to sign and seal. And he brought a new Great Seal, to emphasise the change in government and the King's enhanced authority, the former small seal Durward had made for the boy now superseded. This was now symbolically broken. Gamelyn was carefully respectful, courteous, helpful – but somehow managed to give the impression that *he* was in charge of all, not the monarch or his attendants. Margaret, who was not apt to be critically disposed, was confirmed in her opinion that he was the man to watch and beware of. But he did promise to have better furnishings and effects sent up to the castle. And he offered to find Bishop Clement quarters in Greyfriars Monastery.

He brought surprising news, too. Durward had left the country. He had gone to France, of all things, to join King Louis' crusade. The reasons behind this extraordinary move were unclear, but presumably it was to curry favour with the Vatican again, and the French King, possibly even to pleasure King Henry himself, who was interesting himself, at a suitable distance, in this new crusading venture.

So at least the danger of civil war in Scotland seemed to be lifted meantime. And as though to emphasise the fact, the Earls of Menteith and Buchan had left Holyrood for their northern territories, leaving only Mar in Edinburgh. That man was not the brightest of the trio; and it seemed obvious that Gamelyn was considered well able to guide him.

That young former college tutor was on the way, in fact, to becoming the true ruler of the land, the power behind the regency, Margaret feared. David, considering it, was inclined to wonder whether that would be so ill a situation? For clearly Gamelyn was able, clever and far-sighted – better perhaps for the realm than these sword-ready earls?

Inevitably, when they had been only two days at Edinburgh, Alexander was clamouring to be taken to Luffness, or at least to Aberlady Bay, his idea of heaven – even though this was not the wildfowling season. It suited David well enough, for already he was beginning to wonder how he was going to fill in his time, roosting up in this fortress. An active man by nature, being cooped up on a rock summit was not for him; nor indeed was city life either.

So, only four days after their arrival, the trio were on the road again, heading eastwards, past Holyrood Abbey and round the base of the dramatic hill of Arthur's Seat or Craig – which Alexander declared he must climb very soon – and on down the coast of Scotwater, or Firth of Forth, to cross Esk at Musselburgh and so on past Salt Preston and Cockenzie, to Seton. There David called upon his old friend and associate, Alexander Seton, glad that they could now see more of each other – and prepared to confront his over-friendly sister, armoured in his own new married status. To his surprise, however, he discovered that she had certainly not pined long for him, but had indeed beaten him to it, being now wed to his other friend, Dundas of that Ilk, and living near Queen Margaret's Ferry. So much for enduring passions.

Seton, happy to see them, rode on with them to Aberlady, able to inform his liege-lord that it had been a great winter for the geese, with more thousands overhead than he could ever remember before – which drew forth the comment that the boy wished that he had been there instead of wasting his time down at York, England; although, of course, he had

236

attained to knighthood there, which was something, marriage not being mentioned. He said that he would make Seton a knight one of these days, if he liked?

The Lady Elizabeth greeted her elder son with a mixture of her restrained affection and less-than-restrained warnings. He had been most unwise in marrying as he had done, and need only look for trouble. Even if the Comyns did not take steps to undo the union, up-jumped adventurers as they were, Alan Durward was by no means finished yet, let him remember. He would be back, nothing surer – unless the Saracens got him, which she continually prayed for – and might well have other plans for his wife's half-sister. He would now also be further-ben with the Pope of Rome than ever, after his crusading, and if he could get his wife legitimised he could also get Margaret's marriage annulled – although he might think it cheaper just to have David disposed of one night. To all of which her son shook an exasperated head. Her reception of Margaret, in consequence, was markedly cool, although that young woman tried her effective best to be friendly.

John de Lindsay had shot up noticeably even since last they had seen him, and he and Alexander were quickly deep in consultation on shared interests. The first priority, of course, was to visit down into the bay, even though there would be no fowling at this time. The geese had all left for their summer haunts in the frozen north, and it was breeding season for the ducks and other wildfowl. But Alexander had always wanted to go on beyond where they were apt to do their shooting, out to the mouth of the great bay, a mile and more further, to the dune country and the two-mile-long sand-bar, where the roar of the waves competed with the gabble of the roosting geese of a winter's night. So, nothing would do but that they must set off for the tidelands and saltings without delay, Alexander, John, David and Seton, leaving Margaret to try to improve her relationship with her new mother-in-law.

The tide was half in but ebbing, and they were able to save much plowtering through salt-marsh and pools by most of the way walking on the firm sand-edging of the tideline proper, a progress which set up many redshanks, oyster-catchers, pairs of mallard and teal, and flocks of dunlin, sanderling and other small waders, to Alexander's excitement, John instructing him on the recognition of the various species. But as they got ever further out, the barrier of sand-hills, to their half-right ahead, more and more held the boy's attention. He had had no idea that sand could pile up so high into a miniature mountain range, extending for a mile and more eastwards, to end in the rocky cliffs of a headland. David explained that this long line of dunes had been created by windblown sand, off the wide bar, on the prevailing westerly winds, with marram-grass seeding itself on the slopes, this catching and holding more sand, so that the hills grew yearly in bulk and height and numbers. Alexander then demanded why the bar itself did not grow less, in losing all that sand, to be told that it must be replenished by sand washed up from the bed of the firth itself, a dozen miles wide – an answer which did not entirely satisfy the royal enquirer.

When they reached the first of the dunes, Alexander demanded a race to the top, through the long rustling marram grass, his breath coming short in consequence of the steepness and soft sand, as he exclaimed at the rabbits popping and bolting all around them. Could they not come out here and shoot rabbits with their crossbows, the monarch asked, when there was no fowling? That would demand very expert shooting, he was told.

But at the top of their dune all was forgotten in the prospect which opened before them. Below the sandhills stretched fully a mile of golden beach, wide and fair, unsullied by rock or stone or reef, enticing, along which the waves broke in rolling majesty, this eventually reaching a distant thrusting point of small cliffs round which the breakers crashed. Westwards, the sand-bar, drying out now, could be seen to be almost half a mile wide, stretching right across the mouth of the bay, the roosting-place for the goose thousands. Even Alexander was lost for words.

Not for long, of course. Soon he was racing down to that splendid beach, shouting aloud, to the tide's edge, suggesting that they should wade; and when this was met with adult objections, plunging into the water, boots and all, challenging the waves – and being warned that he would have uncomfortable walking back, in consequence.

They went to the end of the long beach, picking up a great variety of shells, explored the headland and its coves and inlets; and turning back, the boys insisted on clambering up and down the score of sand-dune summits, whilst their elders contented themselves with the level strand. The long tramp back along the bay proper's tidal edge thereafter was admittedly something of a trudge, but Alexander made no complaint despite his water-sodden footwear.

Delighted with his day's discoveries, the boy was in a state of elation. Why could they not live here at Luffness, instead of in that gloomy Edinburgh Castle, he demanded? That would be far better. When assured that the regents would never consider such a thing, he asserted that if he was the King he ought to be able to live where he liked in his kingdom. He retailed to Margaret all that she had missed by not accompanying them to the dune country, but promised that he would take her there again soon. And in his enthusiasm he announced that he was going to make a knight of his friend Johnnie, who had been his guide this day.

David had to put a damper on such notion, pointing out that his brother was too young and had yet done nothing to deserve such honour. It would cause offence to others more worthy. One day, perhaps. But Alexander remembered he had been given the accolade so that he could bestow it on others of note. Only a knight could make a knight, so he made a demonstration of his authority by calling on Pate to fetch a sword, and there and then bestowed knighthood on an astonished and uneasy Alexander Scton, forgetting the exact wording but banging down the blade on the shoulders effectively enough.

When, after a meal, they left for the return to Edinburgh in the early evening, it seemed that Margaret had made some progress with her mother-in-law, for she received a farewell kiss, brief and all but grudgingly, but spontaneous – which much pleased David. Alexander besought Pate Dunbar to come and lodge with them at Edinburgh Castle, where his half-brother and namesake, the Earl Patrick, was now keeper; but David had to veto this also, pointing out that Pate was much needed here at Luffness to steward the baronies. Moreover, the Earl Patrick might not approve, in the circumstances. However, the new Sir Alexander Seton, when they left him at Seton Palace, en route, acceded to a similar request to join the court at Edinburgh. Uncomfortable at having these days so often to hold back his young liege-lord's enthusiasms, David heartily endorsed this and suggested some suitable appointment should be found for his friend.

On the onward ride of ten miles to the city, Alexander took up the idea with his usual enthusiasm, and came out with sundry official-sounding styles, none of which, for one reason or another, seemed appropriate to his advisers. It was then that David voiced a notion which had occurred to him more than once since their visit to the English court at York. At Alexander's coronation, and at his first parliament, the High Sennachie had ordered the arrangements, acting as chief usher. But that old man had died, and no successor had been appointed as yet. It was an ancient Celtic office, admittedly, and a worthy one; but it was not entirely suited to this present age, the reciting of genealogies and the recounting of traditional stories and legends of bygone ancestors being hardly what was frequently required. At this last parliament, he himself had had to act almost as usher and master-of-ceremonies, ordering entries and exits, precedences and the like. But in England they had a chief herald, under the Earl Marshal, whose duties included the official ushering, precedence-ordering and the making of announcements; also other important concerns such as the issuing of coats of arms, in the King's name, the checking of heraldic styles and titles, the tracing of blood-lines, and so on. France and Flanders had similar officers, he understood. So perhaps Scotland should have something of the sort. And, of course, by royal appointment.

That was taken up at once, with acclaim. Make Sir Alexander Seton chief herald.

David proceeded a little more slowly. They surely would not want any slavish copying of the English model? Something typically and uniquely Scots, such as would cover the crown's granting of baronial status, decisions as to clan chiefs and the chieftains of septs, proper marks of cadency on coat-armour and the like. The English chief herald was not a royal officer of state but held his appointment from their Earl Marshal. Better if a Scots one was a direct officer of the crown, acting in the King's own name, all supporting and substantiating Alexander's own increased authority. King's Herald, or King's Officer of Arms.

"Why not King of Arms?" Margaret put in. "Crown Officer of Arms, or Herald or Usher, sounds too long, awkward. Royal Usher means less, does not convey the importance of the officer, or his direct appointment from the King."

Alexander looked doubtful. "But *I* am the King," he objected. "Sir Alexander Seton could not be a King."

"King of Arms would establish his links with *you*, Alex. No other could appoint a King of Arms. Not your Knight Marischal Keith. Or a regent. Or any other earl."

"I agree," David said. "That would be a good style. Significant. *Your* officer. So through him you would have say over so much. Much that others might covet to use. King of Arms sounds better than King's Herald. Heralds wear tabards, loose over-tunics lacking sleeves. The English one has on his the three Leopards of Plantagenet, quartered with the arms of their Earl Marshal. Yours, Alex, should have the royal Lion Rampant, red on gold."

"Yes, yes – that would be good. The Lion King of Arms! Shall we spell it with an i or a y? My grandsire William always spelt it with a y."

"Use you that, then. Y let it be. Lyon King of Arms sounds splendid," Margaret approved. "Think you Alexander Seton will accept the appointment?"

"Why not? He should be glad to," David said. "He has a good, strong voice for making the announcements. And has a kind of dignity to him. He will be much honoured, I would say."

"We will have a, a . . . what was it you called it? The coat? A tabard, yes. Made with a big red lion on it."

"Two, Alex – one front, one back . . ."

Settling all that brought them almost back to Edinburgh.

It was strange how long those summer days in Edinburgh seemed to be, for David de Lindsay at least. There were the same number of hours of daylight as at Roxburgh, but somehow they seemed to take longer to pass. It was undoubtedly partly the fortress atmosphere which caused it, rather like being shut up in a prison; that and being enclosed also by a city. He had never known city life, and the proximity of so many people, so many houses, the congestion of streets and wynds and smells. However widespread the views from the castle, this constricted feeling was always there, for him. Alexander complained of it too, and if he had had his way, every few days they would have been off to Luffness and Aberlady Bay. Margaret did not seem to feel it so much. Perhaps it was a male problem, the need for physical activity. They could climb Arthur's Seat, of course, and did frequently. Also the other hills close by, of Calton, Craigmillar, Blackford and Braid, although these were minor heights by comparison and as such could be ridden up, so that Alexander found them little challenge. Not far to the south were the Pentland Hills, a major range, scores of miles of them, and these constituted a magnet for the boy also. But the Regent Mar frowned on such constant expeditions by the monarch, for one reason or another, declaring that he might be endangered, assaulted, even kidnapped, by enemies or broken men, and insisted on adequate escorts of the royal guard – which much impaired any satisfaction. For the same reason, wandering about the town streets was not encouraged for the sovereign, and friendly contact with the populace disapproved of, Alexander's subjects as they were.

So a mixture of constraints and lack of freedom tended to prevail.

Alexander Seton, gladly assuming the style and tabard of Lyon King of Arms, proved to be a help in this as in other matters, for he had a fondness for indoor games, something left out of David, and was able to entertain his liege-lord, sometimes even Queen Margery, whiling away many a dull hour.

They saw quite a lot of John de Gamelyn, and practically nothing of the Earls of Mar and Menteith. The Chancellor was always civil, courteous, but left none in doubt as to who was in command of the situation. In effect, although not in name, *he* was the regent, extraordinary a situation as this was for so young and hitherto unimportant a man, a cleric of no eminence, and a bastard into the bargain. It was not long before, without actually saying so, he began to make it clear that his masters, the Comyn earls, were not happy with David de Lindsay's so evident influence with the young monarch. Quiet hints were dropped that such influence must be used to help the regency, never to hinder it; that the boy should be guided towards proper co-operation; and that his new increased authority was nominal rather than actual. Veiled hints also were given, however subtly, that any contrary attitude would result in de Lindsay being removed from the royal presence. It was indeed indicated that more attention to his new position as Justiciar-Depute of Lothian, and less of Cup-Bearer and personal adviser to the monarch, was advisable.

This troubled David and Margaret increasingly, needless to say. It was unthinkable that they should be separated from Alexander; but with power concentrated now in Comyn hands, and their domination of the Privy Council, undoubtedly they could effect this. So it behoved them to go warily, at least to seem to co-operate, in some degree. Bishop Clement was not much help, ageing noticeably and becoming ever more of a cipher as regent, a sick, old man. So, although on the face of it, David, Margaret, de Ros, Seton and to a lesser degree Earl Patrick of Dunbar remained in charge of the sovereign, their positions were clearly very much under review. And undoubtedly Gamelyn was the reviewer. When, for instance, it was suggested that perhaps too frequent visits to Luffness Castle and Seton Palace were inadvisable, as possibly productive of unsuitable attitudes and behaviour in the King of Scots, David could not ignore the warning as he would have wished. For undoubtedly the regency and the council could implement a decision to have him dismissed, whatever Alexander said.

So they trod cautiously. It was no way to pass a summer.

Strangely, aid in some degree did come, in this situation, and from an unexpected source – in no less a person than Simon de Montfort, Earl of Leicester, King Henry's brother-in-law. He arrived at Edinburgh unannounced in late August, with a Sir Geoffrey de Langley, whom Henry apparently had sent up to replace de Balliol as a guardian of the young Queen, Balliol's ineffectiveness being as obvious as were his absences. Presumably de Ros had found ways of sending messages and reports to Henry as to conditions prevailing in Scotland, and calling for improvement. And this was the result.

Earl Simon's arrival produced prompt reactions, for none could underestimate *his* influence and the authority he represented. Mar, as well as Gamelyn, was up at the castle within the hour; and the Earl of Menteith was sent for from his Highland Line territories.

The English mission was basically to emphasise King Henry's claims to a say in the governance of his son-in-law's Scotland, through the terms of the marriage-settlement of his daughter. Obviously it was considered that this was being overlooked if not ignored by the present regency. They had heard, in England, and now Earl Simon saw with his own eyes, the unsuitable conditions the young Queen was having to endure and the restrictions imposed on her husband. This must be improved forthwith, he declared. Then there was the old story of Borderland raiding and rapine, which was to have ceased under the settlement terms. Nothing appeared to have been done about this by the regents, indeed conditions grew worse, and Henry's Northumbrian and Cumbrian barons were in constant outcry. This problem and cause of conflict between the two realms would never be solved until the borderline itself was clearly defined. At present large stretches of it were not, especially in the Middle and West Marches, great areas of hill-country claiming to be either in England or in Scotland, or in neither, allowing utter lawlessness to prevail in consequence. This must be rectified, and English commissioners would be appointed to meet with Scots, to demarcate the boundaries, as a joint endeavour. Moreover, there was the matter of the crusade contributions which the princes of Christendom had agreed to provide, for the present crusade King Louis of France was to lead. Scotland had been committed to subscribing by Durward, as regent, but no moneys had been forthcoming. Now King Henry, who had at one time intended to join the crusade himself, and finding that now impossible because of troubles in his French territories of Guienne, was sending a large contribution in men and moneys; and as adviser and Lord Paramount to the King of Scots, was demanding a contribution of one-twentieth of the ecclesiastical revenues of the Scottish Church, this with the backing and authority of the Archbishop of York, metropolitan of the north.

This last demand, to be sure, much perturbed the present Scots regency – although Earl Simon privately admitted to Robert de Ros that his Plantagenet brother-in-law scarcely expected the money, or all of it, to be forthcoming, making the demand more as a gesture to please the King of France, the Pope and his own churchmen. So the Primate, Bishop de Birnam, would have to be sent for, from St Andrews. Meantime, Mar and Gamelyn agreed that the royal quarters and conditions should be improved, the Queen be better provided for, and be allotted personal revenues. Also the border perambulation acceded to.

When David de Birnam arrived, he was of course wholly against any mulcting of Church revenues, one-twentieth or other, denying the archbishop's claims of authority to demand it. He would urge the College of Bishops to make some contribution to the crusading fund, but that would be an entirely voluntary gesture.

Simon de Montfort, a reasonable man however formidable, was prepared to accept all this as the best that could be achieved, in the circumstances. But he warned that a careful watch would be kept on the Scottish situation, and any failure to implement what was being promised would produce serious results for Scotland. With that he departed, leaving the Englishman, de Langley, behind, a character who did not commend himself to any of them, including de Ros.

So Alexander, David and Margaret found their conditions considerably improved, both within the fortress and in their freedom of movement. They were again able to make their expeditions, not only more frequently but without always being saddled with a large escort of armed retainers. The young Queen was allotted the old palace of Dunfermline, in Fothrif, across Forth, as a dowry-house, with part of the revenues of the sainted Queen Margaret's abbey there, as most suitable. Thither visits were paid on occasion. But although other jaunts, such as riding in the Pentland Hills, were popular with Alexander, it was Luffness and Aberlady Bay which drew them most frequently, so that they all but beat a sixteen-mile trail thither, staying overnight when the goose-flighting season commenced.

It had never occurred to David de Lindsay that the King of England would have come to their rescue.

16

David's appointment as Justiciar-Depute of Lothian took some time to become anything more than nominal. Sir Thomas de Normanville was apparently perfectly capable of carrying out his duties without assistance, and David himself had no particular ambitions in that direction. The thing had been more or less an impulsive demonstration on Alexander's part. It was Chancellor Gamelyn who eventually made some reality of the situation, curiously enough, by deciding that the Justiciar of Lothian and the Merse, and his deputy, were the right persons to lead the Scots commission on the desired demarcation of the borderline, at least as far as the East and Middle Marches were concerned, the West March being more or less reserved for appointees of the Lord of Galloway. It is possible that Gamelyn saw this as one means of getting David a little more detached from the young Alexander's presence.

In the spring, then, Gamelyn brought de Normanville to the castle for a meeting and conference, with word that the English commissioners were now appointed, de Ros one of them. De Normanville proved to be a friendly enough character, of middle years, massive of build and with a strange barking laugh which he used frequently. David felt that they would probably get on satisfactorily, and since de Ros was his brother-in-law, the boundary negotiations with their English opposite numbers might not be too difficult.

Gamelyn had had maps of the area produced, these leaving much detail to the imagination, indeed *being* largely imaginary, and using these, gave them their instructions. There were no problems, starting from the east, for the first twenty miles or so, for the River Tweed was the recognised boundary there. But thereafter, at Birgham, soon after Wark, the border became indeterminate, swinging away from the river to the south-west and into the Cheviot hillfoots country. Decisions here could be controversial indeed, for these valleys of the Bowmont, Kale, College and lesser waters constituted, as it were the back-door and hidden routes into the two kingdoms, for invaders, Border reivers, drovers of cattle-herds, travelling friars and the like, who wished, for one reason or another, to avoid the official crossing-places at Berwick, Carter Bar, Deadwater and Kielder; and there would be English pressure to use these to *their* strategic advantage. And some of the Northumbrian barons were hungry for more land. There would probably be attempts to place the boundary where these could benefit, at the expense of the Scots land-holders. In the high Cheviots themselves it was not so important, barren moorlands; but the English would think the same. The resultant border, therefore, would be a matter of barter and bargain. It would not be apt to present any very straight or consistent line.

All this David could have guessed for himself. He was in fact quite looking forward to the venture – the more especially when, later, de Ros declared that, since *he* was appointed one of the English representatives, they should all make his Wark Castle their headquarters, as would be convenient. And why not bring the young King and Queen with them, with Margaret? It would be a welcome change from Edinburgh, and something of an adventure for the boy. The regency could hardly refuse to let them go, for was not he, de Ros, the girl's guardian and King Henry's adviser to her husband? This suggestion was adopted, with acclaim, by all concerned, however unenthusiastic was Gamelyn when he heard.

It was late May, and the weather suitable for the perambulation, when word reached them that the other English commissioners, Sir John Russell and Sir Thomas de Clare, brother of the Earl of Gloucester, were ready to play their part, and could be at Wark in a few days' time. So all was prepared for departure. Since it seemed that there were to be three English representatives, another Scot was called for, to equalise, and young Alexander's insistence that this should be his new Lyon King of Arms met with no opposition. It was something almost like a family group, therefore, which set off for Maxton, in the Merse, to pick up de Normanville.

This was not quite so far to go as to Roxburgh, Maxton being near to St Boswells, on mid-Tweed; and with no laggards in the party, they reached there in five hours' riding. Its castle proved to be very much another waterside one, standing high on a knoll where the steep ravine of a burn reached the great river, with its village on the rising slopes of Longnewton Forest behind. Here they were well entertained overnight, meeting the ailing brother Waleron. Next morning they moved on down Tweed, passing Roxburgh and Kelso, and twenty miles to the ford over to Wark.

They found the English commissioners awaiting them, with what seemed an over-large retinue of assistants. Sir John Russell was an elderly man, haughty and inclining to corpulence, a seemingly odd choice for the task in hand; but Sir Thomas de Clare was young and active enough, proving to be very much a lady's man, according to Lady de Ros, who seemed relieved to see her husband. Margaret, younger and so good-looking, promptly became the object of his attentions. Both Englishmen were surprised to find the King of Scots and his Queen in the party, needless to say.

That evening the six commissioners got round a table with their maps – the English ones being no more accurate and detailed than Gamelyn's. An animated discussion, almost argument, developed practically from the beginning, with differing opinions as to even where the borderline started, once it left Tweed. The village of Carham, two miles upstream from Wark, on the English side, was the Scots notion of where it commenced; but the English declared that it should be over a mile further west, where the Redden Burn entered the river – which of course would give England a slice of good fertile land right away, to Scotland's loss. But de Ros could not side with his Scots friends on this, declaring that this area was really an extension of Wark Common and so should be in England. De Normanville could not assert that it was part of the Hadden property, even though Redden Burn rose therein. And so they lost the first round, as it were, even before they set foot on the ground. David perceived that this was going to be a disputacious exercise indeed, calling for quick thinking, anticipation and determination – as well as patience.

In the morning, they made quite a sizeable company for the start, with the English auxiliaries, six of them, added to the commissioners themselves – and the King of Scots announcing that he was coming too. Although David warned him that he could well be bored by the proceedings and that there could be unseemly argument at times, none were in a position to deny the monarch's attendance, for after all it was his kingdom's limits which were being defined. Margaret did not think to accompany them.

So they rode the two miles to beyond Carham, where all had to agree that the line should leave the Tweed and strike southwards, opposite Scots Birgham. But in half a mile, reaching the Redden Burn, which here ran almost parallel with the Tweed, the first dispute developed. The English said that the line should cross the burn and proceed more or less straight on; but there were cattle grazing here and some way eastwards, belonging to the nearby Scots farmery of Nottylees, and de Normanville declared that this ground could not just be taken from the farmer, de Ros agreeing that this Nottylees grazing had always extended half a mile eastwards, till it met his own Wark Common. Russell objected that they could not make special enclaves and loops to suit individual farms' pastures; it was the borders of kingdoms they were concerned with. But this first test was important, the Scots felt, and insisted that old and established boundaries were not to be ignored. David tactfully suggested that they should go and consult the farmer or his laird. De Ros said that the farm belonged to Hadden of that Ilk, who was after all his neighbour and on friendly terms. Their objective, in this exercise, was to bring peace to the Borderland, not cause offence, and bickering in the future. *He* would advise making a bend in the line as far as Wark Common, the bounds of which were well marked. Russell and de Clare did not agree; but since the three Scots did, that made four to two, palpable decision. So the second round went to Scotland, to Alexander's hand-clapping and English snorts.

They rode the perimeter of the half-mile-sided enclave,

where de Ros pointed out the earthen dyke which marked the edge of Wark Common, and the assistants and henchmen were ordered to dismount and gather stones to make little cairns to establish the border, Alexander assisting in this cheerfully. Fortunately there were stones aplenty.

To the south, however, this Wark Common extended further to the west, and although this projected into any straightish line from the first established boundary, the Scots could not object to it seeming to make something of a salient into *their* territory. A mile of this brought them to another quite large stream, running again east and west, the Pressen Burn, and here further debate took place, the Englishmen holding their maps to show the lines bending westwards along it, the Scots claiming it as straight on southwards and uphill. De Ros again had to agree that he had always recognised the property of Hoselaw, just to the west, with its loch, as in Scotland. His two English colleagues were in a disadvantage here, not being local, whilst he was. They could not disprove it, save by referring to their so vague maps – even though they eyed their fellow-commissioner sourly. So the line went straight on, with little cairns to prove it. All agreed that these cairns must be enlarged and added to.

The quite high summit of Camp Hill directly ahead was the next problem to be presented. Although not steep, it was bare and stony, scarcely valuable land. Should the line go round it to the east or to the west, or over the top? De Normanville thought that it might be good policy to make a gesture on this one, and proposed that they might accept the line round it to the west. So Camp Hill went into England. Alexander awkwardly asked whose sheep those were grazing upon it, an uncomfortable question left unanswered.

Thereafter they were on to lofty open moorland, indeed de Ros said that it was known as Wideopen Muir. Many sheep and a few cattle were scattered over its expanse. Where the boundary should be was anyone's guess. But beyond this was a still higher ridge system, quite long, with three distinct summits. The one to the east was called Bowmont, or Beaumont, Hill, and was clearly in England; that to the west was Venchen Hill and as certainly in Scotland. The middle

251

one was Castle Law, so called after a Pictish fort on its summit. And since the Picts were Scots, or their ancestors, the argument was that this also must be in Scotland. Grudgingly this was allowed, and the line went over the ridge between it and Bowmont Hill.

Now the quite deep and large valley of the Bowmont Water opened before them, a sizeable river, and they headed down to this, the Scots prepared for further dispute, for though the Bowmont *rose* in Scotland, many miles to the south-west, it was in fact a tributary of the English River Till. However, there was less trouble than might have been anticipated, for the admittedly English hamlet of Shotton sat in mid-valley, under Shotton Hill, yet the demesne farmery of Yetholm, a Scots lairdship of ancient standing, sat only a quarter-mile from it, upriver. So the line had to go across between the two. Ahead were now the steep, high ranges of the Cheviot Hills, proper.

They had by this time come eight miles from Tweed, and it was decided that this was sufficient for one day, especially as their followers were falling behind with their stone-gathering and cairn-building. They would leave their high hills start for the morrow.

The return was made to Wark Castle, Alexander announcing in a gleeful but penetrating whisper that Scotland had had the best of it, for sure.

Margaret was given an almost yard-by-yard account of it all that evening, in between fending off de Clare's gallantries and trying to soften Russell's frowns.

Next day's progress was very different, in more than just the scenery, in character and debate as well as in distance covered, this because they were now into the high hills, mountains by English standards, mile upon mile of jumbled heights, towering ridges and peaks, great scars and corries and deep hidden glens, empty, devoid of human habitation. How to plot a borderline through all this? After mounting that first soaring escarpment south of Shotton-on-Bowmont and gazing over the endless prospect of crests, hogsbacks and shadow-filled troughs and dips, seemingly to all infinity, the commissioners were at something of a loss as to how to begin. It was all just high wilderness, with nothing to guide them, even as to routes and preferences, save a recognition that, to reach the eventual recognised crossing-points of Carter Bar and Deadwater, they would have to head fairly consistently southwards. De Ros, with at least some awareness of it all, had brought with them today one of his own Wark shepherds, who had been reared at Shotton and who knew these hills from boyhood, at least for some distance. Also they had brought with them pack-horses laden with posts, stakes, to drive into the ground at given points, to save the delay of building cairns – which could be done on a later day.

Nevertheless, it was cairns which in the end guided them now, not their own little markers, but great well-built ancient mounds of stone which dotted the summit ridges here and there. These were no boundary marks but monuments, former Pictish burial-mounds, some still with standing-stones around them, the chiefs of those long-ago folk seeming to choose the most prominent heights for their interment, presumably as a matter of prestige, vying with each other for the most notable eminences. These cairns were hollow, chambered, according to their shepherd, the warriors laid therein, usually with valuables of a kind, ornaments and weapons – although many had been robbed, down the centuries.

For want of a better guiding-line, therefore, they decided to use these cairns as identifying-posts, or such as stretched away southwards, the hilly territory on either side being of no particular value to either interest. So without the previous day's disputation, they rode up and down those wild uplands, often quite difficult going for horses, driving in the odd stake here and there, but in fact more interested in the wide prospects and what they saw than in delineating national boundaries, Alexander happy and vociferous, David wishing that he had brought Margaret along, who would have enjoyed this exploration.

In fair harmony, then, they rode mile after mile southwards, by a great succession of high hills which their shepherd named as Coldsmouth, Great Hamblet, White Law, Black Hag and the Schil, this last the highest, until they came to a dramatic, precipice-sided corrie or cleuch, where the College Water flowed down to join the lower Bowmont, the oddly named Hen Hole, with great Cheviot itself just ahead.

They had passed only one habitation, save for the dead, in all those dozen upheaved miles, the lonely shieling of Halterburn Head, a summertime grazing location for the Yetholm community, and so definitely Scots. They decided to make the summit of Cheviot the focal point of their line for this stretch, even though this involved something of a diversion eastwards; but it seemed an obvious landmark. Satisfied with a mighty day's riding, not so much in distance as in heights and mounted challenges, they turned back, more amiable towards each other than yesterday.

The next day was wet and unpleasant, followed by a Sunday. So that it was two days before another exploration was made – days in which Seton's aptitude for indoor games was appreciated, even though de Clare's ideas ran on rather different lines. On the Monday, however, the sun shone again, and Margaret this time made one of the party.

They had to recommence at the summit of Cheviot itself, and to spare themselves the up and down journey they had made to it previously, they took a more round-about but so much easier route by the drove-road up the Bowmont Water, by Yetholm's two villages, by Attonburn and Mow, to Cocklawfoot, high amongst the hills still but not difficult riding. From this hub of burns and former Pictish forts and settlements, it was only three climbing miles up the Cheviot Burn to their starting-point. They had picked up a couple of Yetholm shepherds to aid them.

Margaret was enthralled by the tremendous spread and challenge of the scene from Cheviot, Alexander now adopting a proprietory tone towards it all, for her edification.

Even from their inadequate maps, the commissioners had perceived, over the weekend, that, while Cheviot's summit certainly should be important on their borderline, it was really considerably further east than was the general trend of this to bring them to the recognised crossing-place of Carter Bar, which lay a dozen miles south of Jedburgh. So a major turning westwards was now necessary. Still, however, they used hilltops as their guides, and were able to make more or less straight lines from one to another, circling peat-bogs, ravines and cliffs, on what was basically high plateau-land, all amongst the yittering curlews, the loping blue hares, and the grouse which flew off on down-bent wings, a quite exhilarating exercise. The summits of Score Head – which Alexander called Sore Head – an unnamed peak which they called King's Seat in the boy's honour, and another, a couple of miles on, which, to keep the English happy, they named Russell's Cairn, all this they covered without argument. But thereafter dispute arose, with the Scots wishing to head south by an upland ancient track, actually called the Street, presumably of Roman origin, to the River Coquet, the English insisting that the Coquet was wholly an English river, so that its headwaters must be in England. There was a place called Coquet Head, and their line must head for that, westwards. No amount of comparison with the Bowmont situation would appease them, and since the land involved was really worthless, however spectacular, the Scots gave in, for the sake of future give-and-take.

So, by a further succession of peaks, with names like Beefstand Hill and Raeshaw Fell, they made for Coquet Head, leaving their marking-posts, eight more hilly miles.

Reaching the Coquet source, they found themselves on the great Roman road of Dere Street, with the green embankments of fortlets, these marching camps marching up all the way from Hadrian's Wall in Tynedale, a wonder indeed. But, tempting as it would be to follow this ancient highway southwards, that would not bring them to Carter Bar, the recognised meeting-place for the Scots and English Wardens of the Marches, and so undeniably on the border, another seven miles south-westwards. They could scarcely make a beeline thereto, in this terrain, but at least they were able to pick a hilltop route, following Pictish rather than Roman relics – and the Scots were able to win a sizeable slice of territory at Leithope, on account of those burial-cairns again.

At length, at Carter Bar at last, above the loch of Catcleuch on the English side, they called a halt, for they were now a long way from Wark, and their mounts tiring from the rough going. But, happily, there was a small monkish hospice for travellers here, where they could obtain refreshment for the thirty-mile ride back, by Jedburgh and Kelso to Tweed, and by established roads.

Weary as they were when they reached Wark, Margaret declared that she had seldom enjoyed a ride so much.

That night, the commissioners all agreed that they had done enough for the time being. The next stage of the border definition could not be done from Wark, requiring a base perhaps forty or fifty miles to the south-west. Moreover, their cairn-builders had more than enough to do meantime. They would meet again after harvest-time for another venture. On the whole, both sides were fairly satisfied with their efforts, even Sir John Russell comparatively affable. Queen Margery was loth to leave Wark, for she had got on well with the de Ros daughters of her own age.

The Scots left de Ros himself at home, for an overdue spell with his wife and family, and returned to Maxton and then Edinburgh, de Normanville assuring David that he would be summoning him shortly to assist him in a justice-ayres circuit of Lothian and the Merse, for their real duties as justiciars.

17

Margaret was pregnant. Great was the delight. To be a father much appealed to David, to have a son of his own – it did not seem to occur to him that it might be a daughter – and Margaret saw it as fulfilment of their love. Alexander was reaching an age to be interested in the rudiments and procedure of it all, somewhat embarrassingly so, desiring as it were chapter and verse, and declaring rather scornfully that he did not think that Margery would ever be able to produce a baby. When could it be put to the test?

This rejoicing was welcome, for they had returned from the Borders to the sad news that Bishop de Birnam had died suddenly at St Andrews. The Primate's departure was a major loss to the realm, but also to Alexander and those close to him, for he had been a friend and a loyal supporter as well as an able leader of the churchmen. Moreover, unfortunately, his demise set off a dire schism in the Church, which had its inevitable effect on the rule of the kingdom. The canons of St Andrews elected Robert de Stoutville, Dean of Dunkeld, to be Bishop of St Andrews and therefore Primate, whilst the majority of the bishops and mitred abbots wanted Archdeacon Abel, the late King's chaplain and friend, who had acted ambassador and was a man of authority. So there was trouble, with appeals to the Pope. Indeed Master Abel went off to Rome in person, to plead his cause. Meanwhile the Scots Church was without a Primate, a situation leading to much confusion.

De Ros returned to Edinburgh after a month, and it was rather extraordinary how glad all at court were to see him back, this English lord who could so easily have been objected to as King Henry's nominee to interfere in the affairs of Scotland. But as well as being a friendly, cheerful and able individual, he was proving to be more Scots than English in his attitudes and preferences, not so strange perhaps, with his royal Scots mother, illegitimate daughter of William the Lyon, his Scots wife, and living where he did. He, in fact, demonstrated his usefulness by getting rid of that other Englishman at the Scots court, Geoffrey de Langley, an objectionable character who had been making a nuisance of himself during de Ros's absence, and who was now sent packing unceremoniously. Whether, in fact, de Ros had the authority to do this was doubtful, and King Henry might well be displeased. However, Henry Plantagenet himself had left for Guienne, in France, that August, with a small army, and so was otherwise preoccupied, leaving Simon de Montfort of Leicester to manage England for him.

That summer David de Lindsay became a practising judge, after a few lessons on the business from de Normanville, indeed taking over the justiciary duties in Lothian while the other attended to the Merse and Border area. Hearing causes and pleas and making judgments was not entirely new to David, of course, since he had had to sit in on his own baronial courts; but these were informal and minor affairs compared with the justiciary courts, where much more serious offences, crimes and causes were tried, and graver sentences meted out. He hated having to condemn to death or even to mutilations and public lashings, the which he had to attend; but these were laid down by law for certain felonies, and he had no choice. He was glad that he did not have de Normanville's territory, where hangings were all too frequent, on account of endemic border feuding, reiving and rapine. Sometimes Alexander accompanied David to these Lothian courts, as an educational exercise, for one day he would be called upon to administer justice on the grand scale.

More enjoyably, they were able to spend much time at Luffness, and in the warm summer weather delighted in excursions out to the sand-dune country and beaches of outer Aberlady Bay, where swimming, sand-modelling, shell-gathering and other simple pursuits were the order of the day, Alexander interested to observe and comment upon the unclothed Margaret's swelling of figure. He was also introduced to the local sport of spearing flounders in the shallows, using the toes of bare feet to locate the fish, by feel, just below the sand surface, to some danger of spearing the said toes in the process.

In the autumn, another perambulation of the borderline was made, based this time on Bonchester on Rule Water, Margaret remaining behind. Her delivery was expected around Christmas-tide.

On their return from this duty, which defined the border as far as the Deadwater Pass and Larriston Fells, leaving only a short final stretch of some score of miles to the bounds of the Middle and West Marches to complete, it was to learn strange news. King Henry was having difficulties in gaining possession of his territories in Gascony, and Alan Durward, domiciled presently in France, had gone to his aid. He had apparently been well received by the Plantagenet, glad of help. These tidings struck an ominous note in Scots ears. Durward gaining English gratitude and approval could once again perhaps menace Scotland's peace.

This recognition had its effect on the court at Edinburgh, and not happily. For the Comyns reacted. With King Henry out of his country and Durward now in his favour, the latter's supporters and former associates in Scotland, who had been lying low these last years, might well begin to stir again, for almost certainly Durward would be sending them urgings to do so. As a consequence, there could be plots, preparations and preliminary moves. So precautionary measures were advisable. Amongst others, these included imposing restrictions again on the royal freedoms, in the name of safety and security. The King might well be assailed, captured, kidnapped and taken away to some remote fastness and held hostage until Durward's return, giving him a notable accession of strength. Alexander and his wife were safe in Edinburgh Castle; let them leave it seldom, and always under heavy guard.

This depressing development much spoiled the run-up to Yuletide, especially as regards the goose-shooting season, for that was an activity where close guarding was scarcely possible. David pleaded, but without success, and de Ros said that he would write to Simon, Earl of Leicester, declaring that the young Queen's conditions were deteriorating and that she was in fact all but a prisoner in Edinburgh Castle – a report which might have quite major results. But the Comyns, almost wholly through Gamelyn, were obdurate. The King's security was all-important. David de Lindsay could ride abroad where he would; but not the monarch nor his wife. Also, the regency dismissed Patrick, Earl of Dunbar, as keeper of the castle, considering him to be less than reliable, and appointed Sir Nicholas de Soules in his place, a stern individual who revelled in his new authority and became all but the royal gaoler.

So the Christmas of 1253 was a fairly joyless one for the court, although Alexander's friends did their best to improve the occasion. David, of course, was not a little preoccupied with Margaret's condition, nearing her time as she was. She kept well, fortunately, reasonably active and making no complaints; but she wished that the birth did not have to be in their gloomy, prison-like quarters in Edinburgh's fortress. She and David could admittedly have moved to Luffness or Seton, but that would have meant deserting Alexander. They remained in the castle.

After a fairly protracted labour but no complications, the required son was born early in the morning of Holy Innocents' Day, 28th December, to great rejoicing, giving a new dimension to the subdued Yuletide celebrations. By royal command, Alexander insisted that the infant be named after himself. It all made an auspicious start to 1254. And that itself was to be welcomed, for the chances for that year were otherwise less than auspicious. The scandal of the Church split over the primacy showed no signs of abating, despite word from Rome that the Vatican was accepting Archdeacon Abel as Bishop of St Andrews, this subject much dividing the nation as well as the clerics, and delaying necessary appointments. Patrick of Dunbar, incensed at his curt dismissal by the Comyns, joined forces with Bruce of Annandale, always the Comyns' enemy, to announce that Durward had been better in the regency than Menteith and Mar, urging that he should be brought back. And Alexander, the High Steward, surprised all by publicly agreeing with them. Others undoubtedly would follow this lead, including the anti-Abel clerics. So there was muttering and misgiving in the land that spring, not helped by the fact that Pope Innocent died suddenly, and it was not known whether his successor as Pontiff would support Abel or Stoutville.

Then, coinciding with young Alexander's thirteenth birthday, Henry Plantagenet, after another reverse for his army in France, actually summoned aid from Scotland. Needless to say this demand was ignored by the Comyns; but with Durward fighting at Henry's side, it was recognised that this was bound to strengthen that man's position, as regards Scotland. In fact, fairly soon thereafter, Henry returned to England, humiliated and resentful, and Durward with him, being granted a pension. Trouble loomed the nearer.

The new Pope, Alexander the Fourth, did accept Abel as Primate in Scotland, and the prelate came home, but a sick man. Allegedly to strengthen his position, Gamelyn got himself appointed as Archdeacon of St Andrews, a cunning move, so that he could now help to sway the Church, through the Primate, as he swayed the regency as Chancellor.

All this did not personally affect the little court at Edinburgh Castle, all but prisoners as they were therein now; but it did concern them. What worried them a deal more, however, was an unexpected order from Henry for Robert de Ros to relinquish his position of guardian to the young Queen and adviser to Alexander, and to return to England – this because he was being held partly responsible for the unsatisfactory conditions in which Henry's daughter was being kept, and his failure to persuade the Scots to send military aid to him in France. New guardians would be appointed.

There was much dismay at this on the part of de Ros's friends – and surprise but gratification when that man announced that he was going to ignore his monarch's commands and remain at the Scots court. He recognised that this might well have serious repercussions. He might even be declared outlaw and have his castle of Wark forfeited to the English crown. But he had come to the conclusion that he was now more Scots than English, and wished to remain on as part of Alexander's entourage. That thirteen-year-old cheerfully declared that he would find some suitable style and appointment for him. Meanwhile de Ros went off to Wark hurriedly, to make his arrangements there and bring back his wife and family to Edinburgh. Strangely enough, the Comyns approved of all this, or Gamelyn did, presumably seeing de Ros as a useful ally.

Meanwhile, Margaret's baby bloomed, flourished and developed into a chortling pink bundle, a joy to them all. And produced an unlooked-for situation, in that Margery became enamoured of the infant and began to spend much of her time with him, admiring him, playing to him on her lute, singing and ever seeking opportunity to take him up and cuddle him – the first real enthusiasm they had discerned in her. Alexander was a little put out, and announced that she should get a baby of her own. Growing up fast, he was developing into a well-made, vigorous youth, his masculinity unmistakable. For that matter, Margery, six months older and nearly fourteen, was herself showing signs of coming womanhood, with breasts beginning to appear – which did not go uncommented upon by her husband. Not that they engaged in any intimacies, as yet, and kept their own quarters of a night.

The problem of having two Alexanders in the family, as it were – three, if Seton was counted – was got over by all calling the baby by the name of Sander or Sandy.

No replacement arrived for de Ros from England. Henry Plantagenet had other matters on his mind. He was having trouble with many of his nobles, especially the northern ones, who resented his taxes on them, in money and men, to pay for his failed French venture – and also to pay, in gold, for his promised support for the King of France's crusade, the which was now in arrears. Also he was negotiating a financial arrangement with the new Pope, in order to have his son Edward appointed as King of Sicily, which seemed to be within the papal grant. Why he should desire this his lords did not know, but they were distinctly unco-operative. And it was said that Simon de Montfort himself was becoming increasingly out of sympathy with his brother-in-law. That it was the northern nobles who, without actually rising in rebellion, were the most disgruntled, suited de Ros, for it meant that Henry was the less likely to order any of them to take over Wark.

This de Ros situation, and Gamelyn's approval, did have the effect of ameliorating the royal confinement in Edinburgh Castle somewhat, that summer and autumn. The visits to Luffness and Seton were permitted again, on occasion, but always under heavy guard. Fortunately, when, with October, the wild-geese came back, the soldiers of the guard saw no real need to accompany their young liege-lord out on to the cold, windy and muddy salt-marshes for every dawn or dusk flighting, much preferring the ale-houses of Aberlady. So some sport was possible.

The Lady Elizabeth quite fell in love with her new grand-son, Sander, and as a by-product of this, grew much more amiable towards his mother.

So that year passed, with trouble looming but nothing dire actually developing. But none imagined that the clouds would disperse of their own accord, in time – not with Alan Durward the man he was, and the Plantagenet desiring to act overlord of Scotland. It was only a matter of time, probably. The Comyns used that time to drum up the promise of armed support and to strengthen their grip on the land. And, indeed, on the rich and powerful Church. For the ailing new Bishop Abel died in December, having not had a year in office; and who should get himself, by devious means and bribes from the national Treasury, appointed in his place but John de Gamelyn, who now became suddenly Bishop of St Andrews and Primate of Scotland, to add to his chancellorship of the realm, his slender hand now seen by all to be steering the ship of state.

Margaret had been right, from the first, about that smooth operator.

18

The year 1255 saw those ominous clouds open, the year of
Alexander's fourteenth birthday. It started, after a quiet
spring, with only a modest downpour, in the arrival in Scotland of the Earl of Gloucester and the noted churchman
and secretary, Robert de Maunsell, Provost of Beverley,
as Henry's representatives to replace de Ros. These came
breathing threatenings and demands – and met with a frosty
reception from the regents and Gamelyn. In the circumstances they did not remain for long, and departed breathing
still louder threats, not to say slaughters, asserting that it
would not be long before they, and others, would return,
but with an army to speak louder than their words.

A week after the English departure, Gamelyn came to the
castle again. For a Bishop of St Andrews he did not spend
much time at the ecclesiastical capital in Fife. He summoned
David and de Ros to his presence.

"My friends," he said, without preamble, expressionless,
"I fear that you must leave this castle and city."

They stared at him.

"It is necessary," he went on. "Your continued presence
with the King constitutes a danger. You must go, and forthwith."

David drew a deep breath, but de Ros beat him to words.

"You cannot so say, my lord Bishop," he declared forcefully. "*I* am here as guardian to the Queen, and adviser to
His Grace. None can dismiss me."

"King Henry has already dismissed you, my lord of Wark.
But even had he not, the regency of Scotland is not bound
by the King of England's arrangements. You will leave."

"This is folly!" David jerked. "We are part of King
Alexander's household. We cannot be separated from
him."

"You can, and will, Sir David."

"Why?"

"Because there is a plot, a venture to take the King. An English plot. But aided by your cousin, the Earl of Dunbar. So His Grace must be put in greater security. You, and my lord of Wark, represent . . . weakness. Seton also. We may have to remove the King elsewhere, in these circumstances. Your attendance is no longer required."

"But . . . this is not to be considered! His Grace will forbid it."

"In matters of the King's security and the realm's well-being, His Grace will do as his regents say, sir!"

"What fool's tale of a plot is this?" de Ros demanded.

"Foolish perhaps, but no tale," the Chancellor said. "It is fact. And treason against the crown. An English force has landed at Dunbar Castle under the Earl of Gloucester and the man Maunsell, and has been well received by the said earl. With them is Durward, Earl of Atholl. And to them are flocking sundry traitor lords . . ."

"Durward!" David eyed de Ros, astonished, and that man wagged his head, speechless.

"So – you will go," Gamelyn went on. "Dunbar is only thirty miles away, and your continued presence in this castle is a danger. You will leave at once. Before nightfall. By order of the regents."

"*We* are in no Durward's plot! We know nothing of this . . ."

"Sir Nicholas de Soules will have you escorted to the city gates." Bowing briefly, Gamelyn turned and left them.

Shaken, angry, the pair were left to tell the dire tidings to the King.

Margaret, with the baby, and Margery, were with the boy. Predictably appalled was their reception of the news. They gazed at each other, exclaiming, protesting, disbelieving.

"No! No! No!" Alexander shouted. "You will not go, you *must* not go! You cannot leave me. They cannot do this."

"I fear that they can, Alex," David told him unhappily. "They have the power, in men and in authority."

"But I am the King! I *command* that they do not."

"Until you are of full age, Alex, the regency is in charge.

265

They can overrule your commands. Gamelyn acts for them. And de Soules, here, has the garrison of the castle to do as he says."

"Then I will come with you, Davie."

"They would never allow that. They intend to separate us."

"One day I will have that Gamelyn killed!"

Margaret spoke. "Is there no way that we can make them change their minds, David? Give them assurances? Make some offer?"

"What can we offer? They see us as a danger, if we remain with Alexander. They may remove him, and the Queen here, to some other secure place. Some Comyn stronghold belike. In the north, out of reach. They do not want us."

"Oh, Alex! And, and Margery! This is . . . beyond all belief!"

The boy beat his fists against the walling. "I will not *let* them!" he yelled.

Helplessly they eyed each other.

The door opened to admit Sir Nicholas de Soules. "Sire," he said curtly, "Sir David de Lindsay and his wife, Sir Robert de Ros and his family, and Sir Alexander de Seton are to leave this castle and city. At once. By order of the regents. I will take them to the town gates, just as soon as they may make ready. Make their arrangements without delay. The gates close in two hours from now."

"No!" Alexander shouted.

"I have the regents' commands, Sire. These I must and shall obey."

"I am the King! I *command* that they stay."

"I regret, Sire, but I am here by the regents' appointment. I must do as they say."

"As that weasel Gamelyn says! You obey an upjumped clerk rather than your liege-lord?"

"I am sorry, Highness." De Soules turned to the others. "You will be ready to leave within two hours." And, bowing, he left them.

As Margaret, shaking her head, picked up the baby Sander, Margery let out a wail, her first contribution, and ran to clutch the infant, sobbing.

266

The others, oppressed by their utter inability to alter the situation, at this stage, went to inform Seton and Lady de Ros, followed by a young monarch all but in tears.

Later, with de Soules coming to announce that the horses were saddled and laden and the escort waiting, farewells had to be said. It was the first time that David and Margaret had been parted from Alexander, for more than a day or two, in almost six years. It was, needless to say, a heart-breaking, desolating occasion for them all, words utterly inadequate to express feelings and emotions. The boy clung to his friend and his half-sister, standing together, arms round them both, and would not let go of them until David actually had to push him off, to free them. This parting had to be cut short, for all their sakes, sore as was the achieving of it.

"We will be back, Alex – never fear," he got out. "This is not the end." He glared at de Soules, standing watching. "Be brave. You are a King. We will move heaven and earth to come to you, to rescue you, I swear it!" Abruptly he turned away, to assist Margaret, with the baby, to mount.

They reined round, to leave the boy standing there, guards flanking him, beneath the gatehouse archway, a forlorn figure, features working, fighting tears. Margery had already fled the scene.

Surrounded by a large armed escort, de Soules himself in command, they clattered off down into the town streets, to make for the St Mary's Port, the easternmost gate of the city's walls. They would thereafter head for Luffness.

That night, they did not require any conference to decide what they must do, for there was little option. In the morning they must make for Dunbar, to discover the situation there. Where so needful aid was concerned, beggars could not be choosers.

It was less than a score of miles from Aberlady to Dunbar by the coast road, skirting the Tyne estuary. Leaving the women and children in the care of Lady Elizabeth, the three men reached there by noon. Dunbar, set just outside the mouth of the Firth of Forth, on the main Norse Sea coastline, unlike the firth harbours on the south shore, was not tidal, never drying out at low water, and so a useful port – no doubt why

267

the English contingent had been able to arrive here by ship rather than hazard the crossing of the land borders further south. Dunbar Castle, overlooking the harbour, indeed able to block it, was one of the most extraordinary in the kingdom, based on a high knoll of the mainland at one end but built out on individual rock-stacks into the sea, these linked by covered bridges of masonry. Under one of these bridge-like corridors was the entrance to the harbour, with the consequence that the castle garrison could close it at will by dropping a wood and chain barrier, thus controlling all entry and egress. The castle itself had no fewer than seven great towers, providing major accommodation; but sited as it was, there was no room for horses therein, and these had to be left and stabled down in the town immediately below.

The newcomers, dismounted and approaching the gate-house on its rocky knoll, were left in no doubt that the town was full of men-at-arms, with many also camped around. The harbour was packed with shipping, not only the fishing-craft of the locals, and merchanters, but two larger vessels which no doubt had brought the party from England.

The trio had no difficulty in gaining admittance to the castle, with David announcing that he was the Lord of Luffness come to have speech with his cousin the Earl Patrick. They found all as crowded within as was the harbour – and were surprised at the identities of some they met before ever they reached the place's lord. Alexander the High Steward was there, with Malise, Earl of Strathearn. Then they came on Bruce, Lord of Annandale, and his son's father-in-law, Nigel, Earl of Carrick, these with Walter, Lord of Brechin and William de Moray. They met another Lothian lord, Hugo of Gifford, with John Crawford of that Ilk, and one from beyond the Highland Line, Robert de Meyneres, or Menzies. So quite a large proportion of the anti-Comyn lords evidently were already here. And progressing to the furthest tower rising sheer from the stack-top above the boiling waves, they were brought to Earl Patrick himself, sitting at a table with the Earl of Gloucester, the English churchman Maunsell, and none other than Alan Durward, Earl of Atholl, with two or three others.

The visitors' reception by this company was varied, to say the least. Dunbar welcomed them warmly enough, Gloucester and Maunsell looked askance at de Ros, and Durward glowered at them all.

David, as cousin of their host, spoke for them. "My lords, we have come from Edinburgh Castle, learning of your assembly here. We have been evicted from the King's presence by the regency, greatly against His Grace's royal will. He and the Queen are now as good as prisoners there, under de Soules, a grievous situation."

"So – you also, David!" Patrick exclaimed – for he too, of course, had been ejected by the Comyns. "Why you? And Seton?"

"They conceived us to be a danger. To their hold on the King. With this gathering of their enemies so near at hand. Or Gamelyn did."

"I am surprised to see my lord of Wark with you, expelled – if so he can still be called!" That was Gloucester thinly. "I would have thought that they would have . . . cherished *him*!"

"They seek to be quit of all the King's friends. And the Queen's," de Ros said. "And I am that."

"Which King?"

"Both, my lord Earl."

"And what do you want with us here?" Durward demanded, in a growl. "*I* never found you friends!"

"We are, as my lord of Wark says, King Alexander's friends," David answered levelly. "Always we have been that, and always will be. The King needs help now, release from durance and duress. Should we not come to those who can effect it, perhaps?"

"Well said," Patrick declared. "The more we can muster, the better. And, new come from Edinburgh Castle, you can supply us with information, no doubt."

The others there grunted.

"What information do you require, my lords? What do you intend?"

"We intend to take young Alexander and that girl out of the Comyns' clutches!" Durward rapped out. "That is what. And cleanse this realm of such scum!"

"Yes, my lord Earl. But – how?" David was perhaps greatly daring in that company.

"That we seek to decide on," his cousin answered. "There are problems, all recognise . . ."

"None that sharp swords and stout hearts cannot resolve!" Durward interrupted.

"It will take more than swords, however sharp, to take Edinburgh Castle!" David said.

"That we understand, David." Patrick looked uncomfortably round the company, all so evidently at odds. "But this is not the moment to discuss our strategies. Later, my lords." And he nodded significantly at his cousin.

David and his friends took the hint and bowed themselves out.

The Dunbar chamberlain allotted them quarters in that crowded wave-girt castle; and fortunately they got on better with most of the other visitors, some of whom they knew well enough. They learned that while most of the Dunbar men-at-arms were now assembled, to the number of some seven hundred, the other lords had not yet had time to gather their strengths, but orders were out for a great muster. And King Henry was bringing a large army north to their assistance.

This last information much troubled David and his friends. The last thing they wanted was to be involved in any English invasion of Scotland, whatever the cause. Indeed, war of any sort was to be avoided, they claimed. There must be a better way than that.

In the evening, after a bountiful meal in the great hall, a council-of-war was held, for all the lords and magnates present, David and his companions being given comparatively lowly places at the long table. Earl Patrick was, of course, nominally in charge, but in fact Alan Durward took the lead from the start. And he spoke, apparently, with the authority of King Henry Plantagenet. His concern was the massing of every available man against the Comyns, which lords were to be approached, how many of a tail each could be expected to bring, what inducements or threats should be offered, where a sufficiency of arms and horses were to be obtained, the availability of siege-engines, liaison with the

270

hoped-for English forces, and so on, very much a warrior's lead. The discussion of all this, in detail, went on and on.

David, listening, grew ever the more concerned, impatient indeed. In his opinion this was not what they should be considering, at all. At length, when there was a pause, with goblets being replenished, he rose.

"Hear me, my lords," he pleaded. "We are talking of war, outright war. Is that what we should be seeking? Is our cause not to rescue King Alexander and Queen Margaret from Edinburgh Castle? This is not how we will achieve that, I say. We have just come from that fortress. And my lord of Dunbar was keeper there. He, and we know, if you all do not, that that citadel, in the midst of Edinburgh city, is all but impregnable. No army will take it by force. Only, possibly, by siege. Do we want that? Long siege? With the King and Queen therein, as hostages. To be starved into submission? I say no. Do we desire to fight through Edinburgh town, slaying its citizens – as we must do even to reach the castle rock? Will that serve our cause? Do we want to arouse the people of this realm against us – as we will, if we bring in an English army to aid us. Nothing will so unite the Scots folk against us as that! And can we wait for the English, anyway? Or the companies of all the lords spoken of here? Have we time? The Comyns are mustering also, you may be sure. And they may well decide to remove King Alexander and his Queen from Edinburgh to some remote hold in their northern fastnesses. I say that we must move fast. And use our wits. The mailed fist is not the only way, nor the best." That was a long and daring speech to make in that company. But it got some applause, and not only from David's friends.

"There is, perhaps, much in what my lord of Luffness says," Patrick began, when inevitably Durward's voice over-rode his.

"Lindsay, who has never drawn sword in anger in his life, I swear, speaks folly!" he exclaimed. "What does he know of war and battle? To raise voice against his betters!"

"I am no warrior, my lord, I admit," David answered. "But I know my fellow-Scots and how they think as regards

271

the English. And I would seek to use my head rather than my fist."

That produced a moment of almost shocked silence.

"*Your* head!" Durward bellowed. "How is that pretty head of yours going to get us into Edinburgh Castle, without the sword, the siege-engine and the battering-ram? Tell me that."

"I do not tell you that, my lords. I but say that is what we should be discussing here and now, not of amassing men and seeking English aid."

Into the noise and dispute which followed that, Patrick banged his goblet on the table for quiet. "David," he said urgently, "you must have *some* notion, to speak as you do? Some way for us, other than the battle you decry. Wits rather than swords." Patrick of Dunbar was no warrior either, and that was evident in his voice.

David hesitated, as well he might. "My lords," he began, less certainly than before, "I but thought, as all this of men and armies was spoken of, that we might do better. A ruse, a device. Approach Edinburgh with our host, yes. But pause outside. Offer to parley with the Comyns. They will have their own army coming. But, since their strength is in the North and in Galloway, they will not have reached these parts yet, I think. So – say Stirling? A parley at Stirling? Between the two sides. They cannot *wish* for battle, in especial with an English army threatening invasion – "

"Who wants a parley, man?" Durward interrupted. "*I* did not come here for talk and chaffering!"

"The parleying would be but a device, my lord Earl. To keep the regents and the Comyn forces out of Edinburgh. There need indeed be *no* parley, just the name of it. And while they wait, some few of us will go secretly to Edinburgh Castle and seek to rescue the King and Queen."

"How?" That was a bark. Others than Durward also asked that. How to get into the fortress?

"I think that I know how," David went on, his voice gaining in confidence. "Wood, is the answer – or could be. Wood for the castle fires. Many fires have to be fed, even in summer. Every day carts of logs come in. They enter over the drawbridge – they must. I have thought, before now, that men could get into the citadel that way, hidden under the wood. The carts are large. And once in . . ." He left the rest unsaid.

There were moments of hush as men considered that proposal, even Durward silent for once. Then an outburst of comment and exclamation, mainly admiring, favourable.

"Clever!" Bruce cried. "But – how many? These carts – how many could they take in? Hidden?"

"Not many under the wood-bags. Three or four, no more. But enough for our purpose, I think."

"What could three or four do?" That was Durward now.

"Sufficient, my lord. If they knew the fortress, the keeper's and the royal quarters and the rest, as I do. Sufficient to get the King and Queen out, secretly. We have friends in that castle."

Talk and discussion became general. Clearly most there were impressed. Durward, of course, was less so than others. He thumped on the table.

"Is this all we came for?" he demanded. "To win those bairns out of Edinburgh Castle? I came for more. To take over the *rule*, with King Henry's help."

There was another silence, only Gloucester and Maunsell and their English colleagues applauding. The Steward raised his voice.

"At this stage, what is important is to gain the custody of the King. And the Queen, of course. The rest can follow." That met with general approval.

David spoke again. "My lords, the High Steward is right. Do we want an English army coming to occupy our land? Can we not make the necessary changes in rule without that? And has my lord of Atholl considered the timing? We must act quickly, before the Comyns have assembled *their* strength, great strength. They have three earldoms and thirty and more knights, as well as their friends' forces – Grahams, Soules, Maxwells, Randolphs, Cheynes, Sinclairs, Frasers. And many bishops and churchmen. They could set ten thousand men against us in a short time. How many have we? As yet? *One* thousand? Two? Are we ready for battle?"

"The King will be at Newcastle. With sufficient." That was Gloucester.

273

There was a murmur, almost a growl, from most of the company. It was evident that few there were eager for any English invasion.

Bruce, almost as tough a character as Durward, banged the table. "Lindsay is right," he shouted. "If we can get the King this way, we can decide on the rest later."

Earl Patrick, obviously relieved, rose. "So be it, my lords. We shall move tomorrow, since time appears to be short. Meanwhile, some of us will work out who does what . . ."

The council broke up.

David and his friends did not get to their couches until late that night, busy indeed.

They had but little sleep, for an early start was made, and around one thousand men to ride. They would pick up a couple of hundred or so more at Luffness and Seton and Gifford, en route, and would make their halt between Musselburgh and Edinburgh, near enough the city to let it be seen that there was an armed host approaching but not so near that its numbers could be counted. Then a deputation would go forward, to propose a conference at Stirling, in the centre of the land – which would be an obvious venue, with the Comyn forces coming from Menteith, Angus, Mar, Buchan, Badenoch and the Highland west.

The deputation's membership was important. It would be Gamelyn that they would see, presumably. Durward, Gloucester and Maunsell should be there, of course, but also representatives of the Scots lords must go – Dunbar, Strathearn, Carrick and Bruce. They would tell Gamelyn that they were assembling a mighty army, and that King Henry was massing at the border. But to avoid bloodshed and battle, if possible, both sides should meet at Stirling and discuss their differences, to see if they could come to terms. When the deputation came back, a small party would make secretly for the city, before the gates shut. David would have been content for Seton, de Ros and himself to form that party, but was surprised when Durward himself announced that he wanted to be one of the little group, and Patrick of Dunbar also. The latter *might* be useful, as a former keeper of the castle, and knowing it well. But Durward . . .?

That man was not to be gainsaid, however, and the others had to make the best of it. Although five was too many, beneath the wood.

So, in the early afternoon the host halted at Restalrig, where it could be seen from the high ramparts of Edinburgh Castle, and the selected deputation rode on for the city. In collecting some of his own men at Luffness, David had also collected some old and inconspicuous clothing for the five to wear on their secret foray.

It was almost evening before the deputation returned, and David was concerned that the city gates might be closed for the night before they could reach them, especially with this host in view and as the final approach would have to be made on foot, their fine horses all too conspicuous. Gamelyn had apparently heeded the deputation carefully and seemed agreeable to a conference.

Being wished well by all, the oddly assorted five set off, Durward no longer scoffing at the project. He said the Stirling conference had been set for two days hence.

They were just in time to gain entrance before the gates closed, David having the temerity to warn the earls that it would be wise to carry themselves rather more humbly than was their wont if they were not to attract attention to themselves from the town guard.

They moved in along with a party of salt-carriers from Salt Preston.

The woodyard, one of many in the city, was situated in a lane off the Cowgate. David knew it, of course, and had spoken many times to Jock Brodie, the wood-merchant; indeed they were on almost friendly terms, for young Alexander had until a year or so ago often helped to unload the wood in the castle courtyard, and thought of Jock and his man as companions. Now, leaving his companions at one of the many ale-houses nearby, David went to seek out Brodie.

He was received by that hearty character cheerfully, who listened to the project with interest, which grew even to enthusiasm. Jock did not like de Soules, who treated him like dirt and was a bad payer, and would be glad to see him brought down a peg. He recognised, of course, that if the plot did not succeed he might well suffer for it, but was loyal

275

enough to the young monarch to take that risk. As to the mechanics of the business, he saw no difficulty in contriving a framework of boughs above the floors of the two carts, over which canvas could be draped and under which the plotters could lie, with the firewood heaped in bags and logs on top. He would see to that. He delivered in the afternoon, the morning being spent sawing up the logs. He even offered David a bed for the night in his house.

David's fear, for the interim, was that the others, the two earls in particular, would behave in a fashion to draw attention to themselves, Durward especially. He returned to the four of them, urging that they did not all spend the night in the same inn. Durward surprised by declaring that he would spend the night with a whore he had already picked out – which was probably as good cover as any for that man, in the circumstances. They agreed to meet at the woodyard next noon.

David was up early again, next morning, and out to roam the streets, especially in the vicinity of the Canongate and Holyrood Abbey. He sought news. And in mid-forenoon he learned what he sought to know – and better than he could have hoped. For he was able to watch a notable company ride out from Holyrood, heading westwards, with Gamelyn himself at its head – but not only Gamelyn but Nicholas de Soules with him. This was a gift from the gods indeed. The deputy keeper up at the castle, one Dalry, was not a man of great wits or initiative. This cavalcade would be heading for Stirling, no doubt.

Back at the woodyard, the conspirators assembled and were agreeably surprised at the comparative comfort Jock Brodie had contrived for them in his carts, the frames of boughs higher than expected, giving more space below, and blankets to lie on. David, Seton and de Ros went in the first cart, Durward and Dunbar in the second. It was a novel experience for these lords of broad acres to lie there on the floors of carts under their cover, being trundled and bumped over the cobbled city streets.

It seemed quite a long journey up, in the darkness, from the Cowgate to the castle, thus, but presently they heard, and felt, their wheels and the horses' hooves on the planking of the drawbridge, an exchange of pleasantries with the guard – and they were under the gatehouse arch and into the impregnable citadel of Edinburgh; it seeming almost too easy to be true.

They waited until the carts stopped, up at the stable-yard, where the wood was to be stored, and they heard Jock and his man get down. A tapping presently on their canvas cover beneath the bags had David peering out. Unloading wood was much below the dignity of the castle men-at-arms and servitors, if not of a boy monarch, and they had the place to themselves. Out the five of them crept, and into the wood-shed.

They had planned their programme carefully. David and de Ros would head for the royal quarters, whilst Seton and the others would seek to capture the deputy governor and use him, at dagger-point, as hostage. Unsuspected as all this would be, they should have a fair chance of complete surprise. The garrison and royal guard was quite large, but quite likely de Soules had taken some away with him. The rest would be dispersed about the castle and attending to their own affairs. Moreover, not a few of them might be well disposed towards David and Seton, or even the former keeper, Dunbar, should there be a confrontation.

So, bearing heavy bags of logs on their shoulders, stooping, David and de Ros trudged up to the quarters which had so recently been their own and, clad as they were and heads down, attracted no comment as they passed through the porters' entrance-chamber, and went on to climb the winding turnpike stair to the living quarters.

There, in the small hall, they set down their bags beside the fireplace – and unexpectedly encountered the Lady Matilda Cantelupe entering. She gasped as she recognised them, hand to mouth.

That woman had never been a favourite with them, but she behaved well enough in this happening, after only a few words of explanation, leading them to another chamber on the floor above, where both King and Queen were being instructed by a new and elderly monkish tutor.

The scene that followed would have been comic had it not been so fraught with consequence. Alexander, who had been

277

staring out of the window rather than heeding his teacher, turning, leapt up, eyes wide, mouth opening to a yell, tripped over his own feet and fell against the tutor's desk, upending it, as he stumbled over to grab David by the shoulders and shake him in a paroxysm of excited surprise and joy. He had become quite a tall and well-built youth now, and all but knocked the other off his feet.

David had to grip his sovereign, both to save himself from falling and to return affectionate greeting, but also had to seek to cut short emotional display and talk in the interests of effective action.

"Later!" he jerked, urgently. "Talk later, Alex. Quick! Now! Do as I say. No noise. Just come. Margery too. Downstairs. Just as you are." He looked over at the astonished monk. "You – do not move. Make no outcry. Or it will be the worse for you! We have armed men here. Wait you here until we are well gone. You can say that we threatened you." He whipped out a dirk and waved it, as gesture.

De Ros had been coping with Margery – who indeed demanded less attention, in silent bewilderment. Grasping her arm, he pulled her to her feet, holding her, but devoting most of his care to the Lady Matilda, telling her that all would be well, that the Queen would be safely delivered, that alarm must not be raised until they were well out of the castle, that she would be well rewarded.

The woman nodded dumbly.

Taking the youngsters, the two men hurried them off through the doorway and down the stairs. It was as well that they knew that tower building so well, for they could never have got their charges past the porters' lodge unchallenged. Instead, they hastened on down the further flight of stairs to the storage cellars in the vaulted basement, which had their own door on to the courtyard.

Leaving them there, under cover, with de Ros, David, forcing himself to saunter now, strolled across the cobblestones to the first cart. Because of that hollow beneath the frame of boughs there had been much less wood than usual to unload, and Jock Brodie and his man were already finished and waiting. At David's direction, Jock led his own cart over to the cellar door, to dump the last two bags therein.

Hastily de Ros brought the youngsters out and urged them up into the cart, to get them creeping under the now part-collapsed frame. Covered by bags and huddled together, the boy was now excitedly co-operating, the girl in panting apprehension but not resisting.

This achieved, David fretted. They could have done without the other three now. Yet if things had gone wrong, the others might still have been able to save the day. But to wait, now, was dire indeed. Surely the trio had had time to grasp their hostage, if it was at all possible?

As still there was no sign of the others, David decided that his first duty had to be to his sovereign-lord. He told de Ros to wait, with the second cart, and come on with their partners when they appeared. At least he could, he hoped, get the youngsters out of the castle first. Telling Brodie to drive on, he climbed into the cart and burrowed under beside the royal pair, whispering for silence.

Creaking and bumping, the heavy waggon lumbered down to the gatehouse. There were shouts from the driver to the guards there that his man was slow with the other cart. Then his hidden passengers heard the hooves and wheels sounding unmistakably hollow on the drawbridge planking over the moat-ditch, and they were out.

Jock drew up a little way down the tourney-yard which formed the approach to the rock-bound fortress, to wait. David, desperately anxious, almost ordered him to move on down into the town. But that would be to desert his colleagues – not that he could do anything to aid them if they had come to grief.

They waited, whispering, Alexander now bubbling over with ecstatic glee, his wife asking where they were going.

The waiting seemed endless, although it was probably only a very few minutes. Then they heard a cry or two behind, and the rumble of wheels on wood. Thankfully David ordered Brodie onward.

The journey down the Lawnmarket, the High Street and the wynd of the Black Friars' monastery to the Cowgate was slow, uncomfortable but uneventful, with no indications of pursuit. At length, at the woodyard, they drew up, and with the gate closed behind them, the hiders could emerge.

And there Alexander's excitement grew vocal indeed and increased, with even David astonished, when, out from the second cart came not four but five men, Durward, naked steel in his one hand, the other on the shoulder of an unhappy-looking Sir Alan Dalry, the castle's deputy governor.

David cut short reports, explanations and congratulations – time for that later. They must move fast now. Some inconspicuous top clothing for the young couple, and they must be gone. Hue and cry would be bound to follow, sooner or later. They must get out as quickly and covertly as possible, not all in a bunch, to the city gate, and away, hoping that there would be no difficulty there. That was why they had brought this wretched Dalry with them, Durward announced. He would get them past the town guard – or get a dirk between his ribs.

That walk to the gate, some four hundred yards, was a testing experience. The girl's long silken skirts could draw attention; but they had the unfortunate deputy governor walk alongside Margery, with Durward at their backs; and Dalry being fairly richly clad, he would seem to account for her. They were not challenged, and at the guard-house actually had no trouble, the town guard eyeing them all interestedly but not presuming to interfere with someone so obviously an authoritative character, even though they might not recognise him for what he was. They probably did not recognise the young lad as the King, either.

Still taking Dalry with them, the escapers headed along the east-going roadway which skirted the foot of the great hill of Arthur's Seat. Less than half a mile on, at the first of the scrub woodland of the royal hunting-park, an escort with horses should be awaiting them.

It was. Abandoning poor Sir Alan Dalry to his fate, the party mounted, to spur off to the host still camped at Restalrig.

Back with that small army, satisfaction was general, Alexander's most pronounced of all, he scarcely able to contain himself, congratulating all concerned, even the hated Durward, but with David of course the prime recipient.

Gratification was all very well, but what was to be their

programme now? David himself had hardly considered anything beyond this actual rescue of the royal couple, and was concerned that there might still be attempts at recapture – although whether there was sufficient manpower in the city for such a venture, against their thousand or so, was doubtful. He was for getting Alexander further away promptly.

Durward took charge now, scoffing at the idea of any of them proceeding on to Stirling for the proposed conference. That was a ruse which had worked, and could now be forgotten, he declared. They should ride south to Roxburgh, and from there send to inform King Henry at Newcastle that his daughter was safe, and that the stage was set, with the young King's recovery, for a resumption of the due and proper rule in Scotland.

This was accepted, although David for one was not altogether happy about that last suggestion. But meantime, Roxburgh let it be. However, he himself would make a diversion to Luffness again, to pick up his wife and son.

This announcement produced an upheaval. For Alexander declared emphatically that he was not going to be separated from his Davie; and Durward and the rest were equally determined that they were not going to let the King out of their sight at this stage, apparently afraid that he might find alternative protectors. So there was nothing for it but for the entire force to head eastwards the fourteen miles, before they could turn southwards for the Borders, adding considerably to their journey. Alexander made the call at Luffness a royal command, and David said that they could halt for the night there, as well as at, say, Soutra Hospice.

19

It was good to be at Roxburgh again, between the great rivers, after the confinements of Edinburgh Castle, Alexander in especial glorying in his freedom. There was no holding in his high spirits, his enthusiasms, his ardours, his designs and aspirations. He was a prisoner no longer. He would play the King indeed, at last. And his gratitude, in particular towards David, was on a par with the rest. Nothing was good enough for Davie Lindsay. Seton, de Ros, Dunbar, even Durward, were beamed upon and were to be rewarded. But Davie – he was to be the first man in his kingdom.

This effervescence, of course, had to be toned down. David was still under thirty, and no great lord, whatever his monarch thought to make of him. And for that matter, Alexander himself was not as yet fifteen, and even if he could not wait until full coming of age, nineteen was the youngest year at which he might take on full rule for himself, over four years yet. None there denied that he must be allowed more authority now, but he still must have a regency.

Durward, of course, assumed that *he* would resume the regency – for it was taken for granted that the Comyn regents could no longer pretend to function as such, now that they no longer had control of the monarch. Alexander's new attitude to Durward did not go so far as to see him in supreme rule – his desire was that *David* should be regent, a step scarcely to be considered by anyone else. But, to be sure, it was not the young monarch's privilege to appoint his regents, but that of the Privy Council, confirmed by parliament. That, in theory. But, in fact, the thing was really in the gift of whoever held the military power in the land and controlled the King; and in present circumstances Durward could probably claim that, especially with King Henry's backing, and a large English army poised to substantiate it. Practically all at Roxburgh assumed likewise that Durward would be regent again, even though not all desired it.

That man himself, whether out of policy or just as a result of the castle escape co-operation, was less abrasive than heretofore. Nothing would make him amiable or other than curtly assertive; but he behaved better towards Alexander and his friends, David in particular. Perhaps he recognised that he had leeway to make up over that unfortunate papal legitimisation of his wife – which had in fact been promulgated, although it was never referred to now – and could well use the goodwill of these effective individuals.

He, and those supporting him, were busy at Roxburgh, sending out mustering orders all over the kingdom, in the King's name now as well as his own. Maximum manpower was to be assembled promptly for a campaign to deal with the Comyns, once and for all. Also, an early meeting of the Privy Council was called, at Roxburgh – and it could be taken that the Comyn earls and their firm supporters would *not* attend. This call had to go out under the King's own signature, since Gamelyn's chancellorship was assumed to be vacant. A parliament would have to follow in due course.

In the midst of all this activity a messenger arrived from Henry Plantagenet at Newcastle – although message was hardly a description of his communication, more like a peremptory command. He, King Henry, would meet the Earl of Atholl and the King of Scots, with his own daughter, at Wark Castle in three days' time.

That command was received with mixed feelings at Roxburgh, Durward eager, others less so. Young Margery, as usual, revealed little excitement. De Ros, who had collected his wife and children at Luffness, with Margaret and the baby, was more than interested that his Wark should be chosen for the meeting. Did this mean that it was being confiscated by Henry? Was it purely fortuitous, convenient? Or might it mean that he was to be forgiven for not giving up his position at the Scots court?

So, on a mellow September day, a large cavalcade set out down Tweed for Wark, fifteen miles, Margaret acting as the young Queen's attendant, Lady de Ros anxious to see her house again, Alexander nervous at seeing his father-in-law again.

At the Wark ford they could see that the English contingent was already at the castle, large numbers of pavilions and tents in view, and the Leopard standard of Plantagenet flying from the topmost tower. Alexander insisted that his own Lion Rampant banner be unfurled for the river crossing.

It was Simon de Montfort, not King Henry, who came to meet them; and after a civil greeting and congratulations to Alexander and Margery on their escape, led them within, flanked by a ceremonial guard of honour, to the presence. The boy was doubtful about this procedure, as possibly seeming too subservient for one King towards another; but David explained that since they were now on English soil, this was correct. In Scotland, it would be Henry who would be escorted into Alexander's presence.

In the hall, the Plantagenet, who was looking distinctly older for the four difficult years which had passed, received them in state, up on the dais, sitting on a high chair, backed by his standing officers. He did not rise.

"Welcome, Margaret! And Alexander," he called. "Here is a happy reunion. After so long. I commend all who have made it possible." That was said in a set voice, a statement of policy rather than any family greeting. He held out his hand. "Come."

There was considerable hesitation on the part of the newcomers. That hand was evidently held out to be kissed. Alexander looked at David for guidance. Margery looked at Margaret. Durward took a step forward, then waved the young couple onward. The others shuffled feet, uncertain as to procedure.

David, appealed to, was doubtful himself. Surely Henry should have come down to greet his daughter and son-in-law, in parental fashion. He glanced at de Montfort, who nodded – which was not a great help. He whispered to Alexander.

"Go up with Margery. Kiss his hand. But do not kneel. Take *her* hand."

The pair went forward and climbed on to the dais. There the girl hung back while Alexander moved on. It was obvious, by the way Henry held his hand, out low and palm down, that he expected it to be kissed kneeling. The boy, frowning, merely nodded his head, and taking the hand, raised it towards his lips, made a kissing sound, and dropped it.

"Greetings, Lord Henry," he jerked.

It was the man's turn to frown. Then he turned to his daughter, who dipped an incipient curtsy and came forward less than eagerly.

Still Henry did not rise, but only reached out to pat his daughter's arm. It was scarcely a warm family encounter.

There was an uncomfortable pause. Durward ended it by marching up and kneeling, to do the required kissing. Alexander glowered at him. He had never knelt to kiss *his* hand. The other Scots stayed where they were; and de Ros stood hesitant, not knowing whether he was welcome in his own home, or not.

Henry rose at last and, looking round on all the company unfavourably, turned and strode out by the dais door, the odd audience and welcome over.

"There is a man unsure of himself," David murmured to Margaret. "For a king . . .!"

Simon de Montfort now took charge. Refreshment would be served in the lesser hall, for the visitors. Meantime he would take Queen Margaret through to her father. No doubt His Highness would come and talk with them presently.

Alexander returned to David thankfully.

Durward was summoned alone to the royal presence, the English one.

Later, in the lesser hall, King Henry did appear, not exactly to mingle with his guests but at least to speak with some of them, Alexander first – de Ros being ignored completely. Since David had his arm clutched by his own monarch, he inevitably was included in a notably stilted conversation. Henry announced that he was glad that his good-son and daughter had escaped from the clutches of the insufferable Comyns, that he and Queen Margaret would now be safe, with the Earl of Atholl regent and an English force ready at Newcastle to come to their aid should it be necessary. He was petitioning the new Pope to annul the man Gamelyn's appointment as Bishop of St Andrews. And he recommended that Alexander remained at Roxburgh Castle meantime so that he could cross safely on to English soil should by any misfortune his enemies stage an attempt at recapture.

Alexander opened his mouth to comment, and then shut it again, narrow-eyed.

Henry moved on to speak, rather more affably, to Patrick of Dunbar and the High Steward, before again departing.

And that seemed to be all. Durward came back and declared that King Henry should be invited to Roxburgh for a return visit. It would have to be in the next day or two, for His Highness had to return south to deal with urgent problems there. Queen Margaret would remain with her father in the meantime.

All seeming to be arranged between Durward and Henry, the Scots party returned to Roxburgh. De Ros, still unacknowledged by his monarch, came with them but left his wife and children at Wark, as indication that he still considered it to be his ancestral property.

Two days later, then, the King of England, with his daughter, arrived at Roxburgh, with his train. Alexander was concerned as to his greeting, emphasising his equality in all but years. He sent the High Steward to meet them, as they crossed into Scotland at Wark ford, and his Lyon King of Arms to welcome them at the castle drawbridge, with a flourish of trumpets. Durward was there also, to be sure, but it was Seton who announced that the High King of Scots was happy to see the King of England, his good-sire, on his soil, and would welcome him to his presence. Also his own royal wife. Come.

Between ranked men-at-arms and the banners of the Scots lords, all the way along to the furthermost tower of that long castle, Henry was conducted, behind a choir of singers and instrumentalists.

At the tower door David de Lindsay was waiting for him, to lead him and his party up the quite narrow turnpike stair – this chosen deliberately. The hall in this tower was on the first floor up, whereas the greatest hall of this castle was on the ground floor of one of the other towers – the point being that Henry Plantagenet would have to climb this stair, a process which did not enhance dignity; and the hall itself was of modest dimensions and was already well filled, so that the English party had almost to squeeze in. The dais-platform was occupied only by an empty throne.

What the Plantagenet thought of this he did not vouchsafe, but he had to stand there in the throng for perhaps a minute until another trumpet-blast brought in Alexander at the dais door, with his King of Arms, who now played the sennachie, from whose office his own was derived, by announcing in measured tones that here came Alexander mac Alexander mac William mac Henry mac David mac Malcolm mac Duncan mac Crinan, successor to one hundred kings, to greet and honour the esteemed King of England to his ancient kingdom. The Plantagenets, needless to say, could not boast any such lengthy lineage. Alexander had devised this reception himself, and enjoyed doing it.

Seating himself on his throne, the boy raised a hand. "Greeting, my Lord Henry," he called out. "Here is pleasure. My Queen I rejoice to see also. Come up." That came out in something of a rush perhaps.

The trumpets sounded once more, and David, bowing, led Henry forward to mount the dais steps. Margaret, from out of the press, took young Margery's hand and led her after her father. The English lords had to stand where they were, mostly looking offended. Simon de Montfort, however, grinned amusedly.

Alexander remained sitting on his throne and, as there was no other seat there, Henry perforce had to stand. He ignored the boy's outstretched hand.

"I see that you delight in mummery, play-acting, Alexander," he jerked sourly. "You are young, to be sure."

"I shall be fifteen years in a few months. When I shall have been a King for six years."

"No doubt." Henry looked about him, his predicament obvious. There was nowhere to sit, save on the occupied throne, and the boy showed no sign of standing. And no one could assist him.

Alexander turned to Margery. "We have missed you," he said, in lordly fashion. "You were comfortable at Wark?"

She did not answer.

"What did you do yesterday?"

287

"Nothing," she said.

"Nothing? Sakes – I went fishing. I caught two salmon and a troutie. You could have fished at Wark. It is the same Tweed."

Henry, having to stand and listen to this, was showing signs of agitation. Actually it was David who came to his rescue, to announce that hospitality was awaiting them in the great hall in the main tower.

More trumpeting, and Alexander arose and led his father-in-law and wife down, and down further to descend those stairs and out, the play-acting over.

Henry did not wait long at Roxburgh. It was, after all, in the nature of a courtesy call – if courtesy was an appropriate term – and he was for the road next day. Earl Simon mentioned to David, as they ate, that there was insurrection in the south-west of England, along the Welsh border, the marcher lords, so used to unruly behaviour, turning to pillage eastwards now, as well as into Wales, which, of course was allowable. The Plantagenet did not have his troubles to seek.

Seton accompanied the English contingent back to the Wark ford, with his trumpeters.

The Privy Council duly assembled – or such of it as was favourable towards Durward again – in early October. It was highly unusual for the monarch to preside in person, but officially there being as yet no regent save for Bishop Clement, who was house-bound in Edinburgh, the Comyn earls being assumed to have resigned, and the Chancellor Gamelyn likewise, there was a procedural hiatus. And the council was supposed to be of those to counsel the King. Alexander's advisers saw it as a further opportunity to assert his increasing authority, and the boy was well pleased to co-operate. Durward was not in a position, as yet, to object or take over; until the council formally appointed him as regent, he was only one of the earls, holding no office, so he had to stand back meantime, however difficult a role for that man.

Seton, who found his position as Lyon and chief herald much to his taste, and was making a colourful and innovative duty of it, devising new and significant procedures and displays to enhance the royal prestige, opened the meeting almost as though it had been a parliament, with trumpet and even cymbals, to usher in the monarch to the same lesser hall in which King Henry had been received. Behind him came Alexander the High Steward and Keith the Knight Marischal. Then David and de Ros. About a score of lords stood around a long table, waiting, Durward near its head.

The boy took his place there, and waved for all to sit. He was nervous, of course, but he had been well versed in what he was to do and say. Indeed, much advice, discussion and even argument had gone into this day's projected doings, for it represented great opportunity for Alexander's advancement. Once the regency was appointed, his wings would be somewhat clipped; but until then no individual was in a position to challenge his decisions. Admittedly once there was a regency, the royal acts, or some of them, of this royal minor might be revoked, but not without some trouble. So it behoved them to tread carefully if firmly. Inevitably, David had had a major say in it all, and while making important and far-reaching suggestions, had had to tone down his sovereign-lord considerably. Now, he hoped that his advice would be remembered and acted upon. Alexander had a paper in front of him, at least.

"My lords, greetings," the boy said. "This council is greatly important for the realm. A new beginning. The former regency is dissolved. Save, save for the Bishop of Dunkeld . . . no, of Dunblane. But Bishop Clement is sick, not able to act meantime. And the Chancellor Gamelyn, Bishop of . . . Bishop *Elect* of St Andrews, is dismissed. My, my royal authority, therefore, only remains. And this is my council. Therefore I require your much attention, my lords." Alexander glanced behind him, to where David, Seton and de Ros had taken seats, not at the table, but at the back of the throne. "Certain appointments I make, these not requiring the council's con . . . conceding. Nor that of the regency. I appoint Sir Davie de Lindsay, my Cup-Bearer and Justiciar-Depute of Lothian, to be Lord High Chamberlain of this realm. And my close advisers, Sir Alexander Seton, the Lyon King of Arms, and Sir Robert de Ros, to be members of this my Privy Council. Let them, let them take their seats." That was almost defiantly said, however hesitant the diction.

The three arose, to move their chairs forward, close to the table itself, amidst murmurs from the lords but no spoken objections or questions. Actually there were no convenient gaps round that table, so David and Seton merely moved in on either side of the King, with de Ros at David's elbow.

Alexander consulted his paper, biting his lip. "I am now in my fifteenth year," he declared. "And so, according to our laws, I require a regency until I reach full age. Full age is twenty-one years. But King Henry of England took his full rule at nineteen years. I, I intend to do the same. Nineteen years. So a regency for five more years only. We cannot unseat Bishop Clement, who has done no ill. But he can do little. I have been aided and counselled now by the Earls of Atholl and Dunbar. I name them as regents. Is it . . . does this council agree?"

All there had assumed that Durward would be regent; but not all expected Dunbar to be, who was not the strongest of characters. The Earls of Carrick, Strathearn and Fife might have anticipated their appointment. But of course it was Dunbar who had hosted that vital gathering at his castle; and because of his port there, could be in constant contact with England and King Henry. None actually demurred, with Durward's glare round the table noted. That man sat forward on his seat as though about to take over the conducting of the meeting.

But Alexander was not quite finished yet. He looked at David. "*I* wanted Sir Davie to be regent," he announced, in something of a rush. "But he would not. So he is Chamberlain instead. And so nearest, closest, to me." He raised a grin. That statement was not on his paper.

David wagged his head, and shrugged.

The boy, consulting his instructions again, said, "We have no Chancellor. Before I say, before I name the regents. Before the regents are *declared* that. By the King-in-Council. I name one here as Chancellor. Bishop Richard of Dunkeld. Is that agreed?"

There was a pause. Richard de Inverkeithing was young for a bishop – although not as young as Gamelyn. He was none other than Alexander's former tutor, who had gravitated more to being Bishop Clement's assistant, and then promoted by that prelate's influence, once Durward was demoted. He did not love the said Durward, who had always treated him harshly. David had suggested that he would be useful in the chancellorship, as a counter to Durward's domination – for, as Gamelyn had shown, the office could be highly influential. He could be relied upon to prefer to take the King's part, in any clash of wills; as indeed could Patrick of Dunbar probably, which was why David had recommended his cousin instead of himself. All in the interests of a balanced national directorate.

None made protest, although Durward scowled.

Alexander sat back, his main tasks almost competed. "I ask this council, then, to declare Bishop Richard as Chancellor, and the Earls of Atholl and Dunbar regents, my lords."

"I so move," the High Steward declared.

"I second." That was Walter, Lord of Brechin. He was the son of an illegitimate son of David, Earl of Huntingdon, the brother of both Malcolm the Fourth and William the Lyon, therefore of royal blood.

The nominations were accepted without dispute.

And immediately Durward reverted to his normal style. He did not exactly bang on the table, but slapped both hands down on it. "As regent, I have this to tell the council," he jerked forcefully. He scarcely glanced at his fellow-regent, Dunbar. "After three actions, my forces have defeated the Comyns, and they no longer represent any grave danger to the realm. But we shall keep watch on them, I do promise you! So I advise that this council now banishes the Earls of Menteith, Mar and Buchan to their own earldoms, not to leave these on pain of arrest and forfeiture. Also all Comyn lords, knights and lairds. I demand that the man Gamelyn be outlawed – I understand that he has fled the country. Likewise banishment for the lords of Soules, Maxwell, Randolph, Graham, Normanville, Dalry, Argyll and those others who have given strong support to the Comyns. And that the Bishops of Glasgow and Galloway and Ross be censured and removed from this council. All this for the safety of the realm."

There were indrawn breaths at all that. It was clear whose hand was now determined to steer the ship of state.

"My lord of Dunbar will remain here with His Grace, at Roxburgh," Durward went on. "Myself, I will be at either Edinburgh or at Stirling, as more central for the governance of the kingdom. I will resume the justiciarship of Scotia. The lords of Carrick, Strathearn, Fife, Moray, Brechin and Annandale will occupy their respective justiciarships. Other officers will be appointed in due course." He paused, and stared around him. "Is there any other business for this council?" Clearly he desired none.

David spoke up. "A parliament must be called. To confirm, or otherwise, this *council*'s decisions. But not the King's."

"The new Chancellor will see to that."

Alexander rose, of his own accord – as must therefore all others. Surely seldom had a Privy Council meeting had less to say for itself.

20

That was a good winter and early spring at Roxburgh, possibly the most trouble-free they had had. They saw little of
Durward, although they heard of his doings – that he was
ruling the land sternly but effectively, more so than the
Comyns had done, but at the same time apparently making
the most of his opportunities for personal advantage, in
especial pillaging the riches and lands of the St Andrews
bishopric, with its bishop outlawed; and requesting the Pope
that certain illegitimacy in his own background be declared
void, which would enable him to lay claim to the earldom
of Mar, now held by one of his enemies.

They did not see a great deal of the other regent either,
in fact, for Patrick of Dunbar, with at least half of Lothian
and the Merse to look after, said that he had more to do
than dance attendance on the boy King, and would leave
that to his cousin David. He was making much of the fact
that he was engaged in a godly exercise, introducing the
Trinitarian Order, or Red Friars, into Scotland, and setting
up their first monastery, at Houston on the East Lothian
Tyne, not far from Dunbar itself. Actually this was something
of a conscience-easing matter, and done largely to keep his
aunt, the Lady Elizabeth, quiet. She held that he ought to
be off on crusade, avenging the death of his father, her
major preoccupation nowadays; and he thought otherwise.
These Trinitarians were a new order of monks, established
for the purpose of raising funds to pay for the crusades,
begging-friars in fact, to tramp the lands seeking moneys
in exchange for blessings and indulgences. So Patrick sought
to gain heavenly credit and peace from his masterful aunt,
without having to go risking life and limb.

All this left Alexander's little court fairly free to live
their own lives, to their satisfaction. David's duties as High

Chamberlain in the circumstances were all but minimal, for in effect he was responsible now for the royal quarters and living conditions. But this he had been doing, more or less, anyway. It made him one of the great officers of state, however, along with the High Steward, the Constable, the Marischal and the Chancellor, which had its advantages, and gave excuse for travelling the land, to supervise the royal palaces and castles. Not that he did much of that, for they were now all in the control of Durward's friends and relatives, but it did give him freedom of movement away from Roxburgh Castle – freedom Alexander made cheerful use of. So they were able to go goose-shooting at Aberlady frequently, which continued to enthral the boy, as well as making other expeditions, particularly to the Merse cliff-girt shoreline, which produced continual challenge and excitement, in scaling precipices, exploring caves, hunting seals, sea-fishing and the like. Also, of course, they went in for much local sport, hunting, hawking and angling.

It was not all recreation, to be sure. Education in its various aspects was important for Alexander, and Bishop Richard, the new Chancellor – who found the regents but little demanding of his services – returned to his teaching activities, bringing in experts on various subjects useful for a monarch. He did chair the parliament duly called at Edinburgh in early December, Alexander presiding. It was strange for them to be back in the fortress there, temporarily, and a great relief to be able to come away thereafter, where the aura of imprisonment still lingered for the boy.

Boy, in fact, was becoming a term no longer applicable to Alexander. He was growing most evidently towards manhood, a well-built, good-looking and forthright youth, intelligent and open-natured, if apt to quick temper. More and more he behaved the monarch, not arrogantly but asserting his authority. At the parliament, even Durward had to treat him respectfully. His fifteenth birthday celebrations were significant in more than just for one more milestone on the road, for on his own insistence he made a major step towards his manhood by contriving a sally to his wife's bedchamber one night. The visit did not last long, and what Margery thought of it she kept to herself. But Alexander confessed to David thereafter that he did not think that she was very good at it, and that he himself had found it not so good as he had been told. Was he at fault, as well as she? His Chamberlain urged patience, and suggested that Margaret might have a word or two with the Queen.

Margaret herself was pregnant again.

News from England was interesting. Henry was having endless trouble with his discontented lords, especially those on the Welsh marches – indeed the Welsh themselves were in almost constant revolt, largely owing to the savage activities of the said marcher-lords, and Llewelyn, the prince of Wales, was a rising figure in the field. Curiously enough, it was learned that the Comyn Earls of Menteith and Mar had sought safe-conducts from Henry to visit him. Their purpose was unclear but presumably to try to detach him from his backing of Durward. Although they were in theory confined to their own earldoms, they could not be prevented from sailing to England from one or other of the Mar and Buchan ports, such as Aberdeen or Peterhead. So the Comyn faction was not yet subdued, by any means. And Gamelyn, visiting the Pope in Rome, had persuaded the Pontiff not to annul his occupancy of the bishopric of St Andrews, so he was still Primate, at least in name, and no new bishop could be installed in his place. Durward could not fail to note all this, but made no gesture towards reconciliation with the Comyn faction.

But it happened that both kingdoms, and Wales also, had preoccupations other than political and military. That year of 1256 was the wettest in the memory of men. From late spring rain fell day after day, week after week. There was flooding everywhere, fields were under water, cattle and sheep drowned, crops would not grow. Frustration and anxiety was general, with talk of inevitable famine to follow. Nothing like it had been experienced before, and men talked about the judgment of God – although on whom was a matter of opinion. Even when the rains ceased at last, in late July, the farmers said that any harvest there might be would not be reaped until November.

Before that, however, there was a diversion, as far as Alexander and his friends were concerned. King Henry summoned his son-in-law and Margery to England. Just why was

295

not explained, other than saying that he and his Queen pined for a sight of their beloved daughter – which scarcely rang true. Also he wished to consult with Alexander. That youth was for refusing to go, but strangely enough it was Durward who came to urge acceptance. He believed that the summons might well be connected with the Menteith and Mar visit, and was anxious to discover why they had gone, had been received, and to counter, if necessary, any harm they might have done to his interests.

So, in August, quite a large cavalcade set out on the long journey southwards – for this time they were not to go merely as far as York but all the way to Oxford, where Henry would receive them at his royal manor of Woodstock. Once persuaded to go, Alexander was prepared to enjoy the travelling and the seeing of new places – even though the countryside everywhere was bedraggled and waterlogged, the rivers in spate and crossings difficult. David went along without complaint, save that he had to leave the pregnant Margaret behind. De Ros, who was still uncertain as to Henry's attitude to him, chose to remain behind at Wark, and Margaret said that she would take Sander and stay with him and Lady de Ros. But Seton came, and Durward.

Despite the sodden terrain and difficult road conditions, they made good time, no slow riders amongst them – for Queen Margery, now almost a young woman in appearance, however modest her other attainments was a good horsewoman, had had to be. They reckoned on averaging forty miles a day, and gave themselves ten days to reach Oxford, the English cleric Maunsell, now Henry's permanent representative at the Scots court, able to ensure overnight accommodation at the abbeys and monasteries en route. It was noticeable that, however short of provender were the common folk of the land, the churchmen seemed to be consistently well supplied.

The journey was less taxing than it might have been, therefore. The sun, so long hidden, smiled on them day after day. And Durward was not too difficult a travelling-companion. There was no doubt that his behaviour had improved since the old days; that escapade of getting the royal couple out of Edinburgh Castle in the wood-carts had definitely caused him to soften towards them all, a sort of fellow-feeling perhaps. Not that he would ever make a friendly character.

In fact they covered the distance in only nine days. Woodstock proved to be a great rambling place, a moated palace amongst the reedy water-meadows of the River Glyme. These level lands, like so many others, were much waterlogged after the rains, and tents put up to serve as quarters for the trains of the visitors and the Plantagenet retainers were dotted about wherever there was dry enough ground.

Henry and his Queen Eleanor received them kindly enough, although that monarch appeared preoccupied. Eleanor exclaimed at the womanly development of her daughter, whom she had not seen for years. There being no Archbishop of York to sour the occasion, and Prince Edward being absent on the Welsh marches, a fairly genial atmosphere prevailed, with Alexander not feeling bound to emphasise his equality.

Earl Simon de Montfort, as usual, acted as link with the visitors, all but host indeed. He it was who revealed the real objective of the occasion. In the main it related to what had, in fact, become a full-scale war against Wales, a campaign in which many of Henry's disgruntled nobles were refusing to co-operate. As a consequence, with this Prince Llewelyn proving to be a potent military commander and uniting his people as seldom before, Scots aid was to be sought. An invasion of North Wales from the former Scots province of Cumbria would greatly help, and draw off some portion of Llewelyn's forces facing the English army – where young Prince Edward was beginning to show his own military aptitudes, it seemed. It was noticeable, however, that de Montfort himself was not with the army, although he was the foremost soldier of England. David was not the only one to wonder why.

No reference to all this was made by Henry in the first two or three days, banqueting, sports, a tourney and other entertainment prevailing. With famine threatening, all this feasting might seem out of place, but that was not for the visitors to declare. Alexander was treated as a monarch indeed, Durward made much of also.

On the third day, rested, they all rode the eight miles to Oxford, to be shown that city and to inspect the ongoing renewal of the old city walls which King Henry had started. The town was huddled in a rectangle where the River Cherwell joined the larger Thames, its centre clustered round the intersection of four major streets, called the Carfax apparently, these pointing north, east, south and west. They admired the cathedral, built almost a century before – handsome, Alexander said, but not so fine as the abbeys and churches that his great-great-grandfather David had built at Melrose, Dryburgh, Kelso and Jedburgh. And they went on to visit the University College, also founded the century before, of which Henry was inordinately proud; so that his son-in-law had to assert that the said Scots abbey-churches had teaching colleges attached, mainly, as was this university, for the training of priests – but no fewer than eight or nine of them, the names of which Sir David was called upon to recite. Alexander might be impressionable, but he was not so easy to impress.

Back at Woodstock that night, after more feasting, his young liege-lord came to David's room in some concern. Henry had asked him outright for a Scots army to invade North Wales, he said. What was he to do? He had nothing against the Welsh, nor had Scotland; indeed they were a kindred folk, were they not, of the good Celtic race? Why should they fight them, to aid the English? He had answered Henry that he could not say without consulting his advisers. That it would require the regents' and Privy Council's agreement. It was difficult. Henry had just promised to give him five hundred merks, the unpaid residue of Margery's dowry, and restore to him the Honour of Huntingdon which had been his grandfather's. Bribes. What was he to do?

David said that they had better go and see Durward.

They found that man drinking with de Montfort. Which was unfortunate. They could not just come out with it all in front of Henry's brother-in-law. However, the Earl Simon, no doubt aware of the situation, quite quickly excused himself, declaring that he must be getting old and his bed calling.

Durward cut short Alexander's recital thereafter, saying that he and de Montfort had been discussing this very matter.

His fellow-earl was himself against this Welsh campaign and sympathised with the nobles who were refusing to join it. The Welsh were, in fact, of no danger to England; they only wanted to be left to manage their own principality and to be freed from the continuing ravages of the English marcher lords. But Henry was insistent, partly because of his heir's, Prince Edward's, warlike nature and his desire to demonstrate his prowess in the field. Edward was, in fact, a much stronger character than his father, and a force to be reckoned with, only seventeen years as he was.

Alexander declared that he did not like Edward Plantagenet. But what was he to do, to say to King Henry?

Durward agreed that they could not give a blank no to Henry. But that did not mean that they had to go to war with their friends of Wales. They could not afford to indeed – the Comyns would take the opportunity to rise again in Scotland. They must use their wits, rather than their swords – as Sir David had advised on that other occasion! They should use the Comyn-Balliol connection, to their advantage in this matter. The Comyns owned much of Galloway; and John Balliol, Englishman as he was, had inherited most of the rest from his mother, Devorgilla, daughter of the last Celtic Lord of Galloway. And their allies, the Maxwells, controlled the remainder. Galloway marched with Cumbria. Let *them*, the Balliol-Comyn-Maxwell strength, mass along the Cumbrian border, seeming to threaten Wales. To threaten only, not to invade. And to ensure that they did not, Bruce of Annandale and the Earl of Carrick, his son, whose lands lay just to the north of the Comyn ones, would amass *their* strength. This would keep the others looking over their shoulders and make them reluctant to move southwards. So nothing would be done, but Scotland would *seem* to be helping Henry. They could send a messenger to Llewelyn telling him that he need not fear any attack from Scotland.

Much admiring this cunning device, Alexander chortled and actually thumped Durward's shoulder – something never before contemplated. David himself was surprised that this aggressive character, whom he had never thought of as in any way subtle, should have devised this clever scheme. He wondered, indeed, whether perhaps it was de Montfort's idea rather than Durward's? Whosoever, it might well be sufficient to get them out of their present predicament.

Next day, it seemed, they were to go to London. They would ride to Windsor, where Henry was greatly adding to that great castle, and then on by barge to the capital. The object of this excursion was not explained; but Henry was very proud of his building activities – the extravagance of which was in fact part of the reason for his unpopularity with his nobility, whom he was taxing to pay for it – and possibly this was opportunity to display it.

Most of their followers, both Scots and English, were left at Woodstock, since the boating must much restrict numbers. So a comparatively small company set off, considering that it contained two kings. The Queens were left behind also. They went down the Thames, by Chelgrove and Watlington to Henley, and on by the oddly named Maidenhead – which Alexander of course wanted to have explained – and so to Windsor, thirty miles. Here, soaring above the river, was the principal royal castle of England, with an enormous round central tower like a huge drum, within a lower and an upper ward. Henry was extending it all, and was eager to inspect and show off progress, in especial his new palace, next to the Horseshoe Cloisters. There was plenty of accommodation for them here, although the night's feasting was not on the same scale as at Woodstock.

That evening David asked Durward whether he had discovered what the Comyn earls had come south for, to see Henry; and it was to learn a strange story. It appeared, de Montfort being the informant, that their protégé Gamelyn had so impressed the new Pope that he had agreed to the excommunication of those who had deprived him of his bishopric and outlawed him, and all who supported these moves. And this was to apply to the King of England also, if he continued to support the Durward party. So the Earls of Menteith and Mar had come to warn Henry and seek to have him change sides, to support *them* instead of Durward in their struggle to gain control of the King and Scotland again. Durward said that *he* cared nothing for excommunication, but that he was not so sure about Henry Plantagenet – another reason why he had not wanted to give a blank no

300

to the demand for aid against the Welsh. He added that the Comyns seemed also to have acquired a new ally, none other than the King's mother, Marie de Coucy, of all people. It appeared that her husband John, titular King of Jerusalem, was a very close friend of this Pope, who had persuaded him and his wife to change to support Gamelyn's cause. That upjumped secretary and college tutor was proving to be a potent force indeed.

David ruminated long before he slept that night.

In the morning they went down to the waterside to board two large, flat-bottomed barges, heraldically decorated, with fine striped awnings and double banks of long oars. Alexander, never having seen the like, was much intrigued and eager to be off. A choir and band of instrumentalists was waiting in the second barge, to provide a musical accompaniment for the day's voyage – for although Windsor was only twenty-one miles from London by road, it was twice that by river. But Henry preferred this to riding.

However large and clumsy-seeming, the barges made good progress, each with sixteen oars – that is, until about halfway when, near Teddington, they slowed considerably. They had been going with the stream hitherto, but now the river became tidal, and with the tide incoming, faint as it was here, the oarsmen had to work harder. To aid them, the musicians changed their tunes to airs with a slow, regular, rhythmic beat, to which the rowers, two to each oar, could respond with grunts of effort. Alexander, savouring it all, would have taken a turn at an oar had Henry permitted it.

The scenery en route was quietly attractive for the first half, meadows and wooded slopes, but less so for the second, as the land grew flatter and more populous.

They smelt London before they saw more than its smoke pall ahead, the air being easterly. Edinburgh smelt too, of course, but there the hills and sea-breezes of that windy city helped to disperse the stench. Flatter London was not so blessed. The Thames itself added to the effluvium, becoming ever more polluted.

The Scots were astonished at the size of this city, as presently it seemed to engulf even the broad river. Apparently endless was the array of tenements and houses, churches, mills, stores, warehouses, yards, piers and jetties, on either side. It was almost awesome.

They went on and on, with Henry pointing out notable landmarks, some of which even Alexander had heard of, including the abbey of Westminster, which Henry was rebuilding. Then, left-ahead, loomed the massive square Tower of London, the royal fortress for which they headed, strangely pale, built of white limestone from Caen in Normandy by Norman William himself. Even here Henry was adding to the establishment, erecting lesser towers and extending walling. It could readily be seen why the cost of all this building-craze was emptying the treasury and increasing taxation.

They landed at the Tower Steps, and had to make a tour of the additions and work in progress before ever entering the fifteen-feet-thick walls of the white tower-keep. Alexander refused to be overawed by all he saw, racking his young brains for Scots equivalents and improvements to cite to his father-in-law. David and de Montfort exchanged amused glances.

They had eaten a meal of sorts on the barge, so an inspection of the huge main building followed at once, its halls and mural galleries, its curious wall-closets and pits, notorious prisons and torture-chambers, then out to the Lion Tower, with its menagerie of captive animals, and out of the Water Gate to mount the rise called the Tower Hill, where the beheadings took place, Henry indefatigable as guide and demonstrator. It occurred to David that he was in fact almost childish in this respect, and possibly in others also. That would explain a lot.

This examination took a long time, for the Tower of London covered over eighteen acres, with thirteen subsidiary towers and lesser buildings innumerable, so all were thankful indeed to sit down to a repast at last, and bed thereafter.

They spent three days at the Tower, seeing the sights of London – and getting used to its smells. Undoubtedly all this was not just a friendly exposition on Henry's part but an exercise to impress on his son-in-law the wealth, ramifications and power of England, and the wisdom of the King of Scots to take note of it.

They returned to Woodstock thereafter, as they had come, by barge and then on horseback. And after a final day of rest, the journey back to Scotland was commenced. Henry had a last significant point to put before his son-in-law and Durward. He declared, almost as an afterthought, that he had invited Magnus, the young King of Man, to visit him shortly, and issued outlawry against Harald Godfreysson, who had wickedly killed the brother of Magnus, former King. This might seem unexceptional enough – but was otherwise. For these Norse monarchs of Man were claiming overlordship of the Hebrides, which term included not only the Outer and Inner Isles off the Scottish West Highland coast but large parts of the Scots mainland itself, invaded by the Norse – and which in fact Alexander's father had been seeking to regain when he had died at Kerrera seven years before. So, if Henry was showing favour towards the King of Man, there was threat in it for Scotland, danger of an alliance which could further threaten its western seaboard – this no doubt to ensure Scots help in the Welsh campaign.

With this parting thrust to mull over, the visitors headed for home. Durward was not the only one who could devise ploys.

21

The year 1257 started uneventfully enough, save for the food shortages, although there were alarming rumours and consequent fears for the future. Margaret, however, produced another son in February, whom they called William and delighted in.

Alexander's sixteenth birthday was suitably celebrated, all accepting that he was now not far off early manhood, and acting towards him accordingly. He saw to it that they did – although to David and Margaret he remained his former self, affectionate, appreciative. But he was already talking about taking over the full rule of his kingdom, and highly critical of most of what was done by the regency in his name – although he still had at least three years to wait before he could dispense with regents.

The Balliol-Galloway-Bruce arrangement did not work quite as planned, ending indeed in a minor battle between the pretended invaders of Wales and their watchers – which in the circumstances might perhaps have been foreseen. What Henry Plantagenet thought of this was not ascertained, for he had other matters to preoccupy him at this time, his forces on the Welsh border suffering a major defeat by Llewelyn, much to the chagrin and fury of Prince Edward – and the further disaffection of his critical nobility. Indeed Simon de Montfort had to go to the marches to rally the scattered royal forces and seek to restore morale.

Then, in May, an extraordinary report reached Roxburgh. With Gamelyn, the Primate, still at Rome apparently, Bishop Clement of Dunblane was the senior churchman in Scotland – whether he was still also a regent nobody was quite sure. It looked as though he himself scarcely thought so, for of course he had not acted the part for so long. And now, it seemed, he had received a command from the Pope to perform the full excommunication of the other regents and such others as were responsible for Gamelyn's expulsion from his bishopric and outlawry. And this, despite age and decrepitude, he had done, travelling to Cambuskenneth Abbey near Stirling and there, with the Abbots of Melrose and Jedburgh and with full ceremonial of bell, book and candle, had proclaimed Durward, Dunbar and sundry others officially outwith Holy Church's care and recognition, denied not only communion but all Christian consolations and service, including absolutions, weddings and burials. Great was the sensation.

This remarkable development had prompt repercussions inevitably. Durward arrived at Roxburgh in angry mood. Not that he cared personally greatly about the excommunication, for he was not a religious man despite all his previous approaches to Rome on the subject of legitimisation; they gathered that Patrick of Dunbar was shattered, especially after his pious gestures of establishing the Red Friars in Scotland. Durward's fury was against Bishop Clement. Also to some extent against the said Dunbar whom he declared to be a weakling and useless as a regent. The King and council must promptly depose both from their status as regents. In future he, Durward, would rule as sole regent. Bishop Richard, as Chancellor, must call a Privy Council meeting at Edinburgh to proclaim the situation.

Alexander, to whom this announcement was made, came to David and Margaret in a state of indignation. "Durward will *not* order me thus!" he declared hotly. "He is *not* going to be the sole regent of my kingdom. I will not have it! He was insufferable again – as he used to be."

"In effect, Alex, he has been that for some time," David pointed out. "Bishop Clement has lain low, taken no part. And my cousin Patrick is little better, of no use as a regent."

"That I know. But I will not have Durward as my only regent – if regents I must have! *You* must be a regent, Davie, you must! I command it – a royal command!"

"Alex, no! Not me. I am not of the stature. And too young . . ."

"The Earl of Dunbar is little older than you."

"He is a great earl, one of the magnates of the kingdom. And, as we say, no effective regent either. No, no, Alex . . ."

"But yes! You *will*. I tell you, it is my royal command. You cannot disobey that, Davie Lindsay!"

Margaret spoke up. "David, I think that you should agree. You would do well, I am sure. Another regent is needed, if not two, to help keep Durward in his place. Alex *requires* that. And who better than you?"

"But regent, Margaret! Myself, Davie Lindsay! The highest position in the land, next to the sovereign!"

"What of it? You are Lord High Chamberlain now, are you not? And Justiciar-Depute of Lothian. And Cup-Bearer." That was Alexander. "Anyway, I am going to tell Durward that you are to be second regent. He cannot say no – and neither can you!"

David stared from one to the other.

In the event, Durward made little fuss about the matter, although he shook his head, frowned and then shrugged. Perhaps he judged that David would be little danger to him, and might even be of some help in controlling Alexander. He said that it was a matter for the council and a parliament.

Alexander insisted on being present at any such council meeting. So a move had to be made to Edinburgh shortly thereafter. Durward dominated the eventual gathering, to be sure, but his sovereign-lord was not to be silenced and, after Bishop Clement and Patrick of Dunbar – neither of whom put in an appearance – were duly relieved of their positions as regents, he announced strongly that he demanded that Sir David de Lindsay, High Chamberlain, should be made regent in their stead. Seton, Lyon King of Arms, immediately made a motion to that effect, and the High Steward surprised David by seconding. Durward made no counter-motion, nor in the circumstances did anyone else. So, as the councillors moved on to other business, especially the extraordinary and dire matter of the excommunications and the attitude of the bishops and mitred abbots, David found himself, all but casually it seemed, to be promoted to be one of the two highest-placed subjects in the land, a regent for the King of Scots. It would require to be confirmed by a parliament in due course, but there was little likelihood of any rejection there.

Scarcely able to take in the significance of it all, he accompanied Alexander back to Roxburgh, Durward making no suggestion that his services might be needed at Edinburgh. Now they would show how Scotland should be governed, the gleeful monarch declared. David found himself having to revert to a toning-down role. What had he let himself in for?

He did not have to wait for long to find out. Within the month visitors arrived at Roxburgh, welcome but demanding – none other than the King and Queen of Jerusalem, Alexander's mother and new stepfather John de Brienne. They had not come on any merely parental visit. They had indeed come more or less on behalf of the Pope, King John being a king-pin in the crusading campaigns and so having to have strong links with the Vatican. They wanted the excommunicated Durward ousted and got rid of, and the Comyn earls restored to the regency.

John de Brienne proved to be a striking-looking man of middle years, tall and slenderly built, with piercing eyes and a prominent chin. And Queen Marie was a new woman, confident, almost loquacious now, and obviously happy in her marriage. She was greatly taken with her growing-up son, exclaiming over him – to his embarrassment. She was pleased to see Margaret and David, and petted young Sander and William.

But despite all this familial appreciation, their arrival presented David with his first major problem as regent. The visitors assumed, from the first, that he would co-operate in unseating Durward, and began to discuss plans for bringing this about, and asking who could be relied upon as allies. Alexander himself was not averse to this, but David saw his duty otherwise. He was, after all, now a fellow-regent and colleague with Durward, and although he did not love the man, he conceived himself to owe a certain loyalty towards him and could not betray him. He had to tell the royal visitors that, placed as he was, he could not actively support steps to depose Durward. Moreover, he did not consider the Comyn earls to be any great improvement, and was loth to work for their return.

Queen Marie was grievously disappointed in him; but fortunately Margaret supported his stance. Alexander was of little help, *his* stance being that since he was not fond of the Comyns either, Pope or none, they should use them to get rid of Durward, but not to restore them to the regency, Davie to be sole regent.

This of course left that anyway reluctant regent all but speechless.

Eventually David came to some sort of compromise. He would not co-operate in bringing Durward down, nor in any way deliberately aid the Comyns. But nor would he warn Durward that such plans were afoot. Even this left him uncomfortable, and satisfied none. Alexander was reproachful, for the first time in a major matter, especially when David distanced himself from helping to make up a list of lords who might be prepared to join the plot. He warned Alexander not to get too deeply involved, the more so when the visitors informed them that Gamelyn was coming secretly back to Scotland, might already be here indeed, and was fully conversant with it all. David had a healthy respect for that man's wits and abilities, and wondered if the entire project was of his devising.

Marie and her husband did not remain long at Roxburgh. In pursuance of their endeavours on behalf of Alexander – or was it the Pope? – they were going north to the Earl of Menteith's secure castle on its island in the Loch of Menteith. They would have liked Alexander to go with them, secretly, but David persuaded him against this. It could mean civil war, and would indeed warn Durward to take urgent remedial action. Let him remain quietly at Roxburgh meantime, until the situation was a deal clearer.

Disappointed, the royal guests departed as unobtrusively as they had come.

David's regently advice about staying quietly at Roxburgh was not long in being made invalid. For Durward himself, no doubt well supplied with spies, arrived in anger, having been informed of the Jerusalem pair's visit and something of their objectives. He was highly critical of David for not having sent him word. He even knew of Gamelyn's return, and thought that he would be at the Menteith castle also. So David had the worst of both worlds, condemned by each side, his first venture into regency an abject failure.

Durward was not content with mere denunciation. He accepted that Gamelyn was behind it all, and that almost certainly an attempt would be made to get Alexander into Comyn hands, and possibly David also, as a regent. So they were both going to somewhere more secure than was Roxburgh, more secure even than Edinburgh Castle, which they had proved could be penetrated. They were going to Kinross, an old royal castle which Durward had taken over, set on a promontory jutting into Loch Leven, and not only strongly situated, but backed by the outliers of the Highland hills, the Ochils, which would enable Durward to bring down large numbers of men, if necessary, to protect it from his Perthshire lands and Atholl. He would have used Stirling, the strongest fortress in the kingdom, but unfortunately the Earl of Mar held it.

So the court was ordered to pack up promptly, save for de Ros and his wife, who were sent back to Wark, and under powerful escort all headed north.

Since Stirling had to be avoided, they crossed Forth at Queen Margaret's Ferry, after halts at Soutra and Edinburgh, and spent the third night at Malcolm Canmore's old palace of Dunfermline. From there it was only about fifteen miles to Loch Leven, a large, islanded sheet of water at the western end of the Lomond Hills of Fothrif. Kinross, as its name implied, was at the far head of the loch, a little town with a monastery, clustered at the root of the promontory which thrust out towards the nearest of the islands. On the high ground at the edge of this the old castle soared, protected from landwards by a deep artificial ravine-like ditch, water-filled, a strong hold indeed.

Here Durward installed Alexander and his Queen and court, whilst the armed escort was quartered in the town. Actually it was a pleasant enough place, with fine vistas in all directions; but they were most frankly prisoners, David as much so as the royal pair, regent or none, Durward

309

making no pretence otherwise. Alexander was indignant, but powerless to change the situation. It was an interesting thought that not so very far away to the south-west, less than a score of miles, Stirling Castle, in Comyn hands, frowned towards them; and only another fourteen miles further west, Alexander's mother and her husband, with Menteith, were ensconced, probably Gamelyn with them, all in what might be called the waist of Scotland. It might seem a strange area to which to have brought the royal hostage; but it was also near Durward's power-base.

So passed September. Forces were massing on both sides, all knew. It was only a matter of time until the inevitable show-down occurred. But Durward seemed confident – for of course he was the most competent soldier in the land, better than any of the Comyn lords; moreover, in a week or so, a high-powered English embassage came to Kinross from Henry Plantagenet, under Roger de Quincy, Earl of Winchester, promising support in exchange for future aid against the deplorable Welsh. This, apparently, Durward was prepared to agree – though whether he had any more intention of fulfilling it than on the last occasion was doubtful. In this connection, Winchester informed that Henry had forgiven John Balliol's inaction and general weakness, on the Welsh and other fronts, on payment of a large subsidy for his empty treasury. Balliol would have an army waiting near the Scots border should Durward require it.

So perhaps the latter had reason for confidence.

The period of waiting looked like ending at last in mid-October when word reached Kinross from various sources that the Comyns were on the move and in strength. The Earls of Buchan and Ross – the latter married to a Comyn – were marching south with the forces of most of the north country – Buchan, Mar, Ross, Badenoch, Lochaber and Caithness; and Menteith, with supporters from the south and west, was heading to meet them, total numbers put at some ten thousand at least.

Durward did not wait for them. He sent Moray of Bothwell off southwards to request Balliol and the English host to cross Tweed into Scotland, as threat only at this stage rather than real invasion, but to be ready to advance north if necessary.

He himself left Kinross, to head up into the skirts of the Highlands, at speed. His main strength was mustered in the Dunkeld area of South Atholl, apparently. He aimed to prevent the two Comyn armies from linking up; and if possible to ambush the northern force in one of the Highland passes which it must thread, possibly at Birnam. Alexander, David and the rest were left in the care of David the Graham, with a strong guard.

It was three nights later, in the small hours, that there were developments at Kinross Castle. David, in bed with Margaret, was rudely awakened by two men with dirks in their hands, and behind them none other than his one-time colleague, Sir Thomas de Normanville.

"I regret to arouse you thus, Sir David and Lady Margaret," the former Justiciar of Lothian declared, low-voiced. "But the circumstances leave me no option. Despite this naked steel, no harm will come to you if you remain quiet and do as you are bid. You will be taken to Stirling, with the King, forthwith. Secretly. So dress you, quickly. Lady Margaret, you need not do so."

David gripped Margaret's arm, and looked from those dirks to de Normanville. "If I go to Stirling, my wife and bairns go with me," he announced tersely. "Otherwise, I make . . . trouble!"

"No! Here is no ploy for women and bairns."

"But, yes. However you got in here, you will be taking the King, you say?"

"Yes."

"Then you will be wise to take these of mine, if me you must take, also. See you, leave these here, and Durward will use them against me. Nothing more sure. I will do nothing to risk ill to them. And I am a regent now. The Comyns will get nothing from me so long as Durward can hold my family. Use your wits, man!"

The other shrugged. "As you will. But there will be little room in the boats."

"Boats, is it! Well – they go. Or I shout aloud!"

"And die!" one of the dirk-holders jerked.

"Dress then, quickly . . ."

Hastily they donned their clothing, Margaret silent but

making no fuss. She went over to a mural chamber where their two children slept, to dress them, whilst de Normanville fretted.

"I regret this, my friend," he said. "But in war, one has little choice."

"And Alexander?"

"He should be down at the boats by now."

"How did you . . .?" David stopped. Such questions could wait.

Margaret brought Sander to him, still half asleep, the baby William in her arms, eyes shut.

They were led out, and by a mural passage in the thickness of the ancient walling to a minor stairway which went down to the vaulted basement cellars. Out in the courtyard they found Menteith himself, with some men-at-arms, waiting impatiently. He exclaimed at the sight of the children but wasted no time in hurrying them off to a postern-gate, which opened on to a flight of stairs which led down to a jetty at the loch-shore, where three boats were lying, crowded with folk. Here they were hustled on to the first boat, where they found Alexander, Seton and Bishop Richard the Chancellor – but no Queen. Also David the Graham, the castle's keeper, and his deputy, de Brechin, both only half-clothed and looking unhappy, men with drawn dirks at their back.

Alexander greeted David excitedly. "They woke me! I tried to shout, but they would not let me, Davie. They did not hurt you? Or Margaret?" He did not sound unduly depressed.

"No. Where is Margery?"

"They do not want her. She is only a girl! We go to Stirling, they say. At least we are freed from Durward!"

Menteith told Alexander, roughly, to keep his voice down. Then he turned to Graham and his deputy. "You, Brechin, go back to the castle," he directed. "You will not raise the alarm so long as you can see these boats. Or *we* can see the castle. Or else Graham dies! You have it? No alarm, no pursuit, or the Graham dies. Now – off with you!"

Brechin, muttering, climbed back on to the jetty, clutching his scanty garb. The boats pulled out, their rowlocks muffled with cloth to prevent any creaking noise.

The captives exchanged commiserations, Alexander the least upset. He seemed to look on it all as something of an adventure.

They were rowed for quite a distance due southwards, a mile at least, and then in to the reedy, low, western shore of the loch, this no doubt to ensure that they would outdistance any possible pursuit, the swampy nature of this shore allowing no tracks for horses. When they landed, however, they found quite a large number of mounts awaiting them, so there had to be an access of some sort to this point. Abandoning the boats, they all mounted, David holding Sander before him, Margaret cradling little William, Menteith cursing de Normanville for having brought the children.

They set off by a twisting route through the bogland, approximately westwards.

That was a strange ride through the night-bound valleys between the Cleish and Ochil Hills, along the winding Devon to the River Forth, twenty-five miles. It was dawn before they reached Stirling. Fortunately young Sander and William slept most of the way, jolting notwithstanding.

David found himself uncertain as to how he felt about it all. They were, to be sure, merely exchanging gaolers, and the Comyns no worse than Durward. Conditions indeed might be better, with Alexander's mother and her husband in the Comyn camp now. Margaret accepted it all, her usual, quietly effective self.

Up in Stirling Castle atop its vast rock they found Marie de Coucy and King John, also Bishop Gamelyn, awaiting them, and were treated as though this was a blessed delivery for them rather than any mere change of imprisonment; a strange situation, nothing of daggers and naked steel being mentioned. Gamelyn was coolly courteous, and seemed entirely sure of himself. He was about to leave for the north, with Menteith, to join the southern Comyn force under Mar, with more men. It seemed that this former college teacher now aspired to be a military leader as well as all else.

So, perforce, they settled in at Stirling, more comfortably in fact than at Kinross, and with even more panoramic views; considerably better quarters than at Edinburgh Castle also. Alexander did not seem greatly concerned about Margery's position, left at Kinross, although David and Margaret were. But they felt that no great harm would come to her, since she was Henry's daughter and the Durward faction would be anxious not to offend the Plantagenet.

David asked himself what being regent of Scotland meant, as far as he was concerned? Merely being a fellow-prisoner with his sovereign-lord, it seemed, powerless to affect events, much less to rule.

However, events changed his mind somewhat, quite quickly. In only three days the situation was transformed. Menteith, Mar and Gamelyn arrived back, with Buchan and Ross, in high satisfaction. By an effective stratagem, possibly Gamelyn's, they had managed to surprise, outflank and defeat Durward's force in the Dunkeld and Birnam area, dispersing them entirely. Durward himself had fled southwards, presumably to safety in England, and the victors, who held the King, were now supreme in Scotland. And, of course, since Durward's regency could be accepted as no longer effective, David was in fact sole regent until others might be appointed by the Privy Council and a parliament. In name, at least, Davie Lindsay ruled Scotland on its monarch's behalf.

This, to be sure, was *only* in name, in theory; in practice, the Comyns made the decisions. But David's assent and signature were necessary to make all lawful and effective, likewise the Chancellor's Great Seal. So he had to be consulted and treated with respect. On the face of it, the situation was transformed.

The very next day Queen Margery arrived at Stirling safely, sent by de Brechin, with assurance of a new goodwill.

There could be no resting on laurels. English invasion was likely once Durward reached Balliol, and this development must be countered if possible. A hasty conference decided that a move had to be made at once, southwards; first the Comyn lords and Gamelyn, with the King and his regent; and then, following on, the victorious army.

They would head for Roxburgh, and from there seek to negotiate with Balliol, wherever he might be. They would take young Margery with them, to emphasise that she was safe and in good hands.

It was the road again, therefore, and no delay. Margaret insisted on coming along also, children or none. The Lindsays were becoming well-travelled infants, as it were bred to the saddle.

It was decided, at Roxburgh, that only a small deputation should go on to try to confer with Balliol, and presumably Durward, under a flag of truce. David was urgent that their first priority was to prevent any English army's invasion of Scottish soil. He was also strong on making some sort of arrangement with Durward, if possible. This ding-dong struggle between the Comyns and that man must be brought to an end, for the kingdom's sake.

Alexander rather reluctantly backed him in this. He much disliked Durward, but recognised the realities of the situation. And the Comyns, still more reluctantly, acceded. It would take some time for their large army to reach these parts, and meanwhile the English could do much damage, and get themselves strongly entrenched in Scotland. Negotiation from strength was probably wise.

David sent a messenger to Wark immediately, for information, and de Ros himself came back with him. Balliol was at Norham Castle, he announced, Durward and Moray with him, and a force of some four thousand men camped nearby; Norham, also on Tweed, lay some ten miles east of Wark. He, de Ros, had been having trouble with these English soldiery, idle, and too near for comfort. So far as he could tell, there was no sign as yet of this host crossing Tweed.

Alexander wanted to go with the deputation, but he was persuaded that it would be unwise and unsuitable. Durward and Balliol might ignore their white flag, if by doing so they could capture the monarch. So only Menteith, Mar, Seton and de Ros went, with David and a sizeable escort.

They made an early start, for the November days were short, reaching Wark by noon. There de Ros crossed Tweed to his own side, while the others proceeded along the north bank to Ladykirk, opposite Norham; he would go to the English camp and inform Balliol of the mission, and request the necessary meeting, under a truce. It was to be hoped that he would agree. After all, neither he nor Durward had anything to lose by it.

315

A little way past Ladykirk the great river took one of its many bends, and at this a central islet had formed, the shallows of it forming the Norham ford. Above this they waited. Norham Castle was in sight quarter of a mile downstream. They could see the great camp on the slightly rising ground behind.

They had quite a wait before they descried quite a large mounted party coming from the castle. The Lion Rampant standard, carried by Seton, was unfurled, to show due authority, and they rode down into the river, to splash across to the islet, on what might be termed neutral ground, there to wait.

They saw that the opposition consisted of Balliol himself, with Roger de Quincy, Earl of Winchester who, like the former, had a Scots wife and Scots lands, Durward and Moray, with de Ros in attendance, plus the expected armed escort. These also splashed across the water, to rein up on the sandy islet about a score of yards away. All sat their mounts, staring at each other.

David took the initiative. "My lords," he called, "I greet you, in the name of King Alexander's Grace, I, David de Lindsay, his regent. We come to seek resolve some of the problems of our two realms, other than by armed struggle. Do you agree that is a commendable course? We have ten thousand men on their way here," he mentioned, as a seeming afterthought.

Balliol conferred with his companions before answering – but the fact that he had come at all would seem to indicate willingness to talk, at least.

"We have our thousands also, sir," that man said at length. "King Henry's men. What have you to say which should give us reason to heed you?"

"Sufficient, my lords. Battle we are prepared for. Having already won a trial of strength with the Earl of Atholl there! But bloodshed should be avoided, if other means can prevail. His Grace Alexander requests that you remove your armed host, which threatens his realm, to a deal further into your own land, if not disperse it altogether. And either to hand over the Earl of Atholl, and those who support him, to our care, or else remove him and them also, from any possible menace to Scotland."

316

Durward hooted. "So cheeps a cock-sparrow!" he jeered. "Let those behind you bray their loudest, Lindsay! *That* they are good at!"

"We will teach you better, Durward ! Have already taught you!" Menteith cried.

Balliol spoke. "Your demands, sirrah, are foolish as well as insolent. Give us one good reason why we should heed them. Since we do not fear your arms."

David began to speak, but Menteith interrupted. "More than one, Englishman! If you would serve your King well, you will heed them indeed. Do *you* wish for excommunication, and King Henry also? At word sent to the Pope at Rome by the Lord Bishop of St Andrews, and the renowned King of Jerusalem, that will follow. We have the papal assurance."

Durward snorted, but Balliol and Winchester did not.

"Moreover we – that is His Grace, on good counsel – have made a treaty with the Prince Llewelyn of Wales, of mutual aid and support. Cross the Tweed into Scotland, and the Welsh strike north. And when we have defeated your arms here, *we* march south to their aid! How say you, Englishmen?"

Silence.

This last was news to David: at least, he knew of moves towards the Welsh, but scarcely that of a treaty. Alexander certainly had not signed anything of the sort. Only a threat, then – but a potent threat in view of the present series of Welsh victories on their marches. He cleared his throat.

"My lord, all this need not be. If you will but withdraw armed support from the Earl of Atholl. That is all that we ask meantime. We wish to make no threat towards the King of England. His daughter is our Queen, and well cherished and esteemed by us. His Grace would send his salutations, not threats. So – hear us."

"I think that you speak with two voices, my lords!" Winchester said. "Which do we believe?"

"Neither!" That was Durward.

"I speak in the name of King Alexander. As his regent," David said simply.

Menteith opened his mouth to speak, and then shut it again.

317

For long moments nothing was said on either side, as the horses sidled and pawed the soft sand. Then Balliol reined his mount round.

"We shall consider what has been said," he got out. He waved to the others. "Come."

Winchester shrugged, and followed. Durward seemed loth to go, but could scarcely remain alone. He glared then, as he turned. De Ros did not accompany them back but came over to join the Scots.

That appeared to be that. There did not seem anything else to do but to return to Roxburgh.

Two days later word came from de Ros's wife to say that the English army had left the area, heading up Till, southwards, Durward presumably went with them.

There was general relief at Roxburgh Castle. The Comyns went off to meet their host and turn it back, whilst David took Alexander and the court to Edinburgh.

In the circumstances, they could surely now expect a fairly peaceful winter.

22

The required meeting of the reconstituted Privy Council was held at Edinburgh, just before the start of Yuletide, Gamelyn back in the secretary's chair, David presiding but Alexander present. The changing composition of the said council was almost amusing, most former Durward supporters discreetly absenting themselves and the Comyn ones reappearing, as Alexander put it, like coneys out of their burrows. Some there were, of course, not definitely identified with either side, such as the High Steward and the Earls of Fife, Strathearn, Lennox and Angus. On this occasion Patrick of Dunbar seemed to consider himself sufficiently distanced from Durward to attend.

The first business was the matter of the regency. Menteith and Mar, needless to say, assumed their reappointment to be automatic. Alexander was prepared to *demand* that David continued in the office; but curiously it was Gamelyn who beat him to it, proposing that the excellent High Chamberlain, Sir David de Lindsay, brought distinction to the position and should remain a regent. David was surprised at this and wondered as to the wily cleric's intentions. Was he to be manipulated in some fashion? The thing was accepted, anyway, without controversy. But the appointment of the other two regents would not become valid until a parliament confirmed them. And it was decided that such parliament should not be called until April – this because there were always complaints about winter parliaments, with the snow-filled Highland passes all too apt to prevent commissioners from the far north and west from attending, and most of the Comyn support lay thereabouts. So it meant that, officially, David would remain sole regent until then, however much the actual power lay with the others.

The council agreed that the proposed Welsh treaty should

be promulgated, and envoys were appointed to go to Llewelyn, Alexander applauding this. But also, at David's suggestion, envoys were to be sent to King Henry, assuring him that no hostility was intended against him so long as there was no attempt to reinstate Durward, and that the Welsh were left to govern themselves. Also to be informed that his daughter's well-being and care was important to them all.

Sundry necessary appointments were made, especially to justiciarships, nearly all being Comyn-related, and the meeting broke up.

It was Alexander's suggestion that Yuletide should be spent at Luffness, still his favoured location. The Comyn earls did not object, nor did Gamelyn; their concern, of course, was that Alexander should be safe from any possible attempt to capture him, and they considered Roxburgh too close to England for safety, accepting that he and his Queen should not be shut up again like prisoners in Edinburgh Castle. Luffness they considered near and secure enough; but they ensured safety by insisting on a large guard going with him.

What the Lady Elizabeth thought of this invasion could be guessed, for although growing old she was scarcely mellowing. But, with the King and Queen of Jerusalem amongst the guests, as well as Alexander and Margery, she could hardly display her feelings openly. At least her two little grandsons delighted her, and their mother benefited from their popularity. And Seton helped, by decanting some of the company and guards to nearby Seton. It had been a good season and harvest, after the previous grim year, and there was no lack of provision.

So they kept Yule and Christmas happily enough, although there was too much goose-shooting and ploutering about on mud-flats for many there, including Alexander's stepfather, who considered it a strange way of enjoying themselves. It was very frosty weather, which was good for the geese – or at least for their shooters. And Alexander was also introduced to the sport of curling, on the frozen pond which was an extension of the castle moat. In this connection, he found satisfaction in going, with Johnnie Lindsay, to seek suitable roundish, smooth stones on the nearby beaches, a development from the sea-shells he used to gather.

John, now a young man, was tall as his brother, solidly built, cheerful and good company. He and Alexander got on as well together as ever – so well, indeed, that to celebrate New Year, Alexander insisted on knighting him, for no particular reason other than friendship – to Johnnie's distinct embarrassment.

David's mother had not forgotten her preoccupation with crusading zeal, allied to vengeance over her brother's death – especially with the King of Jerusalem present. She made a point of publicly reminding David of his promise to do something about it in due course, he pointing out that until Alexander came of age, and his own duties as regent were no longer required, crusading must wait. She had to agree with that, but suggested that there ought to be something that he could do meantime, influential as he now was. Even his feeble cousin Patrick had achieved some virtue by introducing those Trinitarian friars into Scotland, to gather funds for the crusades. Could David not at least help in that endeavour? Needless to say, John de Brienne supported her in this proposal, and David promised to see what he could do. To prove willing, he organised a visit one day to the new Redfriars Monastery at Houston, on the Tyne nine miles away to the south-east, taking King John and Alexander with him.

It was, in fact, an interesting and worthwhile little expedition – although such brothers as were not away on their peripatetic alms begging duties were quite overwhelmed by the arrival unannounced of two monarchs, a regent and other notables. The monastic premises were still abuilding, in the warm local red stone, so suitable as to colour at least. A chapel, refectory and dormitory were already in use, a granary was nearing completion, and a mill was planned, with a lade being excavated and lined with stone to bring the water for the mill-wheel from the nearby Tyne, all the labour being done by the friars themselves and their lay-brothers.

Alexander was enthusiastic. Where could Davie set up a similar or even better place? His fellow-monarch seconded.

David, recognising that between these two and his mother

he was going to be pressed on this matter, decided that he had better do something about it. Chatting with Pate Dunbar thereafter over the possibilities, that useful individual – who was, of course, now to all intents managing Luffness, The Byres and Garleton estates – suggested that there was a former farm near the boundary of their Byres property and that of Seton, indeed just below Setonhill, where a constantly overflowing burn from the high ground got trapped on its way to Gosford Bay, just west of Aberlady Bay, producing floods and bogland. It was not valuable land therefore, indeed almost unproductive. But if it was drained and the burn harnessed, this could much improve the area, and also give power for a mill. Why not give this property to the Trinitarians, to set up another of their monasteries, or a hospice at least, where they could do the drainage, and provide a much-needed resting-place for travellers between Edinburgh and Dunbar? So it would all serve a useful purpose, reclaim spoiled land and give David credit.

That man clapped his cousin on the back, and said so be it. Let the Red Friars take over the site, drain the land and build their house. Give them every assistance.

For once, his mother expressed herself as pleased with her elder son.

So it was back to Edinburgh and duty.

Duty was the word. Ever more notably Alexander was becoming aware of his role, responsibilities and indeed opportunities. Strangely, it was his mother who was partly the cause of this; not so much on account of parental urgings, as out of a kind of jealousy on his part, for Marie and her husband were taking an ever larger part in the ruling of the kingdom, the Comyns evidently prepared to accept this as counter-balance to the English pretensions. Menteith, the leading Comyn, was a sick man these days, and Mar and Buchan less effective; so that gradually the King and Queen of Jerusalem, odd as it might seem, became very influential in Scotland, often taking decisions in the name of Alexander and his regency. This spurred the youth on to asserting himself and demonstrating that *he* was the real monarch here. There was no animosity but some competition.

David, never eager to play regent anyway, watched and supported.

Alexander's seventeenth birthday, that April, was a significant occasion. Seventeen was all but the threshold of young manhood, with youth, like childhood, being left behind. He had been King for nine years.

Within a few days of the birthday the required parliament was held at Stirling. It produced few surprises, save that Menteith was too unwell to attend. However, he was still appointed, with Mar, to be a regent. Gamelyn steered all efficiently, especially getting the terms of the Welsh treaty accepted – which obviously was mainly of his own devising. It was, indeed, more of a device than anything else, none there anticipating that any actual armed expedition to Wales would eventuate. But it could all be a potent threat to Henry Plantagenet.

Alexander asserted himself from the throne, making it very clear that he was no longer any mere symbol of kingship but a monarch – in fact, he told them that in two years he would be taking over the full rule of his realm, with side-glances at his mother and stepfather, sitting nearby.

David, who as always was concerned with peaceful negotiations rather than threats and possible bloodshed, proposed that, as well as the terms of the Scots-Welsh treaty being conveyed to Henry, a more conciliatory message should be sent from this parliament, indicating that no hostility towards England was involved, merely that the Scots and Welsh should be left to manage their own affairs in peace. He suggested that Henry should be invited to send an embassage to Scotland to discuss mutual relations and problems. This was scarcely enthusiastically received by the assembly, but it was accepted.

Another parliament was scheduled for September, when it was hoped that the situation would be clearer and more resolved. Meanwhile considerable application was necessary for the internal government of Scotland, which had of course been sadly neglected for years, in all the faction-fighting. New sheriffs in especial were appointed – some sheriffdoms had been vacant for long – although admittedly most of the new men were Comyn-related.

Then it was back to Edinburgh, with frequent visits to Luffness.

That summer saw developments in more than Alexander's reaching out towards rule. He began to show an interest in women, young women, remarking on their persons and attributes more and more often, and seeking their company. This did not seem to apply noticeably to his wife, whom he still evidently found less than stimulating, quiet, withdrawn, rather mouse-like creature as she was, an unlikely Plantagenet.

Margaret and David had a discussion about this one night, in their bedroom at Luffness, after an interlude with a visiting neighbour's daughter.

"It is but natural," David said. "We should not be surprised. And Margery is scarcely the one to satisfy him. But it is awkward, in the circumstances. We do not want him to start forging links with other young women . . ."

"Not with *an* other, anyway," Margaret agreed. "That would much upset Henry. To be sure, his father, and *mine*, was bedding women by his age. My half-sister, Durward's wife, was conceived before my father was twenty, unlawfully, although he was wed by then. Kings can be like that. *His* father was, likewise."

"True. But they did not have Henry Plantagenet as good-sire! Who claims to be Lord Paramount of Scotland."

"Most lads learn by trial and error, no doubt. As probably did you? For you were fairly proficient when you came to me! But a king is different, reared apart. Not able to try girls out, in a barn or behind a bush! He needs an instructress. Some decent woman. A widow perhaps. Of some upbringing. No girl, but young enough to be able to attract him, at his age. And teach him. In bed. Without . . . ill consequences."

"Then Alex *himself* could teach Margery. If he would. Yes – that would serve."

So courses of instruction were instituted, Pate quite quickly finding a suitable lady, recommended apparently out of personal experience, widow of a small laird on the Garleton barony, a sonsy, friendly creature in her mid-thirties, who expressed no distaste for the idea of guiding her liege-lord in the pleasant paths of physical stimulation and fulfilment, and whom Alexander found much to *his* taste, from the first encounter. Thereafter, visits to Luffness had more than geese to recommend them. Whether Margery gained in consequence was hard to tell.

The summer of 1258 passed with less event on the national scene. King Henry responded to the placatory message of the Scots parliament by announcing that he would send the High Sheriffs of York and Northumberland to hold discussions as to better relations between the realms; but month succeeded month, and these envoys did not appear. Henry, of course, was having dire troubles, unable to control his rebellious nobles, and his foreign adventures going agley, with Welsh warfare in abeyance. It was rumoured that Simon de Montfort was deserting his brother-in-law. Durward was said to be lying low in Northumberland somewhere.

The Earl of Menteith died in mid-summer, so the regency was reduced to David and Mar. That earl was unreliable, no strong character, and in effect did only what Gamelyn told him. David personally found the situation very unsatisfactory, feeling his regency to be little more than nominal, with Gamelyn in fact ruling the country – which was not a satisfactory situation in his opinion, however efficient that prelate. David had always considered himself to be more of a guardian of the young King than any true regent, ruler; and now with Alexander almost a man, and an urgent one and forceful, his position seemed to be neither one thing nor another. He and Margaret thought a deal about amending it. If matters continued as they were, Gamelyn would soon be so securely entrenched in power that he would be able largely to nullify Alexander's looked-for coming of age, controlling Church and state both. Something would have to be done.

At the arranged parliament in September then, again held at Stirling, so much more effective for good than a Comyn-dominated Privy Council, he and Alexander took a concerted lead. They could hardly say that Mar was useless and Gamelyn something of a menace to the kingdom but, with Menteith dead, the regency had to be reconstituted anyway. So David proposed the setting up of a regency council rather than individual regents, Alexander backing this strongly. Gamelyn could not be excluded, of course, but he might be hedged in and controlled in some measure by a judicious selection of fellow-councillors. It was not just to be the Privy Council under another name, but a distinct and less Comyn-dominated entity to wield the supreme power in the land for the two years until Alexander was nineteen. There were objections and counter-motions, to be sure, but with the monarch himself so vehement, David pressing, and Gamelyn there only as Chancellor, having to act as a sort of seemingly neutral chairman, the commissioners of parliament passed the measure by a fair majority. The regency council was to consist of Queen Marie and her husband, David, de Ros, Gamelyn, Mar, Buchan, the High Steward and two of Durward's former supporters, Sir Gilbert de Hay and Sir Robert de Menzies.

This achieved, with the Comyn say on it countered, Alexander himself proposed that, in the interests of peace, reconciliation and balanced government, the Earl of Atholl himself should be offered the opportunity to end his exile, come back, and join this council, provided that he agreed to sign a solemn document that he would abide by the expressed will of the majority thereon and make no moves to impose *his* will on the realm – on pain of high treason and its punishment, death. This royal suggestion, needless to say, took a deal of swallowing for many there, the Comyns in especial, and Gamelyn declaring that they could not have a man excommunicate on any regency council. David said that if indeed Durward agreed and signed the document and expressed contrition, His Holiness of Rome could, no doubt, be persuaded by my lord Bishop of St Andrews to lift the excommunication, in the interests of peace, harmony and good government.

Parliament eventually passed that also. David helped by declaring that he desired to resign the office of High Chamberlain, and proposed that it should be offered to Sir Aymer de Maxwell, another former Durward supporter. He was, however reluctantly, learning the art of government manipulation.

Other business was less controversial, and the parliament adjourned.

Thereafter envoys, Sir Robert de Menzies and Sir Robert

de Ros, were sent off to Northumberland to seek out Durward and try to persuade him to come to Wark for the required meeting and presentation of the document. And just in case that aggressive character thought to again bring an English host with him on this occasion, orders were issued for the assembling of a small Scottish army to accompany the King's party to the border.

In the event, all went well. Durward duly appeared at the Wark ford of Tweed, with only de Ros, de Menzies and a small group at his back, scarcely humble-seeming but prepared to agree to the terms offered and to sign the required document before all as witnesses. Gamelyn did not come on this expedition.

Durward declared that, with His Grace's permission, he would make his own way back to Atholl and his northern territories which had not seen him for so long. Alexander was glad to be spared his company.

On the face of it, then, that winter was the first in which peace had reigned in the Scottish realm for many a year.

23

Alexander was eighteen. Only one year to go. They spent the birthday at Luffness, which had become almost a second home for that young man, and where indeed he was happiest. Especially now that he had Meg Stotherd to visit, his instructress – although her duties had largely got beyond mere teaching now, providing rather recreation than education. She suited Alexander's vigorous, enthusiastic, warm and friendly nature, and the fact that she was twice his age seemed to trouble neither. Not that his interested, instructed and roving eye did not on occasion turn elsewhere also, in his concern to prove that her tuition was not fruitless, Margery by no means the sole beneficiary; but at least husband and wife seemed more at ease together, although nothing would make the latter an outgoing and congenial personality.

With David, de Ros and Seton, Alexander spent much time at the new monastic establishment between Setonhill and Gosford Muir, which was already being called locally the Reidspittal or Red Friars Hospice. About a score of monks and lay-brothers were hard at work there, partly on the building work, partly on drainage, with a mill and lade one of the first priorities, as a source of income. They had erected a temporary and makeshift chapel and dormitory, of timber, and were bringing in the reddish stone from the quarry at Luffness, out of which the castle itself had been built; the Lady Elizabeth, who was showing a great interest in this project, to be sure, putting the quarrymen and carters at the friars' disposal. She frequently visited there herself, although her physique was deteriorating and age making itself felt. The royal party themselves took a hand in the building process, Alexander coming to fancy himself as a mason, although better at drystane-dyking than actual stone and mortar work, which required a deal more patience. It was a pleasant spot, not much more than a mile from the castle.

Henry's promised envoy had arrived in Scotland at last, not either the Sheriffs of York or of Northumberland but one Master William Horton, of St Albans, a shrewd cleric who was not long in crossing pastoral staffs with Bishop Gamelyn. One day, while they were all at the new hospice, this envoy arrived there, seeking the King, and with him an individual whom he announced had come on a special mission from King Henry, another churchman. He declared that his master wished Alexander to visit him secretly, and as soon as possible. Just like that.

"Secretly!" Alexander exclaimed. "Me? Secretly?"

"Yes, Highness. Secretly."

"Why?"

"His Majesty so requires, Sire."

"But . . . how can I do that? And why? I am King of Scots. I cannot secretly leave my kingdom. Travel down through England like some packman."

"You could go by ship, Highness. To London town."

David spoke. "I am Lindsay. A regent. This is an extraordinary proposal. What reason does King Henry offer for it?"

The messenger looked at Master Horton, who shrugged. "His Majesty does not vouchsafe his reasons, sir – only that it is his royal will. And for the benefit of both realms."

"*His* royal will!" Alexander burst out. "What of *mine*, sir?"

The two Englishmen looked uncomfortable but tight-lipped.

"I cannot think that this is possible," David said. "For whatever reason. If King Henry comes to the border here, His Grace of Scotland might go to meet him. If a meeting is required. But – not any lengthy journey into England, in secret."

Silence.

"I will not do it," Alexander declared. "For whatever reason."

"His Majesty is Lord Paramount of Scotland,'" the envoy mentioned.

"Claims to be, but is not!"

"Surely, sirs, you must have some notion as to why King Henry so desires?" David pressed. "For so extraordinary a request. Kings do not make secret journeys to others' kingdoms."

"His Majesty is King Alexander's good-sire, the Scottish Queen his daughter."

"What has that to do with it?"

"Authority!" Horton said, succinctly.

"He has no authority over me, or my realm," Alexander jerked. "Tell him so."

"Your Highness is being . . . ill-advised. King Henry has means at his disposal to show his royal displeasure."

"Do not threaten me, sirrah!"

"This matter will have to go before the regency council," David put in. "But I have little doubt as to rejection."

"I will not go, whatever the council may say!" Alexander exclaimed. "Tell Henry so. And tell him also that I am still awaiting the payment of my wife's dowry-moneys. We have been wed eight years and still look for them – although promised time and again."

On that awkward note the visitors departed, leaving an angry and mystified group of hospice-builders.

When, later, the regency council heard of this strange summons, they were unanimous in rejection. It was wondered whether his many troubles had caused Henry Plantagenet to lose his wits. No further action was taken.

That summer Gamelyn gave evidence, if that was necessary, of his influence, cleverness and effectiveness. It came in the form of an announcement from Pope Alexander to the effect that the Scottish abbey of Arbroath, now very much under the control of the Bishop of St Andrews – although actually in the see of Brechin – should have the revenues of the wealthy church of Haltwhistle in Northumberland. While on the face of it, this might seem a small enough matter, of interest only to clerics, in fact it was a vital disposition. For the papal dictate added, "Haltwhistle, in the *Scottish* King's land of Tynedale". This represented a triumph for Gamelyn, as well as a useful increment to his income. For, of course, Tynedale, with Haltwhistle, were inset in England's Northumberland, and here was a papal acceptance that they belonged to the King of Scots. This arose out of a bargain struck with King Stephen of England a century before, usurper as some called him. The ancient kingdom of Strathclyde, long incorporated in Scotland, had included Cumbria and some western parts of Northumbria, Tynedale in the midst. Stephen, in exchange for Scots help to retain his throne, had ceded fairly vaguely defined territories here to Scotland. Little had been done about this, but now, with this pronouncement, Gamelyn had brought it to the fore again – and in doing so had provided Scotland with a valuable card to play against Henry, a negotiating-point indeed.

And such was useful, at this stage. For, as threat against Wales, at his son Edward's urging, Henry was supporting the aggressive and ambitious King Magnus of Man, a Norseman and great raider of the Welsh seaboard. But Magnus was also laying claim to the great Somerled's ancient Lordship of the Isles, the kingdom of the Hebrides, as sub-King under Hakon of Norway, that part of the Scottish realm which Alexander's father had been seeking to bring under control when he had died on the Isle of Kerrera in 1249. So this Magnus was a threat to Scotland also, and Henry's support of him dangerous.

Alexander, delighted with Gamelyn for once, insisted on immediately sending a message to his father-in-law that unless he retracted his support for the King of Man, the Scots would consider moving south and taking into possession the lands of Tynedale in Northumberland. He also required his wife's dowry to be paid forthwith.

The King of Scots was beginning to show the mettle with which he was forged.

Undoubtedly Bishop de Gamelyn was recognising this also, and with less than a year to go until Alexander assumed full royal power, was concerned to improve his image with the monarch.

This threat regarding Tynedale had its effect. Earl Simon de Montfort and the cleric Maunsell were sent north in haste, and Alexander and his regency council met them at Jedburgh in August, Durward amongst them, a changed man these days, likewise well aware of the way that the tide was flowing.

Alexander took charge of the meeting from the start, not exactly brash but forceful, leaving no one in doubt that here was a ruler who meant to rule, and without waiting for a few more months to pass.

De Montfort and Maunsell accepted this, the former his smiling, courteous self, the latter inscrutable. They alleged that King Stephen of unhappy memory had been acting outwith his due powers in granting the lordship of Tynedale to Scotland; but accepted that this could be hard to prove in the law of either realm, an inconvenience as it was. It would be a great pity to get involved in any conflict, armed or otherwise, over such a small and doubtful matter, and King Henry was prepared to withdraw active support from Magnus of Man – which support, of course, had never been aimed against Scotland anyway, nor Wales either indeed, but rather against the wretched Irish petty kings who preyed on English shipping in these waters.

No one believed this, of course, but refrained from saying so. Alexander expressed modified satisfaction. Now – what was the reason for King Henry's extraordinary request that he, Alexander, should make a secret journey to England?

The ambassadors looked suitably mystified over this, and expressed their disbelief over any such demand. But they did declare that Henry was most anxious to see his son-in-law and daughter – as was not unnatural, surely. Would they not come to visit him and Queen Eleanor, not secretly but in royal state?

Alexander looked around his council and encountered no hostile reaction, only warnings that there should be no decisions made as to matters of state, lacking the regency's agreement. Their monarch smilingly demonstrated his own grasp of the situation, for he asserted that any such visit would not be convenient until the suitable travel conditions of April or May next – by which time he would have reached his nineteenth birthday and no longer need a regency council! He would, to be sure, seek to be guided by his good advisers, but the decisions would be his own. However, he agreed that there should be no important matters of state dealt with on such a visit, and no pressure brought to bear on him. And he took the opportunity to add to this that another condition should be the payment of that dowry; and also that his personal rights in the Honour of Huntingdon, for which he had received no revenues for long, should be put in order. If these conditions were agreed, he would be pleased, with his wife, to visit his father-in-law the following late spring or summer.

The envoys conceded that these terms might well be acceptable.

That evening, David had a private word with de Montfort, with whom he had always got on well. The earl was careful about what he said, but he did admit to grave misgivings about his brother-in-law. Henry was in a strange frame of mind, he conceded. Always he had been moody, wilful; but now he was being difficult indeed, his advisers all but in despair. The nobles, always restive in this reign, were ripe for outright revolt. How happy the realm whose monarch's wits did not go astray! Henry was being ever more dominated by his elder son Edward, who fancied himself a warrior and whose sole objective seemed to be conquest, of efforts towards which the nobility had had sufficient, since they provided the troops. He, de Montfort, had tried to interest young Edward in going crusading, which might usefully harness his warlike zeal, but so far without success.

David asked again about Henry's strange summons for a secret meeting, but the other seemed honest about his ignorance, even of an envoy being sent. But it was not untypical of Henry's behaviour these days. How fortunate was Scotland to have a young monarch of Alexander's stature and spirit. And with such able and devoted advisers!

David could make only non-committal noises.

De Montfort and Maunsell were sent away with assurances that Scotland desired only peace with England – but warned that Wales should be left in peace also. Privately David wished Earl Simon well in his efforts to turn Prince Edward into a crusader. Let him vent his killing instincts on the Saracens. He did not add that might heaven help England, and perhaps Scotland also, when that young man succeeded his father on his throne. Henry was bad enough, but Edward as King . . .!

24

The vital year of 1260 started significantly, with Alexander ordering that late Yuletide and Hogmanay celebrations all over the country should include bonfires and beacons lit on hilltops and prominent places, to signal to all that this year Scotland would have a monarch who would govern as well as reign. His people would have reason to rejoice, he promised, and should do so now rather than merely wait until April. This was typical Alexander, of course, urgent, impatient, always anticipating. But his intentions were sound, responsible. David believed that he would make an excellent ruling King, even if at first the better of some continuing restraint. How that restraint was to be effected would be the problem, with no regency to impose it. Margaret declared that, in fact, only David, and to a lesser extent herself, could achieve it, as Alexander's lifelong and trusted friends. It would be a year or two yet before they could think of retiring from the active governmental scene, as was David's wish, he ever a reluctant administrator.

David was not forgetting his crusading promise, either – not that his mother would ever let him do so.

As gesture in that direction, the Reidspittal venture was making good progress, and the establishment should be in working order and almost complete by Alexander's so notable birthday, the nineteenth, and the friars able to go out therefrom on their fund-raising missions. Not unnaturally, John de Brienne much interested himself in this work, as one more small step on his long road back to his Jerusalem throne; he indeed convinced Serle de Dundas to set up another Trinitarian establishment on his lands in the west of Lothian.

Although Alexander would have liked to celebrate his coming of age at Luffness, he felt that some public demonstration was called for, some highlighting of the occasion on a national scale. So there was much consultation and debate about this and it was decided that there should be a parliament held, at Edinburgh, at which the regency council would formally resign and the King officially accept full responsibility for the rule of his realm, with the aid of course of his valued Privy Council. This would be followed by a procession, possibly torchlit, through the streets of the city; and thereafter a royal progress around the country, far and wide, the monarch showing himself to his people, receptions in the cities and towns, receivings of the keys of the royal fortresses, and so on. A new chapter would begin for Scotland. Notices for the parliament were sent out.

The great morning dawned at last. They had spent the previous few days at Luffness, but went up to Edinburgh Castle the night before, to ensure that all was in readiness.

That was probably the best-attended parliament for many a long year, the castle's great hall packed, the minstrel gallery filled with ladies, including Margery, Queen Marie and Margaret. The regency council members were ranged on the dais-platform behind the Chancellor's table, and the throne, to the left, had a new scarlet canopy and Lion Rampant backing.

Alexander dominated the occasion, leaving the Chancellor with little to do and say; indeed, despite the crowded benches, it was almost a one-man parliament. The normal business of state affairs, foreign relations, appointments, complaints and so on was postponed until the morrow. This was Alexander's day – and he did justice to it. He thanked his regents for their services, advice and attentions in the past, expressing especial gratitude to Sir David de Lindsay, his familiar friend and mentor since childhood. He declared that he had been well instructed in the duties, arts and responsibilities of government, and intended now to demonstrate that such instruction had not been wasted. He would take full charge and care of his kingdom, inherited from a line of a hundred kings, existing before history was told, before this Scotland was an entity or ever the Scots came from Ireland, and Alba of the Picts was their nation. He would, to be sure, ever seek and heed the advice of his Privy Council and the will of his parliaments, but the final decisions would be his, and the responsibility therefor. Let his people not fear. He loved them, and would cherish them always, to protect them from all who would threaten or oppress them whomsoever, as was his royal duty, playing the father to his realm. Wrong-doers would be punished however lofty, and good-doers rewarded, the law upheld and if necessary improved. He would endeavour firmly to put down rebels within and enemies without, and expel Norse invaders and exterminate pirates and raiders. All this, and more, he promised, God helping him. Did any here wish to give him guidance now?

Only cheers, loud and prolonged, answered that.

David, since he had been specifically mentioned, took it upon himself to first raise voice, although briefly, not wishing in the least respect to lessen the impact of that resounding pronouncement. He merely declared how great had been the privilege of his wife and himself to serve His Grace over the years, however inadequately, how sure he was of the nation's well-being under its monarch's personal rule hereafter, and how fortunate they were in having Alexander, third of his name, as their liege-lord. God save the King!

Others in high places added their esteem and congratulations, from the King of Jerusalem downwards, Durward managing to jerk out a few complimentary words, Gamelyn eloquent.

Then Alexander announced that he was going to lead a great procession down into the city and through the streets, to the Abbey of the Holy Rood established by his great-great-grandsire David, of blessed memory, where they would make a short act of worship and prayer for the realm in this new dispensation, with the Lord Bishop of St Andrews guiding them. If there was just a hint of irony about that last, few there would perceive it, probably. He declared this especial session of his parliament adjourned until the morrow, and called upon Sir Alexander Seton, Lyon King of Arms, to assemble the procession.

So, amidst a great blowing of trumpets and clashing of cymbals, almost the entire gathering formed up under the heralds' directions, not without some argument as to precedence, to march down from that rock-top fortress into the town, something highly unusual for most of them who so seldom went on foot anywhere. With their sovereign-lord to lead them, instrumentalists to regulate the pace and heralds to keep all in approximate order, they wound their way, with some coughing from the smoke of torches, not directly down the Lawnmarket, High Street and Canongate, but making diversions to the Grassmarket, the Cowgate and elsewhere, so that as many of the citizenry as possible might see it all. What the townsfolk thought of this extraordinary spectacle was not to be known; but at least they would realise that a new start was being made in Scotland.

After a second short session of the parliament, there was only a few days' delay before the more ambitious perambulation commenced, necessarily on horseback this time and a much smaller party participating, with only a minimum of armed escort. Alexander was determined to visit as many parts of his realm as possible, to make himself known to the people; and since the Borders area and the Merse, with Lothian and Stirlingshire, already knew him better than the rest, he decided to start with Fife, across Forth, and work northwards, across Tay and on up through Angus and the Mearns to Aberdeenshire and Moray, coming back through the Highland areas of Badenoch, Atholl, Strathearn, Menteith and the Lennox to Glasgow and the Clyde. All this would, of course, take weeks, most of the early summer indeed. Whether there would be time thereafter to cover the south-west as well remained to be seen. Margery was to go with them, important that the Queen should be seen by all also; but Margaret, because of their young children, had to stay behind, much as she would have wished to accompany them. She would wait at Luffness.

The great tour commenced, at the beginning of May, apt to be one of the finest months in Scotland, with the cuckoos calling, the larks singing, the gorse and broom blazing and leafage everywhere hearteningly new and green. Although Alexander's impatient nature inclined him ever to press ahead, get as far each day as feasible, he recognised that this was not the objective, and reined himself in to *show* himself and his wife to as many as he could. So they did not hurry unduly, visiting all the succession of Fife towns from

Dunfermline eastwards to St Andrews, not only along the delightful Forth coast but inland also, to Falkland and Corn Ceres and Cupar. Then over Tay to Dundee and the Angus country.

Although they, perforce, had to pass the nights in establishments large enough to accommodate the royal entourage, castles, abbeys and monasteries, they made a point of Alexander and those closest to him going on foot into the towns and villages, strolling along boat-strands and harbours, entering inns and ale-houses, having brief prayer-sessions in churches. If the King had the love and support of his people, he could deal with the magnates, lords and bishops.

The days lengthened into weeks and weeks into months, as they progressed ever northwards, discovering the great territories of Angus and Mar, Buchan and Strathbogie, to Moravia or Moray and beyond Inverness even, to Easter Ross and Cromarty. The personnel of the expedition kept changing, for few could be expected to spend all this time away from their duties, estates and responsibilities. David stayed the course, although he had never before left Margaret for so long, and missed her sorely.

As it fell out, it was an unexpected development which halted their onward journeying into Sutherland, for Alexander was eager to reach the very limits of his kingdom. Margery, uncomplaining, quiet Margery, became unwell, and the monkish experts on health in the party had no difficulty in diagnosing the trouble – or no trouble, but joy. The Queen was pregnant.

Alexander was at first astonished, then elated and greatly proud of himself. He was going to be a father, have a son – it never occurred to him that it might be a daughter. His coming of age was demonstrated indeed. Great was the excitement – although the mother-to-be scarcely reflected it.

Now, nothing would do but that they must not only cut short the tour but get back southwards as quickly as possible, with no more visitings. He would have had a horse-litter contrived for the young woman, but she declared that she was perfectly able to ride – one of her few assertings of herself.

Thereafter Alexander was torn between the need for speed,

getting as far as possible each day, and not tiring his suddenly so precious wife, as they turned to head down through the mountainous centre of the land, by the Findhorn and Spey valleys, Badenoch, Atholl, Braid Alban, Strathearn and Menteith to the Forth. Margery indeed proved to be very little trouble and even seemed to be more comfortable in the saddle than in strange quarters overnight. They got her back to Luffness at last, none the worse apparently, where Alexander put all in the capable hands of Margaret, with vast relief, hardly able to accept that all this had happened a number of times before, and that Margery had months of fairly normal living ahead of her until the great day of delivery. Meanwhile, however, a man had to get on with ruling his kingdom.

When reminded of his promise to pay the desired visit to his wife's parents, he was in a quandary. At first he decided that this would have to be put off indefinitely. But Margery herself made a further demonstration of developing a will of her own, asserting that she *wanted* to go to be with her mother and father. In fact, she would like her child to be born at Windsor, where *she* had been born.

This produced much discussion, not to say heart-burning, and not only on her husband's part. For the Privy Council came into it, concerned that an heir to the throne should not be born in a foreign land, and where the King of England might seek to hold the child as hostage for Scots compliance with his wishes. They strongly advised that the visit should go ahead only if a written and witnessed promise was made by the Plantagenet that mother and child should be returned to Scotland whenever capable of travel and without any preconditions. There was secondary concern. The journey south should not be made too near to the Queen's calculated confinement period, needless to say. But that would mean that the King, if he was to wait in England until the actual birth, could be away from his kingdom for months, highly unsuitable in the circumstances. To this Alexander agreed. He would take his wife to Windsor, see her safely and comfortably settled, and then come home on his own, making all arrangements for Margery and his son to be escorted back in regal style in due course.

A messenger was sent south to Henry with all this made clear.

Then, of course, the question of timing arose. It was calculated that the birth could be expected in February. Therefore to avoid any risk of premature delivery because of the horse-riding – Margery still would not hear of a litter – they would have to travel no later than November which was only six weeks ahead, and with much to do before then in the matter of government. David found himself to be as busy as ever he had been as a regent, even if now he bore no especial title, but active nevertheless as a sort of deputy.

On the subject of title, Alexander was eager to show his appreciation of all David's service, offering lands, appointments, honours. That man declared that he was quite happy to return to being Cup-Bearer, but Alexander scoffed at that. At least he should be Master of the Household – which in effect he had always been anyway. But if he would accept no office of state, an earldom at least? Earl of Luffness? Or Garleton? The Byres would scarcely sound sufficiently dignified. Crawford, then? Or Craigie?

Gratefully, David declined. He did not seek to be an earl, and have to keep up that sort of style and dignity. Earls all had their private armies, chamberlains, officers and the like. Not for him, not yet anyway. If he was an earl, when he went on crusade as vowed, he would have to take with him a great contingent, as his uncle of Dunbar had done. His thanks, but no.

David was not given any option as to accompanying the royal party to England in November, a prolonged progress with comparatively short daily journeys which would not overtire the mother-to-be – not that she made any fuss or complaint – the father-to-be all attentive care. They took the English envoy, William Horton of St Albans, with them, to ensure suitable overnight accommodation, in King Henry's name, and of course required more frequent halts than on previous wayfaring. But there were plenty of abbeys and monasteries for them, and Henry's daughter always was assured of a warm welcome from the clerics, however little from the barons, even if the King of Scots was less popular.

It took them two weeks and two days, at this pace, to get to Windsor, after calling at London, Simon de Montfort coming to escort them from there.

Henry and his Queen received their daughter and her husband with great ceremonial and lavish entertainment, giving no hint of the financial crisis which plagued the English court and treasury, nor mention made of discontented and rebellious nobles. They were given handsome quarters in the great fortress-castle – where of course Margery would be installed for three months at least. The royal physicians, examining her, declared that all was in order and no complications looked for.

Typically, Alexander, having done what he had set out to do, was all for getting away again as soon as he decently could, with those months before he could play the father, and a realm waiting for his attentions. But he was concerned to make all necessary arrangements for care and safety of his heir-to-be – and, to be sure, of his wife. He demanded of his father-in-law an assurance that should he, Alexander, be unable to come south again to collect them, should he be prevented by anything soever, by sickness or even by death, then mother and child should be handed over to a deputation of representatives of his Privy Council; he even stipulated the composition of such deputation, namely four bishops, five earls – including two Comyns, two others and the man Durward – and four barons, one of whom must be Sir David de Lindsay, this notwithstanding any controversy there might be at the time between the two kingdoms. Henry, while tut-tutting that any such conditions were quite unnecessary, was persuaded to sign an agreement thereto. But he did not do more than promise to find one thousand pounds of the long-owed dowry-moneys, to be ready on that occasion.

After only a few days, then, Alexander bade his wife farewell, with repeated instructions as to the care and handling of his son and heir, and departed for Scotland again.

They made notably better time on their return than on the outward journey, taxing their horses to the limit, with even David protesting that there was no such great hurry. They soon left Master Horton to find his way north at his own speed.

25

Word reached Scotland in late February 1261 that their
Queen had been safely delivered of a child, and that all
was well. But it was a daughter. At first, Alexander was all
but dumbfounded. All his thoughts and plans had concerned
themselves with having a son, heir to his throne, to be reared
in his own image, taught how to behave as a monarch-to-be,
how to rule a kingdom – even how to shoot geese. He was
to be called David. But . . . a girl!

However, he adjusted presently, to some extent, and even
began to look forward to seeing his daughter. He hoped that
she would take after himself, rather than her mother, he
confided to David; Margery was improving, but if he had
to have a daughter she should be a spirited one. She would
be called Margaret of course. And the next child, pray the
good God, a son, would be David.

This acceptance of the situation did not go so far as to send
the monarch all the way down to Windsor again to collect
his family; his good friend David could do that. There was
no need, in the circumstances, to send all that deputation
of bishops, earls and barons; a small escort was all that was
necessary, with the man Horton to arrange overnight stops.
There was no hurry . . .

So the royal twentieth birthday was celebrated before
David set off on this mission in early May, with de Ros
and Horton. In the meantime, Margaret had presented him
with a daughter, whom they named Elizabeth after her
grandmother, a dainty little creature, welcomed a deal more
joyfully than had been the new Princess Margaret.

David found Margery much changed, plumper and more
of the Queen, motherhood evidently agreeing with her. The
infant, now three months old, was well made and hale, if less
bonny than the baby Elizabeth, or Beth as they were calling

her, but obviously the apple of her mother's eye. There was no trouble about them leaving Windsor; King Henry was away superintending another building project in the west, and Queen Eleanor, ever a somewhat shadowy figure, made no difficulties.

That progress back to Scotland, with so young an infant and a nursing mother, was inevitably a slow one. Fortunately the weather was good, and Margery was patient, while taking queenly charge as to when they should stop, how far they should go daily. Horton and his clerical aides were the most concerned, in selecting halting-places and going ahead to arrange suitable reception. Not all of the monasteries and hospices they stayed in were of as high standard as Horton would have wished, but Margery made no complaint. It was noteworthy that they did not approach castles and manor-houses for accommodation, in England, presumably on account of Henry's unpopularity with his landed folk, whereas he seemed to have general support of churchmen.

They took almost a month to that journey, so that it was late June before they got back to Edinburgh. And there Alexander promptly fell in love with his young daughter, despite previous doubts. Margery gained by this also, to be sure, and her access of confidence and poise helped their relationship. At Luffness, however, Laird Stotherd's widow was still providing Alexander with her own help, on occasion.

During David's absence two developments had taken place. Norse incursions in the Hebrides and on the West Highland coasts had increased, some of them on quite a major scale, and Alexander was concerned, indignant. He had indeed sent an envoy to King Hakon of Norway, protesting, and demanding that all such cease and that compensation be paid for damage done. Whether Magnus of Man was behind this was not clear, but he was a protégé of Hakon and a Norseman himself. The second item was the unexpected death of Pope Alexander. This could result in unforeseeable changes, for the Vatican had such enormous influence on all the Christian nations, and new pontiffs could alter the courses of even the most formidable monarchs, with their powers of excommunication and withdrawal of all sacraments, Christian anointing, baptism, marriage and burial. The new Pontiff was to be Urban the Fourth, so far an unknown quantity as far as Scotland was concerned. Gamelyn, who had got on so well with Pope Alexander, was considerably perturbed. He would like to be an archbishop, and had been manoeuvring towards that goal – which, of course, would be not only to his own glorification but to Scotland's great benefit, for it would put an end to this ridiculous claim of the Archbishops of York to have spiritual hegemony over the Scottish Church, as the most northerly metropolitan, as well as the rival claim of the Archbishop of Nidaros in Norway. Now this advance was put in doubt by the advent of this Urban.

Alexander, not concerned over Gamelyn's status but very much so over the metropolitan situation – since the claims of the English Church helped to bolster up the English royal pretensions towards overlordship of Scotland – was, typically, urgent to do something about it, not just to wait on events. Gamelyn was talking about making a visit to Rome once the new Pope was duly enthroned; and Alexander thought to send his own ambassador with him, since he did not altogether trust his Chancellor. How would David like to make a pilgrimage to Rome?

That man reserved judgment on this suggestion. He pointed out that he was bound by his promise to his mother to make a different sort of pilgrimage, on his release from regency duties, namely to take part in one of the crusading efforts – to which Alexander countered that Rome was all but on his way to the Holy Land, so he could do both at the same time. David was still doubtful. The fact was, of course, that he was in no hurry to go crusading at all, a reluctant fighter for the faith in that respect. He would much prefer to settle down at Luffness, with Margaret and his little family, and get on with the management of his estates and baronies, relieving Johnnie and Pate of some of their responsibilities, which were really his.

However, the summer produced pressures other than royal and ecclesiastical. The health of his mother, the Lady Elizabeth, deteriorated badly, and strong-minded woman as she was, she took to her bed. And from there she renewed her pleas, all but commands, for her son to fulfil his vow and go to serve Christ's cause and avenge the slaying by the Infidel of her brother. She was going to join that brother, and her husband, she knew, very soon, and would only go in peace if she knew that David was on his way. He had delayed overlong already.

As July and August passed and his mother's state worsened, David recognised that he would have to go, and soon; he had no choice.

One day in early September he came down from Edinburgh, alone. After greeting the children cheerfully, hearing their eager small adventurings, and visiting his mother's bedside – she now a gaunt and sorry portrayal of her former self – he took Margaret's arm, to lead her off to a private stance on one of the tower-top battlements, where they looked out over the wide bay to the hills of Fife.

"Last night, my dear, Gamelyn got news that the new Pope, Urban it is to be, was duly enthroned. Now he, Gamelyn, intends to waste no time, and will set off for Rome, by ship, in a week or so. And Alex wants me to go with him."

She sighed. "Yes. This has been looming up for long," she said. "You have to go." That was not a question but a reluctant assertion.

"I fear so. And my mother . . ." He spread his hands helplessly.

"Yes. It is not only Rome, but this of the crusading, I know. You have to do it, I know. We have spoken of this so often, but . . ." Margaret clutched his arm. "Need it be much more than a . . . gesture? There is no real warfare going on at this present, is there? I am very ignorant about it all."

"Not that I know of, no. I have spoken to King John about it. He says that King Louis of France, who leads all, is trying to assemble a great army. Not in the Holy Land at all, meantime. He was doing this at Damietta, in Egypt – that is at one of the mouths of the Nile River, some two hundred miles west of Jerusalem. But the new Mameluke, Sultan Baybars, has forced them out. Now they assemble at Tripolis, on the Syrian coast. But John says that the Knights

Hospitallers' fort at Acre, near to Tyre, is still in Christian hands, not far from Galilee. In any assault on Jerusalem, this would be an excellent spear-point. *He* thinks to go there."

"And they fight, from there?"

"Not meantime, I think. The knights but hold it. They have a great fortress and harbour, which the Infidels do not seem able to take. So they hold it, and wait for the great army to start its assault from north and south. Then . . ."

"And this might not be for long?"

"Who know? There has been no serious battle for some years now. Just probings and sallies. The Christian princes cannot agree, Louis and the Emperor ever at odds. The new Pope, this Urban, is a Frenchman, and like to support Louis against the Emperor. It is all difficult."

"So it could be, then, if you go, that you will just be waiting, with the others? Doing little or nothing? Is it worth the going, then?"

"I know not. But I have promised. Vowed."

"Go, then. And stay only a short time, David. Come home, having fulfilled your promise. You have duties here, have you not? To me and to your children, your bairns and mine. And to your lands, baronies. To Alex also. A gesture, as I said . . ."

They left it at that.

Ten days later, it was farewell, with a ship ready to sail from the port of Leith. David spent the night before at Luffness, and had a loving but direly anxious wife in his arms, and a modicum of sleep. In the morning, he took leave of his mother, receiving her quavering blessings and last advice – for she would not see him again in this life, she asserted; but in the next, they would know fullest joy and satisfaction, at last. He was enrolled now in God's good cause. He said goodbye to Johnnie, Pate and then, hardest, to the children, telling them to be good to their mother until he came back. Margaret insisted on accompanying him to Leith, with Seton.

Alexander came down from Edinburgh to see them off, with his letter for Pope Urban. King John and Gamelyn were already aboard the ship. Queen Marie was staying behind with her son in Scotland, meantime.

It was, like so many leave-takings, awkward, unsatisfactory, too emotionally charged to be otherwise. Alexander was all hearty cheer, except when he had sudden pauses of constraint. Seton and de Ros were silent, stiff, finding the activities of shipmen and dockers to stare at. Margaret put up the greatest, lip-biting struggle, knowing that if she broke down, David would also, to the distress of all.

Finally, she flung herself into his arms, grasping, in quivering silence, head buried on his chest, body heaving.

Somehow he got the words out. "We will be waiting . . . for each other . . . whenever, wherever. Waiting . . ." He could say no more.

"Yes! Yes!" she gulped, and pushing herself away, turned and ran from him.

David could not so much as incline his head towards his sovereign-lord, much less bow, as he hurried below.

The subsequent waving to those ashore as the vessel edged out of Leith haven was, as far as David de Lindsay was concerned, a blurred and wilting effort.

Postscript

It was the year 1264, midsummer, and the heat and humidity appalling. Sir David de Lindsay lay on a plank-bed in an airless cell of the mighty triple-walled castle of Acre – and if he could have seen himself, he might well have been struck by his likeness to his mother, that last time that he had seen her, thin, gaunt, wasted, eyes glittering, breathing fast and shallow. The man who sat beside him, in his ragged brown monk's habit, bent head to listen, as now and then the other sought to speak, from dry, burning lips, however damp all else.

What the knight was trying to say the monk already had a fair grasp of; but the dying man was clearly urgent that there should be no mistake. He kept seeking to repeat parts of it, dire effort as it obviously was.

His sorrowing companion spoke soothingly, in a voice very similar, if so much stronger, than that of his patient – for it so happened that he was a fellow-Scot, indeed another Lothian man, Friar Kentigern de Lauder, of the family of the Bass Rock in the Firth of Forth, one of the monks from Mount Carmel, dispossessed by the Infidel from their famous monastery, and now acting as nurses and attendants to the crusading knights. And the said knights much needed their services, for fully half of them at Acre were sick of the terrible fevers which scourged that coast, in the insanitary quarters of this harsh fortress, dying not of wounds or in battle but of wasting disease. David de Lindsay was only one of them.

Friar Kentigern had pieced together the incoherent request of the man he had served and nursed so caringly. Sir David, once he had died – and that could be any day, any hour, now – wanted his body to be embalmed, and when ship was available, taken back to Scotland, to Luffness. And there his brother, Sir John de Lindsay, would give the friar land

and aid to set up a new monastery, a Carmelite monastery on Luffness land, probably the first in all Scotland, in the chapel of which his body was to be interred, beside the altar. Friar Kentigern was to write this out on a paper, and he would sign it. Or, if he could no longer sign, his seal was there and he might make a cross – the only cross that he had been able to make, to advance this ill-starred crusade. And he was to say to his Lady de Lindsay not to forget that he would be waiting, wherever and whenever, as promised – a peculiar message.

And so it was.

It took four long years to get that embalmed body shipped and back to Scotland, and to set up the new Carmelite monastery, having Friar Lauder as its first Prior. In the chapel thereof a stone coffin, with a knight in effigy above, was fashioned lovingly, in a shirt of chain-mail, shield on chest and sword at side, in the chancel, left of the altar. It is still there today, seven centuries later.

NIGEL TRANTER

THE YOUNG MONTROSE

The first volume of Nigel Tranter's classic two-part story of one of Scotland's greatest heroes.

James Graham, Marquis of Montrose.

One of the greatest and most attractive figures in all Scottish history: a general of genius and an inspiring leader, dashing and brave, yet cultured and humorous, a man of tolerance in an age of bitter sectarianism, a man to lead a nation not just a faction.

From the initial snub he received from Charles the First, the monarch he was to devote his life to serving James Graham was loyal through intrigue, violence, treachery and battle.

But one man alone could not alter all, when intolerance, despotism, folly and weakness held the stage — even though James Graham tried hard, and almost succeeded.

HODDER AND STOUGHTON PAPERBACKS

NIGEL TRANTER

KENNETH

Kenneth Mac Alpin: the man who made and named Scotland.

Norse-slayer and nationbuilder, Kenneth, son Alpin Mac Eochaidh, King of Galloway, was the warrior hero and visionary who brought together the ancient kingdoms of Alba, Dalriada, Strathclyde and Galloway to create the country of Scotland.

Yet his vision was wider still. He dreamed of a great coming together of all the Celtic people, Scots, Irish, Welsh, Cornish and Manx, united against the Norse and the Anglo-Saxon invaders.

Fighting not only his country's enemies but also the fractious, obstinate wilfulness of his own people, his legacy was a nation, with its own patron saint, the apostle Andrew, that would endure from the ninth century to the present day.

Nigel Tranter is at his imaginative best as he brings to life not only a man, but recreates a time and place in history when a nation was emerging from a dark and violent world.

'Tranter's style is compelling and his research scrupulous'

Daily Telegraph

'The story goes along with an admirable swing, and is at the same time convincing as a bold reconstruction of a dark period of history . . . Nigel Tranter's enjoyment of his own creation is infectious'

Allan Massie, The Scotsman

HODDER AND STOUGHTON PAPERBACKS